W9-BMF-981

**Praise for the Fatal Series
by *New York Times* bestselling author
Marie Force**

"Force's skill is also evident in the way that she develops the characters, from the murdered and mutilated senator to the detective and chief of staff who are trying to solve the case. The heroine, Sam, is especially complex and her secrets add depth to this mystery... This novel is *The O.C.* does D.C., and you just can't get enough."

—*RT Book Reviews* on *Fatal Affair* (4.5 stars)

"Force pushes the boundaries by deftly using political issues like immigration to create an intricate mystery."

—*RT Book Reviews* on *Fatal Consequences* (4 stars)

"The romance, the mystery, the ongoing story lines... everything about these books has me sitting on the edge of my seat and begging for more. I am anxiously awaiting the next in the series. I give *Fatal Deception* an A."

—*TheBookPushers.com*

"The suspense is thick, the passion between Nick and Sam just keeps getting hotter and hotter."

—*Guilty Pleasures Book Reviews* on *Fatal Deception*

"The perfect mesh of mystery and romance."

—*Night Owl Reviews* on *Fatal Scandal* (5 stars)

**The Fatal Series
by *New York Times* bestselling author
Marie Force
Suggested reading order**

One Night with You (prequel novella)

Fatal Affair

Fatal Justice

Fatal Consequences

Fatal Destiny

Fatal Flaw

Fatal Deception

Fatal Mistake

Fatal Jeopardy

Fatal Scandal

Fatal Frenzy

**And look for the next book
in the Fatal Series from Marie Force,
*Fatal Identity***

MARIE FORCE

Fatal
FRENZY

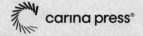
carina press®

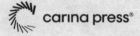
carina press®

ISBN-13: 978-0-373-00410-2

Fatal Frenzy

Recycling programs
for this product may
not exist in your area.

www.CarinaPress.com

Printed in U.S.A.

ONE

"I DON'T WANT to be here." Surrounded by familiar buff-colored cinderblock walls, Sam felt claustrophobic and panicky. Even the burnt-coffee smell of the place nauseated her. She needed to get out of there. Now.

"Sam."

She glanced at Dr. Trulo, who gazed intently at her, his gray eyes never wavering. His hair had gotten thinner since the last time she was forced to spend time with him, after young Quentin Johnson died at the hands of her officers in his father's crack house.

"What?"

"I can't clear you to go back to work until you talk about it."

"What's there to talk about? I did a stupid thing, and I paid the price. Should I have gone in there alone? No. I know that. I knew it then, but I had no reason to suspect that Marissa Springer was going to turn into a murdering lunatic or that she'd partnered up with Stahl. As far as I knew she was a grieving mother, a disgruntled wife and a source of information." Sam shrugged. "There. I talked about it. Can I go now?"

He continued to stare at her without blinking. How did he do that? Everyone needed to blink once in a while, didn't they? Perhaps one of the job requirements for being a police department shrink was a freakish staring ability.

She shifted in her seat, crossed her legs and then her arms. "What else do you want me to say?"

"I want to hear about what happened with Stahl. How you coped during the assault. What you're thinking about now. How you're sleeping. You could start by telling me what it was like to be wrapped in razor wire by a man you once reported to."

"It was sharp."

Trulo finally blinked—and sighed deeply. "Maybe we should reschedule for next week."

"Next week is kind of busy. The inauguration and all that."

"Are you aware that your squad is frantically trying to find the person responsible for a series of knife attacks?"

For the first time she felt a twinge of guilt at letting down her closest colleagues. "I'm aware of that." The city was on edge after a series of brazen and seemingly random attacks that had left two people dead and two others gravely injured. Sam was sorry she wasn't able to help this time, but she couldn't single-handedly catch every killer who roamed the city's streets.

"Do you *want* to come back to work, Sam?"

"Yes! Of course I do. What kind of question is that?" Her heart began to race at how close he'd come to uncovering her recent anxiety about work and safety and the loss of her famous mojo. It would come back. Eventually. It had to come back. Didn't it? Who was she without it?

"It's an honest question. You've been in this game long enough to know that if you don't *play* the game, you remain on the sidelines. I can't clear you to come back until I'm certain you've dealt with the trauma of what happened and are in the right place mentally, physically and emotionally to resume your duties."

Sam was never more mulish than when pushed into a corner, and now was no different. "How am I supposed to prove to you that I'm fine?"

"You have to talk about it."

"What if I don't want to talk about it? What if talking about it makes it worse?"

"Have you talked to anyone? Your husband? Your friends, colleagues, your dad, sisters? Anyone?"

"Yeah, I've talked to them," she said, squirming again. She hated the feeling that he saw right through her bullshit the way Nick did too. He'd been watching her like a hawk recently—to the point that she'd been actively avoiding her overly devoted husband for the first time ever.

Sam knew she wouldn't get away with that for much longer, and Trulo wasn't about to buckle either. "I'd like to leave now."

"No one is forcing you to be here."

She gave him her best "yeah right" look. Did he actually think any cop saw him voluntarily? "Hello, Command Referral. Like I have a choice."

"You know what I mean. This process is on your schedule. When you're ready, make an appointment. I'm here for you whenever you need me."

With the lure of freedom in her reach, Sam began to stand.

"Before you go, though..."

Foiled, she sagged back into the uncomfortable hardback chair.

"I want to say one thing." Trulo cleared his throat and seemed to force himself to look at her. What was that about? "I read the report on what happened that day at the Springers' house, and I just want to say... I've been doing this for a long time, and what happened to you, well, it was bad, Sam. Really bad. And there's no shame in admitting that you're traumatized by it, that maybe you've lost your taste for the job, that—"

"No." Sam leapt to her feet. "Whatever you're going to say, just save it. I'm fine. I haven't lost my taste for anything except this meeting. Some people don't feel the need to air out all their shit in some touchy-feely room where it's supposedly *safe* to spill their guts. We aren't safe anywhere. That's the lesson learned here."

"Now we're getting somewhere," he said with a small, satisfied grin that infuriated her. "Call me when you're ready to talk about why you don't feel safe anywhere."

Pissed with herself and with him, Sam stormed out of the office, slamming the door behind her. She was on her way to a clean escape when Captain Malone waylaid her, taking her by the arm and escorting her into his office where she shook him off. "You need a refresher in sensitivity training if you think you can manhandle your female officers that way."

"So report me."

"What do you want?"

"Nice to see you too, Lieutenant. We've missed your charming self around here."

Sam rolled her eyes. Charming. Whatever. "Is there something you need?"

"Have a seat."

"I prefer to stand."

"I wasn't asking."

Since he so rarely pulled rank on her, she dropped into the chair he pointed to and crossed her arms again, keeping with the mulish theme of the day.

"How've you been?"

"Great. You?"

"I'm down one of my best officers, so things have been a little hectic, especially since someone is going around killing people with a hunting knife. But we're coping."

She refused to feel guilty about sitting this one out. Her team was highly trained, and they'd figure it out. They always did. "Glad to hear it."

"How's it going with Trulo?"

"You're not allowed to ask me that."

"Add it to the report you're going to submit on my bad behavior."

"I have been attending the appointments as required. Would you like me to tell you what we talk about in there? It would only take a minute. Probably less than a minute."

Malone sat back in his chair, exhaling loudly. "So you're not cooperating."

"I didn't say that."

"Don't you want to get back to work?"

Sam shrugged. "I'm kinda enjoying the time off. I like taking my kid to school—even if the Secret Service has to butt into our time together—and taking my dad to his appointments and hanging out with my husband and cleaning my house."

Malone sat up straight, his eyes wide with alarm. "You're *cleaning* your house? What the hell is wrong with you, Holland? You'd rather be cleaning your house than chasing down murderers? Things are worse than we thought."

"We? We who?"

"All of us! We're wondering what the hell is going on with you and why you don't seem to have any desire to come back to work. Every other time something crazy has happened, we've had to practically lock you to your sofa. But not this time. This time something's different."

Sam made a conscious effort not to squirm as he stared her down, looking for answers she simply didn't have. She didn't know why she had no desire to go back to work. She didn't know why she felt dead inside or why she wondered if she would ever again be able to trust her own judgment when it had failed her so dramatically. She didn't have the answers they all wanted so badly, and until she did, they weren't going to let her come back. So she'd decided to enjoy the unexpected time off. What else could she do?

"Sam, this is *me*." He'd been her mentor and friend since the day she made detective. "Talk to me, will you? Tell me what you're thinking."

His concern touched off another wave of guilt at knowing she had caused him—and others—such dismay.

When she remained silent, he said, "I want you to know… We, all of us, from the chief on down, we failed you in this situation with Stahl. It never occurred to us that he would take it as far as he did, and that's on us."

Sam rose to her feet. "I gotta go, Cap. It was good to see you."

"Sam, wait."

Before he could make it around his desk, she was out the door and headed for the morgue and the closest exit. She burst into the frigid January day and took deep breaths of the cold air. Her eyes darted around the parking lot, on the lookout for enemies. After fourteen years on the job, she'd made more than her share of them. Now she knew they weren't afraid to come after her, to try to take everything from her. She'd learned to be wary and more afraid than she'd ever been before.

When Nick accepted the president's offer to become his new vice president, he'd declined Secret Service protection for her so she could continue to do the job she loved. That she was actually thinking about requesting a detail was indicative of how screwed up everything had gotten since Stahl attacked her.

She got into her car and drove home, the one place she felt safe these days, surrounded as they were by Nick's detail and Scotty's. The house was like a fortress, and she liked it that way. No one could get to her there.

SAM PULLED ONTO Ninth Street and was waved through the checkpoint by a Secret Service officer. She parked in front of the house and was surprised to see Nick's black BMW parked at the curb. What was that doing here? He'd told her he'd sold it since he could no longer drive himself.

Grabbing her purse, she got out of the car and went up the ramp to the home she shared with Nick and Scotty. An agent greeted her at the door and opened it for her. "Thank you," she said.

"My pleasure, Mrs. Cappuano."

Not that long ago, Sam would've told the agent to call her Lieutenant Holland, but lately she'd grown used to hearing her married name from the agents that surrounded her family. It didn't rankle the way it once would have. In the ten months they'd been married, some of Lieutenant Holland had given way to make room for Mrs. Cappuano.

Speaking of the devil who'd made her his missus, Nick came out of the kitchen wearing a gorgeous dark gray suit with a cranberry-colored tie that was one of her favorites.

As he had from the moment she first met him years ago, he took her breath away just by walking into the room.

"Hey, babe. How was the appointment with Trulo?"

"More of the same." She dropped her coat and purse on the sofa, earning a frown from her neat-freak husband. In a mocking tone, she said, "'Tell us how you feel, talk about what happened, blah, blah, blah.' I don't know what they want me to say. It happened, I survived, it's over and he's locked up."

Nick kissed her forehead and gazed down at her, taking in every detail with gorgeous hazel eyes that saw right through her—and her bullshit. "You know what they want from you, Samantha, and the sooner you give it to them, the sooner you'll be back on the job."

The Secret Service had given them the room, so she ran her fingertip down the silk tie and dipped it under his belt, pleased to realize he'd delayed the start of his day to be here when she got home. "Maybe I don't want to go back to work. Maybe I'd rather be the second lady for a while and tend to my vice president anytime he needs tending to."

His Adam's apple bobbed in his throat. "Um, who are you and what've you done with my wife?"

For the first time in hours, Sam laughed.

"No, seriously. You want to be the second lady rather than a cop?" He pressed his hand to her forehead. "No fever, but maybe we should call Harry just to be safe."

"Knock it off." She batted his hand away. "Is there anything wrong with enjoying a little break from the rat race?"

"If you were anyone else, I'd say of course not. But because you're you, I see reason for concern. Perhaps even alarm. You love the rat race. You live for it. Or you did until Stahl lost his mind. Since then, you haven't been quite yourself, babe. We've all noticed it."

Sam wasn't surprised that he was tuned in to her as always and wouldn't settle for the platitudes she'd given Trulo. "I'm working through some things having to do with the attack and the job and where I go from here." It was the most she'd said to anyone since that awful day. "I just need some time. As long as I'm on leave, I may as well enjoy it, right?"

"I suppose. But the cleaning and all that… You're kind of freaking us out."

Smiling, she put her arms around him and leaned into the comfort of his embrace, breathing in the familiar scent of home. "I'll knock off the cleaning."

He held her tight against him. "Thank God."

"How come your car is outside? I thought you sold it."

"Yeah, about that, I lied."

She lifted her head off his chest to give him the wifely evil eye. "You *lied*? Start talking."

"When we declined Secret Service protection for you, I didn't exactly do that without some significant fears— and that was before everything happened with Stahl. So I decided… Well, come with me. Let me show you." He held her coat for her while she put it back on and then took her by the hand to lead her to the door.

The agent on duty stopped them. "Are you leaving, sir?"

"Just going outside for a minute."

The agent spoke into the microphone attached to a wire that hung from his ear. "Hotshot and Fuzz are on the move."

"Fuzz?" Sam said, looking up at Nick. "That had better not be a reference to my hair."

"Did I forget to mention we've been assigned code names? And I believe yours is more about your job than your hair."

"It had better be. *Fuzz?* Really? How come you get to be Hotshot and I'm *Fuzz?* Is there an appeal process?"

Hand over his mouth, the agent laughed silently.

"It's not funny! I have a reputation to uphold here. Fuzz is a puppy or a kitten. It's not a badass cop."

"I'll take it up with those in charge," the agent said solemnly, obviously trying not to laugh out loud.

Sam scowled at him. "You do that."

"You may proceed, Mr. Vice President, Mrs. Cappuano."

Sam left the agent with a final glare as she let Nick lead her out the door.

"I can't tell you how much I hate having to get permission to walk out my own door," he said.

"You knew it would be like that."

"Still, it sucks balls."

"Speaking of sucking balls—"

"Not here. Not now."

"How do you know what I was going to say?"

His side-eyed glance said it all. Removing a key fob from his pocket, he unlocked the BMW. "Hop in," he said, holding the passenger door for her.

"Um, okay. I thought you weren't allowed to drive yourself anywhere?"

"We're not leaving."

"I'm not making out with you in broad daylight with your entire detail looking on."

"Good to know," he said, laughing. "Now get your sweet ass in the car."

Sam slid into the soft leather seat and breathed in the

familiar scent of leather and cologne that would always remind her of their first days together. They'd spent a lot of time in this car since then, and she'd been sad to see it go after he became vice president.

He got into the driver's side and pulled the door closed.

She leaned across the center console. "You've got me all to yourself, *Hotshot*. Whatever will you do with me?"

Flashing the irrepressible grin that made her panties damp every damn time, he said, "I'll show you around your new armor-plated, specially outfitted bulletproof security vehicle."

TWO

NICK'S CONCERN ABOUT Sam's safety had led to some of the worst insomnia he had ever experienced, which was saying something since he'd been plagued by insomnia for much of his adult life. And that was *before* Stahl attacked her. Since then, he hadn't slept much in the last few weeks as he watched her toss and turn, tormented by dreams she said she didn't remember the next day.

But he knew she remembered. She remembered the dreams and every minute she spent in that hellhole basement with Stahl and Marissa Springer. That day had changed something in her, something they were both still coming to terms with weeks later.

Sam took a close look at the familiar vehicle, where the differences were subtle but significant.

"The car has been outfitted with many of the same features that my limo and Nelson's have—bulletproof glass and tires, armor-plated metal and a panic button that feeds to the Metro PD, Secret Service and FBI," Nick said. "Under the backseat, you'll find enough food for three days, emergency medical supplies, a biohazard kit, oxygen, sanitary supplies and everything you'd need to hide out."

"You're serious."

"Dead serious."

"When did you do this?"

"I began looking into our options after we declined Secret Service protection for you."

"So before Stahl."

"Yes." He stared out the windshield, battling the rage that gripped him every time he thought about what she'd endured in that basement. He'd read the police report, and in the rare instances when he did sleep, it gave him nightmares. "I should've done it sooner. I should've—"

Sam grasped his forearm. "Nick, not even you with all your superpowers could've seen that coming."

He tried to shake off the rage because it wasn't what she needed. "But wait, there's more." At the press of a button on the center console, a tablet screen popped up, complete with an attached keyboard. "Freddie helped with this part. This is the new tablet the department is mandating for field use, so yours is now built into the car with a Bluetooth keyboard since Freddie and I agreed the keyboard on the tablet would make you ragey."

"You and Freddie agreed, did you?"

"Uh huh. He doesn't know about this part, though." Nick turned on the sound system, and Sam's favorite Bon Jovi song, "Living on a Prayer," roared to life. "All Bon Jovi, all the time."

"*Seriously?* Oh my God! Freddie will hate that!"

"But you?"

"I love it," she said with a sigh and the soft smile he loved so much, especially when she directed it at him. "This… It's amazing, Nick. Thank you so much for doing this."

"In addition to a charger for that dinosaur cell phone of yours, the car is also fully tricked out with all the latest in GPS technology. You'll never go missing again. I'll always be able to find you." He produced his smartphone and held it up so she could see the screen. "This app tells me exactly where the car is at any given time." Glancing at her, he forced himself to be truthful with her when he'd prefer to keep this part to himself. "I know it'll make you mad to have me keeping tabs on you, but I can't bear the thought of ever again not knowing where you are for even one minute."

"A month ago, I would've demanded you rip that shit out of the car. Now, I'm glad you'll be able to find me if need be."

He hadn't expected her to say that, and the statement demonstrated how deeply the trauma had touched her. "Really?"

"Yeah, really." Sighing, she sat back in the seat, resting her head on the leather. "I keep going over it and over it in my mind, you know? Like how could I have been so stupid to walk into an ambush? I like to think I can see these things coming, but this one…"

"Why would you have seen it coming? You'd been there before, met Marissa, talked to her about the case. What would clue you in that she was in cahoots with that bastard Stahl?"

"Nothing, I guess, but still, I feel like I should've sensed something was up. But I didn't. I walked right in there like I would any home of any witness. Remember when Freddie got shot at Reese's place and how pissed I was that he went in there alone? I did the same thing."

"Totally different situation. For one thing, Reese had killed his family and Freddie was watching the place, hoping he'd come back. He went in there knowing he could be confronting a desperate killer, which was stupid. You went into the Springers' house to talk to a woman you'd just had a civilized conversation with an hour earlier. How is that the same thing?"

"We were shorthanded. I went in there alone. No one knew where I was. Checking in and calling for backup is police one-oh-one. I *know* better."

"You're second-guessing yourself from the perspective of hindsight. You know what happened *after* you walked in there. But going in? With the info you had available to you *at that time*? You had no reason to believe there was any reason for concern."

The song on the radio changed to "Make a Memory," one of Nick's personal favorites of the steady diet of Bon Jovi he'd been fed since she came back into his life. "I love this song. It makes me think of when we were first together, and I came home to find you reading *Congress for Dummies* with this song blasting in the house. I think of that and 'fill her buster' every time I hear it."

She smiled at him, but he could still see the disquiet in her clear blue eyes. That she was deeply troubled and trying to hide it from everyone was readily apparent to him.

Taking hold of her hand, he said, "You need to talk to someone about this, Sam."

"I'm talking to you."

"And I'm thrilled you're talking to me. But you also need someone qualified to guide you through the PTSD stuff. Harry told me to tell you to call him when you get tired of stonewalling the department shrink."

"How does he know I'm stonewalling the department guy?"

Nick sent her a withering look. "We *all* know you're doing that."

"Could I ask you something and do you promise to take it seriously and tell me the truth?"

"Sam… Of course you can, and of course I will. What do you want to ask me?"

"What would you think if I took an indefinite leave from work to focus on being the second lady? Tell me the truth."

For a brief moment, Nick's mind went completely blank with shock that she was actually asking him such a thing. He'd been concerned about her before, but now he was downright petrified. Something was seriously wrong if she was thinking that way. "Samantha, you're freaking me out right now."

"Why? Because I'm considering some changes?"

"Because this is so not you. You'd hate being a full-time second lady. You're a homicide cop. It's not just what you do. It's who you *are*."

"What if I want to be someone different? Am I not allowed to be anything but a cop?"

"You can be anything you want, but the one thing you can't do is make life decisions when you're still recovering from what happened in that basement. This is not the time to be having this conversation. Talk to me in two or three months when the dust has settled and your first thought every morning isn't about razor wire."

She looked down at her hands, which were folded in her lap. "The car is amazing. I can't believe you did all this. It goes a long way toward making me feel safe again."

"I want you to feel safe. Whatever it takes. Whatever we have to do."

"I'm thinking about requesting a detail."

"Okay…" Wow, the hits kept on coming.

"You know, just in case."

"Yeah, baby. I know. Nothing has to be decided today

or tomorrow or anytime soon. I'm sure you're feeling some pressure from HQ to get back to work, but there's no rush. The job's not going anywhere, and Gonzo has you covered in the meantime." He produced a set of keys that he held up for her to see. "The red button on the key fob is the same as the one in the car. It notifies MPD, the Secret Service and the FBI that you're in trouble and broadcasts your position to them immediately."

She took the keys from him. "You thought of everything."

"I hope so. If there's anything I missed that would make you feel safer, just say the word, and we'll see what we can do."

"Where exactly do you go to get bulletproof tires and armor-plating?"

"I called in a few favors, made a phone call or two." Unlike the president, Nick had come up through the ranks and had friends in every corner of government. He hadn't been shy about calling on every resource he had to make this happen for her.

"It must've cost a fortune."

"Best money I ever spent on anything. Ever."

"So the windows… Is there a setting so I can see out but no one can see in?"

He gave her a "what do you take me for" look and pressed a button on the dash that sealed off the outside world.

"Excellent, now get over here and make out with your wife, Mr. Vice President."

"With pleasure, Mrs. C."

THE SUMMONS TO appear in the chief's office came from his admin through Gonzo, acting head of the Homicide

Division in Sam's absence. They'd been working long hours, following leads on the slasher case, but were no closer to an arrest than they'd been at the outset.

"Chief wants to see you at four," Gonzo had said, leaving Detective Freddie Cruz to wonder for three long hours what the chief wanted with him. In the back of his mind and in the pit of his gut, he knew exactly what this was about. He'd been waiting since the night he tuned up the guy who hurt Elin. It had been stupid and risky and every other word he could think of to describe the way he'd put his career on the line to defend the woman he loved.

He'd do it again in a heartbeat.

Freddie's leg bounced uncontrollably as he sat outside the chief's office waiting to be called in. Since Gonzo delivered the news, Freddie had wanted to call Sam to get her take, but he'd been trying not to bother her while she was on leave. However, he sure would've liked to talk to her before this meeting.

"Detective Cruz?" Helen said. "You can go in now."

"Oh, um, thanks." He'd rarely been to the chief's office without Sam, so he couldn't remember if he was supposed to knock or just walk in. As knocking was the safer of the two options, he raised his hand to the door.

"Come in!"

Freddie opened the door and stepped into the chief's inner sanctum. In addition to Chief Farnsworth, Deputy Chief Conklin, Captain Malone, the new Internal Affairs Lieutenant Wilson and the department counsel, Jessica Townsend, were there. Holy shit…

Farnsworth gestured to the one remaining chair in the half circle in front of his desk. "Have a seat, Detective."

When he was seated, Freddie glanced at Malone, hoping for some insight into what was going on, but the captain was staring at something behind the chief.

"We're here to discuss the events of January 1st, in which Detective Cruz entered the city jail to confront an Andre Elliott, who'd been arrested earlier that day after assaulting a woman at a gym on Sixteenth Street."

Freddie had been waiting for this for weeks now while at the same time hoping it would go away without any additional fallout. No such luck.

Reading from a paper he held in his hand, Farnsworth continued. "Mr. Elliott alleges that while he was in MPD custody, that Detective Cruz entered his cell and assaulted him, leaving him with injuries to his groin and face." Farnsworth looked up at Freddie. "Do you know anything about this?"

Freddie had no idea what to say. Did he tell the truth or did he deny it? It was his word versus Elliott's. By placing his hoodie over the camera, he had made sure there would be no record of him entering or leaving the cell. The sergeant on duty in the jail that night, Sergeant Delany, had looked the other way after Freddie told him what Elliott had done to Elin.

"Detective Cruz?"

"Before you reply, Detective," Wilson said, "I should remind you that you have rights, including the right to request counsel, should you require it."

"Am I being charged with something?" Freddie asked.

"Not at this time," Wilson said. "But we reserve the right to pursue charges if we're unable to resolve this matter internally."

Fixated on the wall behind the chief, Freddie thought about the broken bones in Elin's face, the violent bruises that were only now beginning to yellow, the weeks she'd been out of work and in pain. Yeah he'd done it, and he'd do it again. But somehow he didn't think it would be wise to say that here.

"Let me make this simple for you, Detective," Farnsworth said. "Elliott is demanding we take action internally or he will file suit."

Freddie forced himself to meet the chief's unflinching gaze. "What kind of internal action?"

"Nothing less than a suspension without pay of one week."

Shit, Freddie thought, *a week without pay will hurt, but a lawsuit would hurt more, especially with Melissa Woodmansee's suit against us winding its way through the courts*. In the second he took to weigh his options, he thought about Sam and how hard she'd worked to build their squad into one of the department's elite teams. Another lawsuit could undermine both their careers.

"Elliott has no way to prove that I laid a finger on him," Freddie said.

"Lieutenant Archelotta brought a gap in the security film from that night to our attention the week after the incident in question. It appeared to him that someone had intentionally placed something over the camera, and when it was removed, Elliott was lying on the floor holding his badly bruised testicles and bleeding from his nose and mouth."

Okay, that looked bad and helped to cement what he needed to do. "I'll take the suspension." This was the worst possible time, with Sam on leave and a knife-wielding lunatic on the loose, but what choice did he have?

"It will include an entry on your personnel file that could impair future advancement opportunities," Malone said.

"I understand." If he was never anything other than a detective, he could live with that. As long as he got to do the job he loved, he'd be fine.

"I hope it goes without saying, Detective," the chief said, "that we in no way condone officers taking matters such as this into their own hands. It goes against everything we believe in, as a department, for members of our team, especially officers at your rank and above, to be doling out vigilante justice."

"I understand," he said again—and he did. From the second he left Elin's bedside at the hospital, he'd known what he was risking by confronting Elliott. But even facing a suspension, he couldn't bring himself to be sorry for avenging the woman he loved. "Is there anything else?"

"I'll need your weapon and badge," Malone said, holding out his hand.

It hurt a lot more than he'd expected to turn over his gun and his prized gold shield to the captain.

"Is there anything else you'd like to say, Detective?" Farnsworth asked.

"What will Elliott be told, and will the suspension be made public?"

"He will be told that you've been disciplined internally, but no further details will be made available to him or the media. It will be treated as an internal personnel matter. Assistant U.S. Attorney Faith Miller has agreed to drop the conspiracy charges against Elliott in exchange for his silence. He'll only be charged for the assault on Ms. Svendsen."

Freddie's mind whirled with implications. Stahl had hired Elliott to beat up Elin so Freddie would be out of the way dealing with a personal matter when Stahl went after Sam. It killed him to hear that Elliott wouldn't be charged for partnering up with Stahl.

"That doesn't mean the media won't ever catch wind of it," Malone added. "They just won't hear it from us."

"You understand that viable charges are being dropped in the case against Elliott because of a choice you made, Detective," Farnsworth said, visibly displeased.

"Yes, sir." He wasn't proud of what he'd done, nor did he like being the subject of the chief's displeasure, but he was not going to apologize—ever. The deal was the best he could hope for under the circumstances. Hopefully, Elliott was smart enough to know better than to defy the terms of his agreement with the U.S. Attorney. The assault charges were enough on their own to make sure he would be locked up for a while. At least he'd better be.

Freddie stood on watery legs. "Thank you."

"Detective," Malone said. "You're a rising star in this department. Be careful letting your emotions get the better of you. I'd hate to see such a promising career derailed by self-inflicted wounds."

"Yes," Freddie said, swallowing, "sir. Thank you." He made his escape and kept his head down on the way back to the detectives' pit. At his cubicle, he shut down his computer and grabbed his keys.

"Oh, hey," Gonzo said. "You're back. What's the deal?"

Freddie zeroed in on the still-healing gunshot wound on Gonzo's neck, a reminder that things could always be worse. "I've been suspended without pay."

Gonzo's mouth fell open in shock. "What. The. *Fuck*."

Freddie remained stubbornly silent.

"The thing with Elliott. The thing you won't talk about. It's come back to bite you in the ass."

"Something like that."

"Goddamn it, Cruz. This is the last fucking thing I need with Sam already on leave."

"I know. I'm sorry to cause you added stress."

"But you're not sorry about what you did to land in this situation."

"Nope."

"I hope it was worth it."

Freddie thought of the way Elin's gorgeous face had been bruised and broken by Elliott's fist. What Freddie had done to him was the least of what that guy deserved. "It absolutely was."

"I don't know that I care for this new edgy side of Freddie Cruz. It's not like you to behave this way."

"I'm not expecting it to become a habit, Sarge," Freddie said, in a rare use of his close friend's rank.

"See that it doesn't. How long is the suspension?"

"A week."

"Son of a bitch."

"I'll be a phone call away if you need me, and all my notes are up to date. If I can help with the investigation, call me."

"Yeah, I will. Have you talked to Sam at all?" Gonzo asked.

"Here and there. You?"

"Same. Does she seem weird to you?"

Freddie nodded. "Suppose it's normal after what happened."

"I guess."

What remained unsaid between them was that it was anything but normal for their lieutenant and close friend to stay away from work for any reason other than debilitating physical injury—especially when they had a hot new investigation going on. Even when she'd been badly injured, they'd had to fight with her to stay home until she recovered.

"She'll be back," Freddie said with more confidence than he felt. "When she's ready."

"I hope so. You'd better get out of here before the word gets out about the suspension. You don't want to be around for that."

"No, I don't. I'll call you."

Freddie left the pit and headed for the morgue exit, hoping to make a clean getaway. If there was any upside to the suspension, it was a week alone with Elin, since she was still on medical leave from the gym. As he drove home to their apartment in the Woodley Park neighborhood, it occurred to him that they should go somewhere, get out of town while they had the chance.

Before he did anything, though, he needed to talk to Sam. He placed the call and hoped she'd pick up. The last couple of times he'd called, she hadn't answered or replied to his voicemail messages or texts.

"Hey," she said, sounding breathless. "What's up?"

"Oh, hey." He'd been prepared to leave yet another voicemail message.

"You're just the man I wanted to talk to."

Damn! Had she already heard about the suspension? Had the brass consulted her before they dropped the hammer? "How come?"

"Nick showed me the new car today and told me you were a big help in getting the dreaded tablet in there. Thanks for that."

"No problem. I'll be happy to get you trained on how to use it as soon as you come back to work."

"Oh, joy," she said with predictable sarcasm. "Can't wait."

"The reason I called is I wanted to tell you that I got suspended for a week."

"*What?* What the hell for? Oh damn, Elliott, right?"

"Yeah. They're dropping the conspiracy charges against him in exchange for his silence about what I did."

She was silent for a long moment, long enough that he began to squirm.

"Listen, Sam—"

"No, *you* listen. What you did to him was beneath you. You played right into their hands."

"How was I supposed to know it was all an orchestrated plan? All I knew is my girlfriend's face was broken. He *broke bones* in her face, Sam."

"I know, and you had every right to be furious. But you had no right to go into his cell and do what you did. No right at all."

"What would you do if someone did to Nick what was done to Elin? Would you sit idly by and let them get away with it?"

She sighed loudly. "I get why you did it, but you've used up your one ticket. Farnsworth has a very low tolerance for police brutality, and he won't let you get away with this twice."

"I'm hardly getting away with it. They're docking me a week's pay." Thinking of that had him reconsidering his get-out-of-town plan.

"You could've been busted back to Patrol. You *are* getting away with it. Count your blessings that it wasn't worse."

"I'm not sorry," he said. "I'd do it again."

"If you do it again, I'll personally pack your bags for the trip to Patrol."

As he expected nothing less from her, he smiled at her saucy reply. "Speaking of trips, I'm thinking about taking advantage of my unexpected time off to get away with Elin. Unless you can think of any reason why I shouldn't."

"I don't see why not as long as you refrain from posting pictures on Instagram of yourself holding an umbrella drink."

"I'm surprised you've heard of Instagram."

"Bite me."

"As appealing as that offer is, I'm going to go home and bite my own girl."

"Gross."

"People are worried about you, Sam. Wondering when you'll be back and all that."

"They're waiting for me to kiss Trulo's ass, and that's not about to happen anytime soon. I'm kind of enjoying the break."

"You are? Seriously?"

"Why does everyone find that so hard to believe?"

"Um, because?"

"I have a life outside of that place, you know."

"Yes, I believe the entire country knows about your life outside of work these days."

"Very funny."

"It's just, you know, not like you to be making up reasons to extend a medical leave."

"That's not what I'm doing. Are people saying I'm taking advantage?"

"No one has said anything like that. And if they're

thinking it, they know better than to say it around me or any other member of your squad."

"What do I care what they say? At least I'm still walking and talking and breathing and mostly functioning after what that dickwad did to me."

Hearing her say she was "mostly" functioning didn't exactly put his mind at ease. "We're all thankful you're walking and talking and breathing."

"Awww, thanks, Cruz. I'm touched."

He snorted out a laugh. "Right, on that note, I'm out. I'll talk to you in a week. Try to stay out of trouble while I'm gone."

"I'm not the one serving a suspension."

"Touché, Lieutenant."

"Try to have a good time, Freddie. You deserve a break, and this shit at work is a temporary setback. Nothing to get wound up about."

"Thanks for that. I'll talk to you soon." He stashed the phone in his pocket and parallel parked outside the building where he lived with Elin. Taking the stairs two at a time, he arrived at the door to their third-floor apartment and pulled out his keys.

The door swung open before he could use his key. "What're you doing home?"

Elin wore a bathrobe and her white-blond hair was gathered into a messy bun. Even with the bruises still prominent, she was gorgeous, and the sight of her stopped his heart the way it always did. He had things he needed to tell her, such as Elliott's involvement in the mess with Stahl. She'd been so fragile since the assault that he had kept all but the most essential information from her, including his late-night visit to the jail.

He wrapped his arms around her and lifted her.

"What're you doing? Why aren't you at work?"

"I've got the week off."

"How come?"

"Things are slow and they were looking for someone to take some time off. I have a lot of vacation accrued so I volunteered." Thankfully, she'd been avoiding the news and hadn't heard about the knife assaults or she'd never have bought his "things are slow" story.

"A whole week?" she asked with more enthusiasm than she'd shown for anything in a while.

"That's right. What do you say we get out of town?"

"And go where?"

"Anywhere you want."

Her hand came up to cover her face. "I don't know… My face…"

"Is gorgeous."

"And still bruised."

"So what? We'll go somewhere that no one knows us and just relax and have fun. Come on. When will we ever get another chance like this to get out of here for a week?" With his hands on her face, he ran his thumb gently over the yellowing bruises. "Let's get in the car and just drive. We'll figure out where we're going when we get there."

"We're not taking your car."

Laughing, he kissed her. "My poor maligned Mustang. She's so misunderstood."

"She's perfectly understood."

"Fine, we'll take your car. So is that a yes?" At some point during their time away, he'd have to find a way to tell her the things he'd been keeping from her. But the goal today was to get her to leave their apartment for the first time in two weeks.

"Yes, Freddie. Let's go somewhere."

THREE

AFTER SAM SENT Nick off to work with promises of a proper thank-you for the car later, she took a call from their assistant, Shelby, who'd been felled by severe morning sickness.

"I'm so sorry, Sam," Shelby said tearfully. "Don't pay me for this week."

"Don't be silly, Tinker Bell. You get sick time."

"I'd feel guilty getting paid for doing nothing but puking and sleeping."

"Is Avery with you?"

"Yes, it was so bad today that he called out of work to stay home."

"I hope you feel better soon."

"I do too. I'll call you tomorrow."

"Take the week off. I'm here and can handle anything that comes up. Rest up and feel better."

"Are you sure?"

"I'm positive."

"Thanks so much, Sam. That's a huge relief. I can barely move, so I wouldn't be much good to you."

"What's the doctor saying?"

"Perfectly normal, but they're keeping an eye on me so I don't get dehydrated. Good times."

To Sam, it sounded like the best of times, but she refused to dwell on the unreasonable jealousy she felt anytime someone around her got pregnant. "Hang in there, and let me know how you're doing."

"I will. How are you?"

"I'm fine. Doing better every day. I'll talk to you soon, okay?"

"Sounds good. Bye, Sam."

She put down the phone and poured herself a rare second cup of coffee. Sam wasn't proud of the jealousy, but she couldn't help it, especially when it would soon be a year since the last time she'd been pregnant. Minus a few months on birth control, she'd had a lot of months to conceive again, but it just hadn't happened. It certainly wasn't for a lack of trying.

The part she found so difficult to understand was that she and Nick had successfully conceived once before. Why wasn't it happening again? She blew out a deep breath full of the frustration she'd experienced for years now when it came to her checkered fertility history. After her last miscarriage, the doctors had all agreed—if she'd gotten pregnant once, she could do so again.

Nick had wanted to pursue fertility treatments, but she didn't have it in her to go through that again after having done it before with her ex-husband. The side effects of the treatments were just too much for her, especially with no guarantee of a baby at the end of it.

"You need to find something to do that doesn't involve dwelling on this shit," she said. On the counter was the handwritten card she'd received after Stahl's attack, from her new chief of staff at the White House. She picked it up and re-read the kind message for at least the tenth time.

Mrs. Cappuano—please accept our heartfelt best wishes for a speedy recovery from your injuries.

*You are in our thoughts and prayers, and if I can
be of any assistance to you whatsoever, please don't
hesitate to get in touch.
Sincerely,
Lilia Van Nostrand.*

She had included her direct line at the White House.
Sam stared at the number for another minute before she
picked up her phone again.

"This is Lilia," she answered in the crisp, professional
tone Sam remembered from the only other time she'd
spoken to the woman.

"Um, yeah, this is Sam Hol… Um, Cappuano."

"Oh! Mrs. Cappuano! How wonderful to hear from
you."

Sam cringed and held the phone away from her ear. "I,
um, I wanted to thank you for your note and the flowers
from the staff. That was very nice of you all."

"It was our pleasure. I hope you're on the road to recovery."

"I am."

"I'm delighted to hear that. Is there anything I can do
to be of assistance to you?"

"Since I'm out of work on medical leave, I thought
this might be a good time for that meeting you wanted
to have with me."

"How's today at two?"

"Wow, you don't mess around, do you?"

"No, I don't."

"This is embarrassing to admit, but how do I get in
there? I've only ever been with Nick, er, Vice President
Cappuano." She still wanted to giggle when she called

him that. Her husband, the vice president of the United
States.

"I'll send a car for you. You'll be at home?"

"Yes."

"Excellent. The car will be there at one thirty, if that's
convenient."

"That's fine. I'll see you soon."

"We'll look forward to it."

Taking her phone with her, Sam ran upstairs to take
a shower and figure out what to wear to meet her White
House staff. The cuts to her arms and legs from the razor
wire had mostly healed but remaining scabs on her legs
had her choosing a black pair of pants and a red blazer
that she matched with one of the silk blouses Tinker Bell's
personal shopper friend had bought for her.

Replacing an entire wardrobe took some time, and
after her ex-friend Melissa took a machete to her closet,
Sam had half of what she'd had before. She put on the
diamond key necklace Nick had given her for a wedding gift as well as her rings, which she only wore when
she wasn't working. A pair of silver hoop earrings and
a bangle bracelet finished off the outfit. As she put on
black high-heeled ankle boots and took a critical look
in the mirror, she decided she wouldn't embarrass herself or Nick.

With thirty minutes to kill before the car arrived, she
went downstairs, sat on the sofa and practiced the deep
breathing techniques her sister Tracy had taught her in
the days after the attack. She'd found the breathing and
meditation helped to calm her mind and ease her anxiety.

People were saying she wasn't herself. She could
understand the concern, but she wasn't sure how to be
anyone other than who she was now, after the fact. Some-

thing had changed in the Springers' basement, and it might take a while to figure out who she was now. In the meantime, she continued to breathe.

GONZO SAT AT Sam's desk and sifted through the reports submitted by the third-shift detectives working the knife assault case. He read through the statement taken from one of the victims who'd been lucky enough to survive the attack.

William Enright been walking on a quiet side street in the Gallaudet neighborhood, on his way home from a night out with colleagues when the assailant approached him from behind, grabbed his arm, swung him around and stabbed him in the abdomen. Luckily, the victim had remained coherent enough to fight off the attacker and call for help, but in addition to the life-threatening abdominal wound, he'd suffered significant lacerations to his hands and arms in the battle.

The description of a tall, muscular man wearing a hat pulled down over his face and a black coat fit the description they'd been given by another victim who'd been attacked on the other side of the city in the Glover Park area under similar circumstances.

"Knock," Captain Malone said from the doorway.

"Hey, Cap, come on in."

"Settling in here?"

"Not even kinda. She can come back anytime now."

"That's why I'm here. I saw her this morning, and I don't think she's coming back soon."

"Where did you see her?"

"She was here for her appointment with Trulo."

"And she didn't even stop by the pit to see what's going on? That's not like her."

"None of this is like her. I was hoping you might be able to shed some light."

"I got nothing. She doesn't return my calls and when she texts, it's cryptic, one-word stuff."

"We may have to prepare ourselves for the possibility that she won't be back."

"No," Gonzo said, shocked and amazed that the captain would say such a thing out loud. "I refuse to prepare myself for that. She'll be back. She's too invested in the job to not come back."

"I don't know… She's got a lot of other stuff going on now with Nick's new job. Maybe this thing with Stahl was some sort of wake-up call that she doesn't actually have nine lives and she needs to be more careful with the one she has."

"You can't honestly believe that."

"You read the report. You heard what it was like for her in there. She lived for hours preparing for him to kill her while he beat and tortured her. Who'd want to come back to this bullshit after that?"

"Sam Holland. That's who. She's not a quitter."

"No, she isn't, but she's as human as the rest of us underneath it all, and she took a bad, bad hit on this one."

"I took a bad hit not that long ago." He gestured to the still nasty-looking wound on his neck that served as a daily reminder of how close he'd come to losing everything. "I came back. Hell, I came back before I was allowed to."

"I'm not, in any way, diminishing the impact of what you went through. But this was different, Gonzo. He *tortured* her. That messes with people's heads."

"And nearly bleeding out during a gunfight with a

murdering psychopath while thinking about the fiancée, son and family I expected to never see again doesn't?"

"Fair enough," Malone said with a deep sigh. "I didn't come in here to debate who had it worse. I hope you know that."

"I do, and I get what you're saying about her. What he did… I think we'd all like to get our hands on him for what he put her through."

"Indeed. But for the time being, you're in charge here, and I'm available for anything you might need. We appreciate you stepping up the way you have, but don't hesitate to call on me if need be."

"I won't. Thanks, Cap."

"So where are we with the knife guy?"

"Same place we were this time yesterday. We're working the case, following up on leads and tips. Got a new interview from a vic that I was just going over." Gonzo handed the page to the captain who read it carefully.

"The guy's got a bit of an M.O. Attack from behind and go for the jugular or the gut if the vic puts up a fight."

"Right. The ones who live get 'lucky' that he doesn't connect with any major arteries or organs. Dr. McNamara reported that the two who died bled out very quickly. Both were dead before EMS arrived."

"Any connections among the victims?"

"Not that we've been able to establish—yet. We're working on it, and now we're working on it without *two* of our best detectives."

"I know. We need to make some sort of statement to the media about what we have so far."

"We have next to nothing."

"Let's give them the facts of the case and let them

know we're following every lead. Maybe a briefing will lead to some more tips."

"I'm going to need you to authorize some OT for the squad since we're shorthanded."

"I'll take care of that. You take care of getting me a suspect—after you brief the media."

"Yes, sir."

"Can you be ready in thirty minutes?"

Gonzo nodded.

"Very good. I'll go out there with you."

"Okay."

Malone took off, leaving Gonzo to contemplate what the hell he could say to the media about an investigation that was stalled. He went over his notes again, refreshing his memory about what they knew so far, and typed up some brief comments that included a plea for information.

He also made copies of the composite sketch that had been created with the help of one of the victims that showed the attacker's general height and build as well as the coat he'd been wearing. With fifteen minutes to spare before the briefing, he took advantage of the opportunity to call home.

His fiancée, Christina, sounded breathless when she answered on the third ring. "Hey."

"Hi there. What're you up to?"

"Doing a yoga video while Alex naps."

Gonzo groaned. "Don't put those images in my head when I've got hours to go until I can see you."

Laughing, she said, "Sorry. So hours to go, huh?"

"Yeah. They suspended Cruz, but that's top secret."

"They suspended him? What for?"

"I'll tell you later, but that leaves me even more shorthanded than I already was. We feel like this knife guy is deliberately taunting us."

"You sound frustrated and overwhelmed."

"I'm both of those things. We're going to have to postpone our plans—again. I'm so sorry."

"It's no problem, Tommy. I'm not going anywhere. The next time we have a free weekend, we'll take off and get it done."

"I don't want to think of our wedding as just another thing on an endless to-do list."

Her soft laughter made him wish he were home with her rather than stuck here for the foreseeable future. "Are you laughing at me?" he asked.

"Maybe just a little. Ease up on yourself, Tommy. Our wedding will happen as soon as we have a space of time in which we have nothing to think about but each other and Alex."

"Thanks for being so awesome all the time. It takes a special person to be the spouse of a cop."

"I just want to be *your* spouse. You could be a garbageman for all I care."

"Garbage is starting to look awfully good to me right about now."

"This is an amazing opportunity for you. If you all manage to catch this guy while you're in charge, it'll be so great for your career."

"True, but catching him is a big *if*."

"You can do it. I have no doubt."

"I love you, Christina. I can't wait to marry you."

"I love you too, and I can't wait either. But I'd wait forever, so don't let our plans add to your stress when you have enough on your plate."

"Turn the TV on in a few minutes. Your dashing fiancé has to brief the media."

"We'll be watching."

"I'll be home as soon as I can."

"We'll be here."

Gonzo always felt better after he talked to her. He never could've gotten through the chaotic events of the last few months without her by his side. First being shot and then being suspected of murdering his son's mother... Gonzo shuddered at the memory of that awful day when Lori's body had been found in her car, and all eyes had turned to him.

Stahl had played them all like a maestro, exacting his revenge with deliberation and cold, calculated precision. Cruz had played right into his hands by attacking the man who hurt Elin. Sam had been lured in by the relative safety she felt at entering Marissa Springer's house alone. The incident had rattled all of them, but no one more so than Sam.

Gonzo hadn't told anyone that he was beginning to believe that she wouldn't be back. Why should she subject herself to the shit they encountered on a daily basis on this job when she certainly didn't have to? Her husband was the freaking vice president of the United States. What did either of them need with a job that put her in constant danger?

The thought of doing this job without her, however, was not one he was prepared to fully entertain. It would be a much different atmosphere in this squad without her leadership. He would be her logical successor unless one of the current lieutenants put in for it.

With everything happening in his personal life, Gonzo wasn't entirely sure he wanted to take on more responsibility at work. But he might not have a choice if he was thrust into the role. That's the way things happened in this line of work. Someone flamed out for whatever reason and the guy standing next in line got caught holding the baton, whether or not he was ready.

His partner, Detective Arnold, knocked on the door. "Malone says they're ready for you to brief the media."

"Okay."

Gonzo collected his notes and a bottle of water and headed for the main entrance to HQ, where the reporters gathered year-round to wait for information. It didn't matter if it was freezing, like today, or sweltering hot in the summer, they were always there waiting to be tossed a bone.

Sam had gotten very adept at telling them a whole lot of nothing. He hoped he could do the same.

"Ready?" Malone asked when he met Gonzo at the main doors.

"No, but let's get it over with."

When they emerged into the biting cold, the reporters surged, quickly surrounding him and Malone.

"Back off and give us some room," Malone barked.

They backed off by a few inches, but began shouting questions about the knife attacks, when Sam would be back, what was happening with Stahl and everything else they could think of.

Gonzo went through a rote recitation of what they knew so far about the knife attacks, including an update on the condition of the two victims who remained hospitalized. He distributed the copies he'd made and asked for their help in generating more tips from the public.

"Have you found any connections among the victims?" a reporter asked.

"Not yet. Until we know more, we're operating under the assumption that these attacks are random. We're asking the public to remain vigilant and aware of their surroundings at all times while walking around the city."

"When will Lieutenant Holland return to work?" Darren Tabor asked.

Gonzo looked to Malone to take the question.

"We have no comment on internal personnel matters," Malone said.

"But she will be back, right?" Tabor asked.

Malone glared at the pesky reporter. "We have no comment on internal personnel matters."

"Can you speak to the status of Stahl's case?" another asked.

"He's been remanded for trial and is being held without bail at Jessup."

"Why there and not here?"

"Due to the potential for conflicts of interest in this case," Malone said, "we requested permission to move him out of our jurisdiction, and the court approved the move."

"Captain, what is the mood within the department in light of the Stahl case?"

Gonzo could feel the captain's tension in the way he stiffened. "What do you think it is? We're still trying to get our heads around the fact that one of our own, a man we worked with as a close colleague for many years, was capable of what he did, not only to Lieutenant Holland but to the other victims of his senseless crimes."

"It's been a rough couple of months for the MPD," one of the bottle blonde TV reporters said. "Is there any talk of the chief retiring or stepping down to make way for new leadership?"

"The leadership we have is more than capable of steering us through whatever comes our way. That's it for today. Thanks for your time." He grabbed Gonzo's arm and nearly dragged him through the doors. "Fucking vultures. And they wonder why we have to force ourselves to meet with them in the first place."

"The chief isn't retiring, is he?" Gonzo asked.

"Not that I've heard, and I would've heard."

"You ever think about…" Gonzo had no sooner said the words than he wanted to take them back.

Malone eyed him shrewdly. "Think about what?"

Gonzo sighed and looked up at the captain. "About when too much becomes just that. Too much."

"How do you mean?"

"The thing with Sam and Stahl… What if it was enough to drive her out of here permanently? And the chief. He's got to be about to the point where he's thinking life's too short for this shit."

"Are *you* thinking that, Sergeant?"

"No! I'm thinking about them."

"It's been a rough couple of months around here. No one would deny that. It's been a rough couple of months for you too. Not only did you have a nearly fatal gunshot wound but the mother of your child was murdered, and you were briefly caught in the crosshairs. And that doesn't even take into consideration what happened to Sam and how we all feel about her and the animal who attacked her. Anyone would be having a crisis of faith after all of that."

"I'm not having a crisis. It's not that."

"Then what?"

"I don't know. It's nothing."

Malone never blinked, letting him know he'd have to do better than that.

"Is she coming back?" Gonzo asked.

Malone propped his hands on his hips and shook his head. "I honestly don't know. I thought she'd be back by now."

"So did I."

"She's stonewalling Trulo, even though she knows she has to pacify him to get back to work. That tells me she's in no rush to come back."

"Or she's not ready to air it out."

"That's also possible."

"So I'm not the only one who's concerned."

"Certainly not. Came up this morning in a meeting with the brass and the other captains."

Gonzo wasn't sure if he was comforted to know the brass was worried too, or more concerned than he'd been before he asked.

"Look, just keep doing what you're doing," Malone said. "It's not gone unnoticed that you've really stepped up when you're barely back to full speed after your injury."

"I'm trying."

"I'm here if you need me. Don't hesitate to come to me if you need backup of any kind."

"Thanks, Cap. I'll let you get back to work."

Malone nodded and took off toward his office while Gonzo headed back to the pit to check on the status of the investigation. The sooner they found the knife wielder, the sooner he could see about marrying the love of his life.

FOUR

THE "CAR" LILIA sent for Sam was a black SUV with tinted windows, driven by one Secret Service agent while another rode shotgun. The thought of a Secret Service agent "riding shotgun" was funny to her, but she didn't think they'd be amused by her little joke. They hadn't said much of anything to her since they arrived at the house and whisked her away.

She wondered if they disliked her because she'd chosen to forgo the protection normally afforded the nation's second lady. Didn't that mean less work for them? The devil in her wanted to ask their thoughts on the matter, but she didn't dare. Everything about this situation was new to Nick—and to her—and she didn't want to do anything to cause him any heartburn. Well, any more heartburn than she'd already caused.

They drove through the gates to the White House, where the officer in charge waved them through. Upon pulling up to one of the many entrances, the car came to a halt and the driver jumped out to get her door. A young woman with a dark bob waited to greet her. She wore a pale pink suit, which had Sam immediately thinking of Shelby, along with pearls and sensible heels. Her big dark eyes were serious as her lips curved into a welcoming smile.

"Mrs. Cappuano," she said, extending her hand. "I'm Lilia and it's such a pleasure to finally meet you."

"*You're* Lilia?"

Seeming baffled by Sam's remark, she said, "Why yes. I am."

"I had you pegged as a sixty-something blue hair with a ruler in her hand, determined to whip me into shape."

"Did you, by any chance, go to Catholic school?"

"Briefly. It wasn't a good fit."

Lilia laughed, and Sam decided not to hate her on sight. In fact, it was possible she might even end up liking her.

"Right this way," Lilia said, leading Sam inside the freaking White House. "Let me show you to your office."

"I have an *office*? In the freaking White House?"

"Ma'am, you're the second lady of the United States. Yes, you have an office."

"Call me ma'am again, and we're going to have a falling-out."

Lilia pursed her lips, perhaps trying not to laugh. "Understood." She cleared her throat and recovered her professional demeanor. "The second lady's office is normally housed in the residence, but as you are not using the residence, space has been assigned to you here."

"Space" turned out to be a suite that included a rather grand room for her. "Wow," Sam said as she took in the office that consisted of a gorgeous dark wood desk and matching bookshelves, a credenza that held a vase of fresh flowers, carpet with the presidential seal and portraits on the wall of other women who'd held this office. There was also a sitting area consisting of a sofa and two wingback chairs arranged in front of a fireplace that had been lit in anticipation of her arrival. For the first time since Nick's promotion, it registered with Sam all of a sudden that she really was the nation's second lady.

Watching Nick take the oath of office in the House chamber hadn't done it. Having her house overrun by Secret Service hadn't done it. But this... An actual office in the White House... That was about as official as it got.

"We hope you like it," Lilia said. "We weren't sure of your taste as far as furniture goes."

Sam snorted out a laugh. "If you could see my office at HQ, you'd understand that I have no taste when it comes to office furniture, and this is lovely." She ran her hand over the smooth finish of the desk, thinking of the metal contraption she used at work. Unlike her desk at HQ in which none of the drawers opened properly, she'd bet every drawer in this desk opened the way they were supposed to.

"Are you interested in meeting the rest of the staff?"

"Sure." While she waited for Lilia to gather the troops, she went to smell the flowers on the credenza. A flurry of activity behind her had Sam turning to greet the three women who walked in with Lilia, all of them young, attractive and smiling warmly.

"This is Andrea, your director of communications and spokesperson, Mackenzie, who oversees your schedule and travel, and Keira, our policy specialist."

Sam shook hands with each of them. "It's nice to meet you."

"We're so happy to meet you," Andrea said enthusiastically. Tall and shapely, Andrea was blonde with hazel eyes and a bright smile. She wore a tailored blouse with a pencil skirt that showed off her killer body.

"I, um, I'm sorry it's taken me a while to get in here. Things have been a bit, um, busy."

"We were horrified to hear what happened to you," Mackenzie said.

"Thank you, and thank you for the flowers and the card. It was very nice of you all."

"Let's have a seat," Lilia said, gesturing to the sitting area.

When they were settled, a man came in with a tray that contained coffee and an assortment of Danishes. Sam waited for them to dig in, but then realized they were waiting on her. These women were nothing like the cops she worked with who would've devoured the entire plate in less than a minute. "Please, go right ahead."

While they helped themselves to coffee and a snack, Sam said, "What have you all been doing to stay busy while I wasn't available?"

"We've been fielding inquiries about you and assisting the First Lady's staff on a number of initiatives," Lilia said, reciting a long list of projects Mrs. Nelson was personally involved in. "Of course, you're our top priority, and we're looking forward to hearing your thoughts about how you'd like to be involved."

Sam's brain went completely blank. How she'd like to be involved? In what? "I'm not really sure what you mean. The job, er, *my* job, keeps me pretty busy when I'm not on medical leave."

"We so admire the work you do, Mrs. Cappuano," Keira said.

"Thank you, but please feel free to call me Sam."

All eyes turned to Lilia. "I believe that would be appropriate when we're behind closed doors, but it would not be appropriate for us to call you that in public."

"Fair enough. So here, in the office, I'm Sam, okay?"

Their heads bobbed in agreement even if they seemed uncomfortable by the informality.

"As the second lady," Lilia said, "you have a built-in

platform that could be used to draw attention to issues and causes that are important to you. For instance, Mrs. Nelson's son is a captain in the army so she is particularly involved in organizations that support military family members and veterans. She's active in the arts and has promoted reading and literacy programs for elementary students across the country."

Immediately intimidated by the staggering list, Sam said, "Wow, she keeps busy."

"She's a very active first lady," Lilia said.

"Are there issues that interest you that you'd like to lend your name and support to in order to build awareness?" Mackenzie asked. She had long reddish-brown hair, brown eyes and pale white skin that would require SPF 100 sunblock.

"I, ah…" How personal did she want this to get? Did she want to lend her name to *her* issues or choose others that struck less close to home? If she were going to do this and get involved at this level, she supposed there ought to be some passion so she didn't come off disingenuous. "Spinal cord injuries and research."

"That's a great one," Keira said. She was petite with light brown skin, long dark hair and a smile that lit up her brown eyes.

"My dad is a quadriplegic."

"Yes, we know," Lilia said. "We probably ought to tell you there isn't much we don't know about you."

"Yikes," Sam said with a good-natured grimace. "That's kinda scary. You might be surprised to hear me add learning disabilities and infertility concerns as well as adoption and support for law enforcement to my list."

"Those are all very worthy causes, but before we officially add them to your list and make the list public, I need to prepare you for what you're taking on," Andrea said. "Specifically, I need to know if you're willing to speak publicly about how each of these issues has played a role in your life."

"Speak *publicly*?" Sam asked, her voice squeaking on the last word.

Andrea smiled. "If we tell the world you're interested in these issues, you'll be in even hotter demand than you already are to appear and speak at events, to participate in fundraising, to become the face of your issue areas for the next four years and possibly beyond. You have the opportunity here to bring light to each of these areas."

"Light," Sam said. "What kind of light?"

"Attention, funding, recognition," Andrea said. "You can start a national conversation in each subject. You and the vice president are the most popular second couple in the history of the office. Your poll numbers are through the roof." She held up a stack of paper. "Interview requests and invitations received in the last week. These are just the latest. Every media outlet in the country is clamoring for an interview with you and your husband. We've been overwhelmed with requests."

"And that's unusual?"

"It's highly unusual for the vice president and second lady to get as much—if not more—attention than the president and first lady," Andrea said.

"*More*," Sam said. "Than the Nelsons?"

"Much more." Andrea handed the pile of paper to Sam. "You can go through these at your leisure and let me know what, if any, appeal to you."

Lilia handed Sam several business cards. "Our email and cell phone numbers are on there. We're available to you twenty-four hours a day."

"Don't you have lives?" Sam asked, incredulous.

"Our lives are devoted to you for the next four years," Lilia replied without an ounce of guile.

"This is all a bit, um, overwhelming, I guess you might say."

"We don't mean to overwhelm you," Mackenzie said. "But we're very excited about the opportunity to work with you, to learn from you, to help you take full advantage of your new role. We're at your disposal."

"That's very kind of you, thank you."

"We have a few somewhat urgent matters to address with you," Andrea said. "Including the bio you'd like us to use on the White House website, an appointment with the White House photographer to take your official portrait and the agenda for the inauguration events."

Sam took a deep breath and blew it out. She could do this, right? Of course she could. She caught murderers for a living. What was a bio and photo when stacked up against that?

BY THE TIME her staff—and she still found it surreal that she had a White House *staff*—had finished with her, it was close to five o'clock and already dark outside. "Would it be possible to meet with the vice president if he's available?"

"Of course," Lilia said. "Let me check with his office and if he's free, we'll walk over there."

Left alone in the office, Sam took the papers Andrea had given her and sat behind the desk, feeling oddly official all of a sudden. She began going through the interview requests from some of the biggest magazines in the world—*Vanity Fair, Cosmopolitan, Town & Country, Vogue, Working Mother*, to name a few.

"I thought there had to be a mistake."

At the sound of his deep voice, Sam smiled, but didn't look up from what she was doing.

"When they said my wife was here and looking for me... I thought, *my* wife? Here? Are pigs flying in hell? Is it snowing in the desert?"

"Hahaha," she said, smiling at him as he came into the office, closing the door behind him. "You're going to start a scandal among my staff by closing the door."

"They may as well get used to how we roll from the beginning."

"Good point. Come on over here and say a proper hello to your wife."

He crossed the room, came around her desk and leaned over to put his hands on the arms of the chair. "What would constitute a proper hello?"

Sam curled her hand around his neck and brought him down to show him what she had in mind. The instant his lips met hers, everything else faded away and there was only him. How he managed to do that to her every time they were together was one of the greatest and most amazing mysteries in her life.

When he drew back many minutes later, his cheeks were flushed and his lips wet from their kisses. "I believe there may be rules about making out in the White House."

"You're the vice president now. You need to do something about those archaic rules."

"I'll get right on that. What're you doing here, babe?"

"Trying to be a good wife and second lady."

"You're a great wife and a great second lady."

"Said the man clearly blinded by love. I'm neither of those things as you well know."

"Why would you say that? You're an amazing wife

to me and mother to Scotty. We wouldn't trade you for anyone."

"You're very sweet for saying so."

"I'm hardly being sweet. You're the only woman I've ever had even the slightest desire to marry. Doesn't that say something about how awesome you are?"

"I suppose it's a pretty good testimonial."

"How'd you get here?"

"Lilia sent a car for me and they brought me in. Good thing because I wouldn't have had the first clue where to go. They're all very nice," she said, gesturing to the outer office.

"What's all that?" he asked of the papers on her desk.

"Interview requests. Apparently, I'm in hot demand."

"You and me both." He reached for her hand and when she took it, he pulled her up and led her to the sofa. Sitting beside her, he turned to face her. "Tell me what's really going on, Samantha."

"What do you mean?"

"This," he said, waving his arm to encompass the room, "is not *you*."

"Maybe it's the new me."

"I liked the old you who was screaming at me to do something about the woman at the White House who was calling to schedule meetings you wanted nothing to do with."

"So you don't expect me to be supportive of your new job?"

"There's supportive and then there's this. You coming here without being dragged kicking and screaming is unexpected, to say the least."

"I was getting bored at home."

"Then go back to work, but don't do this for me. I don't expect it."

"I know you don't, but she called and they sent flowers when I was injured and they were really nice today. They talked to me about how I can use my—our—notoriety to bring attention to issues I care about. It doesn't totally suck to think about bringing awareness to spinal cord issues, learning disabilities, infertility struggles, law enforcement challenges and adoption."

"You'd be an amazing spokesperson for any of those causes, but do you know what that would entail? Being a spokesperson?"

"I'm told it requires speaking. Publicly."

Nodding, he said, "Among other things, such as interviews for print and television, intrusive questions about what these issues have meant to you personally. I just want you to be prepared for what you'd be getting into."

"I hear what you're saying, and I have thought about what we might be able to do in these new roles. If me giving a few speeches and interviews about spinal cord injuries leads to more funding, advanced research, better treatment, then I'll do it. Why wouldn't I?"

"Um, because under normal circumstances you'd rather have the skin peeled from your body with tweezers than willingly meet with the press."

Since she couldn't deny the truth of his statement, she didn't try. "You like me better that way? Kicking and screaming and bitching about all the many ways your new job is putting me out?"

"Frankly? Yes, I like you better that way. This docile Stepford wife thing is not *you*. It's not *my* wife."

"Well," she said, looking down when tears suddenly—

and unexpectedly—filled her eyes. "I'm sorry I'm not what you want."

"Samantha! Oh my God! How can you say you're not what I want? I want you madly, desperately. I want you all the time. What I don't want is you pretending to be someone you're not to make me or anyone else happy."

"I'm not sure where I belong anymore," she said softly. "When I'm at home, I feel like I should be doing something else." She wiped away a tear that rolled down her cheek. It made her feel weak and out of control of her emotions. For that she blamed Stahl. "So I came here thinking maybe I'd find something to do until I figure out what I'm going to do about work."

"If you want to be here, legitimately want to do the work, then please, by all means, do it. But please don't do it for any other reason than because it's what *you* want."

"I liked them," she said of her staff. "They were very nice and welcoming and opened my eyes to some of the things that might be possible while you're in office. Some of it interests me. Some of it doesn't."

"As long as you're doing it for the right reasons, I'm thrilled to have you taking a role. But the minute you're ready to go back to work, that's what you ought to do. Don't let any sense of obligation to me or my job get in the way of that."

"Okay," she said, grateful as always for his unending support and love. "Thank you for understanding."

"I want to understand, Sam. I want to get why you're not in an all-fired rush to go back to work. It's concerning to everyone that you're not."

Because, she thought, *to do that I have to talk about what went on in Marissa Springer's basement. I have to talk about how it made me feel to be certain I was going to die, that I was never going to see you or Scotty or my family again. How can I tell you I'd rather be an active second lady than talk about any of that?*

"Sam?"

She forced herself to look directly into his gorgeous hazel eyes. "I'm just not ready."

"Okay, babe." He wrapped his arms around her. "Fair enough. What do you say we go home, make some dinner with our son and hit the loft after he goes to bed?"

"I say there is nothing else in this world I'd rather do."

FIVE

SHE WAS RIGHT here with him, arching into him as he made love to her, and yet she was as disconnected from him, from their son, her family and friends as she'd been after the miscarriage she'd suffered almost a year ago. He recognized the signs, knew them for what they were this time, and worried endlessly about her.

The Sam he knew and loved would not have initiated a visit to her office at the White House. She didn't clean and organize every square inch of their home. She didn't offer to babysit her sister's children in the middle of a workweek. She didn't cook elaborate meals or make marinara from scratch. She didn't avoid making love with him for weeks, flinching every time he touched her.

And she didn't fake orgasms. That she did so now told him things were worse than he'd thought. *Son of a bitch.* She gave one hell of a performance, moaning and squeezing her internal muscles around him until he couldn't stop the inevitable conclusion.

After, he lay on top of her, breathing hard and trying to make sense of thoughts that refused to add up. He'd experienced the real thing often enough to know a fake when he saw one. But why? Did he say something or let it ride? He opened his eyes and looked down at her. With her eyes closed and her head turned to the side she was closed off to him in a way that frightened him.

They'd never made it to the loft. Scotty had struggled with homework and went to bed late. By the time Nick finished helping him, Sam was already in bed in their room.

He kissed her cheek, nuzzled her neck and waited to see what she would do.

Without opening her eyes, she smiled and wrapped her arms around him.

"Everything okay, babe?"

"Mmm-hmm."

Though he wasn't at all convinced, he withdrew from her and got out of bed. He went into the bathroom to clean up and stood there for a long time trying to figure out what to do. He was so rarely uncertain of himself with her that the feeling was concerning.

Splashing water on his face, he decided he'd call Harry in the morning. He needed some advice from a qualified professional, and his doctor friend had training in PTSD from his own experiences in the military as well as his volunteer work with injured veterans. When Nick returned to bed, Sam was already asleep or pretending to be.

Nick lay awake staring at the ceiling, his mind racing with worries about her, about Scotty's struggles with math, about the president's lack of interest in forging any sort of working relationship with him. The insomnia had never been worse than it had been since Stahl abducted Sam. Standing outside the Springer home that day, waiting for SWAT to go in after her, he'd been so sure they were too late this time.

How many lives could one sexy cop have after all? At some point, her luck would run out. Thinking about that, worrying about it, kept him awake night after night after night until the exhaustion was so ingrained in him he was like a zombie on autopilot during the day.

He'd lost his edge in the exhaustion. He'd lost his ability to read her. The irony wasn't lost on him—he who worried endlessly for her safety on the job would give everything he had to see her back where she belonged, running the MPD's Homicide Division with her usual intense focus.

This new post-Stahl Sam wasn't the same person she'd been before she went into that house, planning to re-interview Marissa Springer and get on with her day. This new Sam was fragile and withdrawn, two words he'd never use to describe her under normal circumstances.

Something had to give and it had to happen soon, before she slipped too far from him and the life she'd cherished before she was viciously attacked.

Nick never did sleep that night and forced his weary body out of bed to get Scotty up for school while Sam continued to sleep. After going to bed late, Scotty was unusually cranky and their morning was more contentious than usual.

"I don't know why you're pissed at me," Scotty said over breakfast.

That he sounded so dejected went straight to Nick's heart. "I'm sorry, buddy. I'm tired and stressed, and I shouldn't take it out on you."

"Are you stressed about Mom?"

"Yeah." He glanced at the perceptive boy. "Are you?"

Scotty nodded. "She's been weird since everything happened. She *cleaned* my room."

"Someone's gotta," Nick said, going for a moment of levity.

"When has it ever been her? You're the anal-retentive freakazoid neatnik, not her."

Those words had come straight from his wife's mouth to his son's. "Hey, I resemble that remark."

Scotty laughed, which made Nick feel slightly better. "What are you going to do about it?"

His natural inclination would be to shield Scotty from what was happening with Sam, but their son was too perceptive and too intelligent to get away with that. And at thirteen, he'd been maturing before their very eyes lately. "I'm going to talk to Harry today and see what he suggests we do."

"Will you let me know what he says?"

"Yes, I will. Try not to worry too much. The most important thing to remember is that she's alive. We can work with the rest."

"That's true. I wish she'd go back to work, though. She'd feel better if she were working. That's what she loves to do."

"I agree. When she's ready, she'll go back. Until then, we need to be supportive and let her do what she needs to do to work through what happened." Nick checked his watch. "Go brush your teeth and grab your backpack. The detail will be leaving in five minutes."

"Not without me they won't," Scotty said with a cheeky grin that Nick couldn't help but return.

"Get going, smart mouth."

After Scotty left with his detail, Nick went upstairs to shower and get ready for work. Seeing that Sam was still sleeping, he ducked into his office to call Harry. The sooner they got to the bottom of whatever was going on, the sooner they could get things back to normal around here.

"Is this the vice president of the United States calling?" Harry asked when he answered on the second ring.

Nick smiled at the predictable comment. His friends had been relentless since his promotion. "In the flesh."

"To what do I owe this incredible honor?"

"I need a favor."

"Sure thing, buddy," Harry said, all joking forgotten. "Anything for you."

"I need you to talk to Sam."

"About?"

"Everything that happened with Stahl. Something's not right with her, and damned if I can get her to talk to me about it. The department shrink isn't having any luck either."

Harry's deep sigh came through the phone. "When you say something's not right, what do you mean?"

"She's cleaning everything and organizing things, which isn't like her. Yesterday, she voluntarily went to a meeting with her White House staff when a couple of weeks ago she was begging me to get her out of those meetings. She's in no particular rush to get back to work, and she's faking things. *Important* things."

"Oh yikes."

"Yeah, exactly. Not like her *at all*. Does she think I can't tell?"

"Um, uh, please tell me that was a rhetorical question."

"What do I do, Harry? I've never seen her this way, even after she was nearly blown up, chased down by gangbangers, pistol-whipped in the face or any of the litany of other shit that's happened. This time it's like she's punched out of reality or something."

"How's she sleeping?"

"Better than I am."

"So the insomnia is back?"

"Worse than it's ever been. I can't recall the last time I actually slept."

"Jesus, Nick. You gotta let me give you something for that."

"It messes me up too bad the next day."

"And how's not sleeping been for your productivity?"

"I'm dealing with it. What I can't deal with is seeing Sam struggling to cope with whatever is going on inside her on her own. *That* is killing me."

AWAKENED BY THE sound of Nick's voice, Sam stood outside the bedroom they'd converted into an office after the Secret Service took over the one downstairs. She listened to Nick air out his thoughts and learned for the first time that he hadn't been sleeping because he was so concerned about her.

She cringed when she heard him tell Harry—she assumed and hoped he was talking to Harry—that she'd faked it with him. Of course he knew. Sometimes she suspected he knew her better than she knew herself.

Tears stung her eyes at the thought of him suffering because of her. Of course he would suffer, and of course he would suffer in silence. He'd never add to her burden.

God, how had it come to this? Listening to her strong, unflappable husband expressing his deepest concerns to his friend… It broke her to know she'd driven him to talk about things he rarely said out loud, except to her.

She took a deep breath and rounded the corner to the office.

He stopped speaking midsentence. "Hey, babe."

"Tell Harry I'll see him today if he has time."

"You'll, what… Oh, okay." His gaze remained fixed on

her when he said, "Sam is here and would like to know if you have any time today—" After a pause, he said to her, "Can you be at his office at ten?"

She nodded.

"She'll see you then. Thanks, Harry." He put down the phone and got up to come around the desk to her. "How much of that did you hear?"

"Enough."

"I wasn't talking about you in a bad way, Samantha."

"I know. I'm sorry you've been so upset. I didn't know you haven't been sleeping, but now that I take a closer look, I can tell. I'm sorry that I was too self-absorbed to look closer."

"Stop." He put his arms around her and wrapped her up in the familiar scent of home. "Don't apologize for any of it. It's not your fault."

"I'm going to fix it."

"Babe, please, don't do it on my account. Do it for you."

"If I do it for you, it'll also be for me because I can't bear to know you're losing sleep over me."

"Isn't the first time," he said with the grin that had made him a national sex symbol since he became vice president.

She reached up to frame his face with her hands. "I'm sorry about last night. I don't know why—"

He kissed the words right off her lips, tightening his arm around her and lifting her to walk her into the bedroom.

Since Sam had kept her eyes open, she saw the Secret Service agent who'd just come on duty avert his gaze before Nick kicked the door shut. She began to laugh and couldn't stop.

"What's so funny?" he asked as he came down on top of her on their bed. "That was some of my best work, and I have to say your laughter wounds me."

Sam only laughed harder. "The poor agent is scarred for life after that demonstration."

"They've never had to protect a vice president who's as hot for his wife as this one is." He kissed her neck and made her shiver from the sensations that rippled through her. As always, his touch electrified her, but weighing heavily on her mind was the meeting she'd agreed to with Harry.

She closed her eyes and tried to concentrate on him, to let him carry her away from all her cares, if only for a short time.

"What?" he asked softly. "Tell me what you're thinking."

"I can't think about anything other than Harry and that appointment."

Nick dropped his head to her chest. "So my best work isn't having the desired effect?"

"It's not you. I hope you know that. God, it's so not you."

"I know, baby." He kissed her lips with tenderness that slayed her. "Rain check?"

"Absolutely." She looked up at him gazing down at her with love and concern. "Could we maybe…"

"What? Anything."

"Just hold me for a while?"

"For as long as you want."

"Don't you have a country to run?"

"The country can wait. My wife needs me to hold her, and that just became the most important thing on my to-do list today."

OUTSIDE THE INTENSIVE care unit at GW, Gonzo pressed the call button, flashed his badge and waited to be buzzed in. The nurses were busy, so it took a minute, which gave him enough time to prepare his case to be allowed to speak to one of their patients.

"Didn't we already talk to this guy?" Detective Arnold asked.

"Yep."

"So what're we doing here again?"

"The lieutenant always says when we hit a dead end, go back and start over. That's what we're doing."

A buzzer sounded and the doors slid open. "What can I do for you?" a nurse asked in a harried tone.

"I need to speak with Mr. Enright."

"This isn't a good time. He's had a rough night."

"We won't keep him long," Gonzo said. "I promise. If it wasn't critical that we speak with him, we wouldn't be here."

She hesitated for a moment and then said, "Just one of you. Follow me."

"Wait here," Gonzo said to Arnold, pointing to the waiting area.

Arnold frowned at him, obviously miffed at being left out. Too bad. The last thing Gonzo had time to deal with right now was fragile egos. He followed the nurse to the room where Enright was attached to wires and tubes and machines. Upon spotting the nurse outside the door, his father jumped up from his post next to the bed and came out of the room. "He's in pain."

"He's not due for more pain meds for a couple of hours yet."

"Hours? He needs it now."

"I'll call the doctor."

"Who's this guy?"

"Detective Sergeant Gonzales." Gonzo flashed his gold shield. "Metro PD."

"What do you want? He's already been interviewed. He told the other detectives everything he knew."

"I'd like a few minutes with him to go over it again."

Enright senior shook his head. "Not now. He's not good."

"He's stable, Mr. Enright," the nurse said, earning points with Gonzo.

"I'll be as quick as I possibly can," Gonzo said.

"Fine, ten minutes, but no more."

Before the guy could change his mind, Gonzo entered the room, stopping at the bedside of twenty-seven-year-old William Enright, an associate at a graphic design and marketing firm called Griffen + Smoltz in Georgetown.

When he opened his eyes and looked up, Gonzo could see the pain in his eyes. William licked dry, cracked lips. "Who're you?" His voice was rough and hard to hear.

"Sergeant Gonzales from the Metro PD. I had a couple of follow-up questions I hoped you could help me with if you're feeling up to it."

"I already told the other lady detective everything I know."

"Detective McBride said you were very helpful. I have to be honest with you—we've hit a brick wall in this investigation. We're getting nowhere fast. When that happens, we've found it works best to go back with fresh eyes and start over. I know you've been through a terrible ordeal, but if you wouldn't mind walking me through the attack one more time, it might help to catch this guy."

"What do you want to know?"

Gonzo pulled a notebook and pen from his coat

pocket. "Tell me what you remember about the minutes leading up to the attack. Where you were, where you'd been, where you were going."

"I was out with some friends downtown."

"Where exactly were you?"

"At a bar on 14th Street."

"Do you remember the name?"

"Desi's, I think?"

"I know that place. It's new, upscale. Right?"

"That's it."

"Who were you with?"

William moved to find a more comfortable position and winced.

"You don't have to do this now, son," his father said from behind Gonzo.

"I'm okay, Dad. I'd rather get it over with." To Gonzo, he said, "I was with people from work. One of the guys is getting married next week, and we took him out for happy hour. It was a good excuse to hit up a place we'd heard a lot about lately."

"The group at work is close-knit?"

"We put in a lot of hours together every week. They're good people."

"Did you leave alone?"

"Yeah, I had a basketball game in the morning, so I wanted to get some sleep. They were staying for one more round."

"So you left the bar and grabbed the Metro?"

"Yeah. I got off at NoMa and was walking home, hurrying because it was freezing. Someone grabbed my right arm and spun me around. The next thing I remember was pain and a struggle and blood everywhere. I didn't realize I'd been stabbed until it was over and he was gone."

"You're sure it was a guy?"

"Absolutely. He was big and very muscular. I remember that much."

"Your initial report stated that he was wearing a mask or something over his face?"

"I assume he was. I never caught a glimpse of his face."

"Was anyone else around on the street?"

"Not that I remember, but someone must've come along and called EMS. The next thing I remember is being here."

"Were you having problems with anyone in your life? Roommate, girlfriend, boyfriend, an ex, a client, a—"

"There was a client who got mad when we refused to design a website he wanted us to do."

"What kind of client?"

"At first, he was really friendly, having us build a site for his T-shirt business, but as we got deeper into the project, I suspected the site was going to be used for something other than T-shirts."

"Did you know what he had in mind?"

"Not really, but he kept asking me weird questions about chat rooms and webcams and stuff like that, and it rang some bells for me. I mean, what does a guy who sells T-shirts want with webcams and chat rooms on his website? So I mentioned it to the art director, who took it to the managing partner. They agreed it was weird and decided to drop him as a client."

Gonzo experienced a burst of excitement at the first possible break in the case. This, right here, was why they went back and retraced their steps. "Can you give me his name?"

"An Italian guy named Giuseppe Besozzi. It was

funny, though, one of my colleagues thought he was pretending to be from Italy. My friend has spent time there, and he swore the guy's accent was fake, which was just another thing that nagged at me after he started asking about webcams."

"What else can you tell me about him?"

"The managing partner at the firm could probably tell you more. He's the one who lands the accounts and manages the clients. We just do the work."

"Would Besozzi have known you were the one to blow the whistle on him?"

"He... Yeah, I guess he would know it came from me."

"And does he match the physical description of the man who attacked you?"

"Giuseppe is tall but I don't think of him as particularly muscular like that guy was, but who knows? Maybe he's tougher than he looks."

Gonzo took down the name and address of the firm as well as the name and contact info for the managing partner. "This has been incredibly helpful, William. I really appreciate your help."

"You really think Giuseppe could be behind this?"

"I don't know yet, but you can bet we'll be looking into him. You've given me something I didn't have before—a lead."

"I hope it helps and you can find the person doing this. No one should have to go through this."

"I completely agree, and we're going to find him and make him pay."

"Come back if you need me for anything else. Whatever I can do to help."

"I appreciate that. I hope you're feeling much better soon."

"So do I."

On the way out of the room, Gonzo shook hands with Enright's father. "Thank you," he said.

Nodding, the man said, "Get this guy."

"We're doing everything we can. We'll keep you posted." He left the room and gestured for Arnold to come with him. Clearing the ICU doors, Gonzo called Malone. "We need an officer outside Enright's door at GW ICU in case his attacker tries to finish the job," Gonzo said.

"What gives you reason to believe he might?"

"Some new information." He brought Malone up to speed on what Enright had told him about his ex-client and asked him to do a run on Besozzi. "Let me know if anything pops and see if you can get me a local address."

"On it," Malone said. "And I'll get someone over to GW right away. What about the other victim?"

"He's still in the hospital, so let's get someone on him too. I'm going to Enright's office now."

"Let me know what you find out, and I'll get back to you with anything I find on Besozzi."

Gonzo walked so fast to the parking lot that Arnold scrambled to keep up.

"Where we going now?" Arnold asked.

"To the offices of the graphic design firm where Enright works. We might finally have something." Gonzo could only hope so. He needed to close this baffling case, not only for the affected victims and their families, but so he could finally marry the love of his life. It was also important that he make Sam proud while he was covering for her. He'd never had better incentive to close a case.

SIX

SAM ARRIVED AT Harry's office ten minutes before her appointment time. The hour she'd spent with Nick had helped to calm and center her, and noticing how exhausted he looked fueled her determination to put the episode with Stahl behind her so she could get back to normal. Or whatever passed as normal now.

Harry emerged from a room in the back, escorting an elderly patient to the checkout desk. He caught Sam's eye and held up a finger to indicate he'd be with her shortly.

Her stomach ached the way it used to when she'd been hooked on diet cola and had come here at Nick's insistence. Even though Harry had told her to give up the soda she loved, he had since become a trusted friend to her as well as her husband, and if anyone could help her navigate her way through this situation, he could.

"Sam?" he said. "You can come on back."

She gathered up her purse and coat and followed him down a long hallway that led to his office. There he closed the door and greeted her with a hug and a kiss to her cheek.

He gestured for her to have a seat on the sofa and sat next to her. "You're looking well."

"Thank you. The bruises are finally fading, thankfully in time for the inauguration."

"Thank goodness for small favors," he said sarcastically.

"Right? As long as the second lady is presentable, all is well."

"I still can't believe you two. Vice President and Mrs. Cappuano."

"We can't believe it either."

"Heard you got over to the White House yesterday on official business. I said that can't possibly be true. The Sam I know and love would never go there willingly."

She rolled her eyes at the predictable comment. "I met with my staff. I have a *staff*. Can you stand it?"

"That's pretty funny. I picture you there and can't stop laughing."

She elbowed him playfully. "It's not *that* funny."

"Yes, it really is."

"I suppose it is kinda funny." She ran her hands over her jeans, trying to dry suddenly sweaty palms.

"What's really going on, Sam?"

"Oh, a lot of things."

"Could I tell you a little story?"

Right about now, she'd say yes to anything that put off having to tell *her* story. "Sure."

"I don't know if Nick told you that I put myself through medical school by agreeing to give the Army six years afterward. Those six years happened to coincide with a pretty chaotic time in our country's history. I did tours in both Afghanistan and Iraq."

"I had no idea. He never said."

"It's not something I talk a lot about because it was a tough time in my life—in the lives of everyone who served and deployed. We saw a lot of things. Unforgettable things. Things that stay with you always, that keep you awake at night years later."

"God, Harry. I'm sorry."

He covered her hand with his. "Don't be sorry. I'm thankful to have been able to make a contribution. But I know what trauma does to a perfectly healthy brain. I know how images get in there and won't get out no matter how hard you try."

"This is why Nick wanted me to talk to you."

"That's right. In addition to dealing with my own PTSD after I returned to 'normal' life, I've counseled a lot of veterans who've come back with a wide variety of post-traumatic issues. Without a thorough analysis and examination, I can't say with any certainty that what you're dealing with is PTSD, but it sounds like it might be."

"I think it is," she confessed for the first time. "I keep going over it and over it and over it in my mind, every misstep, every minute from the second I walked into Marissa Springer's house for the second time that day until SWAT came swooping in. I've relived it ten thousand times."

"And nothing's changed, right? It still happens exactly the same way."

"Every time," she said with a sigh.

"What do you think most about?"

"How stupid I was to go in there alone."

"Why do you say that?"

"Everything about the Springer case had been wonky from the get-go. But things were chaotic that day. Cruz was off tending to Elin after she got beat up at the gym, which we later learned was all part of the plan. Gonzo was still on medical leave and reeling from Lori's death as well as the implication that he might've been behind her murder."

"So you were down two of your closest colleagues that day, which means nothing was 'normal.' Am I right?"

She nodded. "I was working the case, pulling the threads, doing what I do. One of Marissa's sons had killed his brother and a bunch of other kids. The house was heavy with grief. The first time I went there, Marissa and her maid, Edna, were so nice. They talked about how they'd been coping together, watching movies and eating takeout and trying to get through each day. It sounded as if Edna had been a source of huge comfort to Marissa, that they were more friends than boss and employee."

Harry didn't say anything. Rather he just waited patiently, giving her the time she needed to collect her thoughts.

"When Marissa shot Edna, I just... I couldn't believe what I was seeing. I never saw that coming. Not for one second."

"How could you have? In all your previous dealings with Marissa had you seen *anything* that would lead you to believe she was capable of that?"

"No."

"You're the best at what you do."

Sam began to protest, but he stopped her with a raised hand.

"You're the very best at what you do, but you are not—and have never been—a mind reader. You've got incredible instincts that guide you, but they are not infallible. *You* are not infallible."

"So you're saying it was only a matter of time before something like this happened?"

"I'm saying no one, not even a superstar cop like you, would've seen this coming. Marissa Springer in bed with *Leonard Stahl*? In what plausible scenario do those two strange bedfellows come together to do what they did? The craziest of fiction writers wouldn't have come up with that."

As she thought about what he said, Sam looked down at the floor.

"From what I can see you made one critical mistake."

She glanced at him. "What's that?"

"You shouldn't have gone in there alone—or without someone at least knowing where you were and why. That much is on you, and I suspect you're already beating yourself up royally for that. The rest was completely out of your hands. Do you understand that?"

"I guess."

"I want you to say it out loud. 'What happened in Marissa Springer's house was not my fault.'"

"I don't know if I can do that."

"You have to, Sam. Until you do, you're carrying around blame that doesn't belong to you. That's what's holding you back from moving forward, from reclaiming your life and your career. It's what's keeping your husband up at night."

"I hate that he's so wound up about me."

"Scotty is too. Everyone who knows you and loves you is worried."

Sam wanted to die on the spot when tears began rolling down her cheeks. Badass cops did not cry, for Christ's sake, but apparently mothers did. She wiped them away with violent sweeps of her hands.

"The tears piss you off, huh?"

"Hell yes they piss me off! I'm not a simpering female who can't handle the shit that comes her way."

"No one would ever dare accuse you of being any such thing. You went through a shocking, traumatic, painful, frightening, life-threatening experience. I have to tell you, I'm kind of relieved to see the tears."

"I'm glad you are. I'm still pissed."

Harry laughed. "I know."

After another long pause in which she realized he was waiting for her to continue, she said, haltingly, "Intellectually, I know it wasn't my fault. I get that. I really do. But emotionally…"

"You feel like you should've known something like this was going to happen after all the years you've been scuffling with Stahl."

"Yeah." She wiped away more tears that refused to stop despite her desperate desire to control her emotions. "Especially after he came at me on my own doorstep. But at least then I could sort of understand it. I'd been pushing his buttons for a long time by then."

"As I recall, he was in a lot of trouble for that, suspended from the job and facing charges."

She nodded. "And using his time, we now know, to plot his ultimate revenge against me and my squad."

"The key words in that sentence are 'we now know.' There was no way you or anyone could've known what he was up to."

"We could've kept a closer eye on him after he was arrested."

"Was that up to you? The decision to keep a closer eye on him?"

"No. I wanted nothing to do with him. I was glad to not have to see him at work anymore."

"That's another thing we need to add to your not-my-fault list. By my count there're now several things on that list." He ticked the items off on his fingers. "It wasn't your fault that Stahl teamed up with Marissa. It wasn't your fault that Marissa shot Edna. It wasn't your fault that they held you hostage, beat you, wrapped you in razor wire or tormented you for hours in which you were certain you were going to die. It wasn't your fault that Elin got hurt or that Freddie probably did something stupid by going after the guy who hit her."

Sam stared at him, incredulous. "How'd you know about that? It hasn't been made public."

"I know Freddie, and I know what I'd do if someone hurt the woman I loved as badly as Elin was hurt."

"He did a really stupid thing and he's suspended for a week because of it."

"He'd probably say he'd do it again."

"He did say that, which concerns me."

"As much as he respects and admires you, that's on him. Not you. He made the choice to risk his career and his reputation. You probably couldn't have stopped him if you'd tried—or if you'd known what he intended to do, which you didn't. Another thing you couldn't control."

"Control. That seems to be the key word here."

"You're seeing that, huh? Once or twice in every career, no matter the profession, something happens that's outside our control and it almost always leaves a lasting mark. For me it was the young soldier in Afghanistan who suffered a miscarriage in the field, and I couldn't save her because she bled out before we could get her to the hospital. There was absolutely nothing I could do. We later determined that her placenta had ruptured, a very rare complication that is almost always fatal for the mother and the baby, but that doesn't mean I don't go over it and over it in my mind even almost ten years later."

"God..."

"The sad part is we didn't even know she was pregnant. She was more than six months along and not show-ing at all. She kept it hidden because she didn't want to be sent home early. She wanted to finish her tour and was scheduled to go home two weeks after she died."

"That's so sad."

"It was awful for all of us, and it took me a really long time to accept that there was nothing I could've done to change the outcome. I even met with her parents when I returned stateside and told them exactly what'd hap-pened."

"I'm sure they appreciated that."

"I guess so. Didn't bring back their daughter or grand-child, though."

"I hear what you're saying about control and things that are outside of my control, and it helps to clarify things."

He reached over to squeeze her arm. "It's hard to admit to ourselves and others that we're not superhuman, de-spite how it might seem."

That drew a small smile from her. "You're taking shots at my reputation now."

"It's a formidable reputation, and one that anyone would struggle to live up to. You need to allow your-self a few moments of being as human as the rest of us before you put your cape back on and get back to being superhuman."

"Will I get back there?"

"Back where?"

"Back to being superhuman?"

"Do you want to?"

"I think I do. I fear that my judgment is shot, that the gut that has always guided me so well let me down pro-foundly here."

"There were no signals for your gut to register."

"This entire case, from the minute we found Brooke on the front porch to Gonzo getting shot to Lori being killed to Elin getting beat up to SWAT bursting into the Springers' basement... The whole thing was freaking crazy. I've never been part of anything quite like it."

"And it all struck very, very close to home. Think about it—Brooke, Gonzo, Elin, Lori, all of them people you love or connected to people you love. That's going to throw off your concentration under the best of circumstances and this was anything but the best of circumstances."

"Everything you're saying makes perfect sense."

"You might be the first woman ever to say so."

Sam laughed. "I doubt that."

"You're going to have to air this out for the department shrink before you can get cleared to go back to work, and you should take all the time you need to make sure you're totally ready to do that. Until then, I really wish you'd stop blaming yourself and start blaming Stahl. Allow yourself to get really, really mad at him and at Marissa for getting into bed with him. But give yourself a break, will you please, Sam?"

"I'll try. I think I know what I need to do now. Thank you, Harry."

"Happy to help whenever you need me."

"You might've missed your calling as a shrink."

"Funny you should say that. I've actually thought about changing specialties but never seem to get around to it. The thought of more school is rather revolting when you've spent as much time in school as I have."

"I bet." She stood and looped her purse over her shoulder. "I've taken enough of your time. Thank you again for squeezing me in."

He stood to hug her. "Anytime. Call me day or night if you need me. I'm always here for you guys."

"You're one of the good ones, doc. We need to find a nice girl for you."

"Ugh, you and my mother."

"I'll see you at the parties next week?"

"Wouldn't miss it for the world. I'm so damned proud of my friend—and his wife."

Sam gave his arm a squeeze and headed out the door and down the long corridor that led to the waiting room. As Sam entered the crowded room, a woman gasped.

"Oh my God! You're, you, Mrs. Cappuano! *You're the second lady!*"

Sam wanted to expire on the spot when all eyes in the room landed on her. All she could think about is that her face must be a red, blotchy mess after crying her eyes out all over Harry.

"Could I have your autograph?" the woman asked.

"Um, sure. I guess."

While the woman riffled through her purse for a piece of paper and a pen, Sam was forced to stand there like a museum exhibit. A flash exploded to her left, making her jolt. It was a reminder that she was still jumpy and skittish, two things she'd never been before that day in the basement with Stahl.

"Ah, here we go." The woman thrust a used envelope and a pen at Sam. "Can you make it out to Janice?"

"Yeah." She wrote, *Janice, nice to meet you. Sam Cappuano*. She'd been about to write Holland when she caught herself.

"Could I get one?" the lady next to her asked.

Oh for fuck's sake, Sam thought. "Of course," she said with a gracious smile. They couldn't see that her teeth were gritted, could they?

"Your husband," a third woman, the youngest of the three, said with a salacious grin, "is *so* hot."

"Um, thank you. I think so too." Sam wanted to poke out the woman's eyes so she could no longer leer at her hot husband, but she somehow managed to contain the urge to get violent.

Before she left, she signed autographs for six other people in the waiting room as well as the office staff. At some point, Harry came out to see what was going on and had silently mocked her with laughing eyes. She would take that up with him when she next saw him.

She left Harry's office and drove directly to HQ, anxious to get this done before she lost her nerve. After parking outside the morgue, she hustled into the building, the bitter January wind cutting through her coat and sweater. Inside, she took a moment to fix her hair and encountered the Chief Medical Examiner, Dr. Lindsey McNamara, in the hallway.

"Hey, Doc," she said to her close friend and colleague. "How goes it in the morgue?"

"Busier than usual with this knife-wielding freak on the loose. How are you? It's good to see you here."

"Good to be seen."

"Are you back on the job?"

"Not quite yet but getting closer."

"Glad to hear it. We've missed you."

"Nice to be missed, and thanks for the calls, the visits, the food and all the support. It's been greatly appreciated."

"It was the least I could do. I still can't get over everything that happened." Lindsey stopped herself. "But you don't need to talk about that."

"Actually, I do," Sam said with a chagrined smile. "Until I air it out with Trulo, I can't come back. I'm heading up to air it out."

"Good luck with that. You've been down this road before. You certainly know how to give him just enough to get him to sign off."

"That's the plan. I'll see you on the way out."

"I'll be here."

Sam went straight upstairs without cutting through the detectives' pit where she was sure to be waylaid. If she put this off, she might not do it, and it had to be done. If not for herself then definitely for Nick and Scotty who'd spent enough time stressing out about her.

Outside Trulo's office, she marshaled her courage and raised her hand to knock. If he were with someone, he wouldn't answer, so she waited.

The door swung open, and the doctor wiped his mouth with a paper napkin. "Sorry, Lieutenant, I was just downing some lunch. What can I do for you?"

Oddly enough, the thought of the impenetrable doctor eating lunch made him more human than he'd ever been to her. "I'm ready to talk."

Trulo stared at her for a long moment before he said, "Come in."

SEVEN

FREDDIE AND ELIN drove until they ran out of land at the Gulf of Mexico in a little town near Pensacola, Florida, called Perdido Key. They rented a room in an ocean-front hotel and took to the beach. Though it wasn't quite warm enough to swim, it was a hell of a lot warmer than it was at home.

He sent his mother a text to let her know where they were and left his phone in the room, determined to punch out as much as he could and take full advantage of the rare opportunity for a getaway with the woman he loved. They had things to talk about before they could head back to their real lives, and this was certainly a beautiful place to kill a week.

"Will you rub sunscreen on my back?" Elin asked, holding out the bottle.

"I'd love to."

She smiled at his predictable response. He was never shy about how badly he wanted her all the time. They'd yet to make love since she'd been hurt, and he was hoping they'd get back on track in that area this week as well.

As he smoothed the sunscreen over her soft skin, Freddie thought about how close he'd come to losing her. During his career as a cop, he'd seen punches to the face kill people on more than one occasion. She could've been killed when she hit her head on the way down or choked to death on her own blood. In so many ways it could've been worse.

"Why'd you stop?" she asked.

"Sorry. I was just thinking."

"About what?"

"How grateful I am that you're okay—or that you're on your way to being okay again. As bad as it was, it could've been so much worse."

"I know."

He finished applying the sunscreen and handed the tube back to her, rubbing what was left on his face and then sitting back in his chair, trying to relax. They were hundreds of miles from DC, but the stress had come with him. So many thoughts circled around in his mind, making him crazy as he tried to reason his way through what'd happened. The way Stahl had set them all up and how he needed to tell Elin that before Stahl went to court again and the whole mess was broadcast to the world.

"Hey, baby," he said.

"Hmm?"

"So there's some stuff we need to talk about."

"Didn't we just talk for two days in the car?"

"Other stuff, about work and the case against Elliott and Stahl and all that. There're a few things I've been wanting to tell you, but it never seemed like the right time, what with your injuries and how you were in so much pain. I didn't want to add to it."

She sat up in her chair and looked over at him. "Add to it how?"

"So the thing with Elliott coming to the gym and stalking you and getting physical with you."

"What about it?"

"It was all part of Stahl's set up. He hired Elliott to

pursue you and to bring things to a head that day because he wanted me out of the picture when he went after Sam."

Her mouth fell open in shock. "Are you kidding me? The whole thing was a big *plan*?"

"Yeah. From what I've been told, Stahl figured I'd do exactly what I did when you were attacked and run to your side, which left Sam shorthanded and alone that day." Freddie reached for her hand, and she gave it willingly. "And then I did something that I probably shouldn't have done, but I'm not sorry I did it."

"What did you do?"

"I went into the jail and beat the shit out of Elliott."

"Freddie! I told you I didn't want you to do that. Oh my God! That's why you're off this week, isn't it? You got in trouble."

"Yes."

"*Freddie… Why* did you do that? You know better."

"After what he did to you, you have to ask me *why*?"

"Yes, I'm asking why! He was in jail, facing charges. Why couldn't that have been enough for you?"

"He laid hands on you. He hurt what's mine after terrorizing you for weeks. There was no way I could let that go."

"You should have."

"Well, I didn't."

"And now you're suspended for a week, presumably without pay that we need. So what're we doing here?" She gestured to the sand and water. "We can't afford it."

"Yes, we can. I have money put away. We'll be fine." He picked up a pile of sand and let it spill through his fingers, nervous about what else he needed to say to her. "We never talked about the rest of what happened with Elliott."

"What do you mean?"

"The stalking and all that. Before the assault."

"Oh. That."

"Yeah, that. Ever since that day, I can't stop thinking about how you kept that from me, and maybe if you'd told me…" He didn't want to say they might've caught on to Stahl's plan, saved Lori's life and Sam from the hell that she went through. He'd never put that on Elin.

"It's all my fault," she said softly. "Everything that happened to me and Sam and Alex's mom."

"No, it's not your fault. None of it is your fault. That's not why I told you. But the thought of any guy hassling you and me being oblivious… We can't operate that way. If you're in trouble, I'm in trouble. If someone is hassling you, they're hassling me. I don't want you keeping stuff like that from me."

"I'm sorry. I shouldn't have. You were so stressed out after Gonzo got shot, and I didn't want to add to it."

"See, that right there, what you just said. You wouldn't be adding to anything. You're *everything* to me. It hurts me that you kept something so big from me. I thought we were better than that."

"We are better, and I wanted to tell you. I'm sorry I hurt you by not telling you, but I was afraid of what you'd do. Turns out I had good reason to be afraid."

"I'm not sorry I confronted him."

"What did you do to him?"

"I punched him in roughly the same place he punched you, and I kneed him in the balls."

"Don't they have cameras in there?"

"Covered it with my hoodie."

"You shouldn't have done it."

"So I've been told, but I don't regret it."

She pushed up her sunglasses and looked over at him with the piercing blue eyes that had captivated him since the first time he met her. "You want me to tell you things, but if I do, is this what you're going to do? Go after someone, assault them, endanger the career you've worked so hard for? Is that who you're going to be?"

For the first time since he confronted Elliott, he experienced the slightest pang of regret for what he'd done. If it meant she'd hold out on him about important things in the future then maybe he shouldn't have done it. "It's not who I want to be, but you can't expect me to just sit on my hands and do nothing when someone attacks you."

"That's *exactly* what I expect you to do. Can't you see? What you did made it *worse*, Freddie. It got you in trouble at work, and I'm sure this incident will go on your record, which could mess up future promotions. It's not worth it. Can't you see that?"

"Felt worth it at the time."

"Do you hear yourself? What happened to the good Christian boy you used to be who was so devoted to his faith that he waited to have sex until he was almost thirty?"

"He met you, fell in love and discovered he'd kill for the woman he loves."

"Even if she doesn't want him to do that?"

"Even then."

She shook her head in obvious dismay.

"I'll make you a deal. If you promise to never again keep something big like this from me, I'll promise you that I'll never again be violent on your behalf."

"I'll take that deal."

He looked over at her and took the hand she offered to shake on their deal. "You know, you really ought to marry me one of these days so we can make our deal a lifetime arrangement."

"Are you asking?"

"What if I was?"

"Do it and find out."

Freddie felt like he'd been shot again. The burst of adrenaline that fired through him felt almost the same as it did then. Only instead of unbearable pain, there was only joy.

He got down on his knees in front of her. "Elin..." There were, he discovered, no words to properly tell her what she meant to him. Forced to take a moment to collect himself, the next time he looked up at her he saw tears in her eyes. "I love you more than anything, and I always will. When you hurt, I hurt. When you're happy, I'm happy. There's nothing I want more than to be happy with you forever. Will you marry me?"

"I thought you'd never ask." She hurled herself into his arms, knocking him back into the warm sand that cushioned their landing.

"Whoa, careful. I don't want you to reinjure anything."

"I don't want to be careful. I just got engaged."

"I hate to be a stickler for details, but 'I thought you'd never ask' means yes, right?"

"Yes, you knucklehead," she said, laughing, "it means *yes*. A thousand times *yes*."

"I only needed one yes, but I'll take a thousand." He pushed the hair back from her face and brought her in close enough to kiss, taking it easy in deference to her injuries.

"Let's go back to the room," she whispered.

"What do you want to do there?"

"You."

"Oh, well, um, okay then."

Laughing at his bumbling response, she got up and held out her left hand for him.

"We'll be putting a ring on this finger as soon as we find one you love."

"I don't need a ring. You just got yourself suspended. You can't afford it."

"You do need a ring, and I *can* afford it." If it took him five years to pay for it, he was getting her the biggest, best ring he could find. He wanted the whole world to know she was his—and permanently off the market.

"You should call your mother."

"I will. Later. My fiancée wants to do me. I'm not thinking about my mother right now."

The sound of her laughter was one of his favorite things, and it had been far too long since he'd heard her laugh. Inside their room, he directed her straight to the shower to wash off the sand. Freddie turned on the water and followed her in, both still wearing their bathing suits. He loved her all the time, but the sight of his gorgeous woman in a bikini was another of his favorite things.

She wrapped her arms around him and rested her head on his chest. "Did that really just happen out there?"

"Yeah, it really did. I've been wanting to ask you for a while now."

"Why didn't you?"

"I don't know. The timing never seemed right, and then after everything happened…"

"This was perfect—on the beach, on vacation, away from everything. I'll never forget it."

"Good," he said, his voice rough with the emotions only she had ever roused in him.

She went up on tiptoes to kiss him, pressing her sexy body against his.

He'd been so careful with her for weeks now that he was officially dying for her. But he'd never do anything to cause her pain of any kind, which was the only reason he broke the kiss. "You're still recovering—"

"I'm fine. I want you, Freddie. Right now."

"Here or in bed?"

"Here. Now." She looked up at him as she reached behind her to untie her top. The bottoms followed, and then she tugged on the waistband to his bathing suit.

Watching her strip, he'd gone stupid in the head as he often did when she was naked. How such a total goddess could've chosen him would be something he'd still be asking himself on his deathbed. But she was his goddess, and judging by the way she pressed against him, she meant it when she said she wanted him right now.

His foot slipped, and he held on tight to her so they wouldn't fall. The last thing they needed was any more injuries. "Not here," he said. "In bed." Reaching behind him, he turned off the water and guided her from the shower with a hand to her back.

They dried off quickly and went into the bedroom where the sunshine peeked in through the drawn blinds. It felt decadent to be getting busy in the middle of what should've been a workday for both of them, but Freddie was determined to enjoy this break from reality. Who knew when they'd get another one?

"I can't believe I get to keep you forever," he whispered. "The whole time…"

"What?"

"I've just been waiting for you to tell me you've found someone you like better. You could have anyone—"

"I want *you*. I've wanted you since the first time I met you when you were so adorable and bumbling as you asked me what kind of sex I had with John O'Connor."

"I'd prefer to forget that." That interview made up twenty of the most mortifying minutes of his life.

"I'll never forget it." With her fingertip, she traced the outline of his lips. "You were so cute and so sexy and *soooo* embarrassed—and pissed with Sam because she refused to rescue you. And when you came back to find me, I was so happy to see you."

"I could barely speak when I saw you again. I still remember the light blue vest you were wearing and how blue your eyes were. I was glad I had worn a trench coat because I was hard from the second I spotted you on the sidewalk coming toward me carrying a tray of coffees."

Her warm soft hand encircled his erection. "You were hard under your coat?"

Groaning from what she was doing to him, he said, "So hard. You should've seen me trying to hide the hard-on you gave me during that first interview from Sam. She never would've let me live it down."

Elin laughed and began to stroke him the way only she had ever done.

"I was afraid to touch you." He cupped her breast and teased the pierced nipple with his thumb. "I was afraid you'd know I'd never done it before. That I'd come the second you touched me because I wanted you so badly."

She ran her finger over the tip of his cock, making him jolt from the almost-painful desire. "You held up admirably. I had no idea it was your first time until you told me."

"And you stayed with me anyway."

"What choice did I have after I got you shot?"

"You didn't get me shot. You got me in trouble by shutting off my phone and my alarm. I got myself shot."

"I'm thankful every day that you survived that. I would've been so sad to lose you right after I found you." She went up on her knees and straddled him.

He'd never seen anything sexier in his life than the way she looked on top of him with full breasts and the incredibly sexy pierced nipples, the toned body, the white-blond hair and those eyes, damn those eyes.

"You shouldn't be up there doing all the work, baby. You should be lying passively, letting me worship you."

"When have I ever been passive in bed?"

"True, but you've been hurt—"

She bent over to kiss him as she took him in, coming down on him slowly but insistently until he was fully embedded and trying to hold back the orgasm that wanted out right this second.

He bit his lip and groaned. "Gimme a second." His hands on her hips kept her from moving until he managed to get things under control—for the moment anyway. It was always a battle when she was naked and sexy in his bed. He had to remind himself it wasn't about instant gratification, but rather making it last as long as he could to make sure she got everything she needed.

After weeks of dying for her, he wanted that more than ever this time. So when she began to move, he bit his lip and let her take over, her hips moving faster and faster as her breasts rubbed against his chest.

"God, Elin."

"So good, *so, so* good."

It was always so good—not that he had anything to compare it to. But he was wise enough to know he could sleep with a hundred other women and never find what he had with her. Not that he wanted any other woman. She was everything he needed and then some.

When he felt her internal muscles contract, he knew she was close so he held her hips in place and thrust into her.

She cried out and hit the peak a few seconds before he did and then slumped down on top of him.

Freddie put his arms around her, thankful to know he had forever to spend with her. "Love you," he whispered.

"Love you too."

Under normal circumstances, Freddie would be freaking out over having been suspended from the job he loved. But under these circumstances, he decided the suspension was worth knowing the guy who'd hurt her would never come near his fiancée again.

EIGHT

THE OFFICES OF Griffen + Smoltz Design were located on M Street in Georgetown. Gonzo and Arnold trudged up the stairs to the second floor where the offices were situated above several high-end boutiques. They pushed through monogrammed, frosted double doors to enter a wide open space that bustled with activity and young people wearing mostly denim and hoodies and other casual attire.

At the reception desk, Gonzo asked to speak to the managing partner, Simon Griffen.

"Whom shall I say is calling?"

They flashed their badges. "Sergeant Gonzales and Detective Arnold, Metro PD."

"Is this about Mr. Enright?"

"Could we see Mr. Griffen, please?" Gonzo asked. He was the one asking the questions, not her.

"I'll see if he's available."

"Make him available."

She scurried off into the fray of the large room where the entire team worked except, it seemed, for those who occupied offices along a far wall. The receptionist ducked into one of those rooms and shut the door behind her. Gonzo noticed that everyone else was looking at them and probably wondering what was up now.

The sort of thing that had happened to Enright changed the people around him as much as it changed the victim.

It took some of their innocence, messed with their sense of safety and left them edgier, warier, on guard. Gonzo had seen it often during his career and sympathized with what they were going through after one of their own had been brutally attacked.

The receptionist returned with a handsome young guy in jeans and a dress shirt that he wore with the sleeves rolled up. He had light blond hair and an athletic build. "I'm Simon Griffen." He shook both their hands. "What can I do for you?"

"Sergeant Gonzales, Detective Arnold. Could we have a minute of your time, preferably in private?"

"Of course. Right this way." He led them through the maze of workstations. Each desk had at least one huge computer screen. Many had two or more.

The workers stopped what they were doing to watch the cops follow Simon into his office.

"Have a seat. Can I get you something to drink?"

"No, we're fine, thanks," Gonzo said, answering before Arnold could accept. "We've just come from seeing Mr. Enright in the hospital."

"How is he today? I'm planning to get over there after work."

"He's weak but improving."

"Thank God. What a shock it's been for all of us. Will is such a nice guy. Everyone loves him. We can't imagine anyone would want to harm him."

"He mentioned some difficulties with a client named Giuseppe Besozzi. What can you tell us about that?"

"He told you about that?" Griffen asked, visibly rattled.

"Why do you ask?"

"We're all about client privacy and confidentiality. If

it gets out that a client's personal business was being discussed with the police, that could put us out of business."

"What if one of your clients was the one who attacked your employee?" Gonzo asked.

"You don't honestly think it was him, do you? These attacks have been so random."

"They've seemed random. Our job is to find out whether or not they really are and to apprehend the person or persons responsible. What can you tell us about Besozzi?"

Griffen took a deep breath and seemed to sag some under the weight of the circumstances. "He came to us through a referral from another client. He was interested in a website for his retail T-shirt business. We met with him, took him on as a client and Will worked closely with him on the design of the site. They were getting close to finished when Will came to me with concerns about some add-ons that Besozzi was suddenly interested in."

"What kind of add-ons?" Gonzo asked though he already knew.

"Webcams and chat rooms. That kind of stuff."

"What would a guy in the T-shirt business want with such things?" Arnold asked.

"That's what Will wanted to know too. It sounded bizarre to him and he thought it was possible that Besozzi might be involved in something illegal. He did the right thing coming to me. We don't want to be part of anything questionable. I consulted with my partner and we agreed to terminate the relationship. We met with Besozzi, returned his deposit and told him we were ending the relationship."

"And how did that go over?" Gonzo asked.

"Not well. He was furious, but I could understand

why. He'd spent months working with us and was close to launching his site. He ranted about the time he'd lost and what kind of business were we running. We anticipated that, but he was angrier than we'd expected."

"Did he threaten any retribution of any kind?" Arnold asked.

"Not specifically, no."

"But?" Gonzo asked, sensing there was more to it.

"He was kinda scary mad, you know? Yelling and screaming and knocking things over on the way out. You heard all the chatter out there," he said, gesturing to the big room. "After he left, you could hear a pin drop for a full minute. My partner and I brought in security for a couple of days, just to be safe. You hear about people coming back with guns to settle a score."

"Did you think he would do something like that?"

"We didn't know, so we acted with an abundance of caution."

"Did you ever see him here again?" Arnold asked.

Griffen shook his head. "Thankfully, no. We haven't heard from him since that day."

"Was this an unusual occurrence? To have things go bad with a client?"

"Very unusual. We've been in business ten years and have had our issues with clients. Design is a very subjective thing. What one person loves, another hates. So at times we've been unable to satisfy a client and parted company as a result. That's an unfortunate outcome that we work hard to avoid to the best of our ability. But the thing with Besozzi was different."

"Do you have a local address for him?" Gonzo asked.

"I can get it, but you won't tell him we gave it to you, will you?"

"We won't mention where we got it."

He got on the computer and clicked around for a minute. Then he wrote down the address and handed the piece of paper to Gonzo. "You really think he might be behind the knife attack?"

"Truthfully, it's the best lead we've had yet."

"Wow," Griffen said. "I can't believe he'd do something like that."

"Well, we don't know that he did," Gonzo said. "All we know is he had a beef with someone who was attacked. We'll be talking to other victims to see if there are any tie-ins. This has been very helpful. If you think of anything else we should know, here's my card. Please call me, night or day."

"I will. I hope you catch whoever hurt Will."

"I hope so too. We can see ourselves out." As they pushed through the double doors, Gonzo handed the paper with Besozzi's address to Arnold. "Call Dispatch and let them know we're going to need some subtle backup. No charging in with lights and sirens, and tell them to stay a block or so away until they hear from us."

While Arnold called Dispatch, Gonzo called Malone.

"What've you got, Sergeant?"

"A hot lead in the knife attacks." He updated the captain on what they'd learned about Besozzi. "We're heading there now, and we've called for backup."

"Are you thinking this is our guy?"

"I'm thinking he had a beef with Enright. That's all I know right now. I'm going to send McBride and Tyrone over to talk with our other surviving vic to see if there's any connection, but I don't want to wait on Besozzi until we know that. He may be a flight risk if he thinks we're on to him."

"Agreed. I'll update McBride and Tyrone and give them their orders."

"Great, thanks."

"Good work, Sergeant. Keep me posted."

"Will do."

"Patrol is set to provide subtle backup," Arnold said.

"Great. Let's go pick this guy up."

SAM FELT CLAUSTROPHOBIC the second the door clicked shut behind Trulo. She took the visitor's seat while he returned to his desk and packed up his lunch. He again wiped his mouth with a napkin that he discarded before he turned to her, his expression expectant.

As usual, he wasn't going to make this easy for her.

"Since that day," she said, haltingly, "I'm afraid pretty much all the time. I relive it, over and over, looking for signs that I missed, signs that I shouldn't have gone back into Marissa's house, especially alone. I go through every minute of that day, from when I left my house until SWAT got me out of there." She placed her hand on her belly. "I can almost always trust my gut. If there's some instinct telling me to watch out, I *feel* it here. I always feel it. But this time, there was nothing. That's the part I can't get past. How could there be nothing when *that* was about to happen?"

"So you think there's something wrong with you because you didn't see it coming?"

"It makes me wonder if I've lost that instinct and how effective I'll be on the job without it."

"Talk to me about Stahl."

Well okay then. Guess we aren't talking about my instincts anymore... "What about him?"

"You've had a difficult relationship with him."

"To say the least."

"Why do you suppose that is?"

"There's bad blood between him and my dad from before I was on the job that carried over onto me. He resented everything about me, from my last name to the fact that I was female to the way I rose through the ranks much too quickly for his liking. The two years I answered to him directly were a living hell. I swore he sabotaged some of my cases to make me look bad, but I could never prove it. Everything got worse when they gave me command of his squad and moved him to the rat squad."

"When you say it got worse, how do you mean?"

"He was always up in my grill, skulking around the pit after hours like he was looking for something he could use against me. He brought me before IAB a couple of times for everything from getting involved with my husband during the O'Connor investigation to failing to invite someone from my squad to my wedding. He was always on me, like white on rice. And I won't deny that I enjoyed antagonizing him, pushing his buttons. His face turns this glorious shade of purple when he's pissed. I loved making that happen."

"Did your difficulties with him continue to escalate?"

Why did he ask her that when he already knew the answer? "We caught him making phone calls to the media from HQ, tipping off the media about ongoing cases. That was the first time he got in serious trouble for the games he liked to play with me."

"Who caught him?"

"Myself and Lieutenant Archelotta put together the evidence and presented it to the chief. Stahl got arrested for interfering with the investigation, suspended, the whole nine yards. He blamed me for the whole thing, screaming that I'd set him up. The attack on my doorstep happened shortly after that. I stepped out to get the paper and he grabbed me by the throat. I managed to knee him in the balls and kick him in the knee, but not until he'd made me wonder if I was going to die right there on my own doorstep with my son in the house."

Her hands still trembled whenever she relived that incident, which she had often in the days that followed his most recent stunt.

"When you think of Stahl from before the two times he attacked you, how would you have described him?"

"I've always thought of him as a bully. He liked to throw his weight around, and I don't mean that as a fat thing. He never missed a chance to remind junior officers that he outranked them. Pulling rank was one of his favorite things to do when I reported to him. If I was on to something in a case, he'd find out and insert himself somehow to derail my progress and then take credit for whatever it was that I'd uncovered."

"Were you the only one he had difficulties with?"

"Oh hell no. No one liked him. My dad would tell you that he was never well liked within the department."

"So he was antisocial?"

"You could say that. Definitely not one to be asked out for a beer after a tour ends."

"How about mentally? Did you ever suspect he had some form of mental illness?"

"I once heard him described as 'off.' Like you couldn't really say what was up with him, but you knew *something* was up. Does that make sense?"

"It does. Did you get the sense that he took seriously the responsibilities that came with the job and the badge?"

"Not really. It seemed more like he was about advancing his own personal agenda, whatever that might've been."

"Do you know what type of person you've just described?"

Sam could think of a lot of words to describe Leonard Stahl, but she suspected that none of her words would be the one he was looking for. She shook her head.

"Sociopath."

The word hung heavy in the air, the implications reaching far beyond this tiny, airless cinderblock room.

"He's a sociopath, Sam. What he did to you that day in the basement has been years in the making. You just talked about how he'd been escalating, going from verbal jabs to physical altercations. Inside he was blaming everyone but himself for his problems. *You* didn't get him suspended and arrested for making calls to the press. *He* did that to himself, but he's incapable of seeing it that way."

"I thought for sure he would kill me that day in Marissa's basement. Especially after he gut-shot her. But more than anything, I feared that he'd try to rape me. I kept telling myself I could handle anything that came my way if only he didn't try that."

"And he didn't?"

She shook her head. "Apparently the thought of touching me that way was as revolting to him as it was to me."

"He said as much?"

"Yeah, at one point. It was actually a relief when he tied my legs to the chair. That's when I knew rape wasn't on his to-do list."

"I read in the report that you were entirely silent through the whole ordeal. Why?"

"Because. I didn't want to give him the satisfaction

of knowing he was getting to me. I was always mouthy with him, and he expected me to be mouthy that day. When I wasn't, I could tell I ruined some of the fun of it for him. He wanted me to beg and plead for my life, and when I refused to do that, he was so mad."

"Do you think he went harder on you because of that?"

"I know he did. He punched me in the face after I refused to engage with him."

"On a totally personal note, I want you to know that when I read that detail in the report, I was amazed. I can't begin to imagine the mental fortitude it required to remain totally silent for all those hours while your sworn enemy beat and tortured you."

"I was screaming on the inside," Sam said with a weak smile.

"What were you thinking about?"

"Mostly about Nick and Scotty, our son. My family, especially my dad… I thought about what it would be like for them to lose me this way. I wondered if they knew I'd been taken hostage, how they were finding out. I relived every minute I'd spent with Nick. If Stahl was going to kill me, I wanted thoughts of Nick to be what I took with me. I was sad that we might not get any more time together. We'd already been denied so many years by another sociopath who plotted to keep us apart for seven years. Mostly, it didn't seem fair to me. I finally had everything I'd ever wanted—I'm married to the only man I've ever truly loved. We have a son now, and I'm finally a mom after so many disappointments. The thought of not getting to see Scotty grow up or get old and cranky with Nick… I wondered if my dad would survive losing me."

"Any one of those thoughts would be enough to make a sane person crazy."

"I can't be certain I was entirely sane during that ordeal."

"The important thing, at the end of the day, was that you found a way to survive. By going silent on him, you made him work harder and longer to break you. You bought yourself the time needed for your colleagues to realize you were missing and to organize a rescue. *You* did that, Sam. I hope you give yourself some of the credit for the fact that you survived."

"I haven't really thought of it that way before."

"Do you see it now? Really see what I'm saying?"

"I guess…"

"Hear me on this, Sam. If you'd broken and given him the tirade he wanted, he probably would've killed you because he'd have gotten what he'd come for. He would've broken you. That he didn't break you is the only reason you're still alive. It's not because of SWAT or the amazing work Sergeant Gonzales did in sounding the alarm and tracking you down. Those things certainly helped, but *you* ensured they had the time they needed to get to you."

Despite the swell of emotion coming from her chest to her throat and the tears stinging her eyes, she said, "So even after I made the huge mistake of going in there alone and without anyone knowing where I was, I still get credit for the save?"

"You get the credit for staying alive long enough to be rescued."

Trulo had a reputation for reducing even the sturdiest to tears before he was satisfied he'd done his job. Sam had been so certain she'd be immune to him, but when he gave her credit for saving herself, the dam broke and the tears fell in hot streaks down her face.

He handed her a tissue.

She wiped her face and blew her nose. "I'm not sure I want to come back." There. She'd said it out loud to someone who mattered, someone who had the power to decide if her career ended here or carried on as planned.

"Why do you say that?"

Dabbing at her eyes with the tissue, she said, "There's a guy killing people in my city with a hunting knife and I feel strangely detached. As if that's not my problem."

"Technically, it's not your problem. You're on leave and thus absolved of involvement in this one."

"But shouldn't I be at least slightly interested in the case, how it's progressing, what my squad is doing… You know, the usual stuff?"

"I think you do care or you wouldn't be asking yourself those questions."

"Normally, I'd come rushing back to work to help out."

"Normally. Is there anything normal about what happened in Marissa Springer's basement?"

"No, but—"

"No buts, Sam. You're on medical leave for a reason, and that case, as baffling and upsetting as it may be, is not your responsibility. There's nothing wrong with taking a step back from your duties to heal from the trauma you experienced. Maybe you feel uncertain about coming back because you're not *ready* to come back. Has that occurred to you?"

"No, not really. How would I know that I'm ready?"

"My guess is that something big will happen that will spur you to action—or it won't. If it doesn't, then you'll have your answer." He reached for a paper on his desk, wrote something on it and handed it to her.

"What's this?"

"Clearance to return to full duty whenever you're

ready. You and I will be the only ones who know you've got that, and you should use it when you feel ready to. Not one minute before."

Sam stared down at the paper where Trulo had checked the box that allowed her to return to work. He'd signed his name below it. "So that's it? No more appointments?"

"Only if you'd like to talk. My door is always open to you. But no more required appointments."

Why did she feel like she was losing a lifeline when she'd never wanted to be here in the first place?

"How do you feel, Sam?"

"I don't know how I'm supposed to feel. Relieved, I guess. No offense, but I'm not big on this kind of thing."

"No, *really*?"

"Ahh, sarcasm. I do so love sarcasm."

He smiled. "As do I."

"I appreciate all the time you gave me, even when I was stonewalling you, but it feels weird to have completed this process or whatever you call it and still be unclear about whether or not I want to go back to work."

"Only you can decide that. And there would certainly be no shame in deciding the job is no longer for you. In fact, you have the perfect out in light of the oath your husband is about to take this week. Anyone would understand if you chose to focus on your duties as second lady rather than chasing down murderers."

"Chasing down murderers is more than a job to me. It's who I am."

"It's who you've been for some time now. Doesn't mean it's the only thing you're capable of being or doing. The whole world is open to you. I'm sure you're hearing from your people at the White House about things you could be doing."

"I am. There's stuff. Lots of stuff."

"Perhaps that's part of the reason you're rethinking your career. Maybe it has little to do with the attack and more to do with the changes occurring in your personal life."

"I hadn't thought of that possibility." In her mind, the whole thing had been wrapped up in what Stahl had done and the moves she'd made that had given him the perfect opportunity to grab her. But Trulo made a good point about the changes in Nick's life and how they affected hers.

"There's no deadline for this decision, Sam. Take the time you need. Weigh the pros and cons. Talk to people you trust and respect. When and if you're ready to come back, you can do it at any time. Should you choose not to return, that's fine too. One thing I like to tell my clients, both here and in private practice, is that you have just one life to live. You ought to live it the way that best suits you."

He had definitely given her plenty to think about. "Thanks again for everything, Doc. Sorry if I was a tough nut to crack."

"You weren't so bad."

"I wasn't? God, that's disappointing. I'll have to try harder if I should have the misfortune of ending up on your case list again."

"I hope to never see you again in this capacity, but I shall always hope to run into you around the house, and I'll be watching as you and your husband continue to captivate this country."

"Aww, shucks. Thanks. He's the captivating one. I'm just along for the ride."

"Don't sell yourself short. You make for one heck of an appealing power couple."

She stood and reached out to shake his hand.

He enfolded her hand in both of his. "Take good care of yourself, Sam, and come see me if there's ever anything I can do for you."

"Thanks again, Doc. You're all right despite the things I've said about you." She left him laughing and headed downstairs to the morgue. Lindsey was nowhere to be found, so Sam went out into the cold and hustled to her jazzy new car. She'd always adored driving Nick's BMW and loved that it now belonged to her. It would take the rest of her life and half of the next life to figure out all the gadgets, but fortunately she'd have Freddie to decode it for her if she went back to work.

If she went back to work... For someone who lived and breathed her work, it was bizarre and unsettling to have such thoughts.

NINE

SAM BATTLED HER way through rush-hour traffic and was waved through security onto Ninth Street. The BMW practically parallel parked itself compared to her department-issued car. She took the ramp to her dad's house and rapped on the door on the way in. "Yo, are you crazy kids decent?"

"Come in, Sam," her stepmother, Celia, said from the kitchen.

Sam crossed the living room to the kitchen where Celia was quickly gathering a stack of paper while Sam's dad sat in his wheelchair, looking on and seeming troubled.

"What's going on?" Sam asked.

"Nothing," Celia said, cheerful as always. "Just sorting through some stuff."

"What kind of stuff?"

"*Personal* stuff," Skip said pointedly.

Unaccustomed to being rebuffed by him, Sam slid into a kitchen chair and said, "Sorry."

"Don't be sorry, honey," Celia said. "You know how it is. Paperwork up the wazoo over every little thing." She stood and bent to kiss Skip's forehead. "I'm going to run this stuff upstairs and make some calls. You two enjoy a visit. There's fresh coffee on if you want some, Sam."

"Thanks." She got up and helped herself to a cup of coffee, stirring in cream and sugar.

"Not like you to drink coffee in the middle of the day," Skip said. "Doesn't it keep you up?"

"Sometimes. But it's so cold out that I need something warm." She produced the signed form Trulo had given her and put it on the table where her dad could see it.

"I see you've graduated. Congratulations. Did he make you cry?"

"A little."

"Awww, baby girl," Skip said with a sigh. "I've been hoping you'd open up to someone. Trulo's the best at what he does. Did it help?"

"I guess. Some."

"So you're going back to work?"

"Not right away."

"Why not?"

She ran her finger around the rim of the mug. "I'm not ready, and I'm not quite sure why I'm not ready. I'm just not." She wanted to tell him the truth. If only she knew how. It was different with him. He was nearly as invested in her career as she was.

"Okay…"

"What would you say if I decided to do something different?" she asked, using the most innocuous phrasing she could think of.

"Something different as in not be a cop anymore?"

"Possibly."

He was quiet for a long moment before he began to speak. "Did I ever tell you how I almost hung up my badge after Steven was killed?"

Steven Coyne, Skip's first partner, had been killed in a still-unsolved drive-by shooting when the two men were Patrol officers. "No, you didn't."

"I didn't work for about two months after what happened to him. That he could be gunned down simply because he wore the uniform... Still gets to me to this day. I couldn't bring myself to put on the badge, to care about the job or anything else for that matter."

"What brought you back?"

"I had a family to feed. It was either go back and get on with it or start all over in another job. I didn't want another job, but at that time, I didn't want the one I had either."

Sam was shocked to see her dad's eyes fill with tears.

"I loved him like a brother. We had an immediate bond in the academy that lasted through the first couple of years on the job. I hate to even say such a thing, but imagine someone gunning down Freddie just because he wears the blue."

"I can't." The thought was too awful to allow into her muddled brain.

"Exactly. It was just that bad. I was inconsolable and filled with an unreasonable amount of rage. I'd never experienced anything even close to that. I honestly didn't know if I had it in me to go back to work, to put on that uniform, to work the beat without Steven by my side. How would I ever again trust a partner to have my back the way he did? How would another partner trust me when I'd failed Steven so completely?"

"How did you fail Steven?"

"He was shot when I was six feet from him."

"Could you have stopped it?"

"It was over before I knew it was happening." As he said the words, Sam could see the weight of the guilt and grief he carried with him all these years later in the grim expression on his face. "I couldn't have stopped it, but that doesn't change the fact that I was *six feet* from him. What kind of cop allows something like that happen to his partner when he's *right there*? What kind of cop never catches a glimpse of the car or the shooter? I was tortured by those questions. The only way I could sleep without continuously reliving the horror of seeing his head practically blown off was if I medicated myself with Jack Daniel's."

"I've always known about Steven, of course," Sam said. "But you've never talked about how it affected you."

"No, I haven't, because I couldn't. Thirty years after it happened it's still right up there as the worst day of my life."

"Worse than when you were shot?"

"Way worse." Grimacing, he added, "He'd just gotten married. He and Alice were crazy about each other. She was all he talked about, to the point that I begged him to shut up about her. I had to go there, to tell her..."

Sam moved to the chair next to his and put her hand over his right hand, the one extremity that had somehow retained nearly full sensation after he was shot.

"Some things you never get over, Sam. You figure out a way to live with them, but you never forget. I think of Steven every day. He's always with me, as is the guilt and the grief and the pain of his loss."

"I'm sorry you went through that."

"I'm sorry you went through what you did too. But if you leave the job, baby girl, that son of a bitch will win. He'll *win*."

She leaned her head on his shoulder. "How'd you find your mojo again after you went back?"

"Took a long time. It was more than a year before I felt sort of like my old self again. I was never again the person I was before that day, but the new me found a way to cope and go on. The support of the brotherhood helped. There weren't as many sisters then as there are now, so the brother- and sisterhood will get you through. They'll prop you up when you feel like you can't go on. The cases helped. They keep on coming whether we want them to or not. The people we serve help. In their lowest moments it's hard to think of our own problems. After a while, you get back into the groove and you stop thinking you can't do it anymore because you *are* doing it. You're closing cases and writing reports and interviewing witnesses and interrogating suspects and testifying in court like you always did. Life goes on. It moves forward and takes us with it."

"What happened to me was nothing compared to losing your partner that way."

"It wasn't nothing. Someone you should've been able to trust with your life tried to take your life. It was *not* nothing. But he doesn't deserve to sit in his jail cell knowing he took from you something you loved. He doesn't get to do that, you hear me?"

"I hear you."

"You're going back to work. If you get there, and a few months from now it's just not happening and you want to hang it up, then so be it. You'll have my full support. But you will *not* give that piece of shit the satisfaction of thinking he *took* it from you. You will *not*."

"No, I won't."

"Good."

"I've decided to take a more active role as second lady."

"Really?" His grunt of laughter made her smile. "Didn't see that coming."

"Neither did I, but I'm seeing it as an opportunity to

shine some light on things that matter to me, including raising money for spinal cord injury research and adoption and infertility and law enforcement. Those kinds of things."

"All worthy causes."

"I think so too." She stood, kissed his forehead and laid her head on his shoulder. "Thanks for this. It was just what I needed."

"Anytime, baby girl."

"How's the pain today?"

"Manageable."

"So the needles are helping?" she asked, cringing. Acupuncture was one of several remedies the doctors at the National Institutes of Health had recommended to combat the pain of Skip's nerves coming back to life after the bullet that had been lodged in his spine for three years was removed.

"Seem to be."

"How's the sensation?"

"Tingles all around, but no real movement."

"Yet. They said it could take months."

"And they said it also might not happen. No matter, I'm better than I was, and that's good enough for me."

"For now."

"Do you know what John Adams once said about the vice presidency?" Nick asked his chief of staff, Terry O'Connor, during a late-day strategy session.

"What's that?"

"Adams said, it's 'the most insignificant office that ever the invention of man contrived.'"

Terry laughed. "It certainly has that reputation."

"I want to change that. I want to do things, not sit

around and wait to be asked to participate." Over the last few weeks, Nick had had a lot of sleepless nights in which he'd had to force himself to think of something—anything—other than the troubles that plagued his precious wife. "Nelson has his team in place, and they've been with him for years—decades in some cases. I'm a Johnny-come-lately, so naturally he has no real use for me. He's got his people, and they're out forwarding his agenda. I did what he needed by boosting his ratings. The country approves of his choice of a vice president, and he's moved on. So there's no reason I can't set my own agenda and give attention to things that matter to me."

"No reason at all," Terry said. "What've you got in mind?"

With his feet propped on his desk and his tie loosened at the end of a long day, Nick tossed the football he'd been given at a recent fundraiser up in the air and caught it, then did it again. "When Sam met with her team, she gave them a list of issues that are close to her heart. Most of them are also close to mine. Adoption, spinal cord injury research, infertility, learning disabilities and support for law enforcement, especially in the rancorous environment cops are working in these days."

"All good causes worthy of the kind of attention you both could bring to them—and none of them are on Nelson's list."

Nick smiled at his friend and closest aide. He loved that his late best friend's brother worked with him. Having Terry around had helped to fill some of the void John's death had left in Nick's life. Some but not all—John was simply irreplaceable. "Exactly," he said.

"How do you want to proceed?"

"Get with Lilia in Sam's office to coordinate our approach. Make both of us available to groups that work in those areas. This is something my lovely wife and I can do together, and you know how I'm all for anything that includes her. I think it'll make it easier for her to get involved if I am too."

"No doubt."

"I don't want to do this the old-fashioned way, though."

"What do you mean?"

The football went up and came back down. "I've been thinking a lot about what's happened in the last year. I've gone from being John's chief of staff to the Senate and now this. My head has finally begun to stop spinning, and I've come to a few realizations."

"I can't wait to hear this," Terry said dryly.

"I'm the first of the next generation that's going to run this country. I'm twenty-five years younger than Nelson, younger by decades than most of the people in Congress."

"And this is news to you?"

"Not that so much as the opportunity to do things differently—to do things *our* way rather than their way."

"How do you mean?"

"Social media for one thing. How many high-ranking officials manage their own Twitter and Facebook accounts? How many participate on Instagram?"

"So you want to start tweeting now?"

"Why not?"

"You've got a perfectly capable staff to do those things for you."

"And they do a great job, but how much better would it be if I did it myself? If we made it known that every message from this office was from *me* and not a staffer?"

"You think you'll have time for that?"

"All I've got is time. Nelson has given us the deep

freeze, so let's go forth on our own path. Besides, how long does it take to compose one-hundred-forty characters?"

"Those hundred-forty characters can get you in a world of trouble if they aren't done right."

Nick waved off Terry's concern. "You're missing the point. I *want* to get into trouble and stir things up and make a difference. I want to get people thinking about things they aren't concerned enough about. I want to get the media reporting on what the VP is tweeting about today and how his Instagram profile has become a daily must-view. I want to be *relevant*."

Terry's pen flew over the pad on his lap as he took notes. "Okay, social media. What else?"

"Before we move on from social media, I want Trevor to set me up with a blog on Tumblr, and I want a Movie-Time channel. Everything I do needs to be posted there—every appearance, fundraiser, speech, etc. Maybe a few personal things too, like hockey and baseball games with Scotty. The kind of stuff that shows that my life is like a lot of other people's lives. I can take those videos myself on my phone."

Terry eyed him skeptically for a long moment and then put pen to paper. "MovieTime. Got it."

"Even though I sort of grew up in Washington over these last fifteen years, I'm not *of* Washington, you know? I'm not an insider."

Terry's eyes went wide before he laughed. "If *you're* not an insider, who is?"

"I'm talking about Lowell and growing up as the product of teenage parents who had better things to do than raise the son they never wanted. Maybe I've *become* an insider, but I came from so far outside the Beltway it's not even funny. I want to show other kids out there who have no hope that there's *always* hope, that they can aim as high as they want and never stop reaching until they get where they want to be. Sometimes they can get to places they never dreamed of." He gestured to the well-appointed White House office to make his point.

"So you want to go into the schools and meet with kids?"

"As often as I can. Middle school and high school kids, in particular, the ones who pretend to be so cool on the outside when they're filled with doubts and insecurities on the inside."

Terry nodded in approval. "We can definitely make that happen."

"I don't want just the affluent kids. I want the inner city kids too. Particularly them."

"Got it. What else?"

"Get me on TV—late night talk shows, the Daily Show and anything that's hip and widely watched by the younger demographic. I want to be where they are."

"You've been invited, literally, everywhere."

"Start saying yes to some of them."

"You'll need to travel," Terry said, knowing how much he hated being away from home, especially lately.

"Or," Nick said with a grin, "they could come to me if they want me badly enough."

"There is that."

"See what you can do. Of course I'd go to New York if I were asked to host Saturday Night Live."

"You can't be serious."

"I'm totally serious. That'd be the ultimate."

"Nelson would crap himself."

"All the more reason to do it."

Terry held up a stack of papers. "These are all the print interview requests you've received since you took office."

"Pick out five of the edgier, less predictable requests, and I'll choose three of them to start with. I don't want to be on the cover of the high-brow intellectual magazines, but I might say yes to *Rolling Stone*, *Spin*, *The Fader* or *XXL*."

"I haven't even heard of those last two."

"They're both music industry publications, but they cover culture and other hot topics."

"You're very avant-garde, Mr. Vice President."

"That's the idea. If I'm the VP for Gen X and Y, then let's go to where they are. I want to engage them in government and the running of their country. I want to hear their ideas and get them talking." Nick caught the football and held it between both hands. "You think I'm crazy, don't you?"

"No, sir. I think you're about to prove John Adams very, very wrong."

Nick smiled, pleased to know that Terry approved of his plans. "That's the idea."

TEN

As Sam walked home from her dad's house, a caravan of black SUVs pulled up to their place. She recognized the agents from Nick's detail and walked a little quicker so she could be there to greet him when he emerged from the back of the car.

His face lit up with pleasure when he saw her there. And just like it always did when he walked into a room—or onto a sidewalk in this case—her heart skipped a happy beat at the sight of him.

"This is a nice surprise, the little woman greeting the conquering hero when he returns from battle," he said with a teasing grin.

"Conquering hero? Have you given yourself yet another promotion?"

"And here I thought the little woman thing would get me in trouble."

She went up on tiptoes to kiss him right in front of his detail, which went against everything she believed in about public displays of affection. "I like to surprise you."

His grin got bigger as he put his arm around her to walk her inside. "And you do it so well. How is my gorgeous little wife tonight?"

"Better than she was this morning."

"Yeah?"

She nodded.

"That's very good news."

They walked up the ramp he'd had installed so her dad could visit their home.

"Good evening, Mr. Vice President, Mrs. Cappuano."

"Good evening, Jim," Nick said to the agent manning the door.

Sam hadn't yet gotten used to having her own front door opened for her, but she expected it would become routine by the time Nick left office—or at least she hoped it would. When Sam would've tossed her coat over the sofa, Nick grabbed it and hung it next to his in the closet while Sam looked on in amusement. "There's one minute of your life you'll never get back."

"It was one minute well spent to keep our home orderly and neat."

She held up a hand to her ear. "What was that noise I just heard? Was it your sphincter tightening?"

He laughed. "*There* she is."

Confused, Sam looked over her shoulder at an empty room. "There who is?"

"There's my smart-mouthed, sarcastic wife. I've missed her the last few weeks."

"She's been right here."

Shaking his head, he said, "No, she hasn't." He glanced at Jim, who was standing inside the door pretending not to listen to every word they said. "Would you give us a minute, please?"

"Of course, sir."

The agent crossed to the room that used to be their study and now served as the Secret Service's office.

"There," Nick said. "That's better." He drew her into his embrace, wrapping his arms around her.

Sam burrowed her nose into his neck, breathing in the

sweet scents of starch and cologne, the smell of home. "I'm sorry about last night and everything—"

He pulled back to kiss her. "No apology needed."

"I don't know why I felt the need to fake it, Nick. I've been screwed up, but I think I'm going to be better now. Talking to Harry helped and my dad. Trulo cleared me to go back to work."

"Wow, you've had quite a day."

"I'm going to wait until after the inauguration to go back. Gonzo is running things on the knife murders, and it's good for him to have that experience. I have dress fittings and other important second lady business to attend to, so the week after next is soon enough."

"Whatever you want to do is fine with me. I'm glad to hear you say you're going back."

"Are you? I sort of figured you'd be happy to hear I was thinking of quitting."

"As much as I sweat over your safety, I'd never want you to give up something that makes you happy, especially not now. Not when it would give he-who-shall-not-be-named such pleasure to think he ran you off the force."

"My dad said the same thing."

"Skip is a wise man, and so is your husband."

"Indeed. Could I schedule a little loft time tonight?" She ran her finger down the silky length of his tie and hooked it under his belt. "I owe you a do-over."

"Um…" He swallowed hard.

"What?"

"I can't remember what I was going to say. All the blood in my body is heading to a party in my pants."

Sam started laughing and couldn't stop.

Scotty came in from the kitchen and made a face at them. "Eww, are you kissing again?"

Nick smiled at her as he released her. "To be continued." Turning to Scotty, he said, "I'm living for the day you have your first girlfriend. Be prepared to pay for all the times you've said how gross kissing is."

Scotty made another disgusted face that had them both laughing.

"How's the homework?" Sam asked.

"All done except for stinking math. Shelby and I made our own meatballs. They are so good. You gotta come have some. It's all ready."

"It smells fantastic," Nick said. He took Sam's hand to walk with her into the kitchen.

"I should be doing this stuff with him," Sam said for Nick's ears only.

"It's probably better for all of us if we let Shelby handle that part of his education."

Sam elbowed him in the ribs. "I'm not that bad in the kitchen."

"Um, yeah you are, but luckily you shine in other rooms."

"Sex-crazed beast."

"I'm a victim of my environment." He gave her a little push that carried her into the kitchen where their personal assistant and friend, Shelby Faircloth, was stirring something on the stove.

The tiny blonde wore an apron that covered the slight bump in her abdomen.

"You're feeling better, Tinker Bell?" Sam asked.

"I might've turned a corner this morning. I only puked twice and then I felt good enough to come spend some time with my best buddy Scotty."

"Glad to hear it. What've you brewed up for us tonight?"

"Scotty gets all the credit. I only supervised."

"Is Avery still away?" Sam asked, casually, not wanting to show too much interest in the FBI agent who'd shown too much interest in her for Nick's liking. But now he was engaged to Shelby, and that was all in the past. Or at least it was for Sam. Nick still showed his teeth a little too often when Avery was around.

"Yes, he's in Charleston for one more night."

"How's his mother doing?"

"Much better. The cardiologist said the pacemaker is working perfectly, and she shouldn't have any more issues."

"The family must be relieved."

"Very much so." Shelby removed the apron, and Sam tried not to fixate overly much on the gentle swell of her abdomen under the fuzzy pink sweater she wore. "I'll get out of here so you guys can eat." She kissed Scotty's cheek. "I'll see you tomorrow after school."

"Why don't you stay and eat with us?" Nick said. "I'm sure there's plenty, and there's no need for you to eat alone when you could be with us."

"I don't want to impose."

"Don't be silly," Scotty said as he set a fourth place. "We love having you around."

Shelby's eyes filled with tears. "Damned pregnancy hormones." She glanced at Sam, seeming to immediately regret complaining about pregnancy.

Sam smiled at her, hoping to send the message that it was okay. She could handle being around yet another pregnant woman when pregnancy had proven challenging for her.

They sat down to enjoy Scotty's delicious meatballs and a rant about the insanity of seventh grade math.

"Can I just say, for the record, that I totally agree with you?" Sam said. The glass of wine Nick had poured for her had given her liquid courage. "Middle school math sucks balls."

"Samantha," her husband said in the chastising tone she loved.

"What? It does! It's the stupidest thing in the history of stupid things. When have you ever used algebra for *anything*?" She looked to Nick and Shelby, neither of whom had a satisfactory answer. "We put kids all the way through school without teaching them a thing about personal finance or nutrition or how to open a bank account or why they need insurance or how to buy a house. We torture them with algebra and chemistry and Shakespeare, but they don't learn much of anything that they'll actually *use* in their lives."

"I love her so much," Scotty said, seeming awestruck by her outburst.

Hearing him say that nearly reduced her to tears, but the glare she received from Nick let her know she needed to fix the damage.

Sighing, she slipped reluctantly back into mom mode. "That said, buddy, you still gotta deal with the stupid crap they make you do so you can get the piece of paper you need to get out of there. Think of your high school diploma as your get-out-of-jail free card."

Nick shook his head in amused disbelief. "*Really*, Sam?"

"I understand what she's saying," Scotty said. "You have to play the game to get to the finish line."

"Yes! Exactly." Sam smirked at Nick. "He gets me."

"Someone's got to," Nick said.

"Har har."

"Y'all are funny," Shelby said, giggling. "Is this what happens every night at dinner?"

"Thankfully not every night or our son might be a dropout by now," Nick said.

"I only speak the truth," Sam said.

"At the risk of getting fired and banned from your house, I sort of agree with Sam," Shelby said.

"I'm surrounded by rebels," Nick said, taking a long swig of his beer.

"Seriously, though," Shelby said, "everything I needed to know to run my business I learned on the job. I would've loved a personal finance class in high school, something about how the stock market works and how to plan for retirement. I think everyone needs accounting more than they need algebra."

Sam held up her hand to Shelby, who high-fived her. "Sing it, sister."

"Dad, you're the vice president. You could actually do something about this."

"Yeah, Nick," Sam said. "You should outlaw algebra. That would get you elected president of the universe."

"What exactly do you propose that I do?" Nick asked.

"You could meet with the education people," Scotty said in all seriousness, "and tell them the current system is messed up."

Nick looked to Sam, his expression challenging.

"Well, um, he can't just go in there demanding widespread changes," Sam said.

"Why not?" Scotty asked. "He's the vice president. He can do whatever he wants to."

"Yes, Sam," Nick said, enjoying watching her squirm. "Why not?"

"That's not how the government works," Sam said.

"First they have to commission expensive studies when we already know what the problem is. They have to analyze it to death until they forget what they wanted to know, and if they figure out some actual solutions, they have to take it to Congress where it will be bogged down in political mumbo jumbo for years, possibly decades. When they finally decide what to do, they won't be able to afford it or maybe it will get passed and then they will send it to the states to figure out how to implement it, but they'll get pissed because they don't have the money, and that's why we won't ever, ever, *ever* get rid of algebra."

"I just fell into a deep depression," Scotty said glumly.

Shelby was in tears from laughing.

Nick stared at Sam, who was no longer sure if he was mad or amused by her recitation. Then he smiled, and she knew everything was fine. "You are a piece of work, my love."

"Am I wrong?"

"She's not wrong," Scotty said with thirteen-year-old wisdom. "Algebra isn't going away, and Congress doesn't get much of anything done. We talked about that in Social Studies class."

"Awesome," Nick said.

"Y'all are gonna make me pee my pants," Shelby said. "I want to eat here every night."

"You see why I love living here so much?" Scotty asked as he got up to clear the table, leaving his parents reeling from what he'd said.

Under the table, Nick found her hand and gave it a squeeze.

Sam was trying not to cry. To hear him say he loved her and loved living here… What an amazing thing that was.

"Speaking of you living here," Nick said, "we've got

a court date to make it all official. What're you doing on January thirtieth at high noon?"

Scotty spun around to face them. "Seriously? Like for real?"

"As real as it gets," Nick said. "I heard from Andy today that all the final paperwork has been filed, and we're good to go."

"Is that a school day?" Scotty asked.

"It's a Friday."

Scotty pumped his fist in the air. "I get adopted *and* I get out of algebra too! Best day ever!"

"You'll have to make up what you miss," Nick reminded him.

"Don't ruin it."

The three adults laughed at the face he made. But then he came over to hug Nick, and Sam found herself swallowing a huge lump in her throat. She glanced at Shelby and saw her dabbing at her eyes.

"Thank you," Scotty said gruffly, his face pressed against Nick's shoulder. "Thank you so much."

"Oh God, buddy," Nick said, hugging him harder. "Thank *you*. You're the best thing to ever happen to us."

After a long hug, Scotty broke loose and came to Sam. "You too."

Sam wrapped her arms around him and held on tight to the child who'd made her a mom—not the way she'd hoped it would happen for so long, but what did it matter when she had the love of such a wonderful son? "Entirely our pleasure," Sam said. Those three words were all she was capable of.

Scotty hugged Shelby next. "Thanks for being such a good friend to me."

"I've never had so much fun at work," Shelby said tearfully.

"I'm going to finish my homework and take a shower."

"Okay," Nick said. "Let me know if you need help with the math."

"I think I've got it." He left the room and they heard his footsteps on the stairs as he took them two at a time.

"Is anyone else's heart about to burst?" Shelby asked.

"Me," Sam said.

"Me three," Nick added. "What a kid."

Sam reached for his hand and shared a smile with him.

"I'm going to get out of your hair." Shelby stood to take her plate and Sam's to the sink, where she rinsed them and put them in the dishwasher. Then she put the remaining food away.

"We can take it from here, Shelby," Nick said.

"Or *he* can take it from here while I watch and drink more wine," Sam said.

"That's how she rolls," Nick said with a weary sigh.

"You're probably the only vice president in the history of the universe who does his own dishes," Shelby said as she put on her coat and wrapped a pink scarf around her neck.

"Which is just fine with me," Nick said.

"Thanks for dinner and the laughs. I love hanging out with you guys. And Scotty… Sigh, what's not to love about him?"

"We keep waiting for the evil teenage years to kick in, but so far so good," Sam said.

"He won't get evil," Shelby said. "He doesn't have it in him, and besides, he's so damned happy to have a family to call his own that he'd never want to cause you any trouble."

"Fingers crossed," Sam said.

"I'll see you in the morning!"

"Have a good night, Shelby," Nick said.

"May I just say," Sam said after the front door clicked shut behind Shelby, "that hiring her was the best idea I ever had?"

"It was a good one."

"What would we do without her?"

"I don't even want to think about it."

Sam watched her sexy husband move around the kitchen as he finished cleaning up from dinner. He'd removed his suit coat and tie and had rolled his sleeves up to reveal his forearms. Even his arms were sexy. Everything about him was sexy to her, and for the first time since the attack, she felt a burning need to connect with him physically—as soon as possible.

She got up from the table and went over to where he stood at the sink, washing the pots and pans. Sliding her arms around his trim waist, she rested her head on his back and was thrilled to feel his belly quiver her hands.

"What's going on back there, my love?"

"Oh, this. And that." The old feeling was back. Her blood raced through her veins, heating her from the inside. An insistent throb between her legs was a reminder of what had been missing during the last few difficult weeks.

"Let me turn around."

Sam released her tight hold on him and he turned, his sharp gaze taking a quick perusal of her face.

"What's on your mind?"

"You are." She rubbed shamelessly against him. "I owe you a make up."

He combed his fingers through her hair. "You don't owe me anything."

"I owe you everything."

"Samantha…" His lips came down on hers with a ferocity she hadn't seen since that awful day that had nearly ended everything for them.

She wrapped her arms around his neck and opened her mouth to his tongue, pressing her body against his with an urgent need for more.

A low growl came from deep inside him as his arms tightened around her. And when he softened the kiss and began to withdraw, she whimpered in protest.

"Not here. Not now." He kept his arms tight around her as his breathing calmed, but the press of his erection against her belly told her he was anything but calm.

"Remember when we could do it right on the kitchen floor when we wanted to?"

"Mmm." His lips vibrated against her ear, making her shiver in anticipation. "But I'd rather have Scotty living here and not be able to do that."

"Me too. Any day. But we should look into a lock on the kitchen door just in case…"

"I'll get right on that."

"So upstairs later?"

"Wouldn't miss it for anything."

She began to reluctantly release him, but he didn't let her go.

"It's good to have you back, babe. I've missed you."

Sam brought him down for another kiss. "I've missed me too."

They went upstairs to check on Scotty and kissed him goodnight around ten. Nick went to take a shower while Sam tried to lose herself in a book her sister Tracy had given her during her convalescence. But the words ran together the way they did when she was tired or stressed or perhaps because she was still turned on from the kiss in the kitchen. She decided she couldn't blame the dyslexia this time.

And then Nick came out of the shower wearing only a towel and the book was tossed aside in favor of far more interesting things, such as his most exceptional chest and abdomen. "Bring that over here," she said.

"He's not asleep yet, and I'm not touching you until I know I don't have to stop." He went into the closet and emerged wearing a T-shirt and basketball shorts.

Looking for something to do for another few minutes, Sam reached for her phone to see if she had any texts. Her niece Brooke had replied to Sam's earlier text asking how she was doing.

Going well, Brooke had written. School is good and I'm seeing the shrink like I'm supposed to. I'm on boring best behavior! How are YOU?

I'm fine, getting better every day. Thinking about getting back to work after the inauguration. Are you coming home for that? And boring best behavior is good. Proud of you, kid.

Aww, thanks. Wouldn't miss my Uncle Nick being sworn in. Looking forward to it. See you then!

Love you, baby. Keep working hard.

Love you too, auntie. Xoxo

"Who you gabbing with?" Nick had stretched out next to her on the bed but left a six-foot gap between them.

"Brooke."

"How's she doing?"

"She sounds great. She's coming to the inauguration. She said she wouldn't miss her Uncle Nick being sworn in."

"That's very sweet. I'm glad to hear she's doing so well."

"So am I." After Brooke had been drugged and gang-raped the night of the killings at the Springer home, Sam and her family had feared that their girl would never be quite the same. But she'd gone back to her private school in Virginia, determined to finish her senior year and graduate with her class.

A bell rang on Nick's phone.

"Let's go," he said brusquely.

"What was that sound?"

"I set an alarm for one hour after he went to bed."

"You are too funny."

"I'm not funny, I'm horny. Now get upstairs and hurry up about it."

"Yes, sir."

At the door to their bedroom, they gathered themselves and prepared to face the agent who would be positioned outside Scotty's door. Sam had put on a bulky sweatshirt over the skimpy tank she had on under it so they wouldn't see anything she didn't want them to see.

As they walked past the agent, she heard Nick say, "We're not to be disturbed for any reason, except for if Scotty needs us."

"Yes, sir. Sleep well."

"Thank you. Goodnight." He guided Sam up the stairs with both hands cupping her rear end. "Hurry."

She whipped the sweatshirt off on the way up, tossed it aside and turned to him, as desperate for him as she'd ever been.

ELEVEN

OUTSIDE THE TOWNHOUSE of Giuseppe Besozzi in the Manor Park neighborhood, the day had grown dark while Gonzo and Arnold waited for their person of interest to return home. They'd been there three hours so far without a sign of him. The last time Gonzo had business in this neighborhood, he'd nearly been killed. Being back here again brought back the insanity of that day.

"How much longer do we gotta stay here?" Arnold asked for the twentieth time, or so it seemed to Gonzo.

"Until he gets home."

"But our shift ended—"

"Our shift ends when I say it ends." Gonzo would love to get the hell out of there. He was hungry, tired and needed to pee, but they weren't going anywhere until they spoke to Besozzi.

The radio crackled to life. "How much longer are we going to wait, Sarge?" asked one of the Patrol officers who was providing backup.

"Until he comes home," Gonzo snapped back. What was with these people? They weren't killing time out here. They were looking for a potential suspect in multiple homicides who had made people afraid to walk on city streets. This wasn't just another day at work. This could be the break they'd been waiting for, and they were damn well going to *wait* until he got home, no matter how long it took.

Arnold let out a loud burp.

Gonzo rolled down the window to let in some fresh air.

"Kinda cold to have the window down," Arnold said.

"Kinda gross to have to smell your burps."

"You're in a foul mood today, boss man."

"I want to catch this bastard, and I'm no happier than you are to be freezing my balls off waiting for him to come home."

"We could turn the heater on for a while."

"We're going to run out of gas if we do that, and besides, idling is bad for the environment."

"Freezing to death is bad for my health, but if you care about the environment more than you care about your partner..."

"Will you *please* shut the fuck up? Just shut up and watch for our guy. If you sit there with your mouth shut until he comes home, I'll even let you take the lead with him."

"Really?"

"Yep, but you gotta shut up about the cold and the time and how hungry you are and every other goddamned thing. You got me?"

"I got you."

"How about you tell me how you're going to approach him so we're ready."

"I'll say, 'Mr. Besozzi, I'm Detective Arnold, Metro PD. My partner Detective Sergeant Gonzales. We wondered if we might have a few minutes of your time.'"

"Excellent. And then what?"

"Hopefully he'll invite us into his nice warm home where I'll ask him about his meltdown with Griffen and Smoltz and where he was the night Enright was stabbed."

"He might get mad at the implication."

"I expect that he will. I'll say that we're looking to rule him out, and if he has an alibi, we'd be happy to speak to that person."

"That's good. Keep it friendly for as long as you can. You're going to want to really dig in on the Griffen and Smoltz thing so we can get a sense for just how mad he was about what happened with Enright and the firm. He's going to ask if they sent us to him, and you'll want to say that no, they didn't send us, but his name came up in the investigation into the stabbings and we wanted the chance to speak with him."

Arnold rubbed his cold hands together and breathed into them, trying to warm them. "How will I know if I should arrest him?"

"You tell me."

"If he gets confrontational, refuses to answer questions, says something incriminating."

"Any of those things, but don't jump the gun until he gives you probable cause."

"Got it. I can't believe you're actually letting me do this."

Gonzo rolled his eyes in the dark. Had he ever been so green? If so, it was such a long time ago now that he no longer remembered. "Don't fuck it up."

"I'll try not to." He was quiet for several minutes. "You won't let me fuck it up, will you?"

"I'll jump in if need be."

"Good."

Arnold was blessedly silent for a long time, holding up his end of their deal. "Could I ask you something that has nothing to do with when we're getting out of here?"

Though he was young and green and still had a lot to learn about being a detective—and a man—he was a good guy, and Gonzo owed him his life. On the day that Billy Springer shot him in the neck, Arnold had applied pressure that kept him from bleeding out in the street. "Yeah."

"You think the LT is coming back?"

"What's a matter? I'm not good enough?"

"How to answer this without losing my job…"

"Haha. Yeah, I think she'll be back. Maybe not right away, but eventually."

"Can't imagine the job without her in the office barking orders at all of us."

"Barking orders… Got to remember to tell her you said that."

"You'd better not!"

Gonzo began to laugh, stopping only when he saw movement on the corner of the block. "Heads up," he said to Arnold and then into the radio to alert the Patrol officers backing them up. "Let's go." He had to remind himself to hold back and give Arnold the lead as promised.

"Mr. Besozzi?" Arnold flashed his gold shield. "I'm Detective Arnold and this is my partner—"

A shot rang out, and Arnold went down, nearly knocking Gonzo over on the way. Besozzi turned tail and ran. Gonzo pulled his weapon and got off a couple of rounds as he screamed into his radio. "Officer down." Somehow he managed to get off the address to Dispatch before dropping to his knees next to his partner, who'd been shot in the face. A gurgling sound came from his throat and quickly became the worst sound Gonzo had ever heard.

"God, Arnold, hang in there," Gonzo whispered, cradling his partner's head in hands wet with blood. "Don't you dare die on me, do you hear me?"

Pounding footsteps behind them indicated the arrival of the Patrolmen.

"Go after him!" Gonzo screamed at them. "Don't let him get away!" Into his radio, he again said, "Officer down! Get a bus here! It's bad. We need more backup. Suspect is in the wind."

The gurgling sound from Arnold continued until it stopped.

"Goddamn it!" Gonzo cried. "Don't you dare fucking die!" He broke down into sobs that he tried desperately to control as he unzipped Arnold's coat and pressed his ear to his partner's chest, hearing no sign of a heartbeat. "No, please *no*."

The EMTs had to pull Gonzo off his partner so they could tend to him.

"He's gone." Gonzo wiped freezing tears from his face. "He's dead."

One of the EMTs put a stethoscope to Arnold's chest to listen. He looked up at his partner and shook his head.

A short time later, screaming sirens preceded the arrival of additional officers, the Medical Examiner and Crime Scene detectives that would record every detail of the shooting, right down to the clothing Arnold had been wearing.

Gonzo stared down at his partner's mangled face, thinking about how he'd let him take the lead and now he was dead.

"Sergeant," a familiar voice said. "Gonzo."

He couldn't bring himself to look away from Arnold as Deputy Medical Examiner Byron Tomlinson zipped him into a body bag. Ten minutes ago they'd been arguing about the cold, and now his partner was dead.

A hand landed on his shoulder, making Gonzo flinch.

"Gonzo," Captain Malone said. "Come on. Let's get you back to the house so we can talk it through."

"I'm going with him."

"They're taking him to the morgue."

"I'm going with him."

"Okay. I'll meet you there."

"Did Patrol get our perp?"

"I haven't heard anything yet."

"We need to call everyone in. I want our entire squad, the FBI, the Marshals' fugitive response team. I want everyone."

"Already being done."

"This is a crime scene," he said, gesturing to the sidewalk that was covered with Arnold's blood.

"It'll be treated as such. I'll see to it myself."

"Someone needs to call Sam."

"I'll take care of it."

"I'll be the one to tell his family," Gonzo said. "No one but me."

"Of course."

As Tomlinson and his team wheeled Arnold to the Medical Examiner's truck, everyone on the scene came to a halt and stood at attention, paying their respects to their fallen brother. Two patrol cars moved into position ahead of the ME's truck and two more would follow, escorting Arnold home to headquarters.

Satisfied that the proper respect was being paid and steps were being taken to catch the man who'd killed Arnold, Gonzo followed the gurney bearing the lifeless body of his partner into the ME's truck for the ride to the morgue.

NICK CAME DOWN on top of Sam, his hands and lips seeming to be everywhere at once until her senses were completely overwhelmed. The aroma of coconut from the scented candles took her back to the blissful days they'd spent on their honeymoon in Bora Bora.

He cupped her breasts and pinched her nipples until she gasped from the painful pleasure.

She grasped a handful of his hair and dragged him into another tongue-twisting kiss. "Nick."

"What, honey?"

"I want you right now. I can't wait any longer."

"I suppose we can go slow next time."

"Mmm, yes, next time." Sam had been ready to explode for hours by the time he finally pushed into her, filling her in every possible way, like only he ever could. "Don't go slow." She dug her fingernails into his back, making him groan as he began to move.

"Samantha, God I've missed this. I've missed *us*."

"Me too. I love you so much. You have no idea how much."

He lifted her legs so he could go deeper. "I do. I know. I always know."

The new position took her right to the edge, and then he sent her flying by pressing his thumb to her clit at exactly the right moment.

"There it is," he whispered. "Nothing like the real thing."

Even in the midst of an epic orgasm, he made her laugh. Her laughter died on her lips when he withdrew from her, turned her over and positioned her on her hands and knees. When he surged back into her, riding the last waves of her orgasm, she realized she was the only one who'd come.

How she loved him like this, when he was all hers and driving her wild with his hands and lips and cock. And then he pressed his finger against her back door, making her cry out from the incredible sensations that overtook her body. When he loved her this way, there was no space left in her mind for thoughts of anything but him and the magic they created together.

Propped over two pillows, she could do nothing but let him have his wicked way with her. And he was very, very wicked as he alternated strokes of his cock and finger to drive her completely mad. Then he reached around with his free hand to tease her clit, and that was all it took to make her come again.

This time he joined her, surging into her over and over until he came down on her back, his sweat joining with hers, his unmistakably appealing scent filling the air around her, his love providing the safety she craved.

Nothing bad could touch her as long as he loved her, or so she'd like to think.

His arm encircled her waist as he kissed a trail down her back before he withdrew from her and removed the pillows he'd put under her. He pulled a blanket up and over her and got up to use the bathroom at the far end of their hideaway. Or at least it had been a hideaway until they'd had Secret Service all over the house. Now nothing was secret.

The irony of that made her giggle.

"What's so funny?" Nick asked as he got under the blanket and snuggled up to her.

"How there're no *secrets* with the *Secret* Service around."

"This is very true."

"You think they know what we're doing when we come up here?"

He trailed his finger down her backbone, making her shiver. "I'm sure they suspect."

"That's so creepy."

"Try not to think about it. We have a right to a life in our own home, and we'll be damned glad to have them if someone tries to get at us or Scotty."

"Let's hope that doesn't happen." Thinking of what could happen to Nick or Scotty was enough to give her nightmares, so she chose not to go there.

"You've got to figure we've used up our share of bad luck." He kissed her shoulder and then took a little bite of her skin. "You want to go again?"

"Already?"

He pressed his reawakened erection against her. "Uh-huh."

"You have to be the randiest vice president in the history of the union."

"I can live with that distinction as long as I get to be randy with the sexiest second lady in the history of the world."

How could she say no to that?

CAPTAIN MALONE PULLED up to the Secret Service checkpoint at Ninth Street and gave his name. "I need to see Lieutenant Holland."

"I'm sorry but Vice President and Mrs. Cappuano are unavailable at this time."

"It's urgent police business."

"We're under orders that they're not to be disturbed for anyone other than their son."

Malone sighed, recognizing a losing battle when he saw one. He rolled up his window and drove off, calling her cell as he went. Her voicemail picked up on the second ring. "Sam, it's Malone. I'm sorry to bother you when you're on leave, but I need you to call me the minute you get this message. It's urgent."

He ended that call and placed another to Chief Farnsworth, who sounded like he'd been asleep when he said, "Farnsworth."

"Joe, it's Jake. Sorry to wake you, but I'm afraid I have some bad news."

"Oh God. More bad news?"

"The worst kind."

After a heartbeat of a pause, Farnsworth said, "Who?"

"Detective Arnold."

"Oh no. How?"

"Shot in the face by a person of interest in the knife attacks."

"Jesus. Did we get the guy?"

"Not yet, sir."

"Have we called in the FBI and the Marshals?"

"Already done."

"I want all the help we can get, but we're the lead. Understood?"

"Yes, sir. Everyone is gathering at HQ. I thought you'd want to be there."

"You're damned right I do. Has Arnold's family been notified?"

"Sergeant Gonzales has asked to handle that personally. I plan to go with him."

"You'll need to do it soon before the press catches wind. Let's call in Public Affairs to help deal with the media, and as soon as his family is notified we'll need the PIO to put it out to NCIC," Farnsworth said, referring to the National Crime Information Center, which would get the word out to police departments around the country.

"I'll make sure everything is taken care of."

"God, Jake, he was only what? Twenty-five?"

"Twenty-seven."

Another deep sigh echoed through the phone. "Does Sam know?"

"I just went by her place to tell her, but the Secret Service stopped me. Apparently, the vice president and his wife are not to be disturbed by anyone other than their son. I left her a voicemail."

"This is going to screw her up worse than she already is."

"I had the same thought. And Gonzales is not good at all. Happened right in front of him."

"We'll need to notify Cruz and the rest of the squad."

"I'll call them in, and I'll get in touch with Cruz."

"Thanks, Jake. I'm going to call the mayor, and then I'll be right in."

"See you there."

On the drive to HQ, Malone called Dispatch. "It's Malone. I need the entire Homicide squad recalled immediately."

"Captain," the dispatcher said, "I'm so sorry about Detective Arnold."

"Thank you. Please don't mention what's happened to the detectives when you call them. Just ask them to report to HQ immediately."

"Yes, sir."

He hung up with Dispatch and called Freddie Cruz, who wouldn't receive the call from Dispatch due to his suspension.

"Yeah, Cruz." He too sounded like he'd been sleeping.

"It's Malone."

"Yes, sir," Cruz said, apparently now wide awake.

"I'm afraid I have some bad news."

"What kind of bad news?"

"I'm sorry to have to tell you this on the phone, but Detective Arnold has been shot and killed in the line of duty."

"Oh my God. Was anyone else hurt?"

"Thankfully, no, but it happened right in front of Sergeant Gonzales, who's not taking it well, needless to say."

"Did we get the shooter?"

"Not yet."

"I'm out of town, but I'll leave within the hour to come home. I want to help."

"You're suspended, Detective."

"I'll work without pay. Please don't tell me I can't help."

"Check in when you get back to town."

"I'm in Florida. It'll be sometime tomorrow. Did someone tell Sam?"

"I left a message for her. The Secret Service is guarding the fortress."

"I'll call her too."

"I'll talk to you when you get back," Malone said.

"Will you let me know if there are any developments?"

"Yeah, I will."

"Thank you. Will you tell Gonzo… Ah damn, I'll call him."

"I'm sure he'd appreciate that. Safe travels."

Malone pulled into the parking lot at HQ and cut the engine. For a full minute he sat staring at the morgue entrance, telling himself he needed to go in there and take care of his people. He needed to reassure them and remind them they still had a job to do in the midst of unspeakable tragedy. In twenty-two years on the job, he'd unfortunately seen this happen before, and losing a colleague had long-lasting effects on the people who worked closest with the officer.

They were in for a rough couple of months when they'd already had a rough couple of months.

Weary and already overwhelmed by the tasks before him, Malone summoned the fortitude to get out of the car, to go inside, and to deal with everything that had to be done when one of their own went down in the line of duty.

TWELVE

FREDDIE THREW CLOTHES into the suitcase with one hand, while getting dressed with the other. When he had everything packed, he went to the bed to wake Elin, who'd slept through Malone's phone call.

"Mmm," she said in the sleepy voice that usually turned him on. "Again?"

"Elin, honey, wake up."

Her eyes opened and she took in the sight of him dressed. "Why? What's wrong?"

"Arnold was shot and killed tonight. I need to go home."

"Oh my God. Freddie. God." Tears flooded her eyes as she reached for him.

Despite the adrenaline that beat through his system, he took a moment to comfort her. "We have to go."

"Yes, we do." She got up from bed, went into the bathroom and came out a few minutes later dressed and carrying her cosmetic bag.

"I'm sorry to cut short our trip."

"Please don't apologize. Of course you have to go home. Who called you?"

"Captain Malone."

"Did he say anything about what happened?"

"Nothing more than that Arnold was shot and killed, and Gonzo's a mess."

"Poor, Gonzo. And Sam has just been through such a horrible ordeal, and now this."

"Yeah."

"Freddie." Her hand on his shoulder made him flinch. "Could you please hold me for a minute?"

"We need to go."

"One minute."

He was afraid that if he stopped moving for even a minute, he'd lose his mind. But he couldn't say no to her, not when he was well aware that the death of one of his closest colleagues was realization of her worst nightmare. He let her put her arms around his waist and put his around her, though everything in him wanted to get in the car and drive until he was back with his tribe.

"I'm so sorry, Freddie."

"Thanks." Her kindness and sympathy were nearly his undoing. Tears burned his eyes, but he refused to give in to them. If he started, he might never stop. Arnold had been everyone's kid brother in the squad, the one they loved to tease and pick on. He took it all in his stride, always smiling and up for whatever came next.

Gonzo would be wrecked by Arnold's death, especially since it had happened right in front of him and the shooter had gotten away.

"We have to go," Freddie said. "I've got to be with them."

"I know." She released him, grabbed her purse and went out the door ahead of him into the dark of night for the long drive home.

OFFICER DOWN. OFFICER DOWN. *Officer down.* The words kept running through Gonzo's mind like a nightmare that refused to end as he stood watch over his mortally wounded partner in the morgue. Any minute now, Arnold was going to pop up and tell him it had all been another big joke. Gonzo wanted to travel back in time to when they'd been bickering in the car.

You take the lead.

He blew out a deep breath when the sorrow threatened to overtake him. He couldn't afford to lose it. Not while Arnold needed him to stay strong until they got the guy who'd done this. It was the last thing he'd ever do for his partner, and he wouldn't rest until the job was done.

"Sergeant Gonzales."

He recognized the soft voice of Lindsey McNamara. Where had she come from? Tomlinson must've called her in. She'd want to begin her work on the body, but he wasn't ready. Not yet.

"Gonzo." Her hand landing on his shoulder made him want to scream at her to leave him alone. Just leave him alone. But things needed to be done. Arnold's parents had to be notified, a thought that had vomit rushing from his stomach to his throat. He choked it back, determined to get through this, to do for his partner what he would've done if the roles had been reversed.

The roles should've been reversed. He should've taken the lead the way he always did. Instead, he'd sent his partner into a slaughter.

"I need something to clean the blood off his face." Or, he should say, what was left of his face.

"I can do that for you," Lindsey said.

"I want to do it."

Behind him, he heard the water running, but he never took his eyes off his partner's face, which had been mangled by the bullet.

Lindsey handed him a wet cloth, and Gonzo began

cleaning up the blood from around the gaping wound in Arnold's cheek. He wiped up the trail of blood that extended from the corner of his mouth to his neck.

Gonzo brushed Arnold's hair back from his forehead, arranging it the way the young detective always wore it. By the time Gonzo finished cleaning his face, other than the gaping hole in his cheek and the waxiness of his skin, he looked almost like he always did.

And then there was nothing left for him to do. "I can't leave him."

"I'll take very good care of him."

Gonzo rested his forehead against Arnold's chest, wishing and hoping to hear the distinctive sound of a heart that would never beat again. Tears leaked from his tightly closed eyes, soaking the cotton fabric of Arnold's T-shirt. *It should've been me. It should've been me.*

Lindsey ran her hand over Gonzo's back, trying to offer comfort when there was no comfort to be found.

Officer down. Officer down. Officer down. This could not be happening. It was a dream, a nightmare he would wake up from, sweating and gasping the way he often had after Billy Springer shot him. He was alive today only because of the actions of the partner he'd berated earlier, the partner who was now dead and cold in the morgue, because of him. *Because I let him take the lead.*

From somewhere deep inside, he summoned the strength to stand upright, to once again adjust Arnold's hair, to mumble a few words of thanks to Lindsey, to leave the morgue and head for the detectives' pit where he would find out where they were with the manhunt for Besozzi. Then he would drive to Maryland to ruin the lives of Arnold's devoted parents.

The pit was deserted, but the lights were on in the conference room so Gonzo went in there to find the entire squad, less Sam, Cruz and Arnold, of course. Captain Malone was standing before them, apparently about to address McBride, Tyrone, Carlucci and Dominguez. FBI Special Agent-in-Charge Avery Hill was also in the room, apparently back from his family leave in South Carolina, along with Chief Farnsworth and Deputy Chief Conklin.

Gonzo looked to Malone, who nodded, offering him the chance to tell the others what had happened. For a moment, he thought about deferring to the captain, but as the acting commander of the squad, it was his news to impart. All eyes were on him. He knew they were wondering why he had blood all over him, why they'd been called in, why his partner wasn't with him. It was now up to him to tell them that his partner would never again be with him.

"I'm sorry to have to tell you that Detective Arnold was shot and killed in the line of duty tonight."

Before his eyes the others gasped and visibly crumpled.

"Oh no," Jeannie McBride said softly, her eyes filling with tears.

"Christ," Hill muttered.

Carlucci covered her face with her hands, and Dominguez stared off into space.

Tears ran unchecked down Tyrone's face as he stared blankly at the wall.

"We'd been running surveillance on the home of Giuseppe Besozzi, a person of interest in the knife attacks," Gonzo began in a flat, rote tone. It was his job to inform them of what'd happened, and he was going to do his goddamned job even if he was dying inside.

"We were there for hours. Arnold was bitching about

the cold and the boredom and how our shift had ended hours ago, and I made a deal that if he shut up about those things, I'd let him take the lead with Besozzi. We went through it a few times, what'd he ask him, how he'd respond to comments from the suspect, etc. When we finally saw him coming, we got out of the car and approached him as planned, with Arnold taking the lead. He said who he was and showed his badge, and Besozzi started shooting. Arnold went down next to me, nearly taking me with him, which is why it took a couple of seconds for me to react, to pull my weapon, to get off a few rounds. We'd had Patrol providing backup, and I ordered them to go after the suspect while I called for EMS and waited with Arnold. He was dead before EMS arrived."

"Gonzo," Jeannie said, preparing to offer sympathy he didn't deserve.

"I want every asset we have on the manhunt for this guy," Gonzo said, brushing her off. "He's taken one of our own, not to mention whatever culpability he may have in the knife attacks."

"What do we know about him?" Hill asked.

"Only what we've been told from victim William Enright and his colleagues at Griffen and Smoltz." Gonzo filled in the others about the falling out the designers had with their client Besozzi and the reasons for it. "Enright said the fact that he wanted webcams and chat rooms as part of a T-shirt store retail site was suspicious. That's what led him to take it to Griffen, the managing partner. It was their decision to end the relationship, news that Besozzi did not take well, according to Griffen."

"Is he in the system?" Hill asked.

"Nothing that we could find, but one of Enright's colleagues suspected the Italian accent and heritage could be fake, so who knows who he really is. Carlucci, you and Dominguez go back to Griffen and Smoltz in the morning and dig deeper on their files. Ask them to produce everything they have, and if they won't, get a warrant. I want a photo of this guy as soon as you have it so we can put it out to the media."

"Speaking of the media," Malone said, "we'll need to brief them about Arnold and the investigation."

"I'll get with the PIO and do the briefing after I get back from seeing his parents," Gonzo said.

"I'll also request a warrant to get into Besozzi's home," Malone said.

"What can we do?" Jeannie asked.

"Go back and re-interview the other victim who survived," Gonzo said. "See if you can establish any connection between him and Besozzi. It's possible that Enright was his target all along, and he went after the others to create a sense of panic over random attacks that weren't random at all."

"We should dig deeper into the ones who were killed too," Malone said. "I like the theory that Enright was his target and the others were hit to ramp up the panic and concern over seemingly random attacks."

"I'll put my people on that," Hill said, "and I'll let you know if we find anything that will help."

"We need the Marshals Fugitive Response Team helping us to look for this guy," Farnsworth said.

"We've already called them in," Conklin said. "I'm due to brief them in thirty minutes. Were you able to get anything in the way of a description that might help before he started shooting?"

Gonzo forced his mind back to those hellish few minutes on the sidewalk. "It was dark, so I couldn't see much beyond longish dark hair, olive-toned skin, a black coat. Everything happened so fast. I didn't get a good look at him before he started shooting."

"What do we have in the way of cameras in that neighborhood?" Farnsworth asked.

"We'll get with Lieutenant Archelotta on that," Conklin said of the lieutenant who commanded the IT division. "And I'll have Patrol go door-to-door to see if any homeowners have outdoor security cameras that might've picked up something."

"The Patrol officers who went after him," Gonzo said. "Did they report in?"

"There was no sign of him by the time they got to the corner where he disappeared on foot," Malone said.

"No blood or anything on the street?" Gonzo asked. "I got off a few rounds. I was hoping one of them hit him."

"Not that they were able to see, but we'll look again in the morning."

"I need to go to New Carrollton to see his folks," Gonzo said, the sick feeling in his stomach rising up all over again at the thought of what he had to do to good people who didn't deserve it.

But then who ever deserved to have a family member murdered?

"I'll go with you," Malone said.

"That's not necessary."

"I wasn't asking."

"What about Sam?" Gonzo asked. "Has she been told? And Cruz?"

"The Secret Service had a fortress up around the lieutenant's home," Malone said. "I've left a message for her and expect to hear from her in the morning. Cruz has been notified and is on his way back to the District."

"From where?"

"Florida apparently."

For the first time since Arnold was shot, Gonzo thought of Christina, who would need to be told before the news hit the airwaves.

"What about the media?" Gonzo asked. "They go nuts anytime they hear the call of an officer down."

"We've managed to fend them off, but we're on borrowed time," Malone said. "We need to go to New Carrollton."

Gonzo nodded. The captain was right. He just hoped he could get through this gruesome task without vomiting.

"I want someone with Arnold around the clock until he's buried," Gonzo said. "I'd do it myself but as acting commander of the squad—"

"I'm his liaison officer," Tyrone said. Every officer chose a colleague to see to the details if they happened to be killed in the line of duty. "I'll do it."

"Thank you." To Malone, Gonzo said, "I need a minute and then we'll go." He left the room and went straight to the restroom to wash the blood off his hands and to splash cold water on his face. His stomach was a disaster, and he'd be shocked if he didn't actually puke at some point.

Officer down. Officer down. Officer down.

Gonzo couldn't get the image of the gaping hole in Arnold's face out of his mind. He suspected that memory would haunt him for the rest of his life.

If you shut the fuck up, I'll let you take the lead. I'll let you take the lead.

His stomach burned, and there was no stopping the vomit that was coming whether he liked it or not. Bolting for a stall, he bent over the toilet and heaved up the meager contents of his stomach. It went on until dry heaves gripped him, and he broke out in a cold sweat. This could not be happening. Any second now he was going to wake up in his bed with Christina by his side to tell him it had all been a bad dream. What he wouldn't give for that to be true.

He wiped the sweat and tears from his face with shaking hands. The sound of the gunshot echoed in his ears. It had taken just one shot to end the life of a promising detective, a young man in his prime. One shot.

Gonzo's legs were rubbery under him as he forced himself to stand and face what had to be done. He flushed the toilet and left the stall. At the sink, he splashed more cold water on his face and rinsed the foul taste from his mouth. His hands trembled so violently that water splashed onto the countertop around the sink.

Christina. He needed to call her, so she'd hear it from him and not on the news. But how did he say the words that would devastate her? How did he tell her this horrific news without terrifying her all over again? Ever since he was shot, she was clingy and needy, and understandably so. The last thing in the world he wanted to tell her or anyone was that Arnold had been killed. But he couldn't let her hear it from anyone but him, or on the news. So he pulled the phone from his pocket and placed the call.

He could tell by the way she said hello that she'd been sleeping. Of course she was sleeping. It was two in the morning.

"Baby."

"Tommy. You're working late."

"Yeah. Baby, listen, are you awake?"

"Mmm."

"Christina."

"I'm awake, Tommy. What's wrong?"

"It's… I didn't want you to hear… I…"

"What?"

"Arnold's dead."

The anguished sound that came from her went straight to his broken heart. "*No*. Tommy. What happened?"

"He was shot."

"Wh-where were you when it happened?"

"Right next to him."

"Oh, God, baby. Are you…" Her soft sobs brought more tears to his eyes. "Tommy. I'm so sorry."

"I have to go tell his family."

"Does it have to be you?"

"Yeah, it does." He ran trembling fingers through his hair. "I gotta go, baby. I don't know when I'll be home, but I'll call when I can."

"I love you so much. I'm so sorry this has happened to you and your partner."

"Thanks. Do me a favor and stick close to home with Alex until we get this guy. He's in the wind, and I need to know you guys are safe."

"We'll stay home. Don't worry about us."

"I'll call you."

"Let me know if there's anything at all I can do for any of you."

"I will. Love you."

"I love you too."

Gonzo put the phone back in his pocket and took a series of deep breaths, preparing himself to deal with the horror show unfolding on the other side of the bathroom door. He had to go out there and face it. He had to go out there and provide leadership to a heartbroken squad.

He had to go out there and tell Arnold's parents what'd happened. He had to go out there and get the guy who'd killed his partner.

Only after all of that was done could he go home to his love and fall apart. Until then, falling apart was not an option. Summoning all the fortitude he could find, he walked out of the bathroom to rejoin the nightmare already in progress.

Malone was waiting for him. "You okay?"

"I've been better."

"I can take care of his family on my own, Gonzo."

Before the words were out of the captain's mouth, Gonzo was shaking his head. "I owe it to him to do it myself. They know me. It needs to come from me."

"We need to go out through the morgue, and we need to go now. The press is all over the main entrance, looking for info about the officer-down call. They've checked the hospitals, so they know it's a fatality. The public affairs people have pleaded with them to sit on that info until we can notify the family, but we don't have much time before someone gets itchy."

Gonzo nodded in agreement. "The others, the squad…"

"Are doing what needs to be done to find the shooter. The activity will help."

"Okay."

He and Malone moved briskly through headquarters, drawing the attention of every officer they passed. No words were spoken. None were needed. Malone insisted on driving, and Gonzo didn't have it in him to argue. They took off out of the parking lot and headed north to Maryland.

"Nothing from Sam?" Gonzo asked.

"Not yet."

Gonzo's heart ached at the thought of her waking up to this unimaginable news. It ached even worse at how badly he'd failed her and the rest of their squad by letting this happen on his watch.

THIRTEEN

SAM CAME AWAKE SLOWLY, LEISURELY. It had been years since she'd had this much time off and she'd begun to enjoy the ability to sleep in. Although "sleeping in" usually meant eight at the latest, and it was only five now. Why was she awake? Beside her, Nick slept peacefully. She hated that he'd lost so much sleep over her, and to see him relaxed and sleeping was a huge relief.

After a few minutes, she realized she wouldn't be going back to sleep and decided to go downstairs to get the book Tracy had given her. She got up, used the bathroom and then put her sweatshirt and sweats back on to go downstairs. Outside Scotty's door, the agent in charge stood to greet her.

"Good morning, Mrs. Cappuano."

"Good morning, Darcy."

"I was asked to let you know that Captain Malone from the MPD was here to see you."

"When?"

"Around midnight."

"Why didn't anyone tell me?"

"We were given orders by the vice president that you were not to be disturbed for any reason except if your son needed you."

"Right," Sam said, recalling Nick's final words to the agent on duty the night before. "Did he say what he wanted?"

"No, ma'am. I believe he said he would call you."

Sam's heart beat fast and her palms were sweating by the time she picked up the phone she'd left charging on her bedside table. The only reason the captain would've come to her home in the middle of the night, while she was on leave, was if something was terribly wrong.

She sat on the bed and flipped open the phone to find multiple missed calls from Malone, Cruz and Farnsworth. "*Fuck*," she whispered. "God, what now?" Sam was half-tempted to close the phone and pretend, for a little while longer anyway, that she hadn't seen the missed calls.

In truth, she was on leave and could ignore the calls without consequence. But she couldn't do that. She *wouldn't* do it. Whatever was wrong, she'd have to deal with it eventually. With that thought in mind, she returned the call to Malone.

He answered on the first ring. "Lieutenant."

His formality only ramped up her anxiety. "Captain. I'm sorry I was unavailable when you came by last night."

"I'm sorry to have to tell you that Detective Arnold has been shot and killed in the line of duty."

A punch to the gut wouldn't have hurt any worse than those words did. All the oxygen left her body in a big whoosh, leaving her lightheaded and nauseated. "When?"

"Around eleven thirty last night. He was on a stakeout with Sergeant Gonzales, waiting on a person of interest in the knife attacks case. When they confronted the suspect on the street, he fired on Detective Arnold, killing him almost instantly with a shot to the face."

Sam wiped away tears that would've pissed her off royally before she'd been attacked. Now she felt everything so much more acutely than she ever had, and this news hurt like a bastard. Poor Arnold. Such a great guy and a promising young detective. And Gonzo… "Is Gonzo nearby? Could I speak to him?"

"Hang on."

She heard low voices in the background.

"Hey," Gonzo said, the single word conveying a world of emotion.

"I don't know what to say."

"My fault. I let him take the lead not knowing what we were dealing with."

"You were doing your job, part of which is to train him."

"Wasn't the time for training, but that's on me."

She'd argue that point with him later, when the shock had worn off. "His family…"

"The captain and I are on our way there now."

"What can I do?"

"Nothing. You're on leave."

"Not anymore I'm not. I'll be at HQ within thirty minutes. Tell me how I can help."

"Shooter's in the wind. Happened right in front of me, and I couldn't return fire in time to take him down."

It was going to be, Sam realized, a very long time—if ever—before Tommy Gonzales got over what had happened to his partner. "We'll get him, Gonzo." As she said those words, the fire in her belly that had been extinguished in Marissa Springer's basement came roaring back to life with the power of a full-blown inferno. "We will get him. Do you hear me?"

"Yeah."

"I'll see you when you get back to HQ. Tell Arnold's parents I'll be up to see them later today."

"I will."

"Call me if you need me, Tommy. I mean it."

"Okay."

She closed her phone and ran for the shower, skipping her hair so she could get to her people sooner. With the fire in her belly still burning hot and fierce, she crossed the hall to get dressed in jeans, a warm sweater and heavy socks. For the first time in weeks, she went back into her bedroom to unlock the drawer in her bedside table and retrieved her weapon, badge and cuffs.

When she was as ready as she'd ever be to face this day, she burst from her bedroom, startling Darcy.

"Is everything all right, ma'am?"

"One of my officers has been killed."

"Oh my God. I'm so sorry. If there's anything we can do…"

"Thank you. I'll let you know." Sam took the stairs to the loft two a time. She hated to wake Nick when he was getting some much-needed rest, but she couldn't leave without speaking to him. Sitting on the edge of the mattress that covered the double lounge, she leaned forward to kiss him.

"Nick." When he didn't rouse, she did it again.

His eyes opened, immediately awake and on alert. "Why are you dressed?"

"Arnold was killed overnight. I have to go into work."

"*What? He was killed?* How?"

"Shot confronting a suspect. The guy's in the wind. I have to go."

"Samantha, wait. Before you go…" He sat up and wrapped his arms around her. "Babe."

"I know."

"Was anyone else hurt?"

"Gonzo was right there when it happened, but he's not physically wounded. Emotionally…"

"Yeah. Jesus. Poor Arnold. He's just a kid."

Sam bit her lip to keep from wailing. She couldn't think about what had been lost. Not now anyway. Not when they had a killer to hunt down and a job to do. "I have to go."

"I want to come with you."

"I can't wait for the Secret Service and all that. I have to go now. Can you catch up?"

"You want me there?"

She pulled back to gaze into his gorgeous hazel eyes. "Yeah, I want you there."

"I'll clear my schedule for as long as you need me."

Sam kissed him. "Thanks. I'll see you there. Go in through the morgue so you don't get hounded by the media, and keep the detail to as few agents as possible."

"I will. I'll call Shelby and get her over here to stay with Scotty." He twirled a strand of her hair around his finger. "Be careful out there, babe. This guy has already gunned down a cop. He's got nothing to lose, and I've got everything to lose."

"I'm always careful, and I expect I'll be even more so now." She didn't have to tell him what *now* meant. There was before Stahl attacked her, and then there was now.

"You're sure you're ready to go back?"

"Nope. But he was one of mine. I'm going back for him. It's not about me right now."

Placing both hands on her face, he kissed her again. "I'll be right behind you."

"Knowing that makes it easier to face this."

"I love you."

"Love you too." Stealing one last kiss, Sam got up and headed downstairs, nodded to Darcy and kept going to the first floor. She grabbed a couple of granola bars and two bottles of water. At the front hall closet, she chose her warmest parka and a pair of sheepskin-lined gloves Nick had given her for Christmas as well as the warm boots he'd bought for her and was shown out the door by the agent on duty fifteen minutes after she talked to Malone.

In the BMW, she took full advantage of the heated seats as she pulled out of Ninth Street and headed for HQ.

Arnold is dead.

The words refused to register as truth in her brain. It was unfathomable. The happy-go-lucky detective who was their favorite whipping boy couldn't possibly be gone. And Gonzo, poor Gonzo. Arnold had so recently saved Gonzo's life after he was shot, and to have his partner gunned down right next to him…

Sam took a deep breath, trying to keep her emotions in check so she'd be able to guide her squad through the tragic loss of one of their own. Before he heard it on the news, there was one person she needed to tell, so she placed a call to her father.

Sam's stepmother Celia answered. "Mmm, hello."

"Celia, wake up. It's me, Sam. I need to talk to Dad."

"What's wrong, honey?"

"My detective… Arnold…he was… He's dead, Celia."

"Oh no. Oh, God."

"I wanted Dad to hear it from me and not on the news."

"Of course. I'll take the phone to him. I'm so sorry, Sam."

"I know." Her stepmother's kindness brought more tears to Sam's eyes. "Thanks."

"Hang on for your dad, honey."

In the background, Sam heard some rustling and shuffling before Skip Holland came on the line. "What's wrong, baby girl?" His voice was gruff from sleep.

"It's Arnold." She realized she was going to have to say those words a lot before the dust settled. And it wasn't going to get any easier the more she said the words. "He was shot and killed in the line last night. The shooter is in the wind. He was our person of interest in the knife attacks."

"Aw, Christ. I'm so sorry. Such a fine young man."

"Yes." It was all she could do not to break down into big, loud sobs at the sound of her dad's voice on the phone. She used her coat sleeve to wipe her eyes as she drove. "What am I supposed to do, Dad? How do I get my people through this?"

"Your job is to lead and to command, to be there for your people as well as Arnold's family."

"I want to be out tracking this guy down and making him pay for what he did to Arnold."

"That's not your job in this case. I assume you've called in the Marshals to help locate him?"

"Yeah and the FBI."

"Let them do the chasing. You all stay focused on building an airtight case against him that'll hold up in court. It'll give you something to do with the grief and rage."

"I can't get far enough past the heartbreak to feel anything but that."

"There'll be rage too. After Steven was killed, I didn't feel comfortable around my own wife for weeks because I was so afraid I might lose control of the rage."

"But you didn't?"

"No, I didn't, but it was one hell of a fight not to. As hard as it'll be today and tomorrow and next week and the week after that, you'll get through this, and you'll get your people through it too."

His confidence in her gave her a badly needed boost. "Thanks, Dad."

"Anytime, baby girl. Take care of you in all of this, you hear me? You've been through a tough time, and you need to ease back in."

"The fire in the belly is back."

"That's good to hear, although I'm sorry it took such an awful tragedy."

"So am I."

"Call me later. Let me know how you're doing, and give my love to the squad and Gonzo in particular."

"I will. Thanks again." She'd no sooner ended the call with her dad when the phone rang. "Holland."

"It's me." Freddie.

"Hey. You've heard?"

"Yeah, last night. We're on the way back from Florida now. I'll be at HQ soon. Where are you?"

"Almost there myself."

"Oh, good. That's good. Sam…"

The despair was apparent in every word he said. "I know. I know."

"I'll see you soon."

She pulled into the parking lot at HQ, which was filled with trucks from TV stations with big satellite dishes on top, and drove around to the morgue entrance. Thankfully, the reporters didn't recognize her in the new car and never gave her a second glance as she darted inside.

Her first stop was the morgue itself, where Detective Tyrone was standing watch outside the lab. His chin quivered at the sight of her. Sam hugged him for a long moment and then went into the lab where Lindsey McNamara was finishing up the exam on Arnold with a CSU detective standing by.

Sam forced herself to look at the damaged face of the handsome young man who'd reported to her for the last year. She made herself look at the hole in his face that the bullet had left behind.

"Sam," Lindsey said. "Don't do this to yourself."

"Why not? He's mine. The least I can do for him is to be here with him." She reached out to touch his hair, the one part of him unchanged by death. "Was it fast?"

"I believe he died almost instantly."

"So he didn't know what was happening?"

"I can't say for sure, but the bullet pierced his brain. If he knew, it was barely an instant before he lost consciousness."

"Helps to know he didn't suffer."

"Gonzo on the other hand…"

"I talked to him."

"Then you know he's blaming himself."

Sam nodded.

"Are you back to work?"

"As of today."

"It's good to have you back, but I hate the circumstances."

"So do I." Sam ran her hand over Arnold's hair again before pulling her hand back and jamming it into her pocket. "Did you get anything we can use?"

"I was able to retrieve the 9 millimeter bullet. I've sent it out for ballistics testing. But there wasn't much else to be gotten."

"That's something anyway. Keep me posted on what you hear from the lab."

"I will."

"Thanks, Doc."

"If there's anything I can do, Sam, anything at all, please don't hesitate to ask."

"Appreciate it." Taking the images of Arnold's wounded face with her, Sam left the morgue and headed for the pit, ignoring the stares and curiosity from colleagues she encountered along the way. Other than her meetings with Trulo, she hadn't been here in weeks, and people were naturally curious about what'd happened between her and Stahl in that basement. They were curious about her new role as the vice president's wife and the celebrity status that went along with it, not that she cared about that. It was more of a nuisance than anything else, at least in her opinion.

They could have their curiosity. She would never speak of what happened between her and Stahl again, except for at his trial. There she would gladly convey the gory details of what'd happened that day—and the day he'd attacked her on her own doorstep—if it meant putting him away for life. He was facing hard time in a federal prison where the inmates wouldn't take kindly to a cop in their ranks. If it was petty to hope that Stahl might be on the receiving end of some jailhouse justice, then she was happy to be called petty. After the way he'd tortured and beat her, it was the least of what he deserved.

She entered the pit, which was unusually quiet.

Jeannie McBride looked up from her computer, saw Sam and got up to hug her. "Thank God you're here."

Never one to easily accept overt displays of affection, Sam returned Jeannie's hug because she needed the comfort as much as her detective and friend did. "How's everyone doing?"

"Shock. Disbelief. Anger. More disbelief."

"What've we got on the shooter?"

"Come into the conference room, and I'll show you."

Sam followed Jeannie into the room where Avery Hill was updating the murder board.

"Lieutenant," he said, seeming surprised by her arrival. "Good to see you, but I'm sorry about the reason. I had a lot of admiration for Detective Arnold. He was a huge help to me during the Patterson case."

"Thank you. He was showing a lot of potential. Tell me what we have so far and how I can help."

McBride and Hill went through the events of the previous day, including what Gonzo and Arnold had learned from William Enright and his colleague at Griffen + Smoltz.

"Have we established any other connections to Besozzi among the other knife attack victims?" Sam asked.

"Not yet," Jeannie replied, "but we're digging deeper on all of them today."

"What about Besozzi himself? What do we know?"

"Not much of anything, oddly enough," Hill said. "He doesn't exist anywhere in the system, which tells us only that he hasn't been arrested or detained under that name. It doesn't tell us if that's who he really is."

"Do we have reason to suspect he might be operating under an assumed name?"

"We have more of a hunch," Jeannie said, "by one of Enright's colleagues who'd thought the accent seemed fake."

"Let's talk to the colleague today, and see if he can tell us more about why he thought so. See if they can get us a photo of him before the press briefing."

"We're working on the photo." Jeannie took a note, adding Sam's suggestion about the coworker to a long list on the pad in front of her.

"The guy is passing himself off as an Italian citizen, correct?" Sam asked.

"That's right," Hill said.

"Can you reach out to the Italian embassy to see if they can help us to determine whether someone of that name is currently in the U.S.?"

"I'll get right on that," Hill said.

"I want to see everything we've got so far in this investigation," Sam said, "and I want this guy's head on a fucking platter."

FOURTEEN

As THE SUN began to rise outside the neatly tended home of John and Brenda Arnold, Gonzo felt like his skin was on fire from the inside at the thought of what he'd come to tell these salt-of-the-earth people who'd taken such pride in their police detective son.

In the two years Arnold had been his partner, Gonzo had been invited here to cookouts and his partner's twenty-fifth birthday party, among other family celebrations. They'd made him feel like an extra son, and now he had to go in there and pull the rug out from under them.

He was going to be sick again. Gonzo threw open the passenger door and the rush of fresh air helped to fend off the surge of nausea.

"I can do this, Gonzo," Malone said quietly.

"No. I have to. They know me. It needs to be me."

"We have to go in there before they see us out here and leap to their own conclusions."

There would be, Gonzo realized, no avoiding this nightmarish task. He had to walk up the sidewalk that had been lined with pretty red flowers the last time he'd been here, in the summer to celebrate Arnold's birthday. He would knock on the door and tell these good and decent people that their only son was dead, that he'd been murdered in the line of duty, that he was a hero. And none of that would matter to parents who'd lost their son.

If something like this ever happened to Alex…

No, don't go there. Don't.

"Gonzo."

Malone's deep voice jarred him from his tortured thoughts.

"All right. Let's go." His muscles didn't want to cooperate as he got out of the car. His legs resisted his brain's command to move, to walk, to do what had to be done no matter how much he might wish to be anywhere else on any other mission.

The four stairs to the porch felt like a hundred.

Malone pushed the doorbell.

Waiting for someone to come to the door, Gonzo focused on drawing breath to his lungs, hoping he wouldn't add insult to injury by vomiting or passing out or drawing attention to himself when this wasn't about him. No, this was about Arnold and his family. He needed to be strong for them. He needed to hold up. There would be time later, a lifetime in fact, to fall apart.

The door swung open, and Arnold's pretty, youthful mother appeared, wearing a robe and smiling brightly at the sight of her son's partner on the front porch. Until she took a closer look and must've seen the despair he was doing a poor job of hiding. And then she saw the captain standing beside him.

She shook her head. Through the storm door, Gonzo saw her lips move in the shape of the word *no*. And then she was screaming.

Malone opened the storm door and Mrs. Arnold all but fell into Gonzo's arms.

"No! Do not come in here and say it. *Just do not!*"

"Mrs. Arnold," Malone said, "may we please come in?"

She never gave them permission to enter her home, but

they went in anyway, with Gonzo all but carrying her to the sofa in a formal living room, the kind that was kept pristine for visitors. On the wall were old school photos of their two daughters and only son as well as another portrait of Arnold in his Patrol uniform.

Gonzo sat with her on the sofa as she sobbed uncontrollably.

"Is your husband at home?" Malone asked gently.

"He… He's in the shower." She continued to sob as Gonzo rubbed her back. "How?" she asked.

"He was shot while confronting a person of interest in an investigation."

"Were you there?"

"Yes."

"Did you get him?"

"I tried, but I made the decision to tend to Arnold rather than pursue him."

"I can assure you, Mrs. Arnold," Malone said, "that we will not rest until the man who killed your son is in custody."

"Tommy…"

"I'm so sorry. I wish there was something I could've done."

"He loved you so much. He talked about you all the time."

Gonzo couldn't bear to hear that. Not now. Not when he felt so responsible for what'd happened to his partner. "He was the best partner I've ever had. He saved my life. I only wish I could've returned the favor."

"It… It must've been bad if there wasn't anything you could do."

"It was. It was…bad."

As she began to cry again, footsteps on the stairs signaled the arrival of Mr. Arnold. "John," she said, her voice filled with anguish.

John Arnold stepped into the room, saw Gonzo and Malone, and came to a stop, his complexion growing ashen in a matter of seconds.

Brenda held out her hand to her husband.

For a long moment, he stared at her hand before he moved woodenly into the room, took her hand and sat on the other side of her. She turned from Gonzo toward her husband, who put his arms around her.

"He's gone, Johnny," she said softly. "Our boy is gone."

"How?" John asked.

"Shot in the line of duty," Malone replied, sparing Gonzo from having to say it again. Once had been more than enough. "We're so very sorry for your loss. Detective Arnold was a valued member of our team, and he will be missed."

"The person who shot him…"

"Is the subject of a massive manhunt," Malone said, "involving local and federal agencies. The FBI and the U.S. Marshal Service are involved. We will find him."

"I want to see him," Brenda said.

Gonzo glanced at Malone, asking without words how to handle the request.

"He was badly wounded," Malone said. "It may be better for you to hold on to the memories of him as he was in life rather than seeing him as he is now."

"He's my son, my baby," Brenda said as tears slid down her cheeks. "I want to see him."

"We'll arrange it for later today if that's convenient," Malone said.

She nodded.

"Is there anyone we can call for you?" Malone asked.

"Our daughters. We need to tell them."

"We'll call them ourselves," John said. "They'll come."

"We can wait with you until they get here," Gonzo said.

John shook his head. "That's not necessary. We want you out looking for the person who killed our son."

"Then that's what we'll do," Malone said, rising. "I'm sorry again to have brought you such devastating news. You'll have the full resources of our department at your disposal for as long as needed, and an Inspector's funeral will be held befitting your son's honorable service to the District of Columbia."

"What does that mean?" Brenda asked. "An Inspector's funeral?"

"It's a term that originated with the NYPD and is actually a song played by pipe and drum corps," Malone said. "The term is now used across the country when a police officer is killed. It signifies a funeral that is worthy of the highest dignity and respect."

"Thank you for that." John shook hands with both of them. "We know this is an awful loss for you as well."

"I want you to know..." Gonzo's voice broke and tears filled his eyes. "I'll never forget that your son saved my life. I only wish..."

Brenda stood and put her arms around him. "There was nothing you could do. It was his time to go. It's God's will."

Where in the world was she getting her strength and how could he get some?

"I'll be in touch," Gonzo said. "And Lieutenant Holland said she'll be by later today to see you."

"That's very kind of her," Brenda said.

They left a few minutes later and returned to the car. In a career filled with difficult situations, this one ranked among the most difficult of all. Gonzo felt as if he'd been skinned alive with every nerve on full alert.

"It never gets easier," Malone said. "I was new to Patrol when Steven Coyne was killed. I remember the utter shock at realizing that cops actually get killed. That it can happen to people I know and care about. You never really get over it, but you move on from it, wiser, more alert, more aware."

Gonzo knew that his captain was trying to help him to cope with the loss of his partner, but in the midst of shattering grief and overwhelming guilt, Gonzo had the presence of mind to know that he would never get over it.

SAM WADED THROUGH the reports that had been taken from the two survivors of the knife attacks, the families of those who died and the interview Gonzo and Arnold had done at Griffen + Smoltz. This case reminded her of the Woodmansee investigation in which nothing had added up until it was almost too late.

But now they had a name—Besozzi. It was time to go back again and re-interview everyone about any potential connections to the man who'd killed one of her people.

A buzz of activity in the pit had Sam looking up from the reports to see the gorgeous blonde woman she'd nicknamed "Secret Service Barbie" outside her door. She wore a wire in her ear that connected to a radio on her hip.

"Mrs. Cappuano—"

"I'm Lieutenant Holland here, as I've told you before."

"Of course. My apologies."

Apologies, my ass, Sam thought. She did it on purpose, and you'd never convince Sam otherwise. "I'm busy. What do you need?"

"Vice President Cappuano is on his way in. I'm here to ensure a secure space is available for him."

"This is as secure as it gets around here," Sam said of her office.

Melinda's brows knitted with consternation as she took in the small, cramped space. "I suppose it'll do."

"Great." When Melinda continued to hover in the doorway, Sam said, "Was there something else?"

"I just wanted to say how sorry I am about your colleague."

The unexpected words of sympathy brought a lump to her throat. "Thank you."

"We'll show your husband in momentarily."

Sam nodded in acknowledgement.

Another flurry of activity and a buzz of radios preceded Nick's arrival in the pit. He came to her office and stepped inside, closing the door behind him. The sight of him—tall, handsome, commanding, sexy and all hers brought tears to Sam's eyes that she refused to give into. There'd be time enough for that after they caught the bastard who'd killed Arnold.

But she wasn't above stepping into her husband's outstretched arms and letting him wrap her up in his unconditional love.

"How's it going, babe?"

"It's awful. He was shot in the face. Gonzo and Malone are with his parents now. I've got to go there at some point today, and that's about the last thing I ever want to do. There's no sign of the bastard who did it, and the investigation is a hot mess. Other than that…"

He didn't say anything. Rather he only held her closer, stroking a hand over her back.

Sam held on to him, breathing in the scent of her love and her home, until duty called and she was forced to release him to pick up the extension on her desk.

"Holland."

"Oh, you're back," Chief Farnsworth said. "I was expecting Sergeant Gonzales."

"He's with Arnold's family at the moment."

"I'm so sorry, Sam."

"Thank you."

"How's Gonzo doing?"

"I only spoke to him briefly, but he seems to be holding up, doing what's got to be done. Underneath it all, I'm sure he's not doing well at all."

"We'll want to keep a close eye on him."

"I'll see to it."

"I know you're busy, but I just wanted to call, to say... Well, losing a member of your team is the most difficult thing you'll encounter as a commander. Please ask for help if you need it in the upcoming days and weeks. You're not alone in this."

"Thank you, sir. I'll do that."

"On a side note, it's good to have you back, but I'm very sorry about the circumstances."

"As am I."

"Now that Arnold's family has been informed, we'll need to make a statement to the media. They've been camped outside since the officer-down call came over the radio last night."

"Can you tell the PIO that I'll take care of that?"

"Yes, and I'll go with you."

"I need about twenty minutes to get my ducks in a row, and then I'll come find you."

"Sounds good. See you then."

When she returned the phone to the cradle, Nick said, "Do what you've got to do, babe. I'm here to help in any way I can even if it's just an occasional hug."

"I appreciate you clearing your schedule today."

"I wouldn't be anywhere else. If it would help, you can talk it through with me."

"It would help."

A knock sounded on the door.

"Come in."

The door opened and Freddie Cruz came into the office. He looked tired and devastated and stressed from the all-night drive to get back to town. "I figured you must be here," he said to Nick. "I had to go through security to get into my own office."

"Sorry about that."

"No biggie." He walked over to Sam, who stood to hug him. "I can't believe this has happened."

"Neither can I." She clung to her partner longer than she ever had before, relieved to see him, to know it hadn't been him, that he was here to help…

He released her and took a seat next to Nick. "Tell me everything." In his normally amiable expression, Sam could see both rage and heartbreak.

"You're not supposed to be here."

"Screw that. I'm not going anywhere until we get the guy who killed Arnold."

FIFTEEN

"THE KNIFE ATTACKS began on Tuesday, January sixth, with a fatal attack on Isabella Rios, a twenty-four-year-old employee at the U.S. Department of Agriculture." Sam read from the meticulously written reports Gonzo had filed. Nick and Freddie listened intently to every word. "She and all the victims were attacked at night. Rios was outside the McPherson Metro station and died from a fatal stab wound to the jugular. Dr. McNamara has determined that Rios was attacked from behind and most likely never saw it coming. Video surveillance from around the Metro station didn't provide a good enough look at the attacker to aid in the investigation. The next attack was two days later on a forty-eight-year-old mother of two, Deborah Gainsville, who had gotten off a city bus in Brentwood and was also attacked from behind. It's believed that she bled out slowly on the street before she was discovered dead about an hour after the attack.

"Next up was thirty-six-year-old Barry Scanlon, a bartender, who sensed the attack was coming, whirled around to confront his attacker and took a knife to the gut. After four days in ICU, he's been moved to a regular room and should be released in the next few days. William Enright, age twenty-seven, is an associate at Griffen and Smoltz, a graphic design and marketing firm in the city. The report says he was on a side street in the Gallaudet neighborhood, on his way home from a night out

with friends when the assailant approached him from behind, grabbed his arm, swung him around and stabbed
him in the abdomen. He remained coherent enough to
fight off the attacker and call for help, but sustained a life-
threatening abdominal wound as well as significant lacerations to his hands and arms in the battle. He's the one
who turned us on to Besozzi, who was a former client."

"Why former?" Freddie asked.

Sam read aloud from the report Gonzo had written
about what Enright had told them. "Apparently Enright
sounded the alarm to his higher-ups when Besozzi asked
him to include chat rooms and webcam capabilities in
the website for a T-shirt store. Gonzo and Arnold met
with the Griffen in Griffen and Smoltz yesterday, and
he said he and his partner agreed that Enright's concerns
were valid and cut Besozzi loose as a client. Because the
website was close to finished when this happened, Besozzi was furious."

"And there're no other connections to Besozzi among
the other victims?" Nick asked.

"Everyone is doubling back today to ask about him,"
Sam said. "And Hill is working on figuring out whether
Besozzi is actually an Italian citizen or if he's just pre-
tending to be, as one of Enright's colleagues suspected."

"He's not an Italian citizen," Hill said as he came into
the office bearing papers that he handed to Sam. "The
Italian embassy was very helpful and they have no record
of anyone by that name entering the U.S. in the last year."

"Interesting," Sam said. "So he's an imposter then."

"Have we pulled a warrant to search his place?" Freddie asked.

"Malone was handling that. Let me check." Sam
picked up the phone and placed a call to her captain.

"Malone."

"It's Holland checking on the warrant for Besozzi's house."

"We're just leaving Arnold's parents' home. I'll call to check on it."

"Um, how'd that go?"

"As you'd expect."

Sam closed her eyes against the now-predictable rush of emotion. "How's Gonzo?"

"As you'd expect. We mentioned to Arnold's parents that you'd be by later today to see them, and they seemed appreciative of the gesture."

She glanced at her husband. "Nick and I will head up there as soon as I brief the press."

Nick nodded in agreement, and she smiled at him.

"That's good of both of you. It'll mean a lot to them. So, um, she wants to see him."

"Oh God, really? Did you tell her he's in bad shape?"

"Yes, and she said he's her son, her baby, and she wants to see him."

Sam sighed deeply. "Lindsey can arrange that for us."

"I've already called her."

"Thanks, Cap. Keep me posted on the warrant."

"Will do."

"So his mother wants to see him?" Freddie asked.

"Yes."

"I'd like to see him too."

"I don't think that's such a great idea. He was shot in the face, Freddie."

"He was my friend, Sam. I want to see him."

"All right. Let me brief the media, and then I'll go with you to see him before we head out to see Arnold's folks."

"I'm going to sift through the reports while you do the briefing and get up to speed," Freddie said.

"I'm supposed to remind you that you're suspended and technically can't be on the case."

"I'm on the case whether I get paid or not."

Sam would do exactly the same thing, so she didn't argue. "I'll be back." On the way out of the office, she bent to kiss Nick. "You can watch the briefing on the TV in the conference room if you'd like."

"I'd like." He squeezed her hand and conveyed all the love and support he could in the way he looked at her.

Jeannie appeared at the office door holding a piece of paper. "Photo of Besozzi from Griffen and Smoltz."

Sam looked into the black eyes of the man who'd killed her detective and made a silent vow to Arnold that they would get justice on his behalf, no matter what. "Thank you. Can you get me some copies for the briefing?"

Jeannie handed her a stack of copies.

"You're the best, thanks." Sam grabbed her coat on the way out of the office and put it on while she walked.

As Sam left the pit, Nick's Secret Service detail stepped aside to let her by.

John "Brant" Brantley Junior, the lead agent on Nick's detail, said, "I'm very sorry for your loss, Lieutenant."

"Thanks, Brant." She kept moving, putting one foot in front of the other, because she had no choice. Curling up into a ball and wailing wasn't going to change what'd happened and it wouldn't do a damned thing to catch Besozzi.

The chief was waiting for her in the lobby. "Ready?"

"As I'll ever be."

They walked outside together. The moment the door opened, reporters started screaming questions at them.

As she always did, Sam waited for them to quiet down before she began to speak. "At eleven thirty-eight last night, after several hours of surveillance on a home in the Manor Park neighborhood, Detective Sergeant Thomas Gonzales and Detective Arnold John "A.J." Arnold approached a person of interest in the knife assault case. Detective Arnold took the lead, and before he could finish announcing himself, the suspect opened fire, striking Detective Arnold in the face and mortally wounding him."

A murmur rippled through the crowd of reporters as she confirmed an officer had been killed in the line of duty.

Sam held up the photo of Giuseppe Besozzi. "We're looking for this man, known as Giuseppe Besozzi, in connection with the shooting of Detective Arnold and as a person of interest in the knife attacks. We have reason to believe that Besozzi is not his real name, but we have not yet been able to confirm that."

"What led you to Besozzi in the first place?" Darren Tabor from the *Washington Star* asked.

"He was connected to one of the knife attack victims. We're looking into whether there're connections to the other victims, but so far we know of only one connection."

"Assume Arnold's family has been notified?" a reporter asked.

"Yes, this morning."

"Can you provide any more details on the shooting? Where was he shot? Was the wound immediately fatal or was he treated?"

"I'll only say he died almost immediately. We're not releasing the other details at this time."

"Was Sergeant Gonzales wounded?"

"No. He was able to fire several rounds, and despite that and pursuit by Patrol officers who were backing up the detectives, Besozzi managed to get away. The FBI and the U.S. Marshal Service are assisting in our efforts to locate and apprehend Mr. Besozzi. We ask the public's assistance in helping to locate him, but we ask that no one approach him directly. If you know where he is, call us. I want to repeat that he is armed and dangerous and has already gunned down a police officer. Do not approach him."

"Lieutenant, you've been on an extended medical leave since you were attacked by Lieutenant Stahl," Tabor said. "Did the death of Detective Arnold bring you back to work?"

Sam gave him her best death stare. "What do you think?"

"It's a fair question," Tabor added. "You've been out for weeks, and you're back today of all days."

"Where else would I be when one of my officers has been brutally murdered in service to this city?"

"Can you tell us what role the vice president is playing here today?"

"He's here in a supportive role because an officer of mine and a friend of ours was killed on the job. I would think his reasons for being here today would be rather obvious."

"You were seen at the White House during your leave," one of the bottle blonde TV reporters said. "Are you taking on a more active role as second lady?"

"Any more legitimate questions about the investigation?" Before anyone could form a question, she was walking away from the podium and into the building with Chief Farnsworth right behind her. "We have an officer killed in the line and they're going to waste my time asking about the White House?"

"I guess they have to get that in during the rare moments when they have access to you."

"It's inappropriate. Especially today."

A young woman approached them. "Pardon me, Lieutenant," she said, nodding to the chief. "I'm Tara from public affairs. We have requests from all the major networks asking for interviews about the shooting of Detective Arnold. The story is making the national news."

"Fantastic," Sam said. "We've got a cop shooter on the loose, and I'm supposed to stop what I'm doing to give interviews to the networks who are only interested because Arnold worked for *the goddamned second lady*?"

Before her eyes, the young Public Affairs officer shriveled.

"Don't kill the messenger, Lieutenant," Farnsworth said. To Tara, he added, "I'll take the interviews. The lieutenant is otherwise occupied today."

"Of course," Tara said. "I'll let them know." She scurried off in the direction from which she came.

"Poor girl," Farnsworth said. "You've scarred her for life."

"She needs to learn about a thing called *timing*. It's everything."

"She's just doing her job, Sam, and I'll let you get back to doing yours. If there's anything I can do to help, just say the word."

"Malone has requested a warrant to search Besozzi's house. If you could move that along, it would help."

"Consider it done."

"Arnold's folks are coming in later to see him. It would mean a lot to them, if you have the time—"

"Consider that done too. Just let me know when, and I'll be there."

Nodding, she said, "Thank you."

When she would've walked away, he stopped her. "Sam."

She glanced up at his kind, compassionate eyes, the eyes of her uncle Joe as well as her commanding officer.

"This is the toughest thing you'll encounter in this job. You're just off a difficult recuperation, and this is a hell of a thing to come back to. Please ask for help if you need it. We're all standing behind you on this."

She had to swallow a huge lump in her throat before she could speak. "Thank you, sir."

"Keep me posted on where we are with the investigation."

"I will. Nick and I are heading up to see the Arnolds. That's the right thing to do, isn't it? I mean I should be out working the case, but—"

His hand on her arm stopped her. "You're his commander. It's the exact right thing for you to do today. We've got plenty of people out looking for the person who killed him. Your job is to lead your team through the investigation as well as to guide them through the painful loss of their colleague and friend."

She nodded. "Thank you."

"You know where to find me if I can help with any of it."

"You've already helped. I'll catch up with you later."

"I'll be around."

"Don't let the network people ask you about the vice president's wife," she said with a small smile.

"They wouldn't dare. I've heard she's a real barracuda."

He left her chuckling as she walked back to the pit where her heartbroken detectives were waiting for direction and guidance.

In the conference room, Nick was with Hill and Jesse Best, commander of the U.S. Marshal Service's Capital Area Regional Fugitive Task Force. The three men were poring over a map of the city that was spread out on the table.

"Gentlemen," Sam said when she joined them. "Where are we?"

Best stood to his full six-foot-six-inch height. He had blond hair and the build of the defensive tackle he'd been on his college football team. He'd turned down offers from the NFL to go into law enforcement and had risen quickly through the ranks within the Marshal Service. "My condolences, Lieutenant."

"Thank you."

"I was just explaining to Agent Hill and Vice President Cappuano that we have officers spread out in a grid formation throughout the city, complementing the effort underway by the MPD and FBI."

"How do we know he's still in the city?" Sam asked.

"We don't know for certain, of course," Best said, "but we've got officers at the train station, bus depot, airport and we're searching Metro video from all the stations near to where the shooting took place. We've got people checking with cab companies and car services."

"Does he have a phone registered under the Besozzi name?" Hill asked.

"We've got requests into all the major carriers asking that very question," Best replied.

"Wow, you guys don't mess around," Sam said. Under normal circumstances, she'd resent the intrusion from federal authorities. But today she couldn't muster the energy it would take to be resentful of help they badly needed.

"This is what we do, Lieutenant," Best said. "We find people. Our entire team is doubly motivated by the fact that the person we're looking for killed a law enforcement officer. We've already had two cell companies tell us they have no one by that name in their customer database."

"What about the possibility that he's operating under an assumed name?"

"As soon as we have the warrant to search his place, we'll get some prints to determine who this motherfucker really is," Best said. "Then we'll have him by the balls."

Sam liked this guy's style. "I want him alive."

"As do we. But if it's a choice between his life and the life of one of my people, we won't choose him."

"I understand. While you oversee the manhunt, we're going to continue to try to tie Besozzi to the knife attack victims. Please let me know what we can do to supplement your efforts."

"We appreciate the cooperation thus far. Your Patrol officers have been very helpful."

While she spoke with Best, she felt Hill watching her closely, probably trying to gauge whether she was about to fall apart. She wouldn't give him or anyone the satisfaction of falling apart before they'd gotten justice on Arnold's behalf. "That's good to hear," she said to Best.

"Avery, I hear your mother is doing well," Sam said, out of respect to Shelby more than anything.

"She is, thank you."

"We'll leave you all to it. Nick, could I have a word in the office please?"

He followed her through the pit and into her office, closing the door behind him.

"What's it going to take to get us up to New Carrollton to see the Arnolds?"

"If I go, we have to let the Secret Service take us. Are you sure you want to turn it into a big circus at their house?"

"Maybe the detail could tone down the circus ever so slightly?"

"I'll talk to Brant and see what we can do. While you were doing the briefing, I got a text from Shelby asking if she should reschedule the final fitting for your ball gown."

The statement was so comically out of place in the context of this day that Sam had to laugh. "My ball gown." She shook her head. "When is all that again anyway?"

"If by 'all that' you mean the inauguration, it's the day after tomorrow as you well know since this entire department has been preparing for months now."

"That soon, huh?"

"That soon."

"Is it appropriate for me to appear at inaugural balls forty-eight hours after one of my detectives was killed in the line of duty?"

"I don't know the answer to that, Samantha. If you feel it's inappropriate, I would understand if you didn't go as long as you understand that I have to go."

"I do understand. What time are we supposed to meet Marcus?" she asked of the young designer from Virginia who'd become Sam's go-to guy for all things formal.

"Six."

"Ask Shelby to push him to nine, and I'll meet him at the house. I'll have to play attending the balls by ear, but at least I'll be ready if I do go."

He put his hands on her shoulders. "I know this is an awful time for you, and the last thing you want to think about is the inauguration, but I need you up on the podium with me Tuesday morning. That part is somewhat nonnegotiable."

She reached up to caress his handsome face. "I wouldn't be anywhere else at that moment. It's the party aspect that may be seen as inappropriate."

"You know who you could ask?"

"Who?"

"Your chief of staff. From what I hear, Lilia is shockingly well informed about all matters of protocol and Washington."

"Good idea. I'll run it by her. In the meantime, we've got to go to Maryland and I guess you're driving since I'm not allowed to drive the VP."

"Neither am I, but in this case that's an advantage. I'll be able to snuggle with my wife all the way to Maryland. I hope the traffic is *awful*."

Sam couldn't help but laugh at how adorably sweet he was and how he brought a ray of sunshine to the darkest of days.

SIXTEEN

DETECTIVE JEANNIE MCBRIDE found Barry Scanlon in a private room at the George Washington University Hospital. A Patrol officer from the MPD stood watch outside the door and required Jeannie to show her badge even though she knew him.

"Thanks, Detective," he said. "Just following orders."

"Totally understand," Jeannie said.

"I'm really sorry about Arnold. He was a straight-up guy."

"Yes, he was. Thank you. What's the situation in Scanlon's room?"

"The doctors were just in with him, so he should be awake."

"Great, thanks." Jeannie knocked on the door and opened it just enough to peek inside. The man in the bed gestured for her to come in. "Mr. Scanlon, I'm Detective McBride, MPD." She showed her badge and gave him a moment to inspect it.

"I've already given a statement," he said in a weak voice that didn't match up with his broad shoulders or muscular build.

"I have some new information I was hoping to speak to you about, but only if you feel up to it."

"Sure, whatever I can do to help."

Jeannie held up her phone with the photo of Besozzi that had been emailed to her. "Do you know this man?"

He took a long look at the photo. "I can't say I do."

"Does the name Giuseppe Besozzi mean anything to you?"

"Not that I recall, and it seems like I'd remember that name."

"Yes," Jeannie said, "I imagine you would. You're a bartender, correct?"

"I am."

"Is it possible Besozzi was a patron, perhaps?"

"I suppose that's possible, but I can't remember ever meeting him at the bar or anywhere else for that matter."

"We appreciate your time and we hope you make a speedy recovery," Jeannie said.

"Sure, no problem. I'm happy to do anything I can to help catch the guy who put me here."

"One other thing," Jeannie said. "Did your attacker say anything to you?"

"Not a word."

"Thank you again for talking to me, and we'll be in touch if anything else comes up."

"You know where I'll be for the next week or so," he said with a grimace. "Out of work and out of money. I don't have health insurance. I was stupid enough to think I wouldn't need it at my age. My bar is doing a fundraiser for me, but I have no idea how I'll ever pay for all of this."

Jeannie handed him her business card. "Please let us know how we can contribute."

"That's really nice of you. Thanks."

She patted his arm. "Hang in there. We're working hard to get the person who did this to you."

"How's he doing?" the Patrol officer asked when she walked out of the room.

"As well as can be expected it seems," Jeannie replied. "Let us know if anything changes here."

"I will."

Jeannie walked through the hallways of the hospital, trying not to think of the brutal days she'd spent there after she was attacked last year, before exiting through the main doors. She took deep breaths of the cold air to clear her senses of the antiseptic smells that brought back the horror every time she stepped foot in the place.

Jeannie placed a call to Sam. "Nothing new from Barry Scanlon, the bartender who was attacked. He didn't recognize Besozzi's name or picture."

"Okay, thanks for closing that loop."

"What else can I do?"

"Check in back at HQ. Hill and Best are there, and may have something else they want you to do. We're on the way to Arnold's parents' house."

"God, I don't envy you that task."

"And they say rank has its privileges."

"No kidding. Please let me know what I can do. Anything."

"Just keep working the case and pulling the threads. You know how something small can break this whole thing wide open. Hopefully we'll have the warrant soon to search his place. The Marshals need prints to figure out who this guy really is."

"I guess I'll see you when you get back to HQ. Good luck with the Arnolds."

"Thanks. Talk to you later."

As she got in the car, she thought about the conversation she'd had earlier with her partner, who was now standing watch over their deceased friend and colleague.

"You okay?" she'd asked.

Will shook his head. "This thing with Arnold…"

"I know. It's awful and tragic and senseless, but we have to go on. We have to keep doing the job."

"Do we though? Do we have to?"

"What do you mean?"

"When does it get to be too much? The lieutenant is attacked and tortured by one of our own. Cruz got shot, Gonzo got shot, you got kidnapped, assaulted. And now this with Arnold. I can't take it anymore, Jeannie. I really can't take it."

Her partner was young, only a few months older than Arnold had been, and the two men had been close friends outside of work. "Can I tell you something I was told after my attack?"

He shrugged with unusual indifference.

"Captain Malone told me that everything will seem very dark for a while after something like that happens. He said it was important not to make any major decisions about anything after a traumatic event. Because one day, the sun comes out again and the first thing you'll notice is the sun, not the darkness. You'll want to recognize your life when that day comes, he said. He was right and so was everyone else who told me to focus on getting through today without thinking too much about tomorrow. Tomorrow takes care of itself."

"How many times have we approached someone on the street, showed our badges, said who we are?"

"Too many to count."

"He was just doing his job."

"I know. He was in the wrong place at the wrong time."

"He had a new girlfriend and his whole life ahead of him." Tyrone swiped at his face. "It's not fair."

"No, it certainly isn't."

"I can't believe he's actually dead. Arnold is dead. I keep saying it to myself but I can't seem to make it stick. It's too unreal."

"It's apt to be for a while."

"Will it ever make sense?"

"Probably not. These things seldom do."

"I don't want to be a cop anymore, Jeannie. I don't want to be the next one to get shot or attacked or tortured. I'm not strong like you and Sam and Gonzo."

"Yes, you are too! You were right there with me through the whole thing when Sanborn attacked me, holding me up and pushing me through to the other side of it. I couldn't have gotten through that without you. You're so much stronger than you think you are."

A sob hiccupped through him and he buried his face in his hands. "I'm not," he said. "I'm not strong. I was so freaked out the whole time you were missing and then after… When we heard what'd happened… I wasn't strong when the LT was missing or when Gonzo was shot. I was scared shitless that they were going to die and leave us to do this awful job without them."

"Why haven't you ever told me any of this? The department has people who can help you deal with these things. You don't have to do it alone."

"I want to be worthy of the gold badge. It means everything to me, but who wants a chickenshit detective on their team or covering their back? You deserve better than me. The squad deserves better."

"You're not a chickenshit. I've seen you in action. You do what needs to be done. I've never once seen you shirk your duty or do anything other than the right thing on the job. You're selling yourself way short."

"Maybe on the outside I look good, but inside…"

"The outside is all that matters, Will! You're doing the job. You're performing admirably. Anyone would say so."

"What if I don't want to do the job anymore? What if I've had enough?"

"Only you can know that, but you'd be a total fool to throw away the career you've worked so hard to have on the day you lost your friend. *Nothing* is normal today. It's not the day for major decisions. If you still feel this way a month or two from now, we'll have that conversation. But we're *not* having it today and that's final."

Jeannie rarely pulled rank on her partner. She rarely had to, but she did it today because she got where he was coming from. Who understood better than she did what it was like to lose the desire for the job? To wait months for it to come back? To question every aspect of her life, her work and her safety?

"I want you to know," she said in a gentler tone, "that I understand where this is coming from. I've been there myself. But I care too much about you to let you do something stupid when you're grief-stricken and shocked and aching over the loss of your friend and colleague."

Tyrone stared blankly as tears continued to roll down his face.

"Today is an awful day. Tomorrow probably will be too. It's going to be a tough time for all of us. But we will get through it together because that's what we do. We stand together and support each other."

He remained stubbornly silent.

"I want you to talk to Trulo when things settle down. They've made people available for us, and we need to take advantage of the help." When he didn't say anything, she said, "Ok?"

"Yeah, I guess."

He'd said what she wanted to hear, but his flat tone of voice and the aura of resolve she felt coming from him had left her on edge.

WHEN GONZO AND Malone returned to HQ, the first thing Gonzo noticed was the department flag had been lowered to half-staff in honor of Detective Arnold.

"I hate to see that," Malone said. "The only time we lower the flag is when someone in the department dies."

Gonzo had nothing to say to that. This was the first time in his tenure on the force that an officer had been killed in the line of duty, and it happened to be his partner. The partner he'd sent out to be gunned down because he wanted to shut him up.

"I think you ought to go home, Gonzo."

That drew him out of his dark thoughts. "I'm not going home. That's the last place I need to be with the man who killed my partner out there somewhere getting away with it."

"The Marshals are hunting him down. That's their job and they're damned good at it."

"You can't ask me to go home and do nothing, Captain. You can make me leave, but I'll be out there working the case whether I'm on duty or off."

Malone's phone rang. He took the call and ended it just as quickly. "We've got the warrant for Besozzi's house."

"Let's go."

"Not without backup and not without CSU," he said of the Crime Scene Unit detectives who would pore over the place looking for clues that could blow their case wide open.

"Call for backup and CSU then."

"You giving the orders now?" the captain asked with a small smile that told Gonzo he was joking. But he made the call for backup and turned the car around.

They'd be returning to the place where Arnold had been killed. He'd have to see the blood on the sidewalk and remember the horror that was still too fresh in his mind. Gonzo had the time it took to drive across the congested city to prepare himself to be there again. It was nowhere near enough.

"From what I hear, neighbors are going crazy over another cop being shot in their quiet little corner of the city," Malone said after a long period of silence. "Stuff like this doesn't happen there."

"Chris and I looked at a place out there before I was shot."

"Of course you already knew, despite what happened with Billy Springer and now this, it's not the kind of neighborhood where shit like this usually happens. You know that because you've been on the job for twelve years and you know this city inside out."

"What's your point?" Gonzo asked because with the captain, there was always a point.

"Just that if you'd been down in Southeast rather than leafy Northwest, you might not have let your partner take the lead. You probably would've thought, in the back of your mind, that he wasn't really ready to take on the kind of stuff we see down there. But up here… This is the nice part of town, the kind of place you'd want your own family to live."

Gonzo understood and even appreciated what the captain was trying to do, but it didn't do a thing to dull the relentless guilt. "He was pissing me off."

"Arnold?"

"Yeah. Bitching and moaning about the cold and the time and the fact that we were off duty hours ago and still watching Besozzi's place. So I made him a deal— stop the bitching and he could take the lead. I was irritated and that's what drove the decision. I wish I could say I did it because of where we were, but it was about shutting him up."

"Whatever the reason, you know the area. You know most of the time, someone isn't going to shoot a police officer in the face when that officer approaches, shows his badge, gives his name. In Manor Park, most of the time, a resident would say, 'Good evening, Officer. How can I help you?' Don't tell me you didn't know that because you did. That information is so deeply ingrained in you that you couldn't *not* know."

Gonzo tried to wrap his head around what the captain was saying, but all he could see was Arnold lying on that cold sidewalk, blood gurgling in his throat as he struggled to breathe.

"Stop blaming yourself," Malone said. "The person who killed Arnold was the guy with the gun, not you. Keep telling yourself that over and over and over again until it sinks into your thick skull."

As Malone turned onto the block where it had all gone down, Gonzo instantly felt sick again. But he forced himself to choke back the bile that surged from his empty stomach so he could focus on the job that needed to be done. The scene was taped off, and someone had washed the blood off the sidewalk. Thank God for small favors, Gonzo thought.

In the short time they waited for CSU and the FBI to join them, exhaustion engulfed him. The night without sleep caught up to him, and the rush of adrenaline that had followed the shooting suddenly wore off.

He rubbed his hands over his face, trying to get it together and find the focus he needed to get through the next few hours.

A knock on the window startled him. Christ, he was jumpy. He recognized the CSU commander and reached for the door handle.

"You don't have to be part of this, Gonzo," Malone said. "I can take it from here if you need to step back."

"I'm fine. Let's go." As he ducked under the yellow crime scene tape and walked up the sidewalk to the house, he pretended not to notice that in addition to being exhausted, he was also lightheaded from the lack of food. Though the thought of eating brought back the nausea.

He accepted a pair of latex gloves from Malone and followed the captain into the house. Gonzo wasn't sure what he'd been expecting, but it wasn't a well-furnished, comfortable residence with magazines on the coffee table, art on the walls, a big flat-screen TV and plants in the window.

"I wasn't expecting it to be so lived in," Malone said.

"Neither was I. Clearly, he's been here a while, whoever he is."

The CSU detectives swooped in and began combing through every corner of the townhouse, starting in the basement and working their way up. They dusted for prints on every surface, including the walls.

Gonzo began to see double as he watched them.

Malone signaled for a Patrol officer. "Please take Sergeant Gonzales home. He's off duty until tomorrow morning."

"Captain—"

"That's a direct order, Sergeant. You're no good to any of us if you keel over."

"I want to hear any updates the same minute you hear them."

"You have my word."

Since that was as good a deal as he could hope to get, Gonzo went with the Patrolman who held open the passenger door of the cruiser for Gonzo, as if he were addled or elderly or something. "Thanks," he muttered before the door closed.

The Patrolman got into the driver's seat. "Where am I taking you?"

Gonzo gave him the address.

"I just want to say… I'm really sorry about your partner. Mine threw out his knee late last year, and I miss him like crazy, so I can't imagine… Well, I'm really sorry."

"Thanks." Gonzo leaned back against the head rest and looked out the passenger-side window, hoping the young officer wouldn't feel the need to fill the silence with idle chatter the way Arnold always had. Tears burned his eyes, and he closed them tight to keep from bawling his head off in front of a junior officer.

The next thing he knew, the Patrolman was gently shaking him awake. "We're here, Sarge."

"Thanks a lot for the ride."

"No problem. You hang in there."

Gonzo nodded to him and got out of the car, eager to get inside the safety of the home he shared with Christina and Alex. As he approached the door, he remembered that his keys were locked in his desk at HQ, so he pressed the buzzer to their apartment.

"Yes?" Christina asked over the intercom, her tone cautious and guarded.

"It's me."

"Oh thank goodness." The buzzer sounded to admit him.

Gonzo trudged up the stairs, the overwhelming exhaustion a reminder that he wasn't yet back to full stamina after his own shooting. Christina waited for him at the door to their apartment and threw herself into his arms. He wrapped an arm around her and lifted her to walk them inside, kicking the door shut behind him.

"Tommy, God, I can't stop crying. I'm so, so sorry."

Wrapped up in the arms of the woman he loved, Gonzo stopped trying to fight the tears that had been threatening all day. The grief, exhaustion, disbelief, rage and despair combined to reduce him to a sniveling wreck of a man. He wasn't proud of the way he broke down, but there wasn't a damned thing he could do to stop it.

Christina led him into the bathroom, helped him remove his clothes and joined him in the shower where she washed his hair and body while he stood numbly under the water. It could've been freezing cold for all he knew. Then she toweled him dry and tucked him into bed.

"Need you," he whispered.

"I'm here."

He reached for her and she got in bed and snuggled up to him.

"I'm right here, and I'm not going anywhere."

"Alex."

"I called your parents and they came to get him for a few days. I wanted to be able to focus on you. I hope it was the right thing to do."

"It was. I don't want him to see me like this."

"Tell me how I can help."

"You're helping more than you know just by being here."

"You saw his parents?"

"Yeah. His mom was so happy to see me until she realized Malone was with me." He shuddered. "It was horrible."

She wiped tears from his face.

"Should've been me, Chris."

Christina propped herself up on an elbow. "What do you mean?"

"I let him take the lead because he was pissing me off. I told him if he shut up about the cold and the late hour and everything that I'd let him take the lead."

"Oh, Tommy. It's not your fault. You couldn't have known."

"That's what everyone has said, but still. I never let him take the lead, and the one time I do…"

"It was his time to go, baby. It's as simple as that."

Gonzo knew she was right. He knew everyone was right. He hadn't shot Arnold, so it wasn't technically his fault. But it would be a very long time, if ever, before he would stop blaming himself for his partner's death.

SEVENTEEN

IT HAD TAKEN hours to arrange the security for Nick to join her in New Carrollton, and since she didn't want to go without him, she'd waited, which is why they were setting out at seven p.m. Since the traffic was, as Nick had hoped, unusually beastly for a Sunday night, Sam took advantage of the time in the car to place a call to Lilia.

She answered on the second ring. "This is Lilia."

"It's Sam. Sam Cappuano." Out of the corner of her eye, she saw Nick smile at the rare use of her married name.

"I know," Lilia said. "I've got you programmed into my phone."

"Oh, well, okay then. I'm sorry to bother you after hours and on a weekend."

"No such thing as after hours or weekends in my line of work."

"Mine either."

"So we have that in common."

"Apparently we do."

"What can I do for you tonight, Mrs. Cappuano?"

"Will you please call me Sam when it's just us and no one else is listening?"

"I will try to remember to do that. And I want to just say that I saw your press conference, and I'm so sorry for the loss of your colleague and friend. If there's anything

I can do to be of assistance to you or the vice president during this terrible tragedy, please don't hesitate to ask."

"Thank you. That's very kind of you. And that's why I'm calling. Nick and I have been talking about Tuesday and how I should navigate the more celebratory aspects in light of the loss of Detective Arnold. While I'm heartbroken over his senseless death and wish to convey that in all my public interactions, I'm also obligated to my husband. I guess you could say I'm torn over what to do about the balls and whatnot."

"I can totally understand your dilemma. If you're asking my opinion—"

"I am. What should I do?"

"Attend the inauguration ceremony and one ball. Do a ceremonial twirl around the dance floor with your husband and we'll put out a statement from your office that Vice President and Mrs. Cappuano have left to spend time with her colleagues and friends on the Metropolitan Police Department as they mourn the loss of one of their own."

"Wow, you're good."

"Why thank you," she said with a laugh. "So you'd be comfortable with that?"

"Yes, I think I would be. Hang on just a second." Sam put her hand over the mouthpiece of the phone. "Would you be okay with one dance at one ball before we return to our friends on the MPD to mourn the loss of Detective Arnold?"

"As always, my love, I want to be wherever you are, so if we're one dance and out, that's fine with me."

Sam leaned in to kiss him. "Have I told you yet today that you're the best husband I've ever had?"

Nick snorted with laughter. "The bar was set awfully low."

"Indeed it was." She returned the phone to her ear. "Lilia, it's a plan. Nick is fully on board."

"Excellent. I'll coordinate everything with his office to make sure it's smoothly done."

"Thank you again, and I'll be in touch in regard to what we talked about the other day. Needless to say, I'm back to work and otherwise occupied for the time being."

"I completely understand. We'll be here when you are ready to proceed with our plans."

"Very good. I'll see you Tuesday."

"See you then."

Sam slapped her phone closed. "I can't believe I'm about to say what I'm about to say, but I actually like her."

"Wow. That is high praise indeed. You don't like anyone."

"I like you. Most of the time anyway."

"Only most of the time?"

"Ninety-nine-point-nine-nine percent of the time."

"I gotta work on that zero-point-zero-one percent." He held out his arm to her, and Sam snuggled into his embrace. "How you doing, babe?"

"I feel sick inside, heartbroken for Arnold and his family, worried about Gonzo and the rest of the squad. It's just so awful."

"It's my worst nightmare come to life. I talked to Christina earlier today, and she feels the same way. The arbitrary, out-of-nowhere-ness of it is enough to shake us all to our core as our hearts break for the one who was lost."

"I'm sorry you have to live with that kind of fear. I hate that for you and Christina and Elin and Arnold's parents."

"I hate it too, but I love you enough to let you be you, even with all the risks and dangers. But this... Arnold being gunned down on a quiet street for no apparent reason... It's shaken me up, Sam. I won't lie to you about that."

"I wouldn't want you to." She checked her watch. "We should call Scotty while we have time. It's probably shaken him up too."

Nick pulled his personal cell phone from his pocket. "Let's do one better." He made a FaceTime call to their son, who answered right away.

"Hey, where are you guys?"

"On our way to see Detective Arnold's parents."

"Oh wow. I'm really sorry, Mom. He was a wicked nice guy."

"Yes, he was."

"Are you, you know, okay and everything?"

His incredible sweetness brought tears to her eyes. "I'm sad, buddy. We're all sad, but we're doing what we need to do to catch the man who shot him."

"I hope you catch him soon."

"So do I. How was your day?"

"It was fine. I went to see Grandpa Skip and hung out with Abby and Ethan for a while this afternoon," he said of Sam's sister Tracy's kids. "Did my homework. Nothing special."

"Sometimes a day in which nothing special happens is a day to be thankful for."

"I guess so."

"Dad and I are going to see Detective Arnold's parents and then we'll be home, okay?"

"Okay. Tell them... His parents... Tell them I said I'm so sorry."

"We'll do that. See you soon. Love you."

"Love you too."

"Bye, buddy," Nick said.

"He's such a sweetheart," Sam said.

"He really is. This is going to hit him hard, you know. That someone he knows could be gunned down the way Arnold was, especially after what just happened to you."

"Do you think we need to get him some preventative counseling?"

"Probably wouldn't hurt."

"We can talk to him about it and feel him out."

They pulled into the Arnolds' neighborhood half an hour later. Numerous cars were in the driveway and parked at the curb. The motorcade only added to the congestion on the quiet street.

"Hey, Brant," Nick said. "Let's keep it to two cars on the street. The others can park around the corner. We're not looking to create a three-ring circus for these people."

"Understood," Brant said. He issued orders into a radio and then got out of the car to open the door for Nick and Sam. "We haven't done advance recon here, so we're a bit nervous about this."

"We'll be in and out," Sam assured him. "We don't want to intrude any longer than necessary."

Surrounded by agents, they walked up the sidewalk. The front door was opened before they could knock, and they were shown inside.

A woman with eyes gone red and puffy from crying shook hands with both of them. "Mr. Vice President, Lieutenant Holland, it's an honor to have you here. I'm Debbie, Mrs. Arnold's sister. I'll let her and John know you're here."

"Thank you," Sam said.

She gestured for them to have a seat in the living room while they waited.

They sat together on the sofa, and Nick wrapped his hand around hers.

"Thanks for coming with me," she whispered.

"I'd never want you to do this alone."

When the Arnolds came into the room, Sam and Nick stood to greet them. Mrs. Arnold hugged them both and Mr. Arnold shook hands with Nick and hugged Sam. Their eyes were rimmed with red, their heartbreak palpable.

"Thank you so much for coming," he said. "I know how busy you both are."

"I want to say how sorry we are, all of us within the MPD, for your loss," Sam said. "Our entire squad is heartbroken."

"A.J. loved you guys," Mrs. Arnold said. "He spoke so highly of you, Lieutenant, and you too, Mr. Vice President."

"Please call me Nick. We thought the world of your son. He was not only a colleague to Sam, but a friend to both of us, and we'll miss him very much."

"That's so kind of you to say." She wiped away tears. "We were proud of him."

"With good reason," Sam said. "He was very well regarded within the department."

"He loved that job," Mr. Arnold said. "Loved the squad, working with you, partnering with Tommy. He loved it all. We take comfort in knowing he died doing the work he loved."

"We're concerned about Tommy," Mrs. Arnold said. "He's in bad shape over this."

"We'll be keeping an eye on him," Sam assured her. "Don't worry."

"It would be an honor if you might say a few words about A.J. at his service," Mrs. Arnold said.

"Of course," Sam said, though the thought of speaking in front of all those people gave her hives. "It's an honor to be asked."

"Is there any news about the investigation?" Mrs. Arnold asked.

"Nothing yet, but we are working it from every angle. The FBI and U.S. Marshal Service are involved in the manhunt for the shooter. As soon as we have anything to report, I'll make sure you're informed."

"We'd appreciate that."

Sam glanced at Nick. "We don't want to keep you from your family. Just please know that our hearts and prayers are with you, and anything we can do, please let me know." She handed her card to Mrs. Arnold. "Anything you need."

"Thank you. Everyone from the MPD has been so nice, and Detective Tyrone has been a godsend, seeing us through the funeral planning."

"I'm glad to hear he's been helpful. You've been in touch with Doctor McNamara to see your son?"

"Yes," Mr. Arnold said. "We're going in the morning. The family is here now, so we decided it wouldn't make much difference if we go tomorrow."

"If you receive inquiries from the news media, we'd ask that you refer them to the department's public affairs office. Then you won't have to deal with it."

"We'll do that," Mr. Arnold said as he walked them to the door. "Thank you. And thank you again for coming. Means a lot to us."

"Your son meant a lot to me," Sam said. "He won't be forgotten."

With more hugs and assurances to be in touch, Sam and Nick were escorted back to the black SUV by his detail.

"They're amazing," Nick said. "So composed."

"I'll never know where people get the strength. I remember the day my dad was shot, and I was out of my mind. I could barely function. Those people lost their only son last night, and they're thankful to *us* for coming to see them?" She shook her head. "I see it all the time on the job. The way the human spirit somehow endures even in the worst of times."

"You're every bit as strong as they are, Samantha. Look at what you recently endured and survived thanks to your own wits and moxie. Don't sell yourself short."

"Maybe so, but I think about something happening to Scotty... I didn't give birth to him or even get to raise him, but I'd lose my mind just the same."

He put his arm around her. "I know, babe. I would too."

Sam's phone rang and she took the call from Captain Malone. "What've you got?"

"CSU got some really good prints. We're running them through AFIS now."

"Let's hope he's in the system."

"That could bust this thing wide open. I sent your squad home for the night. They were running on fumes and emotion, which can make for a dangerous combination. I've ordered them back at zero seven hundred. You should head home too."

"We're doing everything we can to find this guy, aren't we, Cap?"

"Everything and then some. The Marshals are the best at this, and we're supporting them in every way we can. The national news has picked up the story and they're broadcasting the suspect's picture. Someone will see him and call us."

"Call me if anything pops overnight? I'll have my phone with me." She'd never again be without it.

"I will. Try to get some sleep. It's going to be a long week."

"I'll see you in the morning."

"Yes you will, and for what it's worth, it's damned good to have you back on the job, Lieutenant."

"Thank you." Sam closed her phone and stashed it in her coat pocket. "I want to see my kid, do the stupid dress fitting and go straight to bed with my husband, okay?"

"Whatever you want, babe."

"That's what I want."

And that's what she got. They had dinner with Scotty, had a good talk with him about Arnold's death and came away feeling like he was handling it well enough that counseling wasn't necessary. But they left that option open to him if he changed his mind. Nick helped with his math homework and sent him off to shower while she endured the dress fitting with an overly sympathetic Marcus, who had become a friend to both of them since he'd been dressing Sam.

She loved the midnight blue velvet gown he'd created for her to wear to the inaugural balls as well as the gorgeous red dress and matching coat he'd made for her to wear to the actual inauguration.

When he produced a tie for Nick that matched the red dress, Sam smiled for the first time in hours. "I love that, Marcus."

"I'm so glad you do, hon." He had curly blond hair and warm brown eyes. "Nice to see you smile."

"It's been an absolutely dreadful day."

"Tomorrow will be better. I always believe that."

"I hope you're right. Thanks for coming later for me."

"Are you kidding? I get to dress the most interesting woman in America. I'd come in the middle of the night to tend to you, my friend."

"You are far too kind."

He kissed her cheek. "Hang in there, okay? I'll be here Tuesday to help you get ready. We've got hair and makeup people coming. You're going to knock their socks off."

"Oh joy."

He laughed and waved as he left the room she used as a closet with both dresses in garment bags slung over his arm. He'd make final alterations tomorrow and have them back to her by tomorrow night.

Nick appeared at the doorway, glass of wine in hand. "He doesn't get to see you naked, does he?"

"Oh my God. Are you serious?"

"Dead serious."

"No, he does not get to see me naked. Only you do, but that could change."

"I brought this up for you, but if you're going to threaten me that way, maybe I'll just drink it myself."

"Hand it over, and I might forget your green-eyed monster popped in for a visit."

Smiling, he gave her the wine, and Sam took a sip. "Mmm, that's good."

"All set with Marcus?"

"Yep. I'm told there will be hair and makeup people here early on Tuesday," she added with a scowl.

"Can't have you looking like a hag in front of the entire country."

"True."

It was fun, as always, to banter with her adorable, sexy
husband, but the ache in the region of her heart was a
constant reminder of what had been lost.

Nick held out his hand to her. "Let's get you to bed,
babe."

Sam took hold of his hand and let him take over. He
helped her out of her clothes and into an oversized T-shirt
and put warm, soft socks on her feet, which was what
she wore to bed when she had her period. Otherwise, she
preferred to sleep naked with him.

He tucked her in and kissed her. "I'm going to grab a
quick shower and I'll be right in, okay?"

Sam nodded.

"Drink your wine. It'll help you sleep."

"Okay." While he got in the shower, she did as he directed and sipped the wine. The way she felt tonight reminded her of the first dreadful days that followed her
dad's shooting, Quentin Johnson's death, Jeannie's kidnapping and Stahl's attack. The aftermath of all those
events had been eerily similar. Everything had felt a bit
surreal, like it hadn't actually happened or as if it had
happened in a dream. It was like that tonight. She kept
trying to forget that Arnold had been shot and killed,
but the awful reality would creep back in to remind her
it hadn't been a dream.

Even seeing his heartbroken parents and dealing with
her shattered squad hadn't resulted in reality overriding
her desperate desire to pretend it wasn't real. She ought
to be out trying to help find the man who'd killed her
colleague and friend, but the fire that had burned so hot

and bright earlier had given way to despair and exhaustion as the day had worn on.

She'd be back to work in the morning, doing what she could to get justice for Arnold and the victims of the knife attacks. She was comforted to know that while she was off duty, members of the MPD, the Marshal Service and the FBI were looking for Besozzi.

Her phone rang and she took the call from Captain Malone. "Hey," she said.

"Hope I'm not waking you."

"I was awake. What's up?"

"Does the name Sid Androzzi mean anything to you?"

Sam sat up in bed. "You're joking, right?"

"No joke."

Androzzi was on the FBI's Ten Most Wanted List for his role in a human trafficking ring that had been busted in New York City and Los Angeles. While the busts had shut down Androzzi's operations in those two cities, he'd remained at large with his subordinates unwilling to disclose his whereabouts even to save their own asses. "He's been hiding out in plain sight in our city?"

"So it appears. His fingerprints were all over the townhouse."

"Holy shit. And Hill didn't recognize him from the photo?"

"Apparently, he has significantly changed his appearance since he was last seen. Needless to say, the criminal portion of this case has been escalated right out of our hands and into the jurisdiction of the FBI. The Marshals are still overseeing the manhunt."

"What about the fact that we have jurisdiction over the knife attacks and the murder of one of our officers?"

"The way I see it, we continue to work the case our

own way while they work it their way, in cooperation, of course."

"Of course. I do like how you think, Captain."

"I figured you would. So we dig in deep in the morning, yes?"

"You bet. I'll see you at seven."

"See you then."

Nick came out of the bathroom, a towel tied around his waist, leaving his incredibly perfect chest on full display.

Sam stared at him the way she usually did, in awe that such a beautiful man—inside and out—was hers to keep forever.

"What?" he asked.

"You." She fanned her face. "Seriously hot."

"Honestly, Samantha."

She loved how embarrassed he got when she commented on his insane hotness, which was often. "Just stating the truth."

"Whatever." The view got even better when he dropped the towel and got into bed. "Who was on the phone?"

"Malone. You're not going to believe who our shooter really is." She filled him in on Androzzi's place on the FBI's Ten Most Wanted List.

"He was hiding in plain sight."

"Exactly, and it proves that William Enright's theory about the website he was having them build was spot-on. It wasn't about T-shirts at all."

"Human trafficking. Just the words are so vile."

"The Feds have entire task forces devoted to the issue and trying to stop these guys. That we could've had one of the most wanted traffickers living here for who knows how long and doing God knows what. It makes me sick."

"I'm sure you and your team will get to the bottom of it and catch this bastard."

"We've been superseded by the Feds, but we're going to continue to work the case under the radar."

He turned on his side and reached for her. "You need to shut down and forget about it all for a few hours."

With her hand flat against his chest and her head cushioned by his arm she said, "So do you."

"I'm fine."

"I want you to sleep."

"I will, babe."

She tipped her head up so she could kiss him. As her lips connected with his, she slid her leg between his, bringing her thigh in tight against his groin.

He groaned against her lips and she felt his erection press into her belly. "What're you doing?" he asked, sounding breathless from the kiss.

"Kissing my husband goodnight. Is that allowed?"

"Most definitely, but this feels like hello rather than goodnight."

"What if it is?"

"I didn't think you'd be interested tonight."

"I'm always interested, and tonight," she said with a sigh. "Tonight, I just need you. I don't need bells or whistles or any of your usual finesse. I just need you."

"You have me. You always have me." He kissed her with soft, sweet persuasion, giving her the tenderness she craved, along with the love and comfort she needed and could only get from him. The clothing he had lovingly dressed her in was removed with equal reverence. His hands moved over her body with gentle strokes that had her arching into him, asking without words for the connection she needed so badly.

"Samantha," he said on a whisper, his lips close to her ear, his breath sending a shiver of need through her. "I love you so much. So very, very much."

Tears spilled from her eyes, and he kissed them away as he joined his body with hers, making slow, sweet love to her as she sobbed for her lost friend and colleague, for a life ended far too soon, for the family and friends who would miss him and mourn him. All the while she clung to her husband as he moved within her, reminding her that life goes on, even in the most difficult of times.

"Shhh, I'm here. I've got you."

She was safe with him, safe to let go of the despair that had gripped her since she first heard the awful news, safe to mourn and grieve. His love gave her a soft place to land in the midst of the madness that often surrounded her.

Buried deep within her body, he gathered her in close and held her tightly to him. They stayed like that for endless moments, intimately joined, his love flowing through her and giving her the strength to go on, to move forward and to do what needed to be done while her heart broke into a million pieces once again.

Even in the grip of despair, her body responded to him, taking and sharing the sweet relief they found together, the heat of his release filling and sustaining her. For a long time afterward, he continued to hold her until her sobs quieted and the tears dried on her face.

"I could never face this life I lead without you to come home to," she whispered.

"You'll always have me to come home to. You are my home, and I'm yours."

"It says so in our rings."

"Yes," he said with a small chuckle, "it certainly does." That they'd engraved the same thing inside their wedding rings without knowing had provided one of the more memorable moments of their wedding day. He withdrew from her, leaving her with a kiss when he went into the bathroom to clean up.

Nick returned with a warm washcloth that he used to wipe the remaining tears from her face.

Sam closed her eyes and gave herself over to his care. The next thing she knew, her alarm was going off, jarring her from a deep sleep, the heat of Nick's body curled up to hers making her want to wallow in bed for as long as she possibly could.

And then she remembered. Arnold was dead. A known human trafficker had killed him. She was due at work in an hour to work the case. The ache in the area of her heart hadn't lessened overnight, but her resolve had strengthened. Under no circumstances would the death of Detective Arnold go unpunished. The fire for vengeance once again burned hot and bright within her, powering her out of bed and into the shower. It stayed with her as she got dressed, when she kissed her sleeping husband goodbye while whispering words of thanks that he would never hear but would carry her forward until she could be with him again.

Downing an apple and bottle of water as she drove her new car to HQ, she realized yesterday had merely been a dress rehearsal for today. Today, she was truly back. Today, she would focus on what most needed to be done. Today, she would put her own grief aside to tend to the people who would be looking to her for leadership and guidance as they navigated these turbulent waters together. She would be what they needed, and then she would go home and take what she needed from the man she loved, who would prop her up through it all.

Today, she parked outside the main doors and approached the gathering of media with intent rather than her usual avoidance.

They began shouting the moment they saw her.

"Lieutenant!"

"Can we get a statement?"

"Are there any updates?"

"Have you seen the Arnold family?"

She stepped before them and waited for them to quiet down before she began to speak. "As I mentioned yesterday, we are heartbroken over the loss of our colleague and friend. Detective Arnold was a distinguished member of the Metropolitan Police Department for the last seven years. His rapid rise from Patrolman to Detective was a testament to his commitment to the job and the department. We were proud of Detective Arnold and had great hopes for his future within the department. I've been to see his parents, who are suffering as you'd expect but are strong in their resolve to see justice done on behalf of their son. As are we. The U.S. Marshal Service is leading in the hunt for the man who shot Detective Arnold, and the FBI is coordinating the criminal case against a suspect who has been positively identified. I will defer future commentary about the criminal case to my colleagues within the FBI."

"Will you be attending your husband's inauguration tomorrow?"

"Yes, I will. While I owe my allegiance to my brothers and sisters within this department in these difficult days to come, I also owe an allegiance to my husband. As such, I will be dividing my time between my obligations over the next few days. But let there be no doubt that finding the person who killed my colleague and friend will be my top priority."

"Are you concerned about what people will say about you attending the inauguration while your colleagues are grieving?"

"That's a fair question and one I've considered myself. I apologize in advance to anyone who feels that I shouldn't be on that dais tomorrow. But I will be where I am supposed to be, and then I will return to my duties here. In the years to come while my husband serves our country, I will often find myself divided between what I should do and what I must do. I will always endeavor to do my very best for my team here and my family at home. That's all any of us can do, right? Our very best. I hope you'll understand that I need to get to work. Thanks, everyone."

She'd said more than she'd intended to. She'd made the most public statement yet about how she planned to juggle her competing roles. But there was no time like the present, when her loyalties were deeply divided by demands at home and at work, to lay out how she planned to navigate these next four years. She would do her best and let the lumps fall where they may. People would take verbal potshots at her. Those who felt she wasn't a very good cop or those who thought their country deserved a more dedicated second lady.

Let them say what they would. She would continue to do her best and hope it was enough for those who mattered most to her.

Inside the main doors to HQ, Farnsworth and Cruz waited for her.

"That was unexpected, Lieutenant," Farnsworth said.

"For me too, sir, but I suppose it was time to address the elephant in the room."

"I suppose so." He took a measuring look at her. "You're feeling well?"

"I am. I'm ready to get back to work and to help in any way I can to find Androzzi."

"Everyone is gathering in the conference room in fifteen minutes to regroup," Farnsworth said. "I'll be there shortly."

"Thank you, sir."

Sam walked with Freddie to the pit.

"That was quite something out there, Sam," he said. "I think you left them speechless."

"Good. That's how I like them."

"You're doing okay?"

"I'm better than I was. You?"

"I'm sick at heart over what happened to Arnold, but determined to help get the guy who did it."

"Have you spoken to Gonzo?"

"Not since yesterday. I assume he'll be here soon."

"He's taking this harder than anyone."

"We'll be here for him like we always are." He hesitated before he said, "So I have something I want to tell you, and the timing is all wrong, but I thought maybe some happy news might be welcome."

She ushered him into her office and closed the door. "It's very welcome."

"While we were away, I asked Elin to marry me and she said yes."

Sam hugged him. "Of course she said yes. She knows she's the luckiest girl in the world to be loved by you. I'm so happy for you."

"Thanks, Sam. Means a lot coming from you."

"We've got a son of a bitch to find. Let's get busy doing that, shall we?"

Freddie nodded. "Let's do it."

EIGHTEEN

SPECIAL AGENT-IN-CHARGE Avery Hill stood before the gathered law enforcement officers in the conference room and spelled out the FBI's case against Sid Androzzi. In addition to Sam's entire squad, Captain Malone, Chief Farnsworth, Deputy Chief Conklin and Jesse Best from the U.S. Marshal Service were in attendance.

"Androzzi first entered our radar after a raid in New York City in which twenty-five missing women were located in a warehouse in Chelsea where they'd been held captive, sexually abused and starved. Posing as potential buyers, our agents were able to penetrate Androzzi's network and were led to the warehouse where seven members of Androzzi's organization were apprehended. Androzzi himself was nowhere near the warehouse that day."

As he spoke, Hill posted disturbing photos of the emaciated victims discovered in the two warehouses. "Our next encounter with his organization occurred in Los Angeles, where we were again able to gain access to his network. This time, the warehouse was located in Redondo Beach where forty-two women and children were enslaved. We believe we found them days before they were going to be shipped overseas to destinations unknown. Once again, Androzzi wasn't there the day of the raid. Twice burned, Androzzi tightened the ranks. Since the raid in Los Angeles fifteen months ago, we've had no luck getting close to the organization again. Until yesterday when his prints were found all over the townhouse of the home registered to Giuseppe Besozzi.

"Under the Besozzi name, Androzzi contracted with the local graphic design firm Griffen and Smoltz to build a website that we now believe was going to be used for his trafficking business. Designer William Enright, who was one of the victims that survived the knife attacks, provided information to investigators about how Besozzi's requests for chat rooms and webcams for the site he was building for his retail T-shirt business led him to report the unusual requests to his superiors at the firm. We now believe that Androzzi attacked Enright hoping to silence him. We believe the other victims were randomly selected to incite hysteria in the city and confuse law enforcement about the true motive behind the attacks. Our lab is currently re-examining the clothing worn by all the victims, testing it against the DNA sample for Androzzi on file. I'll turn things over to Marshal Best who will update you on the manhunt."

Jesse Best moved to the front of the room. "Now that we have Androzzi's real name as well as the assumed name he'd been using here, we've been able to subpoena cell records for phones in both names. We're also actively tracking GPS coordinates for both phones, but there has been no activity on either phone since Detective Arnold's shooting. That leads us to believe there is a third phone, so we are aggressively looking into that possibility. In addition, we have isolated all means of egress out of the city as well as the region. Our colleagues in New York and Los Angeles are on alert for the possibility of Androzzi's return to more familiar ground. We've also got alerts out to every major airport that leads out of the country, and his passport has been flagged as well."

"Is it possible that he has passports issued in other names?" Malone asked.

"We're exploring that possibility," Best said. "There was a passport issued in Besozzi's name that we have also flagged. His photo has been issued to the TSA, U.S. Customs and airport security in every major point of exit."

"On a local level, I'd like to take a closer look at missing women and children in this city over the last year or two in light of this new information that Androzzi has been living among us," Sam said.

"That would be helpful," Hill said.

Out of the corner of her eye, she saw Gonzo slip into the room and head for the back.

He looked like hell, and Sam's heart went out to him. In order to know what he was dealing with, she'd have to imagine what it would be like to have Freddie gunned down in front of her while she was powerless to do anything to save him or catch the man who'd killed him.

The very thought made her shudder with horror as bile rose from her stomach to burn her throat.

"What else can we be doing?" Cruz asked. "There has to be something."

"I like the lieutenant's idea of looking harder at recent missing persons cases locally," Hill said. "Expand into Maryland and Virginia. Androzzi's organization was only interested in young women and children, so a compilation of names of missing persons who meet that criteria would be helpful."

"We'll get on that," Cruz said.

"That's all we have for now," Hill said. "We'll keep

you posted on any developments that transpire during the day."

"Is it possible that we'll never find this guy?" Gonzo asked from the back of the room, his voice devoid of inflection.

"I don't have to tell you that's always a possibility," Best said. "All I can say is we're doing everything humanly possible to track him and if he's still in the country, I believe we'll find him, but it might not happen quickly."

Farnsworth moved to the front of the room and shook hands with Hill and Best. "Thank you both for all you're doing to find the man who killed Detective Arnold. We are here to support you in any way that we can."

"Thank you, sir," Hill said as he and Best left the room.

Farnsworth stood before them, his warm gray eyes taking in the assembled group of detectives. "You've suffered an unimaginable loss. Detective Arnold was more than your colleague. He was also your friend. His death brings home the very real risks we take every day when we choose to put on the badge and go to work on behalf of the people of this great city. Wearing that badge is a choice all of us made willingly. It's one we will have to make again now that Detective Arnold has been taken from us so suddenly. If you are looking to make sense of what's happened, don't bother. Take it from those of us who have been through this before. It will never make sense. It will *never* make sense. Sam's dad and I were Patrol officers when our friend Steven Coyne was killed in a drive-by shooting that has never been solved. We were young and cocky and arrogant and so incredibly invincible until that day. I can't speak for Skip or any of the

others who were on the force at that time, but I can tell
you I was never any of those things again. I was no longer young, except in age. I was never again cocky or arrogant or certain of my invincibility. I had been shown,
in the most painful way possible, that we are all as human
as the next person. I'd been shown that wearing a badge
and a gun didn't protect me the way I thought it did. No,
if anything it made me that much more vulnerable than
the next person. I've never forgotten the lessons learned
that week, just as none of you will forget what you will
learn as we investigate Detective Arnold's death, as we
bring his killer to justice and as we lay him to rest.

"These events, these days will stay with you always.
They will frame who you are as people and as police officers. If you need help, I urge you to ask for it. Reach
out to your fellow officers, to the counselors we've made
available to you. Asking for help is no sign of weakness.
In fact, in this environment in which people are revered
for their swagger, it's more a sign of strength to know
yourself well enough to ask for help. I give you my word
that asking for help will never be held against you. Not
while I'm in charge." He paused and took another moment to make eye contact with each detective. "If there's
anything you'd like to say, I hope you'll take this opportunity to do it."

The detectives exchanged glances, nervously looking
to each other for guidance.

"I'd like to say," Detective Tyrone began haltingly,
"that A.J. was not just my coworker. He was my friend.
My close friend. We didn't make a big deal out of the fact
that we spent time together outside of work, but we did.
We spent time together. If I were getting married tomorrow, he would've been my best man. I…" His voice broke

and Jeannie put her arm around her partner's shoulders. "I loved him like a brother."

"He was like a little brother to all of us," Cruz said. "He wasn't that much younger than me, but there was something almost childlike about him. Not in his work, which was spot-on, but in the way he lived the rest of his life. He loved to laugh and to make light of heavy moments. When I think of him, I'll remember that big smile and that hint of the devil in him that made us all laugh."

"I'll remember that too," Jeannie said. "After I was attacked, he used to come by my house every afternoon after work with a container of coffee ice cream with chocolate sprinkles. He knew it was my favorite, so he brought it to me every day. He rang the bell and I'd answer the door. Without a word, he'd hand the bag in to me and then he would leave. I never told him that I had to stop eating the ice cream every day, or I would've gained twenty pounds. Michael loved it, though."

The others laughed even as they sniffled with tears.

"That's just who he was," Jeannie said. "Not one to seek out the attention or the glory, but always there for someone in their time of need. The ice cream was such a small thing, but it meant the world to me at the time. Not only did my friend remember how much I loved coffee ice cream, but he knew how much it would mean to me to know the people closest to me were thinking of me."

"You know what I'll think about when I think of Arnold?" Gonzo asked harshly from the back of the room. When no one replied, he said, "How I marched him into a slaughter because he was pissing me off with his complaints about the cold and the long shift and how he had better things to do than sit outside Besozzi or Androzzi's house waiting for him to come home. I'll remember how

I basically blackmailed him to shut the fuck up with his complaints by telling him he could take the lead with our perp when or if he came home. I'll remember how excited he was that I was finally letting him do something other than tag along. I'll remember that his last words were 'I'm Detective Arnold, MPD,' before he was gunned down. I'll always remember the sound of the blood gurgling in his throat as he struggled to breathe and how I let the guy who did it get away because I was too fucking shocked to react the way I've been trained to. That's what I'll remember." Leaving his stunned colleagues behind, Gonzo stormed out of the room, slamming the door behind him.

Freddie stood up, clearly intending to go after his friend.

"Let him go," Sam said.

"But—"

"Let him go."

Freddie sat back down, crossing his arms over his chest, his distress apparent.

"Gonzo is blaming himself for what happened," Sam said. "He'll probably always blame himself even though he knows, in his heart of hearts, that he is not responsible for Detective Arnold's death. Androzzi is responsible and until he's brought to justice, Gonzo has no one else to blame. We need to stand by him and support him the way he would support us if the situation were reversed."

"Lieutenant Holland is exactly right," Farnsworth said. "In fact, I was going to ask Skip to talk to him. He went through a similar thing when his partner was killed a few feet from him."

"That's a great idea, Chief," Sam said. "I know my dad would be more than willing to do anything he can to help Gonzo through this. I'll set it up."

"Before I leave you all to get to work," Farnsworth said, "I'll remind you that my door is always open. If there's anything I can do for any of you, please come to me. Please ask for help if you need it. I'm not looking to any of you to be a hero in this situation. Now, Lieutenant Holland and Detective Cruz are going to work on the list of missing people that Hill requested. I need the rest of you to report to the Inaugural Task Force for tomorrow's assignments. As much as we want to take a pause to grieve for Detective Arnold, we have a very big day to manage tomorrow, and we will do so with all due attention. And then we will turn our sights on ensuring that Detective Arnold receives a funeral befitting his service to this city."

"Thank you, Chief," Sam said. "I know I speak for all of us when I say we appreciate your support and your sympathy."

"Carry on, everyone," Farnsworth said. "There's nothing else we can do but carry on."

He left the room with Conklin and Malone. For a long time after the door shut behind them, the others were silent.

"To echo what the chief said," Sam said, "I'm also here for anyone who needs me. Tomorrow will be a bit nuts with the inauguration, but otherwise, I'm all yours."

"I still can't believe it's happened," Detective Gigi Dominguez said.

"None of us can," Tyrone said. "I keep expecting him to come busting in here asking what he's missed. I spoke with his family last night, so I know they'll appreciate whatever we do."

"All right then, let's get back to work. There'll be time, later, to give into the grief. Now is not that time."

"Yes, ma'am," they muttered one by one as they got up to leave the room.

"I just need a minute," Sam said to Freddie, "and then we'll get to it."

"I'll get started."

Sam went into her office and shut the door, taking a deep breath to ward off the emotions that were piling up inside. Between the chief's heartfelt words and Gonzo's outburst, her nerves were stretched to the breaking point. The phone on her desktop rang and she pushed herself off the door to answer it.

"Holland."

"It's Malone."

"Didn't I just see you?"

"Sam…"

"What?" *Oh God, what now?*

"Mitch Sanborn was found dead in his cell this morning."

Sam sat down hard, reeling in shock from the news Malone had delivered. "How?"

"He hung himself with a bedsheet."

"How was that possible? Don't they have him on suicide watch?"

"Yes, but he chose his time wisely and did it at shift change when he knew the guards would be otherwise occupied."

Sam ran her fingers through her hair as the implications piled up, one on top of the other. Jeannie would never get her day in court, her chance to put away forever the man who'd stolen so much from her. Sam would never get to testify against the man who'd caused her to lose her baby last year. Her baby—and Nick's.

"Sam? You okay?"

"Just thinking it through. I need to tell McBride…" Pausing, she looked up at the ceiling. "God, what a coward. What a fucking coward."

"That he was, but we already knew that before today, and I've got to hope he'll get what's coming to him in the afterlife. And not for nothing, this is like a huge admission of guilt. Why would he kill himself unless he knew he was going down for what he did?"

"But will that be enough for Jeannie? After what he did to her, will that be anywhere near enough?"

"I don't know, Sam. That'll be for her to decide, I suppose. You want me there when you tell her?"

"No, I don't think so, but thanks for offering. I'll take care of it."

"All right then. Let me know how it goes."

Sam put down the phone and dropped her head into her hands, trying to organize her thoughts before she spoke to Jeannie. The detective had been counting down the days until the trial for the man who'd abducted and raped her last winter during the investigation into a call girl ring in the District.

Sanborn, once head of the Democratic National Committee, had free-fallen from grace after they were able to prove he'd not only abducted and assaulted Detective McBride, but he'd killed two of the immigrant women who'd been part of the call girl operation. After preparing herself to testify for months, Jeannie had been disappointed when the trial date had been postponed to late January.

Now this.

Gathering her hair into a ponytail, Sam twisted it and secured it with a clip. Then she took a series of deep breaths, trying to calm her own emotional reaction to the news before she shared it with Jeannie. Sam would never forget her pursuit of Sanborn and how she'd been forced to tackle him to the ground, taking his elbow to her abdomen in the process. She'd never forget the searing pain deep inside as her body began to reject the baby she'd wanted so badly. Despite frequent, vigorous effort over the last year, she never had conceived again and had all but given up hope that she ever would.

With her emotions already raw from the loss of Arnold, she simply couldn't allow herself to revisit that horrific day too. If she went down that road, she wouldn't be able to function, and she needed to function for Jeannie's sake and for the sake of those who were depending on her for leadership.

Sam stood took another couple of deep breaths and went to open her office door. "Detective McBride, could I have a moment please?"

Jeannie popped up in her cubicle and came into Sam's office, notebook in hand. She was a fine, competent detective who'd worked hard to recover from the horrors Sanborn had inflicted upon her in a windowless room where he'd chained her to a bed and repeatedly raped her. When he was through with her, he'd dumped her in an alley with a message for Sam that she'd be next if she didn't drop the investigation into the call girl ring.

Thinking about what she now needed to tell her friend and colleague, Sam broke out in a cold sweat as Jeannie took a seat in her office.

"Everything okay, Lieutenant?"

"We've had some upsetting news."

"Not *more* upsetting news."

"I'm afraid so."

"It's… It's not Michael, is it?" she asked of her fiancé.

"No, no."

"Oh thank God. What then?"

"There's no easy way to say this, so I'm just going to put it out there. Mitch Sanborn killed himself in prison this morning."

Jeannie gasped and covered her mouth with her hand. "He... He..."

"Killed himself. With a bedsheet."

"That miserable fucking coward *bastard*!" Though the words were spoken fiercely, tears rolled down her cheeks. In a whisper, she added, "That fucking bastard."

"Yes, he is."

She wiped her face angrily. "I'd actually begun to look forward to testifying, to having my day in court, to making sure he paid for what he did to me and the others, not to mention what he took from you."

"I know. I was looking forward to it too. More than I've ever looked forward to testifying against anyone."

"And now we'll never get to."

"It's hard now to see this as anything other than the cowardly act that it was, but it also spares you from re-opening wounds that have begun to heal. If you think of it that way, perhaps you'll find it easier to cope with this news."

"Perhaps." She looked up at Sam, her normally soft brown eyes gone fierce with rage. "But I was really looking forward to nailing his ass."

"I understand that even more than I would have before everything happened with Stahl."

"What am I supposed to do now? I don't know what to do with all the rage I've been carrying around with me. It's been keeping me going until the trial."

"It might be time to let it go now. He's gone, and he can never hurt you or anyone else again."

"That's not enough for me. That's nowhere near enough. He'll never be convicted for what he did to me, so people will think that maybe it didn't really happen or that he might've walked away after the trial."

"There was no way he was going to walk, which is why he did what he did."

"You and I know that, but the rest of the world doesn't."

"There's nothing stopping you from talking about it now that he's gone and there won't be a trial."

"No, there isn't."

"You're going to be inundated all over again with interview requests when this news goes public."

"I suppose I will be." A spark of defiance replaced the tears in her eyes, which was a huge relief to Sam. "I believe I'll be accepting one of those invitations this time around."

"For what it's worth, that's what I would do."

"It's worth a lot. Thank you, again, for standing by me through all of this. Your support and friendship has helped to get me through."

"Your own strength and determination got you through."

She stood to leave the office. "I need to call Michael. He should hear this from me."

"Go on ahead. In fact, take a few hours to go talk to him in person. I'll let Malone know where you've gone."

"Thank you. I'll take you up on that."

"Jeannie."

The beautiful young detective turned back to face her. "Yes?"

"I want you to know that I so admire the way you've handled yourself through this whole thing. You haven't let it ruin your life. You're stronger now than you were then—and you were pretty damned strong before. Don't let this be a setback. Okay?"

She offered a small smile as she blinked back new tears. "I won't."

"Okay then."

Jeannie left the office, closing the door behind her.

NINETEEN

SAM DROPPED INTO her chair again, hoping she'd be able to take her own advice as she learned to live with the fact that the man who'd caused her to miscarry would never see justice in this life. She could only hope, as Malone had said, that the afterlife would dole out the punishment he so deserved for his many sins.

Pulling her cell phone from her pocket, she placed a call to Nick's personal cell. He answered on the second ring.

"Hey, babe."

"Hey. I didn't wake you, did I?"

"Um, no. I do have a job to get to, even if it's the most pointless job I've ever had. What's up?"

They needed to have a conversation about his discontent at work, but not now. Not when there were other things she needed to tell him. "So Sanborn killed himself in jail."

"*What?* Are you kidding me?"

"Wish I was."

"Aw, babe, Jesus. Did you tell Jeannie?"

"Yeah, just now."

"How'd she take it?"

"She was upset but resolved to not let it set her back. At least I hope she is. I suggested this might be a good time to accept one of the many interview requests she got while there was a gag order in place. That'll be lifted now that he's dead."

"A very good idea. She should get with Christina for some media coaching if she's going to do that. Chris is the best at preparing people for their TV debut."

"I'll pass that on to her."

"What about you, hon?"

"What about me?"

"You had your own reasons to want to see him go down in flames. Hell, we both had reason to want that."

"I like to think he's roasting in the fire pit of hell as we speak. That brings comfort."

His soft chuckle carried through the phone. "At times like this, I'm so relieved to be on your good side."

"What can I say? When people I love are hurt, I become a vengeful bitch."

"And we're all happy to have you on our side at those times."

"I want to punch something. But since I can't do that, I'm going back to work on the case of the moment and focusing on getting justice for Arnold."

"You can punch me later if that'll help."

"Nah. You're too pretty to punch."

"Thanks. I think."

Sam laughed at his befuddled reply. She loved his inability to take a compliment on his extreme good looks. And since his rise to notoriety as vice president, she'd taken particular pleasure in what other people were saying about her sexy husband. As long as they contained their admiration to mere words, that is. Any actions would be met with the business end of her gun.

"I'll see you tonight."

"Yes, you will. Call me if you need me."

"I just did."

"I'm glad you did. Be careful with my wife today. I can't live without her."

"I'd say I'm always careful, but we both know my recent track record isn't what it could've been."

"Today is a new day and a new chance. Be careful today. We'll deal with tomorrow later."

"I can do that. Love you."

"Love you too."

Fortified by her talk with Nick, Sam got up and left her office. Before she dug in with Cruz on the list of missing people, she needed to find Gonzo and figure out what she was going to do with him and his misguided sense of responsibility for Arnold's death.

JEANNIE'S FIANCÉ MICHAEL worked in the financial services sector in a building across the street from the World Bank on H Street Northwest, just blocks from the White House. As she drove there, she noticed preparations under way for tomorrow's inauguration and decided to focus on that rather than the news she had just received.

Metal barricades lined the sidewalks on Pennsylvania Avenue, where the parade would travel from the Capitol to the White House after the ceremony. By morning, the avenue would be stripped of trash containers, streetlights, mailboxes and private vehicles. Along the parade route, businesses and apartments had been swept, manhole covers had been welded shut and additional surveillance cameras installed that would be monitored throughout the day by local and federal law enforcement officers.

The MPD's Special Operations Division was in charge of the department's role in the event that was expected to bring between eight hundred thousand and one million people to the city for the day. Jeannie had heard that number could be lower due to Nelson's unpopularity. However, the popularity of the vice president and his wife had many officials expecting the higher end of the spectrum. Judging by the crowds of people she had to avoid at every intersection, many of them were already here.

Police and other agencies needed to be ready for anything from happy, celebrating crowds to violent protestors who would take advantage of the festive atmosphere to advance their own agendas. They'd seen everything over the years and prepared for all possibilities in the year leading up to inauguration day. Representatives from nearly one hundred law enforcement agencies from around the country would be bringing nearly two-thousand extra officers to help supplement the local police department's efforts as well as the federal agencies involved in providing security.

Because the inauguration is considered a National Security Special Event, the Secret Service was the agency in charge. Every aspect of the event was closely managed, with buses requiring advance permits to enter the city, and the restricted National Defense Airspace over the city widened for the day by the FAA. The D.C. National Guard was bringing in more than seven thousand fellow soldiers to help provide military ground security.

Communication networks had been established, social media was being employed to provide up-to-date information to those planning to attend, tickets had been issued to the "lucky" two hundred fifty thousand people who'd be the closest to the actual inauguration ceremony. Jeannie thought they were crazy to want to be there when they could watch it at home far more comfortably. If she and the rest of the nearly four thousand members of the MPD weren't required to work twelve-hour shifts on inauguration day, she'd be home watching it on TV in her pajamas.

But she'd be on duty alongside the rest of her brothers and sisters in blue, except of course for her lieutenant, who'd be with her husband the vice president, holding the Bible as he took the oath of office. How exciting for both of them.

Jeannie tried to stay focused solely on the plans for tomorrow, but the memories of the horrific day she'd spent as Sanborn's captive pushed through despite her desperate desire to forget. The yellow room, the bindings that held her to the bed while he cut off her clothing, the repeated, painful sexual assaults, the threats he'd made against her, Sam and others in the department who were pursuing the call-girl murders, the aftermath of the assault, the excruciating physical examination, finally telling Michael what'd happened and struggling to get back to the life she'd known before Sanborn changed it forever.

And now he was gone forever, taking the easy way out and avoiding the trial that would bring his many crimes to light once again. She tried to tell herself it didn't matter if he never stood trial. The whole world knew what he'd done to her. Her attack and the murders of the immigrant women who'd been lured into his sordid web would forever be tied to his name, which had once stood for leadership and vision within the Democratic Party.

She parked in an underground garage and took the elevator to Michael's office. This would be the first time she'd ever come here in the middle of a workday and she hoped he wouldn't mind that she was interrupting him.

At the reception desk, she gave her name and asked to see Michael Wilkinson.

"Please have a seat while I check to see if he's available."

Every nerve in her body was on full alert as she took a seat and hoped she wasn't getting him from something important. He'd tell her nothing was more important than her, but his work was important too. About a minute after the receptionist made the call, he came bursting through the glass double doors that separated reception from the offices within. At six-foot-six inches, he cut an imposing figure in the suit that had been made just for him.

"Jeannie, baby, what're you doing here?" His concern was immediately comforting. "What's wrong?"

"Could we talk for a minute?" She glanced at the receptionist. "In private?"

"Of course." He took her hand and held the door to the inner sanctum open for her to pass through ahead of him. They walked down a long corridor full of offices and inquiring eyes before he guided her into his and shut the door behind them. Then he closed the blinds, sealing them off from the rest of the office. "What is it, baby?"

Jeannie threw herself into his arms.

He wrapped them around her. "You're scaring me."

"Sanborn's dead."

Michael pulled back, only enough so he could see her face. "He's what?"

"Dead. He killed himself in jail."

His face went slack with shock and fury. "Oh my God." He took a closer look at her. "You've been crying." Sliding his thumbs over her cheeks, he said, "That makes me furious. He's hurt you enough. How *dare* he do this to you?"

"I was so ready to testify. And now I won't get to."

He wiped away more tears.

"Sam says I should do one of the interviews so I can tell my story and make sure people know the truth of what he did."

"How do you feel about that?"

"I think I'm going to do it. Why should he get to take those secrets to the grave with him?"

"Why should he indeed, but are you sure you want to talk about it again? You've been doing so well. I'd hate to see you back where you were last year."

"I would've had to talk about it in court, so what's the difference? At least I won't have to be cross-examined if I do an interview."

"That's true."

"Would you do it with me? The interview, I mean?"

"I'd do anything you asked me to do, Jeannie. You know that by now."

She slipped her arms inside his suit coat and wrapped them around his waist, resting her head on his broad chest. "You've stood by me through this entire nightmare. Never once did you waver. I'll never forget that, Michael."

"You really ought to marry a guy like that," he said teasingly.

"You're right. I should. What're you doing in July?"

"Nothing other than marrying the love of my life, the strongest, toughest, most resilient woman I've ever known."

She smiled up at him. "Thanks."

"Aw, baby, don't thank me. Loving you is the easiest thing I've ever done."

When he kissed her, the spinning inside her stopped and her world righted itself once again. They'd gotten through worse than this, and they'd be fine. She'd be fine, as long as she had him and her friends and family to lean on.

AFTER A THOROUGH search of HQ, Sam found Gonzo in the morgue, staring down at the waxy remains of his partner. After the meeting he'd been required to attend earlier, Tyrone was back on watch outside the door.

Lindsey McNamara approached her.

"How long has he been here?" Sam asked of Gonzo.

"About half an hour now. He just stands there and stares. You got this?"

"Gonna try."

"Terrible thing," Lindsey said with the empathy Sam had come to expect from the medical examiner. That empathy made her excellent at her job. The victims of crime received the utmost respect in Dr. McNamara's lab. Lindsey squeezed her shoulder and left her to deal with Gonzo.

Sam walked up to him and nudged his arm. "Hey."

He didn't reply. He didn't blink. Hell, he was so incredibly still, he didn't even seem to be breathing.

"Gonzo."

After a long moment, he glanced over at her, his eyes tortured and ravaged from lack of sleep and endless tears. "What?"

"What're you doing in here?"

"What does it look like I'm doing?"

"Gonzo—"

"I'm not really interested in company. His parents will be here soon. I'm waiting for them. No need to hover."

Under normal circumstances, Sam would tell him to fuck off with the hovering comment, but nothing about these circumstances were normal so she gave him a pass. "I'll wait with you."

"No need."

"I wasn't asking."

"Suit yourself."

"I will, thanks."

They stood in unusually tense silence, him staring down at Arnold and her trying to look anywhere else. The gaping hole in the detective's face didn't look any less horrible today than it had yesterday, and it made her heart ache to think of his parents seeing that. But they'd insisted on seeing him, so their request would be accommodated.

"I want you to talk to Skip," Sam said after a long period of silence.

"About what?"

"This happened to him when he was still in Patrol. His partner was killed in a drive-by that was never solved. Skip was standing feet away from Steven when it happened."

"It's not the same thing at all."

"Isn't it?"

"No, it isn't. Did Skip send his partner out to be slaughtered? Did he antagonize him in the last hour of his life to the point that he felt he had something to prove? Did Steven take a bullet that should've been Skip's?"

"The bullet that hit Arnold was meant for him and only him."

"You think you'd be saying that if this were Cruz stretched out on the table and you were the one who put him out there to take the shot?"

"I'd probably feel exactly the same way you do, and you'd be standing next to me saying the same thing I am—it wasn't your fault. It was *not* your fault, Gonzo. One of you had to be the one to confront this guy. In this case, it happened to be him."

"It was the *first time* I let him take the lead in confronting someone known to be dangerous. The *first fucking time*, Sam."

"I know." She placed her hand on his shoulder. "It's a terrible thing and the fact that it was the first time makes it that much worse. But *you* did not pull the trigger. *You* did not kill him."

"I may as well have." He shook his head in utter misery and dismay. "When I think about the way he saved my life when I was shot and how I couldn't do a goddamned *thing* for him."

"The shot was fatal, Gonzo. There was nothing anyone could've done."

He used his sleeve to wipe his face. "I owed him better."

"You gave him your very best from the first day he was assigned to partner with you. I'll never forget that night in the surgical waiting room, when we didn't know if you would live or die. He was covered in your blood and we kept trying to encourage him to go home and change, but he wouldn't leave until he knew you were okay. He cared for you so deeply. He'd never want you to be doing this to yourself, Gonzo."

"Can't help it."

"Will you talk to Skip? He's been where you are. He understands what you're feeling better than anyone. It might help."

He shrugged. "Yeah, I guess. If you want me to."

"I'll go with you if it would help."

"Up to you."

"After work tonight. We'll go there together."

Gonzo wiped his face again. "I'm really sorry I let you down."

"What? What're you talking about?"

"I was in charge of the squad while you were on medical leave. This happened on my watch."

"It would've happened no matter who was in charge, Gonzo. As much as we might wish otherwise, Arnold's number was up the other night."

"You really believe that?"

"I have to believe it, or the random shit that happens around here every day would make me insane. There has to be some higher power at work here, someone who has a grand plan for all of us. You were spared because you have a son to raise and contributions left to be made."

"He had contributions to be made too."

"Yes, he did, and we may never understand the why of this, Gonzo. But we have to accept that it happened and find a way to go on. That's what he'd want us to do."

His jaw pulsed with tension. "I want this guy to fry for what he did. I want him dead."

"That's not for us to decide, as you well know."

"Maybe not, but that doesn't make me want it any less."

"Sometimes justice comes in the next life. We heard today that Sanborn offed himself in jail."

Gonzo's head whipped around and his eyes widened. "For real?"

"Unfortunately, yes."

"Jeannie…"

"Has been told. She's taken a few hours to go tell Michael and to deal with the news."

"Christ," Gonzo muttered. "This fucking job, these fucking scumbags. It never ends, does it?"

"Only when we turn in the badge and call it a day."

"You ever think about doing that?"

"Fleetingly from time to time. Never seriously."

"Even after what happened with Stahl?"

"More so after that, but the urge seems to have passed."

"I seem to think about it a lot more often lately. After I was shot, then you with Stahl and now this." He rested his hand on Arnold's chest, which was covered in a sheet. "I think about walking away."

"But you won't do that now or a month from now or even six months from now, because we both know you'd regret doing something rash after what's happened recently. PTSD decisions are never good ones."

"Still. I think about it. I think about packing up Chris and Alex and heading south and finding warm weather and something better to do with my life. Anything has to be better than this."

"Today anything seems better than this, but I know you. Six months in the Florida sun and you'd be jonesing to be back in the rat race again. You'd be bored out of your mind."

"Being bored out of my mind actually looks good to me right now."

"Pardon me," Lindsey said. "The Arnolds are here."

Gonzo blew out a deep breath and stood up straight. "I can handle this if you've got stuff to do."

"I'm not going anywhere. I'm right here with you."

He nodded, pulled the sheet up higher and straightened Arnold's hair. The tenderness he showed his fallen partner brought a lump to Sam's throat. "Not much I can do about the gaping hole in his face."

"I can cover it with a bandage," Lindsey said. "If that would help?"

"I think that's a great idea," Sam said. "They don't need to see that. What do you think, Gonzo?"

"Yeah, let's do that."

Lindsey got the bandage and came to the other side of the table to apply it carefully to Arnold's face.

Gonzo released a deep sigh of relief. "That's so much better. I've been stressing out about them seeing that."

"No need to stress alone, Tommy," Lindsey said softly. "We're all here to help you through this any way we can."

"Thanks." He wiped his face again. "I guess you can bring them in now."

"Will you let the chief know they are here too, Lindsey?" Sam asked.

"Of course."

While they waited, Sam slipped her hand through Gonzo's arm and squeezed. She kept it there when Lindsey brought the Arnolds in to see their son. She kept it there when both parents and Arnold's two sisters broke down at the sight of him lifeless on the table. She held on to him when the chief came in to offer his condolences to the family. Sam only released her hold on Gonzo so he could hug his partner's parents and sisters.

After stroking her son's hair for several minutes, Mrs. Arnold said, "I've seen what I needed to see. I'd like to go now."

Her daughters took her by the arms and led her out. Mr. Arnold stayed behind. "Any developments in the case?" he asked.

"The man we're looking for is a known human trafficker named Sid Androzzi, also known as Giuseppe Besozzi," Sam said. "He's from Yonkers, not Italy, and is on the FBI's ten most wanted list for crimes he committed in New York and Los Angeles. After his organization was infiltrated in those cities, he'd apparently set up shop here under at least one assumed name. The U.S. Marshal Service is leading the manhunt in conjunction with the FBI and the MPD. We're doing everything we can to find him, Mr. Arnold, but we're dealing with someone who is accustomed to hiding in plain sight."

"In other words," he said bitterly, "we shouldn't expect any kind of speedy resolution."

"We never know how these things will go down. All I can tell you is that everything that can be done is being done."

"I suppose that's all we can ask for. Thank you for allowing us to see him. Part of me didn't believe it was true until I came here." He blew out a deep breath. "Now denial is no longer an option."

"We're so sorry again for your loss," Sam said. "And we're heartbroken. He was very well loved within our squad and the department."

"Thank you so much for that." To Gonzo, he said, "Sergeant, we'd like for you and the other detectives from his squad to be the pallbearers."

"We'd be honored," Gonzo said gruffly.

"We'll be in touch with the details. Detective Tyrone has been very helpful to us."

"Glad to hear that," Sam said. "You let him know if there's anything we can do for you."

Mr. Arnold fixated on his son's face. "Burying a child... Most unnatural thing I'll ever do in my life."

With those words, he turned and left them, the doors to the morgue swinging shut behind him.

Gonzo bent to rest his head on his partner's chest and wept.

Sam put her arm around him and stayed right there with him, wiping up her own tears as his brokenhearted sobs echoed off the cold, sterile walls of the morgue.

TWENTY

THE NEWS ABOUT Sanborn had cast a pall over Nick's day. He could still remember how excited they'd been when they realized Sam might be pregnant, and before they could even officially celebrate the good news, her altercation with Sanborn had led to the miscarriage.

It had taken months for them to get back on track after she lost the baby. It had carried over into the week of their wedding when she'd finally opened up to him about her private agony. Four miscarriages. His poor, sweet Samantha had been through the wringer. Even knowing that, he still hoped against hope that one day they might conceive again and she might finally realize her dream of carrying her own baby.

He prayed for that every day of his life, but only because he knew she wanted it so badly. If she and Scotty were the only family he ever had, Nick would be perfectly satisfied.

After a brisk knock on his office door, Terry came in holding a stack of papers and a phone tucked between his head and shoulder. He glanced at Nick. "Um, hmm, let me check with him. Hold on." Terry covered the phone with his hand. "There's a woman at the gates claiming to be your mother. She's demanding to be let in to see you."

Nick's stomach took a dive at that news. "Did she give a name?"

"What's her name?" Terry asked into the phone. Holding it aside, he said, "Nicoletta Bernadino."

Nick sighed and shook his head. This was the very last thing he needed today. If he let her in, if he acknowledged her, it would screw him up for days. The very smell of her perfume used to leave him reeling after her infrequent visits during his childhood. He simply didn't have it in him to deal with her today.

"Tell her I'm not available."

"The vice president is in meetings," Terry said. "He's not seeing visitors today." He listened to what was being said on the other end. "I'll let him know." Terry ended the call and put the phone in his pocket.

"What did they say?"

"She's raising hell, apparently, making demands, throwing your name around, telling them she's going to have their jobs."

"Let them know their jobs are safe."

"I'll do that." He looked as if he wanted to say more but didn't.

"It's okay. You can ask."

"It's none of my business."

"It is when she shows up here and makes it your business. The little demonstration at the gate is a metaphor for my entire life. She shows up out of the blue, makes it all about her and leaves me flattened in her wake. It's our pattern. She's long overdue for a visit. I haven't seen her since she tried to crash my wedding and Sam ran her off before she could get her hooks in me and ruin the best day of my life."

"Wow."

"Yeah, with a mom like Laine O'Connor, it would be hard for you to understand a mother like mine." Nick got up and went to the window, trying to see the main gates, which were just out of view. "You don't think the press is going to catch wind of her being here, do you?"

"The Secret Service will take care of it."

"Okay." Staring out the window reminded him of countless Saturdays he'd spent looking out the window from his grandmother's apartment waiting for her to show up. More often than not, she disappointed him. And on the times she did come and leave the distinctive scent of Chanel No. 5 all over him, he'd refuse to bathe for days afterward lest the scent disappear from his life once again. To this day, the scent of Chanel No. 5 disgusted him.

He shuddered at the pain those memories could still invoke in the child who lived within him.

"You okay?" Terry asked.

Shaking off the past, he turned to face the present. "Yeah, sure. What's up?"

"I've got the final schedule for tomorrow from Nelson's office. Just a few things to double-check. You, Sam and Scotty will be joining the Nelsons for services at St. John's in the morning, correct?"

"Yes." He hadn't yet broken the news to her that they were going to church, but she'd roll with it for his sake.

"Here's a copy of your guest list for the luncheon after the ceremony. Just want to make sure one last time that everyone is on there."

Nick scanned the list: his father's family, the O'Connors and Sam's family as well as some of their closest friends including Shelby (thankfully her "boyfriend" Hill would be working and unable to join them), Nick's former chief-of-staff Christina, Terry's fiancée Lindsey McNamara, Derek Kavanaugh, Dr. Harry

Flynn and Nick's lawyer friend Andy Simone and his wife. Freddie and Gonzo had been invited, but they'd be working like every other MPD officer that day, except of course the second lady. Nick had also invited Scotty's former guardian, Mrs. Littlefield, and two of Scotty's closest friends from school. "That's everyone."

"Excellent, thanks." He held up another piece of paper. "Your Twitter account is up and running. Are you ready to take on the world as VPOTUSCap?"

"Oh, I like that handle."

"We wanted you to be able to keep it after you leave office."

"Good thinking."

Terry handed him the page that held his Twitter password. "It's all yours, ready to go whenever you are. You've got a one-hundred-forty character limit on tweets—and we've already had the account verified so people will know it's really you."

Nick opened Twitter and signed into his account where his staff had set up his profile with his official White House portrait and a line of text that said VP of the U.S. "I'm having performance anxiety."

Terry laughed. "Just be you, and they'll love you."

Nick typed his first tweet: Hey Twitter, this is your VP here. Sam and I are looking forward to the inauguration tomorrow and the next four years. Then he read it to Terry. "I still have twenty-eight characters left. What should I add?"

"How about Scotty. Sam, Scotty and I…"

"Oh damn, good call." Nick added Scotty to the tweet. "He would've been all over me for that. He's already mortified that I'm going to be on Twitter in the first place."

"Don't let him fool you. He loves all the attention he gets with his dad as the VP."

Nick posted the tweet and sat back to watch as his number of followers began to increase—rapidly. "Hey, check this out."

Terry came around the desk and leaned in for a closer look. "Holy shit. Is that like a hundred thousand in a minute?"

"Looks that way to me."

"That's incredible. I wonder if you'll break Twitter by joining."

"Let's hope not. We don't need the whole Twitter-verse mad at me."

"Listen to you with the lingo."

"I pay attention."

"That's some crazy welcome to Twitter. Two hundred thousand! Wow. You're a rock star, Mr. Vice President."

"Whatever you say. Getting back to the schedule for tomorrow…"

"Right," Terry said, dragging his gaze off the Twitter numbers. "What've you decided about the balls?"

"We'll go to the Inaugural Ball, take a twirl around the dance floor and leave out of respect to Detective Arnold and his family."

"I think that's a good call. You make an appearance but you don't party the night away."

"Exactly."

"Lindsey said things are pretty grim at HQ. I don't know how they do what they do every day, knowing something like this can happen at any time."

"It's better for my mental health if I don't think about how easily something like this can happen."

"True. Sorry. Didn't mean to strike a nerve."

"It's fine. It's a raw nerve. I wish I could say I don't think about it every day, but I do. I've learned to manage the anxiety, and then Stahl takes Sam hostage and Arnold gets killed. It's the stuff of nightmares."

"It really is. But if Sam could get through that situation with Stahl, she can survive anything."

"Except a bullet to the face, of course."

Terry winced. "Lindsey said Gonzo's taking it hard. He's blaming himself when there wasn't anything he could've done."

"It's that sudden random out-of-nowhere shit that keeps me awake at night. But anyway, we have other stuff to talk about than my nightmares."

Another knock sounded at the door and Terry got up to admit his father, who came bursting into the room, smiling from ear to ear. "Is this the office of the vice president of the United States who'll be taking the oath of office tomorrow?"

"That'd be me," Nick said, pleased by Graham's excitement. "What've you got there?"

From under his arm, Graham produced the O'Connor family Bible. "I hope I'm not being presumptuous that you'd want to use this again."

Nick took it from him. "Not at all presumptuous. It's the closest thing to a family Bible as I'm ever going to get. Thank you."

Graham put both hands on Nick's arms. "Our family is your family as you know." He straightened Nick's tie and patted his chest. "And your family is extremely proud of you."

"I'm here because of you."

"Nah," Graham said. "That might've been true a year

ago when I helped you into the Senate, but this, *this*, my friend, is *all* yours."

That might be true, Nick thought, but none of it would be happening without Graham O'Connor and his late son John. The two of them had shown him the meaning of family and the rewards of public service. There's no way he'd be standing in an office in the White House without Graham.

"I declare this auspicious event requires a drink." From inside his coat pocket, he produced a bottle of his favorite bourbon.

"How'd you get that in here, Dad?" Terry asked, amused by his dad even if he wouldn't touch a drop of liquor. He'd recently celebrated one year of sobriety, and Nick was nearly as proud of him as Graham was.

"I never tell my secrets, son." He poured the liquor into glasses Nick provided and then pulled a bottle of cola from his other pocket and handed it to his son. "At least the color is close."

"There is that," Terry said, laughing as he poured cola into a glass.

"To the vice president of the United States and to four years from today when we'll be toasting the president," Graham said.

"I'll drink to that," Terry said.

Nick, who knew better than to question Graham when he was on a roll, smiled and raised his glass to them.

SAM FINALLY CONVINCED Gonzo to leave the morgue, but not until the funeral home came to collect Arnold's body. Everything at HQ came to a stop and every officer went outside to see off their fallen brother, who would be escorted home to Maryland by two officers on motorcycles leading the procession, as well as four cruisers—two in front of the hearse and two behind. Detective Tyrone was riding in the hearse and would remain with his friend until he was buried.

After the procession left HQ, Sam brought Gonzo into her office and deposited him into one of her visitor chairs. She would've sent him home, but he was in no condition to drive. "How about I ask Patrol to give you a lift home?"

He shook his head. "I'd rather be here."

"No one would rather be here."

"I'm not leaving. I'll go crazy at home wondering what's happening here."

Sam didn't bother to argue with him, because she'd feel the same way in his position. "How about some food? When was the last time you ate?"

"I can't."

Freddie came into the office, saw Gonzo sitting with his head in his hands and glanced at Sam, asking without words if their friend was okay.

She shrugged and shook her head.

"We've got a report from a group here for the inauguration that two members of their party, both female, didn't return to the hotel last night," Freddie said. "Dispatch asked us to take it since everyone else is tied up with the inauguration stuff."

"Let me come with you guys," Gonzo said. "I need to do something."

"All right." Sam grabbed her coat and handheld radio. "Where're we going, Cruz?"

"The JW Marriott on Pennsylvania and 14th."

"Let's go out through the morgue. We're overrun with press outside the main doors." Every heartbreaking second of Arnold's final departure from HQ had been caught on film by the news channels that had set up shop in the parking lot.

Sam led Gonzo and Freddie to the BMW.

"New ride?" Gonzo asked, and Sam was relieved to see him showing a spark of interest in something.

"Yep. Nick had it tricked out for me." As they got in and buckled up, Sam gave him a rundown of all the safety features.

"It's like a traveling fortress," Gonzo said. "So cool."

"And the best part," Sam said, turning on the radio, "is all Bon Jovi all the time." She cranked up the volume on "You Give Love a Bad Name."

Freddie groaned. "I'm filing a protest with the union. I shouldn't have to be force-fed Bon Jovi on the job."

"Go ahead and complain."

Sam glanced in the rearview mirror and saw Gonzo staring vacantly out the window.

"We ought to be out looking for the guy who killed him," Gonzo said. "That's what we should be doing."

"We have people fanned out all over the city looking for him," Sam said. "The Marshals and the FBI are tracking down leads and following up on tips. We're doing everything we can."

"Yeah, but *we're* not working the case. Why aren't *we* working the case?"

"Because it's too close to us, Gonzo," Freddie said. "They're going to want an unimpeachable case against this guy. If we're involved, it could be seen as a conflict of interest because Arnold was one of ours."

"But our Patrol people can be involved? How is that fair?"

"He wasn't in their chain of command," Sam said. "It's better for us to take a step back on this. We want to be able to nail Androzzi. And besides, we're helping by taking another look at missing persons over the last couple of years. The whole squad is working on that. If we can tie some of them to his trafficking business, that'll help the U.S. Attorney to prosecute him."

"We've got about ten to look more closely at," Freddie said. "Everyone has divided up the names and we're going back today to speak to families and reviewing the files, the phone records and social media in light of this new information about Androzzi. Stuff is being done, Gonzo."

"Doesn't seem like we're doing enough."

"We're doing what we can," Sam said. "This guy is good. He's slipped through the FBI's net several times before. He knows how to disappear."

"What if we never find him?"

"We will. He'll screw up eventually, and we'll get him." Not getting him wasn't a possibility she was willing to entertain. "Look how arrogant he's already been. He's obviously invested in moving his organization here. He's not going to just abandon that now. I have a feeling he's very close by."

The District was being transformed before their eyes in preparation for the inauguration. Flags and stars and stripes banners were hung from nearly every building on Pennsylvania Avenue. The metal barricades were in place and crews were working with frantic precision along the parade route.

"Hard to believe you'll be walking this street tomorrow as the second lady," Freddie said.

"*Walking?* No one said anything about *walking.*"

"The president and vice president and their spouses

always get out of the cars for part of the trip from the Capitol to the reviewing stand."

"Nothing like giving the crazies an easy shot," she said, shuddering at the thought of how vulnerable Nick would be.

"The crazies won't get let in. Don't worry."

"Right. Don't worry. What do I have to be worried about?" Her stomach churned with nerves at the thought of the endless minutes when they'd be out in the open, too far from the security of the car and separated by feet from the detail that protected Nick.

She began to pray for rain. If it rained, they wouldn't let them out of the car, would they? Rain-soaked VIPs didn't make for good TV.

Sam drove up to the JW Marriott and flashed her badge to the bellman who greeted them.

"Hey!" he said when she got out of the car. "You're the vice president's wife!"

"Am I? I hadn't heard that. Thanks for letting me know."

"Haha. Nice ride. I'll keep a close eye on it for you."

"I'd appreciate that."

Hotel security was waiting for them inside the door. "I'm Jim Rollins, head of security."

"Lieutenant Holland, Sergeant Gonzales, Detective Cruz," Sam said. "What've you got?" He did a double take when he recognized her, but fortunately he didn't tell her she was the vice president's wife. The guy outside had taken care of that.

"Right this way." Rollins led them to a bank of elevators. "A college group from Northern Connecticut University reported this morning that two members of their party failed to return to the hotel last night." The elevator took them to the tenth floor where a somber group was gathered in the hallway.

Sam, Gonzo and Freddie followed Rollins through a scrum of college kids to a room where several adults were on cell phones. Calls were swiftly ended.

"These are detectives from the DC Metro PD," Rollins said.

"Lieutenant Holland, Sergeant Gonzales and Detective Cruz," Sam said again as they all showed their badges. "We understand two members of your party failed to return to the hotel last night?"

"That's right," a nervous-looking washed-out blonde woman said. She was heavyset and overwrought. "Mindy Cahill and Jennifer Torlino."

Sam wrote the names in the notebook she pulled from her back pocket. "We'll need photos of both of them and cell phone numbers. Cruz, give them your email for the photos."

One of the other adults scurried from the room to get the requested information.

"Do we know where they were last seen?"

"At a bar in Georgetown," the blonde said.

"What's your name?"

"Debbie McLane. I'm one of the faculty chaperones."

"Are the students of legal drinking age?" Sam asked.

"No, they're both nineteen. We're not sure what they were doing in a bar."

"You're really not sure what they were doing?" Sam asked with thinly veiled skepticism.

"They weren't supposed to be there."

"Were any of the other students there with them?" Sam asked.

"Several of them," Debbie said, seeming chagrined

to admit that. Some chaperone she'd been. Her underage charges had been out drinking on her watch.

"I'd like to speak to everyone who was with them. Get them in here."

Freddie's phone dinged with an email. He showed Sam and Gonzo photos of two gorgeous young blonde women.

One of the other chaperones returned to the room with two boys and a girl who looked like she'd been crying for hours.

"Your names?" Sam said.

"Brian Watkins."

"Tyler Johnston."

"Wednesday Alexander."

"Your real name is Wednesday?" Sam asked, her brow raised.

"Yes, I was born on a Wednesday, and my mom liked the name. I go by Wendy." Wednesday had dark hair and eyes and the palest skin Sam had ever seen.

"You were with Mindy and Jennifer at a bar in Georgetown last night?"

The three young people exchanged nervous glances.

"Let me make this really simple for you," Sam said. "Tell us what we want to know here, or we'll take you into custody and escort you downtown where we won't be anywhere near as friendly as we're being right now. That's a lot of headaches and paperwork we'd prefer to avoid."

"We were with them," Brian said. "At a place called McDuffy's in Georgetown. We heard online that's the place to go if you're not quite legal and want to get served." He ventured a glance at Sam. "Are my parents going to hear about this?"

Sam gave him a "what do you think" look.

"How many drinks would you say Mindy and Jennifer consumed while you were with them?" Freddie asked.

"I don't know," Wednesday said, "maybe six? Or seven?"

"What were they drinking?"

"Jennifer likes cosmos, and Mindy prefers vodka on ice," Wednesday said.

"Was it just the five of you?"

"From our group, yes," Wednesday said. "Other people joined us during the night. A couple of guys started hitting on them, and they were dancing with them. When we were ready to leave, they told us to go ahead and they'd catch up. I woke up this morning, and saw that they never came back, and when I tried to call their cell phones, the calls went right to voicemail. Their phones are *never* off. Never. That's when I started to get scared. I let Mrs. McLane know that they hadn't come back, and she notified hotel security."

"Can you describe the guys?" Sam asked, liking this less by the minute. Who leaves their friends alone with strange guys in a strange city?

"One of them had dark hair and eyes. The other one had lighter hair and blue eyes."

"Call up the photo of Androzzi," Sam said to Freddie, playing a hunch.

He produced the photo on his phone and handed it to her. "Was this one of them?"

"Yes!" Wednesday cried, her eyes widening. "Do you know him?"

"Unfortunately, we do."

"Unfortunately?" Mrs. McLane asked. "What does that mean?"

"He's a known human trafficker and is wanted in

connection with the murder of our detective earlier this week."

Sam watched as the older woman's eyes rolled back in her head and moved quickly to catch her before she landed on the floor. She eased her onto the bed. Debbie came to, sobbing hysterically.

"We have to find them!" She struggled against one of the other women who tried to comfort her.

The third chaperone handed Sam a page with the missing girls' cell numbers. "Write down their Twitter and Instagram info too."

While Brian held a sobbing Wednesday in his arms, Tyler pulled out his phone and looked up their accounts and added their profile info to the page.

"Is there anything else we need to know before we go looking for them?" Sam asked. "This is no time to keep secrets. Your friends' lives may depend on you being forthcoming."

Wednesday began to cry harder. "They… They… Tell them, Brian."

The proverbial deer in the headlights, Brian could only stammer. "Uh… Um…"

"They run a MovieTime channel," Tyler said.

"What does that mean?" Sam asked.

"It's like a webcam inside their dorm room where they give…performances…and stuff."

"What kind of stuff?"

Tyler blushed to the roots of his blond hair. "Sex stuff."

"Fucking Christ," Gonzo muttered under his breath. "They were targeted."

Mrs. McLane only wailed louder. "We're going to lose our jobs over this."

"Be quiet, Debbie," one of the other chaperones said,

echoing Sam's thoughts. "What can we do to help find them?"

"Get me the address of this MovieTime channel."

Tyler again took to his phone, his fingers flying over the screen. When he'd located what he was looking for, he handed the phone to Gonzo, who took down the URL.

Sam handed her card to the more rational chaperone. "You're going to want to let their parents know what's happened. Have them call me as soon as possible."

Debbie's wailing escalated to epic levels, which led to the rational one slapping her square across the face.

"Shut up right now. I mean it."

Stunned into silence, Debbie whimpered pathetically.

"Well done," Sam said to the slapper. To the rest of them, she said, "Call me if anyone hears from them in any format—tweet, Facebook post, Instagram, SnapChat, MovieTime, whatever. Any contact from them is to be reported immediately. Got me?"

They nodded and mumbled their assurances.

"For their safety, we're asking that you keep the information we shared with you about their abductor in this room. I will take care of informing their parents about his involvement when they call me. Do you understand?"

More murmurs and nods.

"If I see anything about this case anywhere online, we'll start making arrests." She left them with that and headed for the door, Gonzo and Cruz following her.

"Are they going to be okay?" a tearful coed asked.

"Let's hope so," Sam said.

The second they exited the hotel Sam, pulled out her phone to call Malone. When he took her call on the first ring, she said, "Our big problem just got a whole lot bigger."

TWENTY-ONE

"I NEED AN immediate warrant for the security footage at McDuffy's in Georgetown," Sam said after she'd filled in the captain on the latest development. "We also need to let Best know we've had a sighting of Androzzi right here in the District, so he's close by."

"In light of the information about the MovieTime channel, this meeting sounds like it might've been pre-arranged," Malone said.

"Our thoughts exactly. Get Archie on tracking down their cell phones and getting me a dump of their text messages. Highest level of urgency. We got to get this guy before he ships them out of the country." Sam didn't have to add that their chances of finding them after they left the U.S. would be dramatically lower. "We're heading to the bar now. Get me that warrant nine-one-one."

"I'm on it."

Sam closed her phone. "Put that stupid tablet to use and call up that MovieTime channel. Let's see what our girlfriends have been up to in their cushy dorm rooms."

While she drove through congested roads made more so by the inauguration preparations, Freddie worked on the tablet.

"Holy crap," he said.

At a stoplight, Sam got an eyeful of naked breasts as well as up-close-and-personal shots of other female body parts. One of the girls was lying on a bed, masturbating with a gigantic dildo while the other narrated the scene and handled the camera work.

"Christ, I need a shower," Sam said after thirty seconds of watching the big-breasted girl writhe about on her bed. Under her was a comforter with red poppies on it. Her mother had probably bought that for her sweet kid's college dorm room, never suspecting it would be seen around the world under her naked daughter as she performed sex acts for perverts.

"Is this what college kids are doing for fun these days?" Cruz asked.

"There's a lot of money in it," Gonzo said. "See the label on the dildo? The manufacturer probably pays them to use their products. And they charge for subscriptions to the channel too. I bet they're rolling in dough."

"Androzzi's probably been cultivating them for months," Sam said. "They walked right into his net by coming on this school trip to DC."

"We should call for backup when we raid the bar," Gonzo said.

"Go ahead and do that," Sam replied, pleased to see him engaged, at least partially, in something other than his grief.

He made the call while she drove to Georgetown.

Freddie checked his phone. "Wow, fastest warrant in the history of fast warrants."

"That tends to happen when we're looking for someone who killed one of our own," Sam said.

She double-parked in front of McDuffy's on Wisconsin Avenue. Pre-Stahl, she might've gone charging in there ahead of the arrival of her backup. Now she waited. Whatever was in there would keep for the five additional minutes it would take for Patrol to arrive on the scene.

In addition to the Patrol officers, Marshal Best arrived at the bar too.

"This is where Androzzi was spotted last night?" he asked Sam when she got out of the car.

"Yep. We've got two missing college coeds who were seen drinking and partying with him here last night. They're both nineteen and were here on a college trip for the inauguration. According to the hotel roommate, she and two of their male friends left them here with the guys, one of whom they identified as Androzzi, and didn't realize until she woke up this morning that they never made it back to the hotel. Both their phones are off, which apparently never happens, and we've learned that they were MovieTime stars with their own dormitory peep-show channel."

"How much you want to bet that Androzzi was a subscriber?" Best said.

"I'd bet the farm," Sam replied. Seeing everyone was in place, she said, "Let's do this." They marched into McDuffy's where a small lunch crowd was seated mostly at the bar. She flashed her badge. "Lieutenant Holland, MPD. I need to see the manager or owner."

A wide-eyed female bartender bolted from behind the bar and disappeared into a room in the back of the building. She returned a minute later with a man in tow.

"What's this about?" he asked, taking in the crowd of cops in his bar.

"Who are you?" Sam asked.

"Joe Warren, the owner of McDuffy's."

"Are you aware, Mr. Warren, that your bar has a reputation for serving underage people?"

His eyes bugged and his face turned a shade of purple that had Sam thinking of Stahl. "Who told you that?"

"The nineteen-year-old college kids from North Connecticut University who were in here drinking last night."

"We check ID for everyone we serve."

Sam held out her hand for Freddie's phone.

He handed it over with the screen open to the warrant.

"This here is a warrant for your security footage." She gestured to a camera over the bar. "And don't tell us you don't have it or it's broken or any other bullshit. Two of those college students you served last night have gone missing. They were last seen in the company of a known human trafficker who's also wanted for the murder of an MPD detective this week. He too was a customer here last night, so make it easy on yourself and get us that film."

"Fine."

She nodded at Freddie to go with him. "You," she said to the bartender, "come here."

The woman looked like she might crap her pants as she made her way over to Sam. "What's your name?"

"Vanessa."

"Do you have a last name?"

"Christie."

"Did you work last night, Vanessa?"

"I pulled a double yesterday. I was here all day."

"Gonzo, show her the photos. Did you see these girls or this man here last night?"

"Yeah, they were partying pretty hard until about midnight or so when they left."

"Did you see them leave together?"

"I um, yeah." Her eyes darted nervously between the gathered law enforcement officers. "I saw them leave. The girls were pretty hammered, and the guys sort of seemed to be kind of holding them up."

"Do you frequently over-serve your customers?" Sam asked.

"We didn't over-serve them. I cut them off an hour before they left."

"Drugged," Best said under his breath. "Did you happen to see the car they left in?"

"It was a black SUV that pulled up to the curb as they were leaving. I was clearing tables in the front so I happened to see it."

"Was it a car service?" Freddie asked.

"I didn't see a sign in the car window. In fact, the windows were tinted, so if there was a sign, I might not have seen it."

To Gonzo, Sam said, "Get with Archie to see what cameras we have on the street." She walked to the back office where Freddie had disappeared with the owner. "I want the film from outside too, while you're at it."

Freddie held up a thumb drive. "Already got it."

"I didn't know they were minors," Warren said from his seat at a computer terminal. "You ever seen some of the fake IDs these kids are using? You try to tell them apart from the real thing."

"I don't have to tell them apart," Sam said. "That's your job." She gestured to Patrol. "Take him in."

"Take me in?" He leapt to his feet. "What the hell for?"

"Serving minors is against the law. You have the right to remain silent. Anything you say can and will be used against you in a court of law. Finish it up for me, boys."

"*You fucking bitch!* You think you're so high and mighty because of who you're married to!"

Sam moved in close to his face. "Actually, *douchebag*, I thought I was high and mighty *long* before I was married. Get him out of here." The Patrol officers dragged

Warren through the bar, kicking and screaming about having people's jobs the whole way. "Wow, I enjoyed that."

"Welcome back, Lieutenant," Freddie said with a pleased smile. "Nice to see you again."

Sam cracked her knuckles. "Thank you. Now, let's get that video back to the house and see what magic Archie can do for us."

It was, indeed, good to be back.

ON THE WAY to HQ, Sam received frantic phone calls from the parents of the missing girls. She assured them law enforcement officials were doing everything they could to find their daughters and promised to call with any updates. She had no choice but to tell them what she knew about Androzzi and what they were up against in finding the girls.

Their fear and panic had left Sam feeling queasy. Before Scotty had come into her life, she would've empathized with them as any caring human being would. But as a mother herself now, these situations hit her much harder than they used to. Scotty was turning her into an old softie, she thought, but that wasn't such a bad thing. Her sharp edges were in bad need of the kind of smoothing out that had happened since her son came into her life.

At HQ, Sam went straight upstairs to IT and had the supreme misfortune to run into Special Victims Unit Sergeant Ramsey on the stairs. For some unknown reason, he hated her guts.

"Well, look who's back," Ramsey said with a snide smile. "Have a nice vacation, Lieutenant?"

"Fuck off," she said as she went by him.

"Ohh, someone's touchy. I thought our old friend Stahl

would've taken some of the starch out of you, but I can see—"

Sam would never know what he could see because she whirled around and punched him square in the face, sending him flying backward down the stairs. Ouch. That sounded like it hurt. Without waiting to see if he survived the fall, because who cared if he did or didn't, she continued along her way to the IT Division, which was run by her former sex buddy Lieutenant Archelotta.

"Archie!" she called over the hum of computers and the click of keys coming from cubicles. "I need you!"

"Story of my life." The handsome officer stepped out of his office, his dark eyes twinkling with mirth as he received the disk Sam handed him. "Women always need me for something."

Sam rolled her eyes. "Easy, Romeo. If you can get me a license plate number off the black SUV that made a pickup outside this bar last night around midnight, I'll find someone willing to kiss you square on the lips."

"Wow, you know how to get things done, Lieutenant." The commotion in the hallway caught his attention. "What's going on out there?"

"Oh, I might've punched Ramsey in the face, causing him to fall backward down the stairs."

Archie stared at her, agog. "You did *what*?"

"He had it coming. So about my video—can you look at it now?"

"Um, yeah, I suppose I can do that, but since you're going to be arrested any minute, there's probably no rush."

"There's a big rush. Our cop-murdering human trafficker grabbed two college girls in town for the inauguration. Time is not on our side."

"Jesus. Let me see what I can do." He took the disk into his office, slid it into the drive and got busy clicking away while monitoring two huge screens. "Around midnight you said?"

"Yeah," Sam replied, hanging over his shoulder as he worked.

"Don't breathe on me."

"I'm not breathing on you."

"So you ready for tomorrow?"

"I guess. How does one get ready for that circus?"

"I'd have no idea," he said, chuckling between clicks. "I still can't believe you're married to the VP."

"Neither can I. Not entirely sure how that happened." She leaned in closer to one of the screens. "That. There. Zoom in."

He did as directed and zeroed in on a Virginia license plate number.

"That's it! I could kiss you right now!"

"But you won't."

"But I won't."

He wrote down the license number and handed it to her.

"If you could also isolate the video of our guy Androzzi and his buddy escorting them from the bar, I'd appreciate it."

"I'm on it. I'll bring it down when I have it."

"Thanks, Archie." Sam used her cell phone to call Freddie. "Run a plate for me."

"Did you really punch Ramsey and push him down the stairs?"

"I punched him. The stairs were on him, not me."

"Oh my God, Sam."

"Shut up about Ramsey and run this Virginia plate

right now." She gave him the numbers. "I'll be down when the coast is clear."

Sam headed out of the now-deserted IT department to a crowd gathered in the hallway. At the bottom of the stairs, Ramsey was screaming about having her badge while paramedics tended to him. Damn it. He'd survived the fall. Sam scooted around the crowd and across the hall into the SVU division, which was also deserted. Detective Erica Lucas greeted her.

"I hear you've been up to no good, Lieutenant," she said with a gleam in her eye that made Sam smile.

"I have no idea what you're talking about."

"You want some ice for those knuckles?" Erica asked, nodding to Sam's right hand, which had begun to throb.

"Wouldn't say no to that."

"Right this way." Erica led her into a small kitchenette and filled a baggie with ice that she handed to Sam.

"Thanks. We're overdue for that coffee we were going to have."

"I just brewed a fresh pot. Could I interest you in a cup?"

"Since I'm stuck up here until they get the trash off the stairs, I'd love one."

Erica snorted with laughter. "Did you really push him down the stairs?"

Sam placed the bag of ice over her right hand. "I might've punched him and he might've fallen, but I didn't *technically* push him down the stairs."

"What did he say this time?"

"Something about how surprised he was that Stahl didn't knock the starch out of me or some such thing."

Erica stared at her, mouth open. "Well good for you. I would've punched him too. He's such a prick."

"So you've said. Are you safe to talk here about what you know?"

"Since you put a big hurt on him and there's no chance of him walking in here and overhearing me say that I've been concerned by how much he hates you. He goes off about you at least once a week, if not more."

"Any idea why?"

"He talks a lot about nepotism and things being handed to you because of who your old man was and all the attention you've gotten because of your marriage. He says you're an attention whore." She grimaced. "Sorry, don't shoot the messenger."

"I've been called worse. Just this morning in fact."

Erica laughed. "I'm sure you have. The thing that concerns me with Ramsey is how vicious he is about you. Like you took a spot that should've been his, when we both know that wasn't true. He's failed the lieutenant's exam as many times as he's taken it. His career is dead in the water because of him, not you."

"Can't tell him that, though."

"Nope."

"Stahl was like that too. Always blaming me and others for issues he brought upon himself. Typical narcissist. The old-boy network can't bear to see women getting ahead and doing better than them."

"I haven't had a chance to talk to you since everything happened with Stahl. I just hope you know that most of us were horrified by what he did and very thankful you got through it."

"Thanks. I had a ton of support from people here that really helped. I never did get a card from Ramsey though."

Erica smiled. "I doubt you'll get one now that you've punched him in the face."

"Oh well. And I had such hope for our relationship."

"Listen, Sam… I hope it's okay if I call you that."

"Of course it is. I'm not hung up on pretense around friends."

"The thing is… He's really got his nuts in a twist over you, and that's not going to get better after what happened today. I know I don't have to tell you how to watch out for yourself, but be careful."

"Your warning is well taken. I'm running low on enemies with Stahl out of the picture and my ex-husband on a string of remarkably good behavior lately. I'd hate to get bored and lazy."

"That would be a travesty."

"I appreciate the heads-up, the coffee and the ice, but I need to get back downstairs. Hopefully, they've cleaned up the roadkill in the stairwell by now."

"Don't quote me on this," Erica said, glancing toward the door to the kitchen nervously, "but you might want to look into Ramsey's role in providing inside info to Stahl during the Springer case, not to mention the possibility that he was the one who tipped off Billy Springer that we were on to him for the murders of his brother and the others."

"What do you know?"

"Nothing concrete, but he was acting really weird and secretive for a couple of weeks there, beginning with the final days of the Springer investigation. It seemed to end after everything blew up with Stahl. I heard you suspected he was getting inside info, and I immediately thought of Ramsey and his odd behavior."

"Did anyone else witness it?"

"You might want to talk to his partner, Harper. He's a straight-up guy and though he's never said so, he dislikes Ramsey as much as the rest of us do. Ramsey's a bully, and Harper is his favorite target. It drives Ramsey mad that Harper idolizes you. He thinks you're a badass and says so every chance he gets, which takes Ramsey right over the edge. If Harper knows anything, I think he'd give it up under the right circumstances."

"This is very good to know, Erica. I appreciate it."

"We girls have to stick together around here."

"You're goddamned right we do." A thought occurred to her then, and she took a second to weigh it out before she shared it with Erica. "Unfortunately, a spot has opened up in my squad. If you were to apply for a transfer, I'd do what I could to make it happen. If you're interested that is."

"I'd love to work for you. My only hesitation would be leaving SVU for Homicide. I feel like I'm making a real difference for the victims here. Not that you don't in Homicide, but my victims are usually still alive, you know?"

"I do know exactly what you mean. Think about it. Nothing is going to happen soon. We've got a funeral to get through before we can even begin to think about replacing him."

"I'm so sorry for all of you. He was a good guy."

"Yes, he was. Well, I'd better get back to it. Thanks for the coffee and everything else."

"Anytime."

TWENTY-TWO

SAM LEFT THE kitchen and felt every set of eyes in SVU
land on her as she walked past the cubicles on the way
to the hall where the crowd had dispersed and Ramsey
had been taken away. She went downstairs to her own
office and found Malone waiting for her, hands on hips
and his mouth set into that glower thing he did when he
was pissed.

"Captain."

"Lieutenant. Anything you want to tell me?"

"I've got a few things, actually. We got a plate number
for the car that Androzzi used to take the college girls
from the bar. I also just had a very illuminating chat with
Detective Lucas in SVU, who shared some information
you're going to want to hear."

"You forgot the part where you punched Ramsey in
the face, causing him to fall down a flight of stairs, leaving him with possible broken bones in addition to the injuries to his face."

"I was getting to that."

He crossed his arms, which only added to his stern
countenance. "Were you now?"

"He got mouthy with me. I got mouthy back at him,
and then he said something about how he thought Stahl
would've taken some of the starch out of me, so I punched
him." Sam shrugged. "He had it coming."

"He was screaming about lawsuits and pressing

charges and everything else he could think of on the way out of here."

"Whatever. Let him sue me. Who's going to side with him when he would say such a vile thing to a fellow officer who went through what I did with a criminal?"

"No one, I suppose, but you still shouldn't have hit him."

"Okay."

"You may hear from higher up than me on that."

"Okay."

"What's this other information you mentioned?"

Sam conveyed what Erica had told her about Ramsey's odd behavior around the time that Stahl was planning his last stand as well as the possibility that he'd tipped off Billy Springer. "She didn't have anything concrete, but she suggested we might speak to his partner, Detective Harper. And I'm just saying, with Ramsey out of the building for the day, this might be a good time to have that chat."

"You are not having that chat, you hear me?"

"Of course I'm not. That would be a clear conflict of interest. I know that as well as you do."

"You're a total pain in my ass, you know that?"

"Awww, Captain." She dabbed at her eyes. "I love you too."

He snorted out a laugh. "As much as you drive me nuts, it is good to have you back around here, assaulting your fellow officers aside."

Freddie came to the door. "I've got a lead on the SUV. Shall we?"

"By all means. Let's call SWAT in on this." She grabbed her coat. "Catch you later, Captain."

Malone glanced at the piece of paper with the Alexandria address written on it. "I'll be right behind you."

To Freddie, she said, "Grab Gonzo. I don't want him here alone. Meet me at the morgue."

Freddie veered off to the pit.

At the end of a long hallway, Sam ducked into the morgue. "Doc!"

"In here," Lindsey called from her office.

"Question for you—can we run the DNA from the knife victims against the profile we have for Androzzi now that we've isolated him as our suspect?"

"One step ahead of you. I put in the request this morning."

"You're the best."

"I know. I say that every day."

"And your ego might just be as healthy as mine."

"Don't go too far, Lieutenant." She looked up at Sam, her green eyes brimming with compassion. "How's everyone holding up in your squad?"

"They're keeping busy with what needs to be done. That's helping."

"Have you heard anything about when the funeral will be?"

"Not yet. We're waiting on his family to let us know what they want to do."

"I can't imagine what they must be going through. His parents broke my heart."

"Mine too. I gotta get to it. We've got a lead on our shooter, who's been keeping busy since he killed Arnold. Last night he grabbed two college girls who were here on a school trip to the inauguration."

"Oh lord."

"Apparently, they're a couple of Internet stars with

their dorm-room webcam, so they were ripe for the pluck-ing. But they had no idea what they were getting them-selves into with this guy."

"I hope you find them before it's too late."

"So do I."

EVERY TIME SAM drove over the 14th Street Bridge to Vir-ginia, she was reminded of the night she met Nick and how, after a thorough search of the city for the "right" condoms, he'd taken her to his place in Arlington by way of the bridge and changed her life forever.

Thanks to her malicious ex-husband, Sam hadn't seen Nick again for six long years after that night, but they'd more than made up for lost time over the last year. Rather than give Peter one more ounce of her mental energy, Sam chose to think of Nick and that breathtaking night in which he'd come to her rescue after an asshole player spilled beer all over her.

From the first second she laid eyes on him, she was captivated by his stunning good looks, subtle humor, crackling intelligence and exceptional manners. She'd never forget the way he'd washed her skirt while she slept in his bed so she wouldn't have to wear the damp, stinky garment home. Tomorrow, that same man, a man of in-tegrity and character who also happened to be the love of her life, would stand before the nation and the world to be sworn in as vice president of the United States. She couldn't be more proud.

"Lieutenant," Freddie said. "I think we're ready."

Jostled from her thoughts about her husband, Sam checked her watch to discover it had taken forty-five long, intense minutes to get everyone in place. Out of courtesy, they'd notified their colleagues in Alexandria about the raid they were about to make on a warehouse near the Potomac. Even in the dead of winter, the smell of the river was ripe in the icy breeze that blew in from the water.

Sam shivered from the cold as much as the fear of whether they'd be too late to save the girls who'd been kidnapped. The warehouse's close proximity to the river indicated the possibility that the traffickers were shipping women by sea, which was a truly terrifying thought.

The Potomac and Chesapeake beyond were busy shipping lanes and finding two girls among the many containers, barges and other ships that traversed the local waterways on a daily basis would be like looking for a needle in the proverbial haystack.

"Are you ready?" Freddie asked.

"Have we gotten the go-ahead from SWAT?"

"Everyone is in place."

"All right, let's do it."

Freddie communicated her order to the SWAT commander via his handheld radio.

The men and women in black sprung into action. Sam and her team hung back with Malone and Conklin, who'd come with him to oversee the operation. Wearing helmets and heavy bulletproof vests and with their guns and flashlights drawn, Sam, Freddie, Gonzo, Conklin and Malone followed half the SWAT team into the building. The other half formed a perimeter around the outside so no one could escape from inside.

In the darkness, Sam could see the beams of light coming from the headlamps the SWAT team wore. They looked like lasers in a crazy video game, but this was no game. Shots rang out from above, and SWAT returned fire.

Someone cried out from the upper rafters and fell to

the floor near Sam with a sickening thud. She used her flashlight to check the man's identity. It was the guy who'd been with Androzzi in the bar the night before. She recognized him from the video footage and checked for his nonexistent pulse.

"One of Androzzi's guys is dead," she said into her radio.

More gunfire sounded from deeper inside the building. Sam left the dead body to rejoin the others, who were exchanging fire with at least two shooters. Through the earpiece she wore, she listened to the SWAT commander, Captain Nickleson, issue orders to his team, which soon had the shooters surrounded.

"There's no way out for you," Nickleson said over a loudspeaker. "We have you surrounded. Put down your weapons and come out with your hands on top of your head."

After at least a full minute of total silence, the sound of guns hitting the floor echoed through the cavernous space. Two men appeared out of the darkness, hands on their heads as directed. Neither of them was Androzzi.

"Is there anyone else here?" Nickleson asked as two of his people cuffed them.

"There was one other."

"Where's Androzzi?" Malone asked.

"Who?"

"Don't play dumb. We know you work for him. Where is he?"

"No idea who you're talking about."

"What about the girls?" Sam asked. "Where are they?"

The two men looked at each other.

"Lieutenant!" Freddie cried. "Back here!"

Sam ran toward his voice with Gonzo and Malone right behind her. "Where are you, Cruz?"

He waved his flashlight to direct them. "Keep coming this way."

In the far back corner of the vast building, the two missing girls were asleep or unconscious on a grungy mattress. "Are they breathing?"

"Shallow respirations and slow heart rates on both."

Sam used her handheld radio to call for an ambulance. "Stay here with them," she said to Freddie. She went back to the other part of the building where the SWAT team had the two men facedown on the floor, hands cuffed behind them. Sam squatted and shone her light in their faces. "What're they on?"

"Who?"

"The girls in the back."

"What girls?"

"Oh for fuck's sake. The jig is up, you losers. Tell us what you gave them so we can try to save their lives. Otherwise you'll be looking at two counts each of murder one."

"It's GHB," the nervous-looking one said.

"You stupid motherfuckers. I hope you didn't give them enough to kill them."

"Killing them ain't the goal."

"Shut up," the other one said. "Stop talking."

"Lieutenant, back here!" Cruz said. "There're more women."

Sam, Gonzo, Conklin and Malone followed the sound of Freddie's voice to another room where ten hysterical women were chained to the wall, all of them nude and battered. Sam recognized two of them from pictures of missing local women she'd seen earlier in the day.

"We need to get CSU here to go through every inch of this place," Sam said to Malone. "And let's get SVU here to handle the victims." SWAT produced a pair of bolt cutters and began cutting the women free from their chains.

"Already made the call," Freddie said.

"What the hell is going on here?"

Sam whirled around to face an extremely pissed off Avery Hill. Whoops. She knew she'd forgotten something. "We, ah, got a lead on Androzzi's car and jumped on it."

"You had time to get SWAT here, but you didn't have time to give me a heads-up?"

"Sorry."

"*Sorry?* That's the best you've got?"

"Yeah, it is. We moved fast because the lives of two young women were at stake. And we've found ten others who were in rather dire straits too. I'm sorry if you're offended because you were left out."

Hill took a step closer to her and it took all of Sam's resolve not to back off. The impulse to back off was new, and she had Stahl to thank for that. "I'm in charge of this investigation—not you. I know that galls you, but that's not my problem."

"The only thing that galls me is that your ego is more important to you than the safety of twelve women who were kidnapped, drugged and sold into sexual slavery. But hey, if you're more important than they are, someone should've told me that."

"Enough," Conklin said. "Hill, I'm sorry we failed to notify you. It was an oversight not a slight. Get over it."

Sam wanted to send her deputy chief an engraved thank you note, but this was definitely not the time to say so.

Hill stormed off, and Sam breathed a sigh of relief. Locking horns with him had not been on her to-do list for today.

"He's right, you know," Conklin said. "We should've given him a heads-up."

"I honestly never thought of it," Sam said. "My only thought was getting to those girls before they were shipped out and possibly lost forever."

"Thank God we found them."

"I just hope we weren't too late."

SAM SPOKE WITH the parents of both girls who were on their way to Washington to join their daughters at the hospital. Both sets of parents had been overjoyed to hear their daughters had been found, but gravely concerned in light of their condition. SVU detectives were working to identify the other women who'd been rescued, to get them medical attention and reunite them with their families. The statements that would be taken from them would help to cement the growing case against Androzzi.

Crime Scene detectives spent hours scouring the warehouse, while Sam's team took the two men they'd arrested back to HQ for questioning. By the end of the day, they were no closer to finding Androzzi than they'd been at the start, and the frustration was building with every hour that went by without the arrest of the man who'd killed Arnold and kidnapped so many women.

Androzzi's minions had clammed up, demanded attorneys and weren't talking about Androzzi or his organization. Archie's team had been working on dumping their cell phones, hoping for a number that might lead them to the phone that Androzzi was using.

"Anything?" Sam asked when Archie appeared at her office door at ten o'clock that night.

"Nope. We were able to identify all the numbers called in the last two weeks, and none of them leads to Androzzi. There're a lot of unknown numbers, which leads me to believe he's using burner phones."

"Fucking burner phones." This wasn't the first time an investigation had been stymied by untraceable burner phones.

"He's getting cocky sticking around here after he killed one of our officers," Archie said. "He'll fuck up and when he does, we'll grab him. Gonzo can identify him as the shooter. And we've got ten women who can identify him, and hopefully the other two will recover to identify him as the one they were with at the bar. We're building a case, even if it's taking longer than we'd like."

"I know." Sam released the clip that she'd used to contain her hair and ran her fingers through the mop that fell to below her shoulders, trying to bring some order. "Thanks for all you did today."

"Sorry we couldn't do more. So did you hear you put Ramsey in the hospital?"

"Oh, really? Gee, that's too bad."

Archie laughed hard. "You're all heart, Lieutenant."

"That's what people say."

"Who says that?"

"People."

Archie laughed even harder. "I'd love to meet these so-called people."

"So what's wrong with him?"

"Broken wrist and a concussion."

"That's really a bummer. He probably shouldn't have

said what he did to me. Would've saved us all a bunch of paperwork."

"He definitely shouldn't have said what he did, and for what it's worth, I would've punched him too."

"It's worth a lot. Thanks for the support."

"You ought to head home. There's nothing more we can do tonight."

"I'm going soon."

"See you tomorrow."

"No, you won't. I'm playing second lady tomorrow."

"Oh, that's right! Well, have fun."

Sam glowered at him, and he left laughing. She was packing up to leave when Freddie came to the door. "One of the girls is awake."

"Let's get over there and see if we can get a statement from her."

"I'm with you, LT."

"Bring your own car so you can go home from there. I'll meet you at the ER entrance."

"See you in a few."

As Sam drove to GW, she called Nick. "Hey, I'll be home soon. Just one more thing I've got to do."

"I saw on the news that you found the missing girls."

"Yes, but no sign of Androzzi. He's slippery as an eel."

"You guys will get him."

"I hope so. I can't imagine letting Arnold's killer get away with it."

"That won't happen."

Sam appreciated his show of support. "One of the girls is awake, so Freddie and I are going over there now to try to talk to her, and then I'll be home."

"I'll be here. So, um, are you going to be able to go with me tomorrow?"

She smiled at his adorableness. "I wouldn't miss it."

"Even if there's somewhere else you'd rather be?"

"There's nowhere else in this universe I'd rather be than with you, no matter what we're doing or whether the whole world is watching."

"Awww, baby, you know just what to say to me, don't you?"

"It's true. You know that, right?"

"I do. Now hurry and do what you've got to do so I can have you to myself tonight and show you off to the rest of the world tomorrow."

"I will. Love you. See you soon."

"Love you too."

Freddie was waiting for her inside the main doors to the ER. He'd already scored the room number for the girl who was awake.

"Did you have to flirt with a nurse to get it?"

"Don't question my means. Celebrate my results."

The cheeky reply made her laugh. "I feel guilty laughing at anything when Arnold is dead."

"I feel guilty making jokes, but I can't believe he'd want us to feel like shit forever. He just wasn't like that."

"No, he wasn't. But still…"

"Yeah."

She appreciated that he got it. He usually did. That's what made him the best partner she'd ever had. At the bank of elevators, he pushed the up button. "Hey so, I'm sorry if your big news has been overshadowed by everything this week. I'm really so happy for you and Elin."

"Thanks. I'm happy too. I still can't believe a goddess like her picked me."

"She's lucky to have you, and she knows it."

"We're both lucky. Finding that one person in the sea of people is kind of a miracle, you know?"

"I do. And how strange is it that we both have John O'Connor to thank for leading us to the person we were meant to be with?"

"It's bizarre, but sort of fitting in light of what we do for a living."

"Just don't ask me to be a bridesmaid in the wedding and we'll be good."

"How do you feel about best man?"

"Haha, very funny."

"I'm totally serious."

Sam stopped walking and turned to him. "For real?"

"Yes, for real," he said with an indulgent smile.

"You realize the best man is supposed to be like, you know, a *man*, right?"

"It's supposed to be the groom's best friend, and you're my best friend."

"Well, that's sort of sad for you."

"Shut up, Sam," he said laughing. "Just say you'll do it. You'd get to throw the stag party and can have hookers and strippers and every other dirty thing you can think of."

"I accept," she said with a big gleeful smile that had him groaning. "Lap dances for everyone!" The teasing helped to hide her emotional reaction to his request and hearing that he considered her his best friend. In truth, he was probably hers too. Not that she could ever admit that to him. After all, she was his supervisor. She had to maintain some decorum.

So she punched him in the arm.

"Um, ow?"

"Thanks for asking me."

He rubbed his arm. "You're welcome, I think. Thanks for accepting. I'm sure you'll do all you can to make me regret it before the big day."

"You know me *so* well, Frederico. So very, very well."

"The second lady can't hire lap dancers."

"Where does the rule book say that?"

"I'll find out and get back to you."

"You do that." She had no doubt that Lilia, if asked, could produce some sort of federal law against second ladies hiring lap dancers, which is why Lilia would not be consulted.

The banter and bickering helped, even if it felt inappropriate in light of their loss. But life went on. Like the chief had said, there was nothing they could do but carry on.

TWENTY-THREE

OUTSIDE JENNIFER TORLINO'S ROOM, a group of people had gathered that included an MPD Patrol officer who'd been assigned to provide security for Jennifer while she was in the hospital.

"Excuse me," Sam said. "I'm Lieutenant Holland—"

"Oh Lieutenant!" A woman launched herself into Sam's arms, and only Freddie's quick action behind her kept Sam from toppling over. "It's so awful! Mindy is in a coma and Jennifer is so sick. Those monsters! What they did!"

Sam patted her back awkwardly. She wanted to remind Jennifer's mother that it could've been a whole lot worse, but thankfully that wouldn't happen now.

"Now, Monica," a frazzled-looking man said as he collected the woman from Sam. "Let the poor Lieutenant say what she's come to say."

Sam sent him a grateful smile. "I was hoping to get the chance to speak to Jennifer, if she's up for it. We only need a couple of minutes."

"If it will help you get this guy, then sure," the man said. "We'll allow that."

"Thank you." Sam and Freddie showed their badges to the Patrol officer who opened the door for them.

Jennifer's parents came with them.

A nurse was tending to her, so Sam showed her badge again. "We just need a few minutes."

"Try not to upset her," the nurse said on the way out.

That was a tall order, Sam thought. This whole thing was upsetting. "Jennifer," she said to the frail-looking blonde in the bed, who'd been the star of the dorm-room video Sam had seen. She tried not to think about gigantic dildos while she spoke to her. "I'm Lieutenant Holland, and this is my partner, Detective Cruz."

"You're the vice president's wife," she said softly.

"Yes, I am. I wanted to ask you about the men you met last night at McDuffy's and whether you remember anything about the man named Sid that might help us to find him."

"I don't remember one named Sid."

Freddie produced his phone and showed her the photo of Androzzi.

"That's Jack."

Yet another assumed name. "Do you recall if he gave you his last name?"

She shook her head. "He only said he was Jack."

"And did you meet him that night or did you know him before you came here?"

Jennifer glanced at her parents, who were hovering at the foot of the bed.

Sam realized she would never speak freely with them in the room. "Would you mind giving us just a few minutes alone with Jennifer?"

"Is that all right with you, honey?" her mom asked.

"Yes, it's fine."

Her parents left the room, and Jennifer looked up at Sam. "He contacted me a couple of weeks ago through my movie channel, and we exchanged some emails and texts. He seemed really nice, and offered to help us find some fun while we were here for the inauguration." She wiped away tears. "I can't believe he drugged us and kidnapped us. And Mindy. She's in a coma."

"You don't happen to have the number he texted you from, do you?"

"No, it changed all the time."

Sam wanted to scream at her, to ask her how she could've been so stupid or taken such foolish risks. But she didn't do that. "And you didn't find that odd?"

"No, he said he had a bunch of phones for his business."

"Did he happen to mention what business he was in?"

"He owns a T-shirt shop here in the city."

"Has anyone told you what he really does?"

"N-no."

"He is a human trafficker. Do you know what that is?"

"No. Should I?"

"He kidnaps women like you and Mindy and sells them into sexual slavery, often overseas."

"Oh my God," she whispered, her already pale face leaching of all remaining color. She lunged for the puke bucket on the table next to her bed and was violently ill. Thankfully, Freddie stepped up to deal with that.

Sam handed her a tissue while Freddie went into the bathroom to dump the bucket.

Jennifer's hands were shaking and tears streamed down her face.

"You had a close call," Sam said. "A very close call. Your friend Jack is really Sid Androzzi, who's on the FBI's ten most wanted list."

As Sam spoke, Jennifer sobbed and whimpered. "I didn't know... I had no idea. I thought he was a nice guy. We just wanted to have fun on our trip."

"Is there anything at all you can tell us about where you think he might be hiding out?"

"No, he never said anything about where he lived. Just about the store he owned."

And like a lightbulb had been illuminated in her mind, Sam suddenly knew exactly where they'd find Androzzi. "This has been very helpful, Jennifer. We'll hope for your speedy recovery and Mindy's too."

"Thank you."

"And even though it's none of my business, I'm going to say this anyway. Take down that Internet channel and stop letting strangers into your life. You never know who's watching."

Still trembling and weeping, Jennifer nodded. "We will."

Sam handed her a business card. "If you think of anything that might help us find him, no matter how minor it might be, please call me. Day or night."

"Okay."

As she and Freddie retraced their steps back to the Emergency entrance, Sam said, "For the record, I just want to say I hate the fucking Internet."

"I'll make a note for the record."

"I hate how it provides naïve kids with a place to be stupid with life-changing results. These two girls will never be the same again. Brooke will never be the same," she said of her teenage niece who'd been victimized twice—once when she was gang raped in the Springers' basement and again when video from the assault was posted online. "It gives the pervs a place to troll for unsuspecting victims. I hate it."

"I bet this job was a lot easier before the Internet existed."

"No doubt. It was never easy, but it was better than this shit." Sam called Malone. "So guess what we've missed in this whole thing with Androzzi?"

"What's that?"

"The fucking T-shirt store actually exists." As she walked and talked, she flipped through the pages of her notebook to find the notes she'd taken from the reports on the interviews with Enright and Griffen. "It's on freaking Constitution Avenue. How much you want to bet he's been hiding out there since he shot Arnold?"

"What's the address?"

Sam read it off to him.

"Meet you there?"

"Yes, you will."

"Let Hill know."

"Aww, Captain, do I gotta?"

"Yeah, you gotta. He was ranting to the chief about you earlier."

"And here I thought we were such good friends these days."

"You're making friends all over the place this week. The brass wants to talk to you about what happened with Ramsey, and he's demanding charges be filed."

"Whatever. I don't have time to deal with that scumbag right now. Cruz and I will meet you at Constitution Ave."

"Call Hill," Malone said before the phone went dead.

Sam growled.

"Uh-oh. What's that about?"

"Freaking Hill. Gotta play nicey-nice with his ego."

"He is in charge of the investigation."

"But he's not the one out pounding the pavement, is he?"

"Want me to call him?"

"No, I'll do it." Sam put through the call, and Hill answered immediately, as if he'd been waiting for her to call. Weirdo. "There's going to be a raid on a T-shirt shop on Constitution Avenue where we suspect Androzzi has been hiding out." She provided the exact address.

"What makes you suspect he's hiding there?"

"I don't have time to lay it all out for you. I'm doing you the courtesy of letting you know." She ended the call before he could say anything.

Freddie snickered under his breath.

"What's so funny?"

"You said, 'I'm doing you.'"

"What? I did not?"

"Um, yeah, you did. 'I'm doing you the courtesy…'"

"Shut up. Just shut up."

He snickered again as they exited the hospital and emerged into an icy tundra that had Sam zipping her coat all the way up and tying her scarf around her neck. "Meet you there."

Sam got into the car and whispered a prayer of thanks to the God of heated seats—and to her husband, who she called to thank.

"Hey, babe."

"My bum is loving you right now."

"I have no idea how to reply to that."

"Heated seats, my love. Heated seats."

"Ahhh, I do what I can to take care of your sexy bum."

The way he said that made her desperately wish she were in a bed naked with him. Soon enough. "I'm going to be a little bit longer," she said, updating him on the hunch about the T-shirt shop.

"You're not going in there alone, are you?"

"Nope, we're bringing the cavalry. Second time today

that we've busted out the SWAT team. They're going to be positively spent tomorrow."

"I'm glad they're going in ahead of you. Be careful."

"I will. I'll be home as soon as I can."

"I'll be waiting for you."

"Knowing that makes this very shitty day so much more bearable. See you soon."

Sam pulled up to the address on Constitution Avenue and didn't see anyone else from the MPD yet. She stayed in her car, hunched down, eyes on the dark storefront. God, she hoped she was right about this. It would be so great to nail this bastard tonight and be done with it before the inauguration.

Having an armed murderer on the loose with a million or so extra people in town was law enforcement's worst nightmare.

Freddie pulled up behind her and the others arrived a few minutes later.

She switched her radio to the encrypted channel used for sensitive situations such as this, lest Androzzi be tipped off to their arrival by a police radio that could be purchased anywhere.

"This is Captain Nickleson. My people are in place. We'll be going in via the front and back simultaneously."

"Be prepared for gunfire," Conklin said. "He's already killed one cop. He's got nothing left to lose. Proceed with caution."

Sam got out of her car and met Freddie outside of his.

Hill came storming up the sidewalk, brushed by Sam and went to confer with Conklin.

"Was it something I said?" she asked Freddie.

"He's still thinking about you offering to do him."

"I liked you better before you knew what that meant, back when you were a good Christian boy."

"Here we go, people," Nickleson said over the radio, giving the order for his officers to move in.

"Please let him be there," Sam whispered.

On the radio she heard the doors to the store burst open, followed shortly after by multiple reports of all clear.

"Damn it," she said with a sigh. "I was so sure he'd be there."

"Someone's been living here," Nickleson said. "There're clothes and blankets and a food stash, but he's not here now."

"Let's get CSU in there," Conklin said.

"I guess we're good to go home," Sam said to Conklin, frustrated that they'd been unable to find him before the inauguration. "Call me if anything pops overnight."

"I believe you're off duty until Wednesday, Lieutenant," Conklin said with a teasing smile that had Sam glaring at the deputy chief.

"Have your fun, sir."

"Thank you, I will. I'll wave to you on the reviewing stand."

"Watch for my middle finger."

Conklin took off laughing, and Sam noticed Gonzo standing alone on the sidewalk, staring at the store, which was now lit up. Sam told Freddie to go on home.

"Good luck with everything tomorrow."

"Thanks. Keep me posted on all of this. I'll have my phone, so text me."

"Will do."

Sam walked over to Gonzo.

"Never occurred to me for one second that there was

really a T-shirt shop," Gonzo said. "I should've thought of that. It's brilliant. Hiding in plain sight in the legit business while running his sordid trafficking sideline."

"It never occurred to any of us that the shop was legit, Gonzo."

He continued to stare, unblinking.

"Come with me." She took him by the arm. Her dad would already be in bed at this hour, but she had no doubt he'd be happy to talk to Gonzo no matter the time.

"Where am I going?"

"Just get in the car." Sam held the passenger door for him and slammed it shut when he was settled. As Sam drove to Capitol Hill, she hoped she was doing the right thing by forcing him to have this conversation. At the checkpoint on Ninth Street, Sam was stopped by the Secret Service when they saw she had a passenger. "Show them your badge."

Gonzo retrieved his badge from his pocket and showed it to the agent on duty.

"Thank you, Lieutenant. Have a nice evening."

"You too." Sam parked the car in front of her house.

"Why are you bringing me home with you?"

"Come with me, and I'll tell you." She could tell she surprised him when she directed him to her father's home rather than her own.

"Sam, it's too late for this tonight. We can do it another time."

With her hand on his back, she propelled him up the ramp to her dad's front door where she knocked softly.

Her stepmother, Celia, dressed in a thick robe, came to the door. "Oh, Sam, it's you." She ushered them into the warm house. "And Tommy." She hugged him. "How are you, honey? We've been thinking about you."

"Thank you," he said.

Sam kissed her cheek. "Sorry to bother you so late, but we really need to see Dad. Is that okay?"

"Sure, he's still awake. We just watched a movie in his room. Go on in."

"Thanks, Celia."

"Yeah, thanks," Gonzo said. "Sorry to barge in."

"You're welcome here anytime of day or night."

"Told ya," Sam said, smiling at him over her shoulder. His unusually stern countenance made her ache for him. It would be a long time before Tommy Gonzales found anything to smile about. "Knock, knock, Skippy. I come with friends."

"Hey there," Skip said. "You're up late."

Sam bent over the rail on his bed to kiss his forehead, where he could feel the sensation. "We've been working the case all day. Good news is we found the college girls who were grabbed by Androzzi. Bad news is no sign of him, but all kinds of signs that he's been hiding out right here in the city."

Sam stepped aside to let Gonzo in.

"Sorry to bust in on you so late, Skip," he said. "She made me."

"I know how she can be."

"So listen, I'm going to put it right out there. You boys have something awful in common. You've both had partners killed right in front of you."

Gonzo began to shake his head. "Sam—"

"Gonzo, he's been where you are. Steven Coyne was his very best friend. Let him help you."

"I don't want to—"

"Go on home, Sam," Skip said. "We can take it from here."

That's exactly what she hoped he'd say. She gave her dad another kiss. "See you in the morning."

"With bells on."

She was thrilled to see him so excited to attend the inauguration. Nick had gone to extraordinary lengths to make sure Skip and his wheelchair would be accommodated at every event. Sam surprised herself as much as Gonzo when she kissed his forehead too. "Let him help. He's been there. Call Patrol for a ride home when you're ready to go." She patted his shoulder and left the room, hoping against hope that her dad's experience and wisdom might ease Gonzo's burden.

"It's a good thing you did bringing him to your dad," Celia said softly. "Who knows better what he's going through?"

"That's my thought exactly."

"Poor Tommy. And poor, poor Arnold. I can't stop thinking about his parents and how proud they were of him."

"I know. It's heartbreaking."

Celia hugged Sam. "I don't know how you do it day after day, how you keep getting back up no matter what comes your way, but I so admire you for never giving up."

"Sometimes I want to. Sometimes it all gets to be too much."

"You'll never give up, Sam. You're Skip Holland's daughter."

"You have no idea how badly I needed to hear that right now."

"Go on home to your handsome husband. He always makes you feel better."

"So do you." She kissed Celia again. "Thanks."

"Anytime. And I'll make some coffee for Tommy."

"You're the best. See you tomorrow."

TWENTY-FOUR

SAM STEPPED OUT into the frigid cold and walked the short distance to the ramp that led to her own front door, which opened for her. It was creepy the way the Secret Service watched everything, but that was the small cost of keeping Nick and Scotty safe.

Nick was on the sofa in the living room, where the downstairs TV was now located since the Secret Service had absconded with their den.

"Hi, honey, I'm home." She tossed her coat over the love seat and went over to him.

Smiling, he raised his blanket to let her in.

She scooted in next to him and sighed with pleasure as his arms came around her and his heat warmed her.

"How'd it go?"

"Another dead end. I simply can't think or talk about Androzzi for another second today or my head will explode."

"Then we won't talk about him."

The agent who'd been working the front door locked up, turned out the front lights and left the room with silent stealth.

"Alone at last," he whispered, making her shiver from the touch of his lips against her ear.

"Mmm, this day was endless."

"It just got a thousand percent better for me."

"You wanna make out?" She wanted to lose herself in

him and let him take her away from the heartache and the frustration and the pain of this day.

"You have to ask?"

Smiling at his predictable reply, Sam turned to face him, slid her leg between his and rested her hand on his chest. "Are they spying on us?"

Nick raised the remote and turned off the TV, casting the room into darkness. "If they are, they won't see anything."

"Scotty…"

"Has been asleep for hours. Stop making excuses and kiss me."

She loved that he'd turned off the TV. She loved that he always wanted her so badly and that he didn't care who was watching. She loved kissing him and the ravenous way he responded to her. She loved absolutely everything about him, especially the way he made her forget the torturous day she'd just put in.

His warm hand found its way under her sweater. In a matter of seconds, her bra was unhooked and he had a handful of breast.

"Someone has done this before," she whispered.

"Done what?"

"Made out in a dark living room with a better than average chance of getting caught."

"You can't prove that."

Sam laughed and bit his bottom lip, making him gasp.

He responded by pinching her nipple tightly between his fingers.

She moaned.

He shushed her and then had to be shushed himself when she cupped his erection through his pajama pants. "Samantha."

"Quiet. My parents might hear us. I don't want them to kick you out."

"You make me so hot. I can't help it."

"Try." She slipped her hand inside his pants and wrapped it around his thick cock, stroking him from root to tip.

"Fuck," he whispered when she slid her thumb over the moisture at the tip. "You're such a tease."

"I never tease. I always deliver. All the boys say so."

He pinched her nipple harder than before. "You'd better not let any other boy touch what's mine." Then he pushed her sweater up to her neck and brought his mouth down on her nipple, sucking and biting until she was nearly delirious with desire.

"Nick." *Enough already with the fooling around*, she thought. *It's time to get down to business.* "Let's go to bed."

"Your parents would kill me if they caught me in your bed. Right here, baby."

She couldn't believe they were actually going to do this, right out in the open where they could be seen or caught. But the room was pitch dark, and the role-playing was hot, so she didn't protest. Rather, she ground her body against his, letting him know she was game for anything he wanted.

And what he wanted was to slowly and thoroughly drive her mad with his lips on every part of skin he could get to without removing her sweater.

This so reminded her of sweaty make-out sessions in high school, only it was so much better because he loved her and there were no parents to catch them—only Secret Service agents who were hopefully otherwise occupied at the moment.

His hand traveled over her belly to the button on her jeans, which he pulled open before he unzipped her. He went right for third base without hesitation, driving his finger into her.

"Oh, God, Sam, you're so wet. So hot." He drove her wild with the slow slide of his finger and the occasional bump against her clit.

She was so captivated by what he was doing, she barely noticed when her jeans and panties were tugged down her legs to below her knees. He came down on top of her, his lips devouring hers as he continued to tease her nipple with his free hand. "Let me in," he whispered in her ear as he withdrew his finger and pressed his much larger cock against her.

"It's *so* big. Will it hurt?"

"Fucking hell," he muttered, making her giggle softly, as a huge shudder rippled through his big muscular body that turned her on even more if that was possible. "It only hurts a little the first time, but I'll be so gentle."

Good lord, Sam thought. *Who knew that pretending could be the hottest thing in the history of the universe?* "Yes, Nick," she whispered in response, biting down on his earlobe. "*Yes*. Right now. I can't wait anymore."

True to his word he went slowly, so slowly that she nearly screamed in frustration. She wanted all of him, but he only gave her short, shallow thrusts, as if she were in fact a virgin doing this for the first time.

"I can't believe we're doing this," she whispered. "What if I get pregnant?"

"I'll be so happy if you do."

Though she smiled at what he said, she couldn't break character. "My dad will kill you."

"I'll take my chances." He withdrew almost completely, and then gave her all of him in one deep thrust that had her biting her lip to keep from screaming.

Sam's back arched into him, wishing she could get her pants off entirely so she could wrap her legs around him. Then she remembered a trick from way back when and kicked her way free of one leg of her pants and wrapped her leg around his hips.

"*Yes*," he whispered hotly. "Tell me you want me."

"I want you so bad. I've wanted you for so long. You have no idea."

"Tell me what you want me to do to you."

"Don't make me say it."

He pulled out of her. "Say it or I won't do it."

"Fuck me, Nick," she whispered, scandalized by their behavior. God help them if anyone was paying attention to the dark living room or what might be happening under the blanket that covered them.

"That's it. That's what I wanted to hear. I've been dying to fuck you since the first time I ever saw you." He slammed into her, and she detonated. She couldn't recall a time when she'd come harder than she did then.

"Jesus," he whispered, his fingers digging into her ass as he rode her orgasm straight into his own. "Holy shit," he said on a strangled sounding gasp as he erupted inside her. "What the hell just happened here?"

"I believe," Sam said between deep breaths, "you just showed me how you passed your misspent youth."

"*I* showed *you*? How about that leg move I never saw coming?"

Sam started laughing and couldn't stop until his mouth covered hers and he kissed her into silence.

He broke the kiss slowly, backing off until his lips

were barely touching hers. "How do you propose we get ourselves out of here?"

Sam squeezed her internal muscles tightly, drawing another gasp from him. "I have no idea. This was your big idea."

"I was lying here minding my own business until you came in and seduced me."

"Who shut off the TV?"

"I might've played a small part in what happened, but I'm the innocent victim of an older, wiser woman who had her wicked way with me."

"*Oh*, can we play *that* game sometime?"

He cupped her ass and dipped a finger between her cheeks. "We can play any game you want anytime you want."

"I think I might want to keep you for longer than high school."

"I think I might let you keep me forever."

"Yes, please." Sam kissed him again, hooking her arm around his neck to keep him from escaping. "I've heard," she whispered many passionate minutes later, "that you've got a big day tomorrow so you ought to go home and get some sleep."

"Yeah, I'm getting my Eagle Scout award. Will you fuck me again after that?"

Sam rocked with quiet laughter. "I'll fuck you any-time and any place."

"I have to be the luckiest guy in the history of the world."

"You are pretty lucky, but then again so am I."

After one more long tongue-tangling kiss, he finally withdrew from her before they could forget where they were a second time. "You take the blanket." While he pulled up his pants and removed her jeans completely, Sam wrapped herself up in the blanket. "Ready?"

"Yeah."

They tiptoed up the stairs and into their room, drawing only the attention of the agent who was positioned outside of Scotty's room. He nodded to them and returned to the book he was reading.

Inside their room, they fell against the door laughing quietly.

"You know that someday they're going to write best-selling memoirs about all the stuff they see in our house," Nick said.

"Let them. What do we care if the whole world knows we're wildly in love?"

"We don't care at all."

Sam dropped the blanket and the rest of her clothes into a pile on the floor, locked her service weapon and badge into her bedside table and headed for the shower to clean up. By the time she brushed her teeth and returned to the bedroom, he had folded up the blanket and her clothes, which were in a neat pile on top of his dresser. "Anal-retentive freakazoid," she said as she climbed naked into bed with him.

"I don't know what you're talking about."

"Yes, you do. And this is so much better than high school because we get to sleep together after we fuck on the sofa."

"Did you do a lot of fucking on the sofa?"

"I'm not answering that unless you do too."

"I did my share of fooling around," he said bluntly. "But I never made love until the first time I made love to you."

"That was very smooth. You ought to be a politician when you grow up."

"You think? They always seem so seedy."

"I think you could be anything you wanted. Hell, you could be president someday."

He smiled at her. "You never answered my question about sofa sex."

"I did my share too, although usually not at my house due to the overwhelming fear of the father with the gun." She cupped his face and looked into his gorgeous hazel eyes. "But I never made love until the first time with you."

Nick buried his fingers in her hair and tugged her closer for another kiss and then settled her into his arms, her head on his chest, his fingers running through her hair. This was her absolute favorite way to end a day.

"You going to tell me what happened to your hand?" he asked, running his finger lightly over her swollen knuckles.

"I punched Detective Ramsey in the face, sending him backward down the stairs. Something about a broken wrist and concussion, but he deserved it after saying he thought Stahl would've taken some of the starch out of me."

"Fucking right he did. Good for you. Are you in trouble over it?"

"Who knows? Least of my worries right now. Oh and you'll be glad to know that Hill is pissed with me because I forgot to stroke his ego."

"You'd better not be stroking anything of his."

"Shut up," she said with a laugh.

"Guess who showed up at the White House today demanding to be let in to see me?"

Sam went immediately on full alert. "Who?"

"Nicoletta."

"Are you fucking kidding me? What did she want?"

"I don't know. I turned her away."

"Oh my God, and now you feel guilty because you wouldn't let her in."

He shrugged ever so subtly but Sam felt it.

She raised herself up so she could see his face. "You will not feel guilty for refusing to allow her to screw up this huge moment in your life. Do you hear me?"

"Yeah, babe, I hear you."

He said what she wanted to hear, but the wounded look in his eyes infuriated her.

"I hate that she does this to you. I hate it."

"I do too."

"What right does she have to show up at the White House of all places and demand to be let in simply because she's the one who gave birth to you? She was never your mother. Ever. Laine O'Connor is your mother."

"Yes, she is."

"If you turned Laine away I'd tell you you're a heartless bastard and never to do that again. But turning away Nicoletta is you taking care of *you* for a change. You don't ever need to feel guilty about doing what's best for you when she has never done that."

"I know."

"But you still feel bad, don't you?"

"I wish I didn't, but old habits are hard to break."

"I'm talking to Brant in the morning, and I'll make sure she doesn't get anywhere near you tomorrow or ever. I swear to God I'll claw her eyes out if she tries anything tomorrow."

Nick chuckled softly. "Easy tiger."

"I'm not kidding around."

"I know, baby. In other news, I broke Twitter today."

"You did what?"

"I got more than two million followers in three hours after they made my Twitter account live. That apparently broke some sort of record or something."

"That is so cool. My hubby, the Twitter rock star." She moved so she was on top of him, her lips hovering just above his. "Will you do me a favor?"

"Again?"

"Stop," she said, laughing. "I'm being serious."

He filled his hands with her butt cheeks and squeezed. "I'd do anything for you."

"Will you please focus on the two million people who love you so much they couldn't wait to follow you on Twitter and not give one more second of your time or attention to the woman who has never loved you the way you deserve to be loved? Will you do that? Will you do it for me?"

"Yeah, baby. I'll do that for you."

"Good. Now go to sleep. You're getting sworn in tomorrow. I don't want you looking like shit."

His arms encircled her and he exhaled, relaxing as much as he ever did. Now hopefully he'd sleep rather than lying awake all night thinking about the woman who'd already hurt him too many times in the past.

Never again. Sam would kill her before she'd let that happen.

TWENTY-FIVE

FOR A LONG time after Sam left, Gonzo sat staring at the foot of Skip's hospital bed, uncertain of what he was supposed to say to him.

"Not a day goes by that I don't relive the moment Steven was shot," Skip said after a prolonged silence. "You know what I remember so vividly?"

"What's that?"

"The smell of gunfire and exhaust. It all happened so fast. One minute we were standing on the sidewalk, the next he'd been shot and the car that carried the shooter was roaring away. I didn't know what to do first—see to him or go after the car. I chose him, and I've wondered every day since if I made the right call. He was already gone, and the shooter got away because I made that choice."

Gonzo struggled with his emotions as he listened to Skip.

"He was just picked off randomly because he wore the uniform. I honestly believe that. Over the years, I've come to the conclusion that it was some sort of gang initiation thing or something like that. They didn't care who he was or what he meant to the people who loved him. They set out that day to kill a cop, and they not only succeeded, they've gotten away with it. But what it did to us... I can't even begin to describe the devastation."

"You don't have to," Gonzo said.

"No, I guess I don't. It hurts like a son of a bitch. No other way to say it. And in your case, you feel responsible because he was under your command. Steven and I were the same rank, but I still felt responsible because it happened feet from me and I couldn't do anything to stop it. I didn't even see the car until it was racing away from us. Rank and responsibility don't matter between partners. There's a bond there that supersedes the department BS. When you're out on the streets, it's just the two of you against everyone else and no one cares who outranks who."

"He was pissing me off with his complaints about the cold, the long shift, the boredom, so I said if he shut up I'd let him take the lead. He was all excited about that because I never let him take the lead. Hadn't felt he was ready yet."

"If you're waiting for it to make sense, it never will."

Gonzo had come to that conclusion on his own in the awful hours since it happened.

"You will live with this for the rest of your life. You will relive those few minutes every day, and it will never add up to something that makes sense."

"*How* do you live with it?"

"You just do. What choice do you have? I was like you—I had a young family counting on me and didn't have the luxury of walking away from the job that paid the bills. I had no choice but to go back out there with a new partner who could never take the place of the one I'd lost and continue to do the job. My family needed me to do that. But I didn't want to. I did *not* want to."

"How long did it take before you got over that?"

"Truthfully? Until I made captain and was off the streets. I hated every second I spent pounding the pavement after Steven was killed. It was never the same for me after that. And it may never be the same for you either. But that doesn't mean you can't still be effective on the job. It doesn't mean you can't successfully supervise junior officers. It will just be… It'll be different now."

Gonzo took it all in, processing what Skip was saying and trying to figure out how he felt about it. His mind was so muddled with disturbing memories and anger and despair. So much despair.

"The most important thing you can do now is to not make any big decisions. Focus on getting through this hour and then the next and the one after that and then the funeral. A few weeks from now that painful knot in your chest will begin to ease up a little, and you'll feel like you can breathe again without every breath causing you pain. That will happen. I promise."

Gonzo leaned forward, arms on his knees and head bent to hide his tears from a man he admired so greatly. "His parents were so nice to me, and I just wanted to scream at them that they should hate me for letting this happen to him."

"They'll never hate you. They may hate the man who shot him, but they will never hate you because he loved you, and they know that. You might be blaming yourself, but they never will. Steven's wife never once made me feel like it was my fault. Not once. It took me a long time to understand how it was possible that she didn't blame me."

Gonzo pressed the heels of his hands to his eyes, wishing he could stop the tears.

"I want to say one other thing, and I hope you'll really hear me on this one. After Steven was killed, I was so caught up in how it affected me that I neglected the people who loved me most. I was obsessed with caring for his wife at the expense of my own. I ruined what had been a pretty good marriage up to that point, and we never got back on track. If you let this take over your life, you may wake up one day to find that the people you loved before aren't around anymore. Don't let that happen. You'll regret that almost as much as you regret what happened to your partner. Christina is going to want to be there for you. Let her in. If you freeze her out, you'll be sorry for the rest of your life."

Gonzo nodded in acknowledgment because that was all he was capable of at the moment.

"A terrible, awful thing has happened, Gonzo. But you will survive this, even if it doesn't seem like it now."

"I took him for granted. I hate that, you know?"

"Yeah, I do. It never occurred to me for one second that anyone other than Steven would be my partner for the rest of my life. We all take for granted the people we're closest to. You're no different than anyone else that way."

"He saved my life, but there wasn't a damned thing I could do for him."

"Even knowing what was going to happen to him a short time later, do you think he would've done anything different the day you were shot?"

"No."

"Of course he wouldn't have. He did for you what you would've done for him if you could have. He'd never hold it against you that you couldn't save him."

"But even after what he did for me, I still busted his balls and gave him shit. I should've been more... Appreciative."

"Did you thank him for what he did that day?"

"Yeah, a couple times."

"Then he knew you appreciated it. I bet that other than you yourself, no one wanted things back to normal between you guys more than he did. He was probably thrilled to have you back to busting his balls because the alternative didn't bear consideration. He probably had many a nightmare about the day you were shot and lots of sleepless nights to think about what could've happened. You ever think about that?"

"Not really, no." He was ashamed to admit that he'd spent very little time considering how traumatic his shooting had probably been for the young partner who'd saved his life. "I owe him everything. I feel like he deserved better than what he got from me."

"You're going to have to let that one go, Gonzo. There was nothing in this world you could've done to change the outcome the other night. Somehow you're going to have to accept that. It won't happen today or tomorrow or even next month, but you will find a way to live with this."

"I really appreciate you talking to me about it, especially at this hour."

"I'm always here for you. I hope you know that."

Gonzo took a deep breath and nodded. "I'll get out of your hair so you can get some sleep. Big day for your family tomorrow."

"Indeed it is. Never expected to have a son-in-law who was vice president of the United States."

"I don't think Sam ever expected to be married to the VP."

Skip replied with a bark of laughter. "Ain't that the truth?"

Gonzo stood and reached over the bed rail to squeeze Skip's right hand. "Thank you."

"Take care of yourself, Tommy. You're a good man

and a great cop. Anyone would be privileged to partner up with you."

"Means a lot coming from you, sir." He left Skip's room and went into the living room.

Celia jumped up from the sofa.

"So sorry to keep you folks up late," Gonzo said.

"No apology needed. I hope it helped to talk to Skip."

"It did."

"I hope it's okay that I really want to hug you again right now."

Gonzo forced a smile for her. "I wouldn't say no to that."

She hugged him tightly. "We're all here for you, Tommy. No matter what you need. We're here."

"Thank you. I'll get out of here so you can go to bed. Have a great time tomorrow."

"We will. You've got a ride home, right?"

"Yeah, I'll call Patrol."

"Take care, honey."

Gonzo stepped out in the frigid darkness and walked over to the Secret Service checkpoint, flashing his badge again. The agent waved him through. As he walked toward Capitol Hill, he thought about calling for a ride but then decided to walk, even though it was freezing and home was a couple of miles away.

The talk with Skip had helped to put some things into perspective. Though he couldn't see the light at the end of the tunnel, it was good to know that someday he would. And in the meantime, he would heed Skip's very good advice to not let the rest of his life fall apart. He loved Christina and Alex too much to do that to either of them.

INAUGURATION DAY DAWNED snowy and bitterly cold. Nick had been awake early, so he'd already showered and shaved when he brought coffee up to Sam. He tried kissing her awake, but she didn't budge. So he sent a hand under the covers to find a warm soft breast to play with.

Her eyes popped open. "Oh thank goodness. I was thinking my husband was going to be awfully pissed if someone else was doing that."

She made him laugh even when he was nervous about the day to come and still agitated by the unexpected appearance of his mother yesterday. Thank God for Samantha. He had that thought at least ten times a day, and today, he was doubly thankful that he got to have her by his side for what would be one of the biggest days of his life.

Nothing would ever top last March 26, but this was a close second.

He reached for the mug he'd placed on the bedside table and held it so she could see it.

"Does this mean I have to get up and make myself presentable?"

"I'm afraid so. There are hair and makeup people due shortly."

Moaning and groaning, she sat up in bed and took the mug from him. The sheet fell to her waist and the sight of her rumpled hair and sexy breasts nearly had him forgetting all about what they had to do today.

"Quit that," she said.

"Quit what?"

"Ogling your wife. You don't have time for that."

"Ogling my wife is my favorite thing to do, especially when she's naked, rumpled, sexy and grumpy in the morning." He ran his finger from her chin to her chest, dragging it between her breasts.

"Did you sleep?"

"Enough."

"How much is enough?"

"A few hours."

She caressed his smooth face. "Remember when my stomach was hurting so bad and you made me see Harry about it?"

"I seem to recall something like that."

"I want you to see him or someone about the sleep issues. We can't have our vice president perpetually fatigued. You need sleep. Can I talk to him about it if I get a chance?"

He leaned in to kiss her. "Sure, as long as there are no reporters lurking, looking for a scoop on the insomniac VP."

"Dodging reporters is one of my favorite hobbies."

"While we're on the subject of reporters, Terry and I have been talking about accepting one of those big network offers for a sit-down. Of course they all want both of us. Would you be willing?"

"That doesn't sound like dodging."

"No, it doesn't. And if you don't want to do it, I'll certainly understand."

"Of course I'll do it. I can't send my gorgeous husband out there alone for all of female America to drool over."

His eyes rolled to high heaven. "What-*ever*."

"You have no idea how sexy you are. Sexiest vice president ever."

"Get your sexy ass out of bed and into the shower. We've got a schedule to keep."

"Get off me and I will."

Kissing from her lips to her neck, he said, "Last night was so amazing. It's all I can think about this morning."

"Mmm, we'll have to do that again sometime."

"Absolutely." He gave her neck a little nibble that made her squeal.

She pushed him away. "No hickeys! I'm going to be on TV today!" After placing the empty mug on the bed-side table, she got up and headed for the bathroom, put-ting just enough wiggle in her sexy ass to get his motor running. "Don't even think about it," she said.

The bathroom door slammed behind her and the lock clicked into place.

Foiled.

That's all right. He had big plans for her later and she could make it up to him then.

Sam would never admit to being nervous. If she allowed herself to think about how many people would be watch-ing them, she'd throw up. Rather than dwell on that pleas-ant thought, she tried to sit still while her hair was dried and straightened by a woman she'd never met before.

Another woman applied a respectable amount of makeup and when they were done fluffing and buffing her, Sam decided she didn't look as hideous as she felt on the inside, knowing they'd failed to find Androzzi the day before.

Wearing a robe, she grabbed her phone off the char-ger and went across the hall to her closet, calling Captain Malone as she went.

"You're off today," he said.

"Good morning to you too. Anything new overnight?"

"Other than the second kidnapping vic taking a turn for the worse, no."

"Ah damn it. How bad is it?"

"They're not saying, but she's in critical condition, which is a downgrade from yesterday."

"I want that bastard so bad I can taste it."

"We all do. A bulletin has gone out to every member of the department with a description and everything we know about him. And we've sent it to everyone who is assisting us today. We've got ten thousand people on the streets today. If he's still lurking in this city, we'll find him."

"I really hope so."

"Don't you have better things to do than call me?"

"In fact I do. Shoot me a text if anything pops, okay?"

"I will. Good luck today. Don't trip and fall or anything."

"Your confidence in me is underwhelming."

The last thing she heard before she ended the call was his deep guffaw. He cracked himself up. Sam closed the door to the hallway and removed her robe to put on the sexy black underwear she'd ordered to wear under the red wool dress Marcus had made her. From her jewelry drawer, she retrieved the diamond key necklace Nick had given her on their wedding day and put it on. Next, she put on the dazzling diamond engagement ring she only wore on special occasions.

A knock sounded on the door.

"Who is it?"

"Your husband."

"Come in but only if you're alone."

Nick opened the door only wide enough to sneak in and closed it behind him. He'd gotten dressed in a sharp navy suit with the red tie Marcus had made for him and a white shirt. He looked very patriotic and very sexy. "Ah, damn," he said, taking in the black underwear. "I'm going to be thinking about that all day."

"You've got other things to think about today."

From behind his back, he produced a wrapped box with a card. "For you."

"What's this? It's not my birthday or our anniversary or even Valentine's Day."

"It's just another Tuesday," he said with a smile.

She took the box from him and opened the card. *To my Samantha*, he'd written, *Thanks for taking this crazy ride with me. I could never do it without you and Scotty to come home to every night. Love you forever, Nick.* "Aww, that's so sweet."

"Open it."

Inside the distinctive blue Tiffany box was a stunning platinum and diamond bangle bracelet. "Oh my God! This is gorgeous!" She put it on and held out her arm for him to see. "Thank you so much. If I'd known there were diamonds involved, I would've wanted you to be vice president sooner."

"Really?" he asked, his brow raised in amusement.

"Okay, not really, but still, I love it." She closed the small distance between them and kissed him, slapping away his hands. "Not now."

"Later. Definitely later."

She couldn't wait for later.

TWENTY-SIX

THE DAY UNFOLDED with military precision. Sam, Nick and Scotty joined the Nelson family for services at St. John's Episcopal Church, the so-called "Church of the Presidents" where Sam and Nick had been married last March. The Nelsons greeted them with hugs and a warm welcome that had filled Nick with scorn.

He'd never thought David Nelson to be a fake until recently when he'd clearly used Nick to boost his own ratings and then relegated his popular vice president to the cheap seats of his administration. Nick planned to do something about that as soon as they got through today.

In the motorcade that carried them to the Capitol for the official ceremony, Nick shared tidbits of history with Scotty, such as how the tradition of attending church before the inauguration began with President Franklin Delano Roosevelt in 1933.

"This procession from the White House to the Capitol began in 1837 when Presidents Van Buren and Jackson rode in a carriage made of wood taken from the U.S.S. Constitution."

"How do you know this stuff?" Scotty asked.

"I'd like to know the same thing," Sam said.

"I read up on it. This day becomes a lot more involved when one president is turning over power to another, which is what'll transpire in four years."

"When Nelson turns things over to you," Scotty said.

"Getting ahead of yourself, much?" Nick asked his son.

"I read the paper every day, and I read every word they say about you online. Everyone thinks it's all yours in four years. It's not just me."

Sam squeezed Nick's hand and shared a smile with him. He had put her in charge of the O'Connor family Bible, which she held on her lap along with his hand. She was stunning in the red dress and the sexy black Louboutin heels he'd bought her for Christmas. He'd never forget the way she'd thanked him for the shoes, but he couldn't think about that now or he'd risk an embarrassing situation.

"While I appreciate your vote of confidence as well as your research," he said to Scotty, "a lot can happen in four years."

"Care to make it interesting?" Scotty asked as Sam hooted with laughter.

He eyed his son with interest. "What've you got in mind?"

"I'll bet you a hundred bucks right here and now that four years from today, we'll be on our way to the Capitol for you to be sworn in as president."

"So if I take this bet of yours, I'm basically betting against myself, is that right?"

Scotty mulled that over for a second or two. "All right how about this then… If I'm right, you have to pay me a hundred bucks."

"What if you're wrong?"

"Since you won't bet against yourself, I don't have to pay you anything."

"He's scamming me, isn't he?" Nick asked Sam.

"Sounds like a fair deal to me," she said, earning a big smile from Scotty.

"Shake on it," Scotty said.

Nick reached out to shake his son's outstretched hand. "You've got yourself a bet."

"Easiest hundred bucks I'll ever make in my life," Scotty declared.

"We'll see."

"Mom is our witness."

"I'll make sure he pays you," Sam said.

"So you think I'm right too!"

"I'm Switzerland."

"What does that mean?" Scotty asked.

"Switzerland is known for being neutral," Nick said. "They don't take sides."

"I think I'd like to live in Switzerland."

"It's a very peaceful nation," Nick said, "and the skiing is great."

"We'll have to check that out after you get done being president, but I suppose by then I won't be living with you anymore."

"You can live with us for as long as you want to," Nick said. "The lease has no expiration date."

"Good to know cuz if you're living in the White House, I'm not moving out," Scotty said, making them laugh. "So why is Inauguration Day on a Tuesday? That's so random."

"For a big part of the country's history, Inauguration Day was March 4th, which was also the last day of the congressional session. It was changed to January 20th by the 20th amendment to the Constitution. So it's not always on a Tuesday."

"They had to amend the Constitution to change the date?" Scotty asked.

"Yep."

"That seems like a lot of hassle for a date change."

"Well, they were changing what was outlined in the original Constitution, so it required an amendment."

"Oh. I see."

"I picture your dad teaching government classes at Harvard someday," Sam said.

"After he's done being president maybe."

Nick loved how certain Scotty about his future. If only his son knew what they'd have to go through to make it so. The thought of the fundraising, not to mention a national campaign, exhausted him, and it was years in the future—if it happened at all. That he was even in a position to be having that conversation with his son or anyone was still amazing to Nick.

At the Capitol, they were whisked inside and escorted out to the west front terrace, which had been transformed for the inauguration with red, white and blue bunting, seats for hundreds of VIPs, including Sam and Nick's family and friends who were off to the left while the Nelson contingent took the right.

Accompanied by music from the Navy orchestra, Nick, Sam and Scotty made their way down the stairs to the front row. Nick waved to friends from the Senate, accepted handshakes from the Joint Chiefs as well as several Supreme Court justices. Beyond the Capitol, as far as the eye could see, was an absolute sea of people. He'd never seen more people in one place in his life. His belly fluttered with butterflies at the thought of what he was about to do.

He accepted hugs from his dad, Leo, and Stacy, the stepmother who was a few years younger than him, as well as Graham and Laine O'Connor who sat next to Skip and Celia Holland. Nick took only a moment to wonder if Nicoletta was out there somewhere watching the son she'd ignored accept the second most powerful position in the world. He hoped she was watching. He hoped she was also wishing she'd been a better person and mother so she might've shared the stage with the other people he loved.

And then he was standing before Chief Justice Byron Riley, his hand on the O'Connor family Bible with Samantha and Scotty by his side.

"Mr. Vice President, please repeat after me," Riley said. "I, Nicholas Domenic Cappuano, do solemnly swear that I will support and defend the Constitution of the United States against all enemies foreign and domestic, that I will bear true faith and allegiance to the same and take this obligation freely without any mental reservation or purpose of evasion. I will well and faithfully discharge the duties of the office of which I am about to enter so help me God."

A deafening roar came from the crowd gathered on the mall as they waved to the people in what had to be the most surreal moment of Nick's life to date. The applause went on and on and on. It went on for so long that Nick began to feel sort of uncomfortable. He could almost feel Nelson's eyes boring into his back, as he waited for his moment in the spotlight.

Nick waved one more time and then guided Sam and Scotty to their seats to make way for the president to be sworn in. After the oath of office was administered to President Nelson, he received decidedly less enthusiastic applause than Nick had gotten. He didn't do much to help his popularity with an hour-long address that seemed to go on forever.

Sitting next to him, Sam shivered in the cold so Nick

removed his overcoat and put it over her lap. She was too cold to object.

During the speech, Nelson repeatedly referred to his vice president as if they were the best of friends. Let him continue to believe that. The first time Nelson called on him to represent the administration at some far-flung event, Nick would put his cards on the table with the president and demand a seat at the table within the administration.

He was looking forward to that.

Nelson finally wrapped things up, clearing the way for the Inaugural Luncheon put on by the Joint Congressional Committee on Inaugural Ceremonies. The food featured selections from the home states of the president—bison from South Dakota—and vice president—lobster and New England clam chowder from Massachusetts. More than two thousand people attended the luncheon, held in the Capitol's Statuary Hall. Speeches were made, gifts presented and toasts to the new administration made by members of the JCCIC.

Halfway through the luncheon, Nick saw Sam smother a yawn, which had him holding back a laugh. Yes, it was boring, but it was also tradition. He reached for her hand under the table and gave it a squeeze, reminding her that even in a room full of the most powerful people on earth, they were still them.

She smiled at him. Message received.

Scotty and the rest of the family seemed to love all the pomp and ceremony. Skip Holland's smile was wider than Nick had seen it in months, since well before the surgery he'd had to remove the bullet that had been lodged in his spine for nearly three years. It was good to see him back to smiling again after a difficult recuperation.

Leo Cappuano was equally excited, and Nick's four-year-old twin half brothers bounced in their seats, trying so hard to behave on their brother's big day. From his spot at the head table, Nick could see Sam's niece Brooke sitting next to her mother, Sam's sister Tracy, their heads bent together as they whispered to each other. He was glad to see Brooke looking so well and getting along with her mother after the terrible ordeal they had been through before Thanksgiving.

Everything had fallen into place for their families in recent months. The only thing Nick wanted that he didn't have was the baby he knew Sam wished for, despite her assurances that their family was perfect just the way it was. He agreed—it was perfect, but it would be even more perfect if they could have a baby to love too. Scotty would be an awesome big brother, especially to a baby sister.

Sam leaned in close to him. "What're you thinking about?"

"You, as usual. And Brooke—so nice to have her here and looking so well." He would never tell her how often he thought about the baby he wanted so badly for her.

"Yes, it is."

After lunch, they said goodbye to their extended families and were escorted by the Secret Service from the Capitol into the motorcade that would take them down Pennsylvania Avenue to the reviewing stand for the parade.

"Are you still interested in walking part of the route, Mr. Vice President?" Brant asked.

Nick looked at Sam, who nodded somewhat reluctantly.

"Yes," he said.

"Very good. We'll let you know when."

"This is so cool," Scotty said of the massive crowds that lined the avenue. "All my friends are going to see me on TV."

"You'll be famous," Sam said.

"We're all famous, duh."

"Yeah, Sam," Nick said. "Duh."

She elbowed his ribs, making him laugh.

The car slowed to a crawl and then stopped. Brant opened the back door. "Ready?"

"Let's do it," Scotty said.

His enthusiasm was contagious as Nick and Sam followed him out of the car. The crowd welcomed them with another deafening roar. He kept a tight grip on Sam's hand as they waved to the hordes of people who'd braved the freezing cold day to catch a glimpse of the first and second families.

Nelson and his family were also walking the route in front of them.

Nick heard Sam say something and leaned in closer so he could hear her. "What?"

"I said it's like being married to one of The Beatles."

"Very funny." He wanted to tell her she was exaggerating, but the crowd chanting his name and calling out to them as they walked by proved her point. Though they were surrounded by Secret Service and the parade route had been thoroughly inspected ahead of time, he couldn't help but feel vulnerable standing in the middle of the vast avenue surrounded by tall buildings and people everywhere he looked. It would be so easy for someone to pick them off. So very easy.

He was waving to the people on the left side of the

street when Sam pulled her hand free and took off running toward the right side of the street.

"Mom," Scotty cried.

"*Samantha!*"

She darted between Secret Service agents, leaped over the metal barrier and tackled someone in the crowd. It happened so quickly, Nick barely had time to process that she was running for the crowd before she disappeared into it.

What the hell?

THE THRILL OF the hunt had never been more thrilling than the moment she spotted Androzzi standing in the sea of people watching the parade. He'd tried to disguise himself with a hat pulled down over his hair, but those eyes. Those black eyes gave away his true identity. After hours of staring at pictures of him, she'd know those eyes anywhere. What an arrogant bastard he was to think he could blend into the crowd and get away with it once again. Not this time. He was not getting away this time.

Sam landed on top of him with a bone-crunching thud as the screaming people around them were pushed back by the force of their fall. Burning pain radiated from her knees, but she ignored that to remain focused on apprehending the man who'd killed Arnold.

He'd had nowhere to go to escape her with so many people nearby squeezed in around them. The fall knocked the wind out of him, which gave her just enough time to retrieve the weapon she'd strapped to her thigh.

She pressed the gun to the center of his forehead. "Don't fucking move, you miserable excuse for a human being." It took everything she had to resist the urge to pull the trigger and end him the same way he'd ended

Arnold. But she didn't do it. Rather, she waited the few seconds it took for the Secret Service to catch up to her.

In those few seconds, Androzzi looked up at her with those dark, cold eyes. "You haven't won, bitch."

She pressed the gun harder into his forehead and her knee into his gut, making him wince. "You don't think so? Your days of hiding in plain sight are over."

"Mrs. Cappuano!"

No, she thought. *Right now I'm Lieutenant Holland.*

Secret Service agents and other law enforcement personnel surrounded them, clearing the immediate area and taking Androzzi into custody. He fought them the whole way until one of the MPD Patrol officers hit him with a Taser, which took the fight out of him.

Seeing that, Sam finally exhaled. The whole thing had taken maybe thirty seconds—from the first instant she spotted him on the parade route to the arrival of the other officers. She'd been so laser-focused on him that she'd forgotten all about the inauguration or the parade or her role as second lady. In that moment, she was only Sam Holland, Homicide lieutenant, and she'd gotten the murdering scumbag who'd killed one of her detectives.

With the burst of adrenaline fading, Sam came out of it to find thousands of people watching her in shock and maybe awe. "Sorry, folks."

"That was freaking awesome," one guy said.

"*Totally* awesome," the woman with him said.

"We've been looking for him," Sam said.

"Is he the one who killed one of your officers?" an older woman asked.

"Yes, he is."

"We're sorry for your loss."

"Thank you."

"Mrs. Cappuano," Brant said, his tone tense and harried. "Right this way."

Secret Service Barbie, aka Melinda, looked on in shock. She'd probably never seen a second lady go crowd surfing before. Oh well, they needed to get used to how she rolled.

They led her through an opening in the metal barricades and into the car where Nick and Scotty waited for her.

Scotty beamed with pride. "Oh my God, Mom. You were like Wonder Woman! That was the coolest thing I've ever seen. You *owned* him."

Embarrassed by Scotty's praise she ventured a look at Nick, who was staring at her with a stony expression on his gorgeous face.

"Sorry about that. Today is all about you, but I saw him and I just… I acted."

"What if he'd been armed?" Nick asked. "He could've killed you before you even got to him."

"He couldn't have gotten a gun in there. Everyone who was that close to the parade route went through screening."

"What about a knife?"

"They would've stopped him if he had any kind of weapon. I knew he'd be unarmed."

"I can't believe you just ran into the crowd like that."

"I couldn't let him get away again, Nick! He *killed* Arnold, and he thinks he's going to taunt me by standing right there in the front row like I'm not going to pick his ass out of the crowd and go after him? He thought I wouldn't or that I couldn't. Well, he thought *wrong*."

"You're bleeding," Scotty said.

"What?"

"Your knees are bleeding."

Sam glanced down to see that he was right. Her hose was shredded, as were her knees. Great.

Nick handed her his monogrammed handkerchief, the same way he had the night they first met when an asshole at a party spilled beer all over her. Now, like then, she didn't want to ruin the creamy white cloth. "Take it, Sam." In his voice she heard simmering fury.

Hoping to avoid a fight with her husband on the biggest day of his life, she took it from him and used it to mop up the blood that was running down her shins.

Nick pressed a button on the roof of the vehicle. "Hey, Brant? Mrs. Cappuano needs medical attention."

"I do not. I'm fine. Go to the reviewing thing."

"We'll break free of the parade in a couple of blocks and get her to the ER," Brant replied. Apparently, he took his orders from Nick not her.

"Thank you," Nick said.

"That's ridiculous," Sam said. "It's just a couple of scrapes."

"You're getting it looked at, and that's final."

"Wow. So now you're the boss of me as well as the country. Where did it say that in the oath of office?"

"He's right, Mom. Those are bad cuts and you need to make sure you didn't break anything."

Sam glared at Scotty, who grinned back at her.

"I'll remember this the next time you need me on your side," she said. "No more Switzerland for you, mister." Her cell phone rang, and she took the call from Captain Malone.

"Holy, *holy* shit, Lieutenant."

Sam smiled. "Hello, Captain."

"The TV was on in the command center, and we saw

the whole thing. That was the craziest freaking thing I've ever seen."

"I got him."

"Yes, you did. The TV people are going wild over it. You just made yourself into the biggest celebrity in the country."

"Yeah, well, um, okay. I don't care about that. I got the guy who killed Arnold. That's all that matters. How'd he get in there anyway?"

"I don't know all the details yet, but from what we've heard so far he was under yet another assumed name. John Davidson this time."

"Just another American citizen out to watch the parade."

"Something like that. Are you injured?"

"Some cut knees and a couple bumps. Nick is making me go to the ER, but I'm fine."

"Very well done, Lieutenant, although I'm sure the Secret Service will have a few words for you after that stunt."

"I'm not under their protection, so let them say what they will." As she said that, she glanced at Nick, who was glowering at her, so she looked away. She had no regrets. She'd do it exactly the same if she had it to do over again. "I'll check in later."

"Take a half day, Lieutenant. You've earned it."

Sam chuckled, slapped her phone closed and dropped it into her coat pocket. Then she subtly hiked up her skirt and returned her service weapon to its thigh holster.

"Let's talk about how you were armed on inauguration day too," Nick said.

"I'm always armed. I never leave the house without my weapon. You know that."

He had nothing to say to that. In fact, he had nothing at all to say as their motorcade broke with the parade route and headed toward the GW emergency room. They waited outside while the Secret Service went in ahead of them to clear the way for Nick and Scotty. By the time they took her in, Nick's handkerchief was nearly soaked through with blood and the wounds on her knees were beginning to hurt.

Her phone rang repeatedly, but she ignored it. Nick's quiet rage added to her anxiety. What was he mad about exactly? That she'd taken the focus off him on his big day? That wouldn't be like him, but she wouldn't blame him for feeling that way. It was always about her and her job in their marriage. Today was supposed to have been about him and she made it about her—again.

She'd taken a foolish chance going after Androzzi, but he'd eluded arrest so many times before that she couldn't miss the chance to take him down.

The car door opened. "Are you able to walk, Mrs. Cappuano?" Brant asked.

"Yes, I'm fine."

"Right this way."

"I certainly know the way. I'm a frequent flier here."

Nick and Scotty followed her into a waiting room overflowing with people who burst into applause at the sight of her and her family.

Sam smiled awkwardly at the people and was guided right back to a cubicle where her old pal Doctor Anderson waited for her. "We meet again," she said.

"Her knees are bleeding bad," Nick said, "and she mentioned some bumps."

"We'll take good care of her. You know the drill, Lieutenant." He dropped a gown on the table. "Everything off."

"Why? I cut my knees and banged my hip. Why does everything have to come off?"

"We need to give you a thorough exam to make sure you aren't injured anywhere else. The quicker you cooperate, the quicker you'll be out of here."

"Do what they say, Mom. We've got a parade to get to."

Her son was really racking up the points today. "Everyone out."

"I'll stay," Nick said. "Scotty, go with Darcy, and we'll find you when we're done."

The agent assigned to Scotty was waiting for him outside the cubicle.

Before he left the room, he gave Sam a kiss on the cheek. "Behave, will you?"

"Who's the mom here?"

"Sometimes, it's gotta be me."

Sam laughed at the cute smile that accompanied the comment. She could hardly argue with the truth.

When they were alone in the room, Nick helped her out of her coat and unzipped her dress. As it slid down her body, he said, "Aw, Christ, Sam. You're all banged up. Again."

Her entire left side was bruised, possibly from connecting with the barrier as she went over it or perhaps from crashing onto the sidewalk. She wasn't really sure what she'd hit on the way down. "I'm fine, so you can stop being pissed with me now."

He wrapped the hospital gown around her and tied it closed. "I'm not pissed."

"Yes, you are. I'm sorry if I ruined your big day and took the attention off you—"

"Is *that* what you think? Are you *insane*? I could care less about the attention. That guy could've *killed* you in a matter of seconds when I was only a few feet away and powerless to do anything to protect you. I hope you never have to know how that feels."

"I'm sorry. I never want you to feel that way, but he was standing there almost taunting me to come after him."

"Why not tell the agents that surrounded us? They could've apprehended him."

"Because that's not their job! Their job is to protect you and Scotty. They never would've left you to go after him, and besides, how would they know, in that mass of people, *which* guy I wanted them to grab? And in the time it took me to tell them, he would've been long gone. I *had* to get him, Nick. I had to get him for Arnold and Gonzo and Arnold's parents and all the women he sold into slavery. I had to stop him."

"What you did was incredibly brave, but it was also incredibly reckless."

"Maybe so, but I'd do it again in a New York minute."

"And you wonder why I don't sleep at night."

Sam unbuttoned his overcoat and slid her arms around him inside his suit coat. "I'm sorry to put you through what I put you through. I thought I'd lost my edge after Stahl."

"Safe to say your edge is just fine."

"And isn't that good news? Isn't that what you said you wanted?"

He looked down at her, his eyes blazing with love and

frustration and aggravation, but the love… The love was all she saw. "You are going to be the death of me."

"Nah." She curled her hand around his nape and brought him in for a kiss. "I make your life so much more interesting than it would've been without me."

He finally flashed a smile that broke up the knot of anxiety that had formed in her gut when she realized he was mad at her. There was nothing she hated more than being out of sorts with him. "You can say that again."

TWENTY-SEVEN

X-RAYS SHOWED NO broken bones, to Sam's great relief. Her relief was short-lived, however, when the doctor started cleaning the wounds on her legs. She wanted to scream from the pain. "Are you using fucking battery acid or does it just feel like that?"

"Hang in there," Anderson said. "We're almost done."

Sam clung to Nick's hand while the cleaning seemed to go on forever.

"Good news," Anderson finally declared. "No stitches required."

By then, Sam was sweating and breathing hard and nauseated from the pain.

"I'll write a script for some pain meds."

"Don't bother," Sam said through gritted teeth. "I've got some left over from my last visit."

"All right then. You're going to want to keep those wounds clean and dry for the next few days. Change the dressing once a day or more if needed. Do you still have antibiotic ointment?"

"Yes."

"Use that on them twice a day, and make sure you get your frequent-flier card punched on the way out. You must be due for a free visit by now."

"Hardy-har-har."

"That joke never gets old. By the way, I saw what you did on the TV in the doctors' lounge," Anderson said.

"That was some badass shit. I'm glad you got the guy who killed your detective. I knew him a little bit from seeing him around here, and he was a good guy."

"Yes, he was."

He handed her his card. "Call me if it gets swollen or starts to look infected. Okay?"

"I will. Thanks."

Anderson shook hands with Nick. "Mr. Vice President, I feel a little more hopeful for the state of our union with you in office. Don't let us down."

"I'll do what I can. Thanks for taking care of Sam."

"I'd say it's my pleasure, but…"

Nick laughed. "She's not the best patient."

"No, but she's a damned good cop, and we're lucky to have her on our side. You all take care."

Left alone in the exam room with Nick, Sam took a minute to catch her breath following the painful treatment. After four miscarriages, invasive infertility treatments and a litany of injuries, she ought to be used to pain by now, but doctors and needles and the smell of hospitals always made her sick.

"You ready to get out of here, babe?"

"Yeah." She sat up, slowly and painfully. The old gray mare was definitely not what she used to be back in the days when she could tackle a perp and go dancing the same night.

Nick helped her into her clothes, forgoing the hose that he had trashed.

"Do I look hideous?" she asked, thinking of the room full of people who had recognized them on the way in.

"You're not capable of looking hideous." He straightened her hair and dabbed at the space under her eyes with a tissue. "There."

"I want to say one thing."

"What one thing do you want to say?"

"I'm really, really glad we got Androzzi, but I'm really, really sorry it interrupted your big day."

"I'm glad you got him too, and I don't give a shit about the interruption of the big day. Today was already a great day because I got to spend all of it with you. The part that upset me was you taking yet another crazy chance with your own safety."

"I know, and I'm sorry, but—"

He laid a finger over her lips to stop her. "No apologies. I'm already over it. You're fine, so I'm fine." Kissing her softly, he said, "Let's get out of here."

"I want to go to the parade."

"You're going home."

"No, really! I'm fine. I want to go to the parade."

"And I want to take you home to get some rest so you can dazzle me at that ball tonight."

"Scotty wants to go to the parade."

"I'll take him after we get you settled at home."

She started to argue again but a wave of nausea had her thinking better of it. "Okay, take me home then."

HOURS LATER, SAM stood before the full-length mirror in her bedroom, taking a critical look at herself in the midnight blue gown that clung to every one of her considerable curves. "It's too sexy," she declared.

"It is not," her sister Tracy said. "It's perfect on you."

"I agree," Angela said from her perch on the bed. "It's sexy but classy. Like you."

"Right. I'm one classy broad, jumping barriers and tackling murderers when I'm supposed to be walking with my husband like a dignified lady."

Brooke, who was stretched out on the bed next to Angela, giggled. "Everyone in the world is talking about that tackle tonight."

"Great," Sam said. It was wonderful to hear Brooke giggling like the girl she was once again. For a while after her harrowing night in the Springers' basement, they'd had reason to wonder if she'd ever be the same as she'd been before. "It might be too sexy, but it's the best I can do." She fingered the key necklace that rested right above her cleavage. The bracelet Nick had given her earlier was on her wrist and the stylist had returned to wrestle Sam's hair into a sexy updo.

"Knock, knock," Nick said as he came into the room, stopping to take a good long look at her in the dress he hadn't yet seen. "*Wow*."

"I could say the same for you, Mr. Vice President." She would never, ever get used to how incredibly sexy he looked in a tuxedo. Tonight he wore a white tie and vest under the black suit.

"I'd say that's our cue to get the heck out of here," Tracy said. "You guys look amazing. No wonder the whole country is captivated by you." She kissed Sam's cheek and then did the same to Nick on her way out. "Have a great time."

"Thanks for keeping me company, ladies," Sam said as she hugged and kissed Angela and Brooke.

When they were alone, Nick came over to her and took a much closer look at the neckline that seemed to plunge more deeply than it had at the fitting. She'd have to tell Marcus to cover up the girls a little better next time.

"Look at my gorgeous, sexy wife," Nick said as he planted a kiss on the top of each breast. "You sure you feel up to this tonight?"

She felt like hell. Her entire body hurt and her knees were on fire, but she was going to get through that one dance they'd agreed upon even if it killed her. And then she would come home and collapse. "I'm sure," she said, fussing with the white bow tie that was perfectly tied.

He offered her his arm. "Then let's get going."

Downstairs, Sam was surprised to see Shelby waiting with Scotty to see them off.

"What're you doing here, Tinker Bell?"

"I came to keep my buddy Scotty company while Mom and Dad are off to the balls, and I wanted to see you guys before you left. You look beautiful. Both of you." She dabbed at her eyes. "Damned hormones."

"You're still feeling better, then?" Sam asked.

"Yes, thank goodness."

"That's good," Sam said.

Nick helped her into her coat and then she went to hug Scotty. "Have fun with Shelby."

"We always have fun."

"We aren't going to be gone long," Nick said.

"Take your time," Shelby said. "Avery is still working, so I've got nothing else to do but get my butt kicked in Call of Duty."

"She stinks," Scotty said bluntly.

"You'd better watch your mouth, my friend. I've been practicing."

"Uh-oh," Scotty said with pretend fear. "Let's go see what you've got. See you guys later."

"I'm a terrible mother because the nanny plays Call of Duty with him, and I don't even know what that is," Sam said while they waited for the Secret Service to give them the signal to go.

"You're not a terrible mother. You gave him a story today that he'll tell for the rest of his life."

"About the time his oh-so-ladylike mother tackled a murderer during the inaugural parade."

"Yep, that's the one. He loves you just the way you are. He told me the other day that he hoped you went back to work soon because that's where you're the happiest."

"I'm happiest with you guys."

"He knows that, babe, but he also knows you love your work. You're setting a great example for him in so many ways."

"No, you are. I'm just giving him stories. Lots and lots of stories."

"You've also given him something he hasn't had since he was six—a mom and a real home."

Sam looked up at him. "Will you teach me how to play Call of Duty?"

Smiling, he said, "Sure thing. Whatever you want."

They were in the car when Lilia called. "What's up?" Sam asked.

"It's a world gone mad. We've been overrun with media requests since your heroic feat today. Everyone— and I do mean *everyone*—wants you."

Nick tipped his chin in inquiry.

"Everyone wants me," Sam said. "Interviews."

"Ah, well, let's do one."

"Pick your favorite," Sam said to Lilia, "and set it up for next week."

"You're going to make someone's career with this one."

"In that case, let's make it someone young and hungry," Sam said.

"I'll do that. And by the way, Sam, that was some kind of awesome today. We're all so proud of you."

"Aww, stop. My head is swelling and my husband would tell you it's already gigantic."

Lilia laughed. "With good reason. Have a wonderful time tonight. I can't wait to see the photos."

"Talk soon." To Nick, she said, "She's a lot cooler than she sounded that first day on the phone when she was all stuffy and official." Sam frowned. "I hate stuffy, official people."

"I'll keep that in mind."

"How in the world did this happen to us?"

"What?"

"This. What we're doing today, tonight. You're, like, really the vice president."

"You're just getting that memo?"

"It just sort of finally and completely registered with me today when we were up on that stage in front of the entire world."

"If that doesn't bring it home, I'm not sure what will."

"I'm so crazy proud of you. I hope you know that."

"I do know, but it's nice to hear anyway."

Sam leaned over to kiss him and then wiped the lipstick from his lips. "Thanks for understanding why I need to keep the festivities to a minimum tonight."

"I totally understand and everyone else will too."

Outside the Washington Convention Center, they encountered another massive crowd of people hoping for a glimpse at the president and vice president. The crowd went wild when Nick and Sam emerged from the limo.

He leaned in close to her and said, "That's more for you than for me tonight, babe."

"It's for both of us."

She held on tight to his arm as the Secret Service hustled them inside. Every step hurt, but she gritted her teeth, determined to get through this for him. He did so much to support her career. Tonight, it was his turn.

"Did I mention that I got to invite some of my favorite musicians to play tonight?"

"No, I don't think you did. Who'd you ask?"

"You'll have to wait and see."

The moment they stepped into the ballroom, they were surrounded by people wanting to greet them, to hear about what'd happened earlier, to take photos with them, to be part of them.

Overwhelmed by the crush, Sam held on even tighter to Nick's arm.

Apparently sensing her dismay, Nick put his arm around her and she immediately felt better.

"I'm afraid I owe my wife a dance," he said to the leaders of the Democratic National Committee. "We'll catch up with you later." He took Sam's hand and walked through the crowd of cheering revelers to the dance floor. "Look," he said as he took her into his arms.

She turned her head toward the stage, and Jon Bon Jovi waved to her. "Oh my *God*! You did not!"

"I certainly did too."

Like he had at their wedding nearly a year ago, Bon Jovi played an acoustic version of their wedding song, "Thank You For Loving Me."

"Nick," she said, overwhelmed all over again, this time by the amazingly thoughtful man she'd had the good sense to marry.

"I've never been more thankful that you love me than I have in the last couple of months since I tipped our already crazy lives completely upside down."

"I love you so much, and I always will."

Right there in the middle of the dance floor, with the whole world watching, he kissed his second lady.

THEY WERE HOME two hours after they left, having made brief appearances at two other inaugural events. Shelby was watching TV when they came in, and jumped up to greet them.

"How was it?"

"Fun, actually," Sam said.

Shelby placed her hand over her heart. "I saw Bon Jovi on the news. Very well played, Mr. VP."

"I know the way to my wife's heart."

"Jon kissed me this time." Sam pointed to her cheek. "Right here. I'm never washing that spot again."

Nick threw her a look that had Shelby laughing.

"Not even you can compete with Bon Jovi," Shelby said.

"Believe me," Nick said, "I know. Thanks again for hanging with Scotty tonight. He wanted to go to the balls, but he has school tomorrow."

"I'm always happy to hang with him, and you'll be glad to know I held my own with Call of Duty even if he still kicked my booty."

"If it makes you feel any better, he kicks mine too," Nick said.

"That does make me feel better. I'll see you in the morning." Lowering her voice, she said to Nick, "Everything is ready."

"Thanks for the help."

"My pleasure."

Wondering what they were taking about but too tired ask, Sam said, "Have a good night, Shelby." She headed for the stairs, dying to get out of the dress and the shoes so she could stretch out her aching legs.

"Keep going," Nick said, steering her past their room to Scotty's room where they nodded to Darcy and went in to check on their sleeping son. "Come with me upstairs," Nick whispered after they'd both kissed Scotty.

"Not sure I've got the loft in me tonight, babe."

"Come with me anyway?"

Because she'd go anywhere he asked her to go, she took his hand and followed him up the stairs. Candles cast a warm, romantic glow over their special place. A table had been set for two and covered dishes had been left for them. As the scent of something delicious reached her nose, Sam realized she was starving.

"What's all this?"

"Our own private celebration of the inauguration and the closing of your case."

"How did you do this? *When* did you do it?"

"I asked Shelby to help me out, and she called in a favor from her favorite wedding caterer. I know you're sore and tired, so what do you think about dinner in bed?"

"That sounds lovely."

"Are you in a lot of pain?"

"Not right now. I took a pill earlier. I'm okay."

He helped her out of her clothes, wincing at the sight of the angry bruises on her side. "I hate to see you hurt. I hate it so much."

"I hate how much you suffer when I'm hurt."

Nick was so gentle as he tucked her into bed with a pile of pillows behind her. When she was settled, he delivered her dinner and a glass of champagne. "Can you have this with the pill?"

"A little won't hurt." She glanced up at him. "You

planned this whole thing, and I messed it up by getting hurt again."

"You haven't messed up anything. You're still here with me. That's all I need."

Sam raised a brow. "So you didn't have plans to ravage me?"

"I never said *that*."

"Haha! I knew it."

Laughing, he stripped down to his boxers, and Sam enjoyed every decadent second of the strip show. "Quit your gawking and eat your dinner."

"I'd rather look at you."

"You can do both." He brought his plate to the bed and stretched out next to her.

"This is so good." The tasty meal consisted of teriyaki chicken, pineapple, crisp red peppers and rice.

"I remember how much you loved teriyaki chicken on our trip."

"You remember everything," she said with a sigh. "Your lame wife is lucky to remember what happened yesterday."

"My wife is not lame. She's the perfect wife for me, and the perfect mother for our son. We love her just the way she is, and we'll keep telling her that until she believes us." He put his plate on the bedside table and reached for his glass of champagne. "Mmm, that's good."

"We need a toast."

"You're absolutely right. Let me see…" He rubbed at the sexy end-of-the-day stubble on his jaw. "How about… To you and me and Scotty and the next four years in office. May we and all the people we love be blessed with health, safety, happiness, prosperity, success and love. Lots and lots of love."

"I will most definitely drink to that." She touched her glass to his and then leaned into his kiss, looking forward to all the years ahead as long as she got to spend them with him.

EPILOGUE

MORE THAN TEN thousand police officers came from around the country to the District to help the Metropolitan Police Department lay to rest Detective Arnold John Arnold. The ceremony was touching and humorous and a fitting tribute to a life of service ended far too soon. Sam would never forget the sea of blue uniforms, the bagpipes, the eulogies delivered by his devastated older sisters or the sight of her entire squad acting as pallbearers for one of their own, led by Arnold's grief-stricken but determined partner, Tommy Gonzales. Arnold's parents had been presented with the department flag and his badge number had been permanently retired. He was posthumously promoted to detective sergeant.

She wouldn't forget the way regular citizens lined the streets as the hearse left the church to take Arnold to his final resting place. There were tears and tributes and toasts and songs and more tears. A collation was held at the Washington Convention Center, where Sam and Nick had danced at the inaugural ball a few days earlier. Food and drinks were provided for Arnold's family and friends as well as all the officers who'd come to pay their respects. Chief Farnsworth personally greeted and thanked every one of them for coming.

While they were at the funeral, Androzzi had appeared in federal court, and was charged with multiple counts of murder, including that of Detective Arnold, as well as human trafficking and sex crimes. He'd been ordered held without bail until trial. Mindy Cahill had rallied and was now out of the coma, and Jennifer Torlino had been released from the hospital. SVU had been working around the clock to take statements from the other women who'd been rescued from the warehouse, all of which would be used to build the case against Androzzi.

Immediately following one of the saddest days of her life came one of the most joyous, the day that Scott Dunlap Cappuano legally and permanently became their son.

With the sweep of a pen, a Family Court judge made Scotty's adoption official. "Son," he said, "I hope you know how lucky you are to be adopted by two people who will love and support you for the rest of your life."

"I do, your honor." He looked at Sam and Nick, who were struggling to contain the overwhelming emotions. "I know exactly how lucky I am."

"As do we," Nick said gruffly, releasing Sam's hand to hug his son.

Watching the two of them together, bonded to each other from the first time they ever met, Sam gave up on trying to contain the tears that wanted out. She might never get the chance to carry her own child, but this boy, this child of her heart, had made her a mother, and she would be eternally grateful to the curious twists of fate that had brought him into their lives.

They returned home for a celebration that included their entire extended family and all their friends.

"Crushing lows and soaring highs this week," Freddie said to Sam when they were alone in the kitchen.

"I know. We wondered if it was appropriate to do this the day after Arnold's service, but Nick thought it would be good for everyone to have something to celebrate. And we didn't have the heart to disappoint Scotty by postponing it."

"Life goes on," Freddie said, taking a sip of beer. "I wanted to tell you that I thought your eulogy for Arnold was really nice yesterday. I liked what you said about him being everyone's favorite kid brother. We could tell how much you cared for him. How much you care for all of us."

"I do care. Too much sometimes."

"You can never care too much."

"So when are you getting married?"

"We're not sure yet."

"What'd your mom say?"

"She was happy because she knows I am. Maybe she wouldn't have chosen Elin for me, but it's not her life or her choice."

"That's right. You're a good son, Freddie. She has no reason to be anything other than proud of you."

"Thanks. I hope she's proud."

"She is and she'll cry like a baby at your wedding."

Gonzo came into the kitchen. "Oh hey."

"How you doing?" Sam asked.

"All right. You?"

"Better now that everything is signed, sealed and delivered with Scotty."

"I'm sure." Gonzo got himself a beer and opened it. "Congratulations, Sam. He's a great kid."

"Yes, he is and thanks for being here to help us celebrate."

"Sitting at home feeling sorry for myself isn't getting me anywhere, so I'm glad to have somewhere else to be."

"You're always welcome with us—anytime. I hope you know that."

"Us too," Freddie said. "Don't be sitting around feeling crappy when you could be with friends."

"Thanks, guys. I'm going to be okay. It's just going to take a while."

"We'll be here for you no matter how long it takes," Sam said.

Nick poked his head into the kitchen. "Can you come out for a minute, Sam?"

"Sure thing." To Freddie and Gonzo, she said, "Duty calls. Come with me?"

They followed her into the living room where Scotty was the center of attention.

"Time for some speeches," Skip declared. "I'm going first. I want to say how happy I am to officially welcome my grandson Scotty to the family. Scotty, you've been a part of this family since the first time we met you. Today was about paperwork. It's been official for us for quite some time now. In fact, it's hard to remember what it was like around here before you came along. You make us better than we were without you, so thanks for choosing your mom and dad to be your parents so that I'd get to be your grand pop. I love you, buddy."

Scotty went to Skip and kissed his forehead. "I love you too. Thanks for having me."

"My turn," Tracy said. "To my nephew Scotty, thank you for making my sister a mom. It's the one thing she's always wanted to be that she never was before she had you."

"Aww, jeez, Trace," Sam said, wiping tears. "Pull out the big guns, why doncha?"

Tracy smirked at Sam and then hugged her.

"To my best pal, Scotty," Shelby said. "I just hope my kid turns out half as awesome as you are, and one of these days, I *am* going to kick your butt in Call of Duty, so be ready. Love you, Scotty."

"Love you too." Scotty hugged her and by the time he released her, Shelby was wiping up tears.

"Damned hormones," she said.

"That's what you always say," Scotty said, laughing at her comical expression.

"Scotty," Laine said, "from the first time your dad brought you to the farm, you've been an O'Connor. We love you, your mom and dad, and we're thrilled to have you as part of our family."

Everyone had something sweet to say about their boy, which made Sam realize just how much he'd touched them all since he came into their lives.

"Scotty, I miss you so much in Richmond," Mrs. Littlefield, his former guardian, said. "But I couldn't be happier that you're settled into such a wonderful family. If anyone deserves that, it's you. Thanks for not forgetting about your old friend Mrs. L in the midst of your exciting new life. I'll always love you."

Scotty hugged her tightly and whispered something that brought tears to the older woman's eyes.

"I guess that leaves us," Nick said, when everyone else had spoken. He put his arm around Sam. "I'll never forget the day I walked into that state home for children in Richmond and bonded over our shared love of the Red Sox with a twelve-year-old boy who reminded me so much of myself at that age. Scotty, we want you to know how thankful we are that you decided to take a chance on us as your parents. Our lives are hectic and filled with unreasonable levels of insanity, but you roll with whatever comes our way, and that makes you a perfect fit for us.

We love you so much, and we always will." He glanced at Sam, passing the baton to her.

"And I'll only add that I may never be a typical mom, but no mom could ever love you more than I do."

Scotty hugged them both.

The family around them cheered for the new family the three of them had become together.

"Do I get to say something?" Scotty asked.

"Whatever you want," Nick said.

He took a moment to gather himself. "Before I met Nick, my dad, I would've said I didn't need a family. I would've said I had everything I needed in the home I had. It was a good home, and I was loved there. But this…" Tearfully, he gestured to the wide circle of people around him. "This is more than I ever could've hoped for. Thanks to all of you for making me feel so welcome and so much a part of this awesome family."

"To Scott Dunlap Cappuano," Nick said, his arm around Scotty's shoulders.

"To my parents, Vice President Cappuano and Lieutenant Holland," Scotty said, "the best parents in the whole world."

As she leaned her head against Nick's shoulder, Sam was almost certain they weren't even close to the best parents in the world, but they would be the best parents they could possibly be to the boy they loved with all their hearts.

* * * * *

Look for Sam and Nick's next adventure,
FATAL IDENTITY,
from Marie Force and HQN Books.
Read on for an exclusive sneak peek…

SAM PUSHED THROUGH the double doors and into cool, crisp winter air that smelled like snow. She'd had a conversation yesterday with her son, Scotty, about how air can smell like snow. Scotty said it wasn't possible to *smell* snow, even after she got him to take a few deep breaths to see what she meant. He remained skeptical, but she had a few more weeks of winter to prove her point.

"Mrs. Cappuano."

Sam turned toward the man who'd called to her. He was in his late twenties or early thirties, handsome with dark blond hair and brown eyes. The panic she saw in his expression put her immediately on alert. "That's me, although they don't call me that around here. And you are?"

"Josh Hamilton."

Sam shook his outstretched hand. "What can I do for you, Josh?"

"I need your help."

"Okay."

"Today I was bored at work, so I started surfing the web, you know, just clicking around aimlessly."

As a technophobe of the highest order, Sam didn't know because she'd never done that and certainly not at work, where she was usually too busy to pee, let alone surf.

Josh took a series of deep breaths, and Sam's anxiety ramped up a notch. "I saw this story about a baby who was kidnapped thirty years ago. They had this age-progression photo showing what he'd look like now, and..." He gulped. "It was *me*."

"Wait. *What?*"

With trembling hands, Josh retrieved his cell phone from his pocket and called up a web page, zeroing in on a digitally produced photo that did, in fact, bear a striking resemblance to him.

"Those photos are produced by computers. They're not exact."

"*That's me!* And it explains why I've never felt at home or accepted in my family. What if they *took* me?"

"Hang on a minute. What evidence do you have to suspect that your parents participated in a criminal act to bring you into their family?"

He seemed to make an effort to calm down. "They're extremely accomplished people and so are my siblings. My brother is a board-certified neurosurgeon. He went to Harvard for undergrad and medical school. My sister is an attorney, also Harvard educated, Law Review, the whole nine yards. And then there's me. I barely made it out of state college after having spent most of my five years there on academic probation. After four years working for the federal government, I'm a GS-9 at Veterans Affairs, where I shuffle paper all day while counting the minutes until I can leave. The only reason I have that job is because my father, who has never approved of a thing I said or did, pulled strings to get me in. They're all Republicans while I'm a liberal Democrat who fully supports your husband. I hope he runs in four years, by the way."

"None of that proves your parents kidnapped you."

"Will you take my case? Please? I need to know for

sure. This would explain so much of why I've felt like a square peg in my own family my entire life."

Sam held up a hand to stop him. "I'm a homicide cop, not a private investigator, but if you really believe a crime has been committed, I can refer you to someone within the department—"

"No." He shook his head. "I want you. You're the best. Everyone says so."

"I'm honored you think so, but I'm on a leave of absence for the next few days, so I'm not able to take your case personally."

"It *has* to be you. You're the only one I'd trust to do it right."

"The Metro PD has plenty of very qualified detectives who could look into this for you and help determine whether a crime has been committed, Mr. Hamilton."

"You don't understand. It can't be any random detective. It can only be you."

"Are you going to tell me why?"

He took another series of deep breaths, appearing to summon the courage he needed to tell her why. "It's... He's... Well, my dad, you see... He's Troy Hamilton, the FBI director."

HOLY BOMBSHELL, BATMAN! Sam's mind raced with implications and scenarios and flat-out disbelief. "You can't honestly believe that your father, one of the top law enforcement officials in the country, *kidnapped* a child thirty years ago."

"I wouldn't put it past him," Josh said.

"He's one of the most respected men in our business. He's revered."

"Believe me, I know all about how *revered* he is. I

hear about it on a regular basis." He looked at her be-
seechingly. "You have to help me. I don't know who else
to turn to. Besides some of the people who work for my
father, I don't know any other cops, and you're the best.
And… I'm scared." The last two words were said on a
faint whisper.

Sam wanted nothing to do with the snake pit this case
could turn out to be, but the detective in her was far too
intrigued to walk away. "How'd you get here?"

"I took the Metro."

She took a look around to see if anyone was watching,
but the parking lot was deserted, and the usual band of
reporters that stalked the MPD were taking the day off.
They tended to do that when it was freezing. "Come with
me." She led him to her car and gestured for Josh to get
in the passenger side.

Though she had no idea what she planned to do with
him or the information he'd dropped in her lap, she
couldn't walk away from what he'd told her. "Tell me
more about this website where you saw the photo."

"It's a blog run by parents of missing children."

"How did you end up there?"

"I read a story about a baby who was kidnapped from
a hospital in Tennessee the day after he was born and
how his parents have never stopped looking for him. The
thirtieth anniversary of the abduction is coming up, so
they've gotten some regional publicity. There was a link
in the story that led to the blog where the age-progression photo was."

"So the photo hasn't been picked up by the media?"

"Not that I could tell, but I was too freaked out by what
I was seeing to dig deeper, especially since my thirtieth

birthday is next week. I told my boss I had an emergency. I left the office and came right to you."

"Why me?"

"Are you *serious*? After the inauguration, the whole country knows what an amazing cop you are. Who else would I go to with something like this?"

Blowing off the comment, she said, "You realize that accusing the FBI director of a capital felony is not something you do without stacks of proof that he was involved."

"That's where you come in. I need proof, and I need it fast before that picture gets picked up by the wires or social media and flung around the country. I need proof before he knows that *I* know."

Sam had to agree that time was of the essence before this thing blew up into a shitstorm of epic proportions. With that in mind, she started the car, pulled out of the MPD parking lot and into weekday afternoon traffic that clogged the District on the way toward Capitol Hill.

"Where are we going?"

"My house."

She glanced over at him and saw his eyes get big. "For real?"

"Yes, for real." She paused before she continued. "Look, if you want me to dig into this, I have to do it at home. I'm…off duty right now. I've gotta stay below the radar on this or my bosses will be all over me."

"No one will hear it from me."

After a slow crawl across the District, Sam pulled up to the Secret Service checkpoint on Ninth Street. Normally they waved her through, but she had to stop to clear her guest. "They'll need to see your ID."

Josh pulled his license from his wallet and handed it to her.

She gave it to the agent, who took a close look before returning it to her. "Thank you, ma'am. Have a nice day."

"You too."

"What's that like?" Josh asked. "Being surrounded by Secret Service all the time?"

"About as much fun as you'd expect it to be."

"Why don't you have a detail?"

"Because I don't need one. I can take care of myself." Thankfully, he didn't mention the recent siege in Marissa Springer's basement as an example of her inability to take care of herself. Sam liked to think that was a onetime lapse in judgment, never to be repeated.

Outside their home, her husband's motorcade lined the street. What was he doing home so early?

She parked in her assigned spot—everyone who lived on Ninth Street now had assigned parking spaces—and headed up the ramp that led to their home.

"Why do you have a ramp?" Josh asked.

"My dad's a quadriplegic. He lives down the street. My husband installed the ramp so he could come to visit."

"Oh, that's cool. Sorry about your dad, though."

"Thanks."

Nick's lead agent, John Brantley Jr., met her at the door. "Lieutenant."

"Brant. What's he doing home so early?"

"The vice president isn't feeling well."

"*Say what?*"

ACKNOWLEDGMENTS

THANK YOU FOR reading *Fatal Frenzy*! I hope you enjoyed the latest installment in Sam and Nick's life together. To discuss the story with spoilers allowed and encouraged, join the Fatal Frenzy Reader Group at Facebook.com/groups/FatalSeries. Make sure you're on my newsletter mailing list at marieforce.com.

Please also subscribe to updates from my blog at blog.marieforce.com to ensure you never miss a sale or a chance to attend a local book signing in your area or other news. This is a new feature I've added to my website as Facebook makes it more difficult for me to stay in touch with my readers. Blog readers will also receive occasional surprise excerpts and flash giveaways, so make sure you're signed up to participate!

Special thanks as always to the HTJB team that supports me every day: Julie Cupp, Lisa Cafferty, Holly Sullivan, Isabel Sullivan, Nikki Colquhoun and Cheryl Serra along with our "Designing Women," Ashley Lopez and Courtney Lopes. And an extra thank-you goes to Cheryl for her research help for this book. My appreciation goes to my agent Kevan Lyon, editor Alissa Davis and everyone at Carina Press and Harlequin for their support of the Fatal Series.

Captain Russell Hayes of the Newport Police Department checks my work and helps me keep Sam's experience as a police officer as realistic as I can make it.

Thank you so much, Russ, for always being willing to help me out.

To my beta readers, Holly Sullivan, Ronlyn Howe, Kara Conrad and Anne Woodall, thank you ladies for being the first eyes on all my books and for all your support and encouragement.

Finally, and most important, to the readers who have embraced Sam and Nick's story over the last five years, a huge *thank-you* for making this series so successful. There's much more to come for Sam, Nick and Scotty, so stay tuned for book ten, *Fatal Identity*. Thanks for reading!

xoxo

Marie

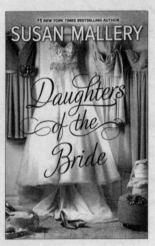

REQUEST YOUR FREE BOOKS!

2 FREE NOVELS
FROM THE ROMANCE COLLECTION
PLUS 2 FREE GIFTS!

YES! Please send me 2 FREE novels from the Romance Collection and my 2 FREE gifts (gifts are worth about $10). After receiving them, if I don't wish to receive any more books, I can return the shipping statement marked "cancel." If I don't cancel, I will receive 4 brand-new novels every month and be billed just $6.49 per book in the U.S. or $6.99 per book in Canada. That's a savings of at least 19% off the cover price. It's quite a bargain! Shipping and handling is just 50¢ per book in the U.S. and 75¢ per book in Canada.* I understand that accepting the 2 free books and gifts places me under no obligation to buy anything. I can always return a shipment and cancel at any time. Even if I never buy another book, the two free books and gifts are mine to keep forever.

194/394 MDN GH4D

Name _____ (PLEASE PRINT) _____

Address _____ Apt. # _____

City _____ State/Prov. _____ Zip/Postal Code _____

Signature (if under 18, a parent or guardian must sign)

Mail to the **Reader Service:**
IN U.S.A.: P.O. Box 1867, Buffalo, NY 14240-1867
IN CANADA: P.O. Box 609, Fort Erie, Ontario L2A 5X3

Want to try two free books from another line?
Call 1-800-873-8635 or visit www.ReaderService.com.

* Terms and prices subject to change without notice. Prices do not include applicable taxes. Sales tax applicable in N.Y. Canadian residents will be charged applicable taxes. Offer not valid in Quebec. This offer is limited to one order per household. Not valid for current subscribers to the Romance Collection or the Romance/Suspense Collection. All orders subject to credit approval. Credit or debit balances in a customer's account(s) may be offset by any other outstanding balance owed by or to the customer. Please allow 4 to 6 weeks for delivery. Offer available while quantities last.

Your Privacy—The Reader Service is committed to protecting your privacy. Our Privacy Policy is available online at www.ReaderService.com or upon request from the Reader Service.

We make a portion of our mailing list available to reputable third parties that offer products we believe may interest you. If you prefer that we not exchange your name with third parties, or if you wish to clarify or modify your communication preferences, please visit us at www.ReaderService.com/consumerschoice or write to us at Reader Service Preference Service, P.O. Box 9062, Buffalo, NY 14240-9062. Include your complete name and address.

MARIE FORCE

00415 FATAL AFFAIR	___$7.99 U.S.	___$9.99 CAN.
00416 FATAL JUSTICE	___$7.99 U.S.	___$9.99 CAN.
00417 FATAL CONSEQUENCES	___$7.99 U.S.	___$9.99 CAN.
00418 FATAL FLAW	___$7.99 U.S.	___$9.99 CAN.
00420 FATAL DECEPTION	___$7.99 U.S.	___$9.99 CAN.
00421 FATAL MISTAKE	___$7.99 U.S.	___$9.99 CAN.
00422 FATAL JEOPARDY	___$7.99 U.S.	___$9.99 CAN.
00408 FATAL SCANDAL	___$7.99 U.S.	___$9.99 CAN.
00410 FATAL FRENZY	___$7.99 U.S.	___$9.99 CAN.

(limited quantities available)

TOTAL AMOUNT	$ _____
POSTAGE & HANDLING	$ _____
($1.00 for 1 book, 50¢ for each additional)	
APPLICABLE TAXES*	$ _____
TOTAL PAYABLE	$ _____

(check or money order—please do not send cash)

To order, complete this form and send it, along with a check or money order for the total amount, payable to Carina Press, to: **In the U.S.:** 3010 Walden Avenue, P.O. Box 9077, Buffalo, NY 14269-9077; **In Canada:** P.O. Box 636, Fort Erie, Ontario, L2A 5X3.

Name: _____
Address: _____ City: _____
State/Prov.: _____ Zip/Postal Code: _____
Account Number (if applicable): _____
075 CSAS

*New York residents remit applicable sales taxes.
*Canadian residents remit applicable GST and provincial taxes.

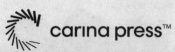

carina press™

www.CarinaPress.com

CARMF0716BLR